J.T.

BOOKS BY JOHN NICHOLAS IANNUZZI

FICTION

Condemned
J.T.
Courthouse
Sicilian Defense
Part 35
What's Happening?

NON-FICTION

Handbook of Trial Strategies
Handbook of Cross Examination
Trial: Strategy and Psychology
Cross Examination: The Mosaic Art

J.T.

A NOVEL

JOHN NICHOLAS IANNUZZI

A MADCAN BOOK

ISBN 978-1-4804-7675-2

Cover image, *New York Cityscape*, by Kurt Schumann

Cover design by Neil Alexander Heacox

Distributed by Open Road Distribution
345 Hudson Street
New York, NY 10014
www.openroadmedia.com

J.T.

NOVEMBER 21, 1960

THE AUGUST SENATE HEARING ROOM was jammed to capacity. Every seat in the large, wood-paneled room filled the instant the Senate pages opened the sluice gates to permit a tide of newsmen, photographers, and curiosity seekers to flood in. The aisles were jammed by camera crews and their equipment; wires and cables were taped to the rugs, running down to microphones at the front of the room.

Photographers, cameras dangling from their necks, roamed the aisles between the television crews, focusing and flashing their cameras on the empty witness chairs and tables, the curved podium from which the interrogation would soon begin. The noise and banter from the spectators was growing louder, swelling with excitement as the moment neared when the Chairman would gavel into session the Select Joint Congressional Committee to Investigate Organized Crime.

"Just a few more minutes," murmured J.T. Wright, the young associate counsel to the committee. He stood just outside the door of an antechamber, studying the restless crowd. Beside him stood Marty Boxer, a law-school intern attached to the committee counsel's office. Boxer, looking out into the main chamber, nodded at Wright's remark.

J.T. Wright was short and physically unimpressive. His dark eyes bulged slightly, his hair was slick and black, his complexion sallow. He was all of twenty-six years old.

Marty Boxer was twenty-four, and still awaiting word from the bar examiners. He was tall, athletically broad, with a strong jaw and dark, wavy hair. He and J.T. had attended the same college and law school.

Behind Wright and Boxer, the antechamber was crowded with committee members, both senators and representatives, and their aides and staff members. A few select reporters had been permitted exclusive access to the committee members for pre-game interviews. Senator Evard Anders, the chairman of the committee, stood near a sideboard on which coffee and pastry were set out; he was surrounded by assistants, other congressmen, and two reporters, making comments that could not be heard beyond the small circle of people around him. The antechamber buzzed with anticipation; the players were up, adrenaline pumping. This was the big game, the one heralded in all the papers, the one that would be on television screens all across the country in a few minutes, and, later tonight, flooding the newscasts in living rooms and bars for all the voters back home.

"Christ, J.T.," Marty Boxer said, not turning his eye from the spectacle, "the hearing chamber is jammed. You can't even walk down the aisle."

"That's just what we wanted," J.T. smiled. He turned, with Marty following, and walked toward Senator Anders.

J.T. stopped suddenly. "Are the guards keeping an aisle open for the committee?" he asked Marty.

"I didn't even notice."

"Well, go back and notice," Wright directed, his attention now focusing on the reporters and committee personnel in the room. "We don't want the committee to have to fight their way to their chairs."

Boxer nodded and turned back toward the hearing chamber.

"Did everybody get this morning's updated schedule and transcript?" J.T. called to Boxer as an afterthought.

Boxer turned back. "Yes, I made sure they did."

Wright nodded rapidly, nervously. He glanced in a wall mirror momentarily, cocking his head, patting his hair.

"You look terrific," Boxer smiled.

"Stop the horseshit. Did you check the aisle yet?"

"I was just going."

"Great, great, you were just going. Listen, Marty"—J.T.'s eyes wandered around the room—"I have a thousand things on my mind. When I tell you to do something, just go and do it, okay?"

Marty nodded and walked toward the door to the hearing room.

"Talk to you a minute, Mr. Wright?" asked James C. R. Duneden, a star columnist for the *Washington Post*. Duneden's column always contained a lot of inside political information. He was a self-appointed watchdog, with contacts in every branch and agency of the government. He was respected, even feared, all the way up Pennsylvania Avenue.

"Sure, Jim." A slit of a smile flickered across Wright's lips.

"What are your views on this investigation, Mr. Wright?" asked Duneden.

"Jim, do you really want an interview, or did you just come over to bust my balls?" Wright said softly, familiarly. His eyes darted quickly from one side to the other, to see that no one could overhear them.

"My interview piece with you is already in type, J.T. It'll run as a special supplement to my column tonight."

"How long is it?"

"I don't know how long it'll be after the city editor gets at it. But you're splashed all over it, featured picture and all."

"One of the pictures we took in my office the other day?"

Duneden nodded.

"Good. How did your interview of the chairman go?"

"Just as you wanted it."

"That'll make his hillbilly heart swell." J.T. smiled. "You're not going to interview anybody else, are you? I mean," he said, looking around, then whispering, "you can interview them all you want. But you don't have to print anything on them for tomorrow, do you?"

Duneden smiled. "Probably not. We'll have enough special material with your interview and the chairman's."

"If things get crowded," Wright whispered even more softly, "cut out the chairman."

Duneden chuckled.

"Whatever you do, don't interview that creature," J.T. said, looking directly across the room at a man of about fifty, with metal-frame glasses, a dark blue suit, brown shoes, and a striped tie. He was looking at Craig Rogers, chief counsel to the committee.

"You mean your boss?" Duneden asked.

"What a creep," said J.T. "He's still wearing the official prep uniform of an FBI agent, or one of those New York United States Attorneys. A hard-assed prig. Did you get an updated copy of today's transcript?" he said, changing the subject.

"Yes, the transcript, the agenda, the whole thing. I see you're leading off with John Entrerri."

"Right. Gentleman Johnny. What do you think about him from a publicity point of view?"

"Might as well start out with some glamour. He's dapper, always in the papers, nightclubs, sporting events. You think he's going to testify about anything?"

"Of course not. He'll take the Fifth, which is just perfect as far as I'm concerned."

"How so?" Duneden asked.

"I can ask him anything I want—'Did you kill your grandfather?'— and he'll refuse to answer on the grounds that it might incriminate him. I love it. I hope almost every one of them takes the Fifth."

"That sounds like you have something up your sleeve. Didn't I get a full transcript of today's activities?"

"Today's, yes. I can't give away all my secrets, though," Wright said slyly.

"Come on, 'fess up, J.T. Let me in on it."

"I will, I will. Let me keep a couple of things to myself until the right moment."

"I won't use it until you tell me. But give me a chance to work something up," Duneden said.

"Talking about working something up," Wright parried, "how did you like that blonde from the party?"

Duneden glanced around, then turned to J.T., a leer dripping from his face. "You son of a bitch, where the hell did you get those wild bozos? That one almost chewed my dong off."

Wright emitted a quick chuckle. "Sorry about that. I'll get you something more sedate in the future."

"Hell, no. Send me two like that one." Duneden had forgotten J.T.'s withheld information already.

"Two? That's a little exotic for my taste, but do a good job with today's coverage, and you'll have three at your own private party."

"J.T.," the chairman interrupted, touching Wright's arm. "Excuse us a moment, Mr. Duneden."

"Of course, Mr. Chairman. I'll talk to you later about those three items, Mr. Wright," Duneden smiled.

"Yes, Mr. Chairman?" J.T. said courteously, turning to face the tall, rawboned man with glasses and a reddish complexion.

"Do you think we should get going now?" the chairman asked, walking with Wright to a place apart from the crowd.

"In a few minutes, Mr. Chairman. Perhaps you can let the others go in and take their seats, get their papers in order. Then you can walk in at the end. Make a dramatic entrance, you know?"

The chairman nodded, smiled appreciatively, then turned toward the crowd. "Gentlemen," he called out.

The noise began to subside.

"Gentlemen, may I have your attention?"

The room was down to a murmur now.

"Would you committee members start into the hearing room and assume your places? I'd like to get things started on time. We have national television for two hours this morning, and I don't want to hold up the networks or our folks back home more than we have to."

The murmurs increased again as the committee members began to gather their papers. As they started toward the chamber, a few of the members glanced in the mirror on the wall, giving themselves a last once-over.

The chairman and Wright conferred to one side, as the members filed out.

"Once at center stage," J.T. told him, "you'll begin the proceedings with your initial statement. Then we'll call Entrerri as our first witness."

"Lucy already gave you a final copy of my opening statement. What do you think?"

"It's fine," Wright assured him. "Just the right tone. I made one slight suggestion somewhere in the middle."

"I saw it, and I thought it was a good one. I've already incorporated it into the statement." He looked at his watch. "I think it's about time we went in, don't you?"

"Just a second, Mr. Chairman. Marty," he called.

"Yes, J.T.?"

"What's happening out there?"

"The committee is all in place. The cameramen and the photographers are all crowded around the podium, waiting for the chairman."

"Sounds like the right moment for your entrance, Mr. Chairman." J.T. smiled.

"Well, here goes nothing," said the chairman, glancing in the mirror, touching his tie.

J.T., behind the chairman, glanced at Marty with a deprecating smirk as he watched Anders primp.

The hubbub that filled the chamber grew perceptibly as the chairman made his way slowly to the center of the high podium. J.T. followed directly behind him. Boxer slipped almost unobserved from the anteroom and quietly made his way to the committee counsel table in front of the podium. Craig Rogers was already seated at the center of that table.

The chairman and J.T. purposely stood at the center of the podium now, chatting casually as the cameras flashed. J.T. finally moved away from the chairman and made his way toward the committee counsel table.

"Are we all set to begin, Mr. Wright?" Rogers asked J.T. acidly. He reciprocated J.T.'s dislike of him, particularly since Wright, still wet behind the ears, had eclipsed him in committee affairs and was considered the chairman's fair-haired boy.

It was no secret that the chairman thought Rogers stiff and mirthless, a man who didn't like to belly up to the bar for some serious drinking. Second only to his love of politics and public acclaim, Anders enjoyed his drink. Not that J.T. ever caroused with the chairman, but he did have the redeeming quality of being clever, and more than that, he got along well with the media people. It was J.T., for instance, who had thought up the entire idea of the organized-crime hearings in the first place. It was J.T. who had calculated that those legendary hearings from the McCarthy days, the fabled witch-hunts for Communists, could be duplicated or even surpassed now that there was unlimited television coverage to bring the hearings into every home in America. He had only to find the right witches to hunt. And it had taken just a little time to find them: the Mafia, organized crime, the syndicate, the mob, the boys. This was an entity as well known in America as Rice Krispies. Anders loved it immediately and saw the coverage such hearings would command. He couldn't stop praising—privately, of course—Wright's idea. Publicly, it was the chairman's brainchild, which Wright didn't protest. After all, he realized, the chairman could hardly put together all the necessary plans by himself. Wright became the real thinking force behind the hearings. Which, of course, incensed Rogers. He couldn't understand how someone with no family background or money, one so obviously not "in," could have jockeyed one of the Wall Street Rogerses, the Park Avenue/Palm Beach Rogerses, into such a corner. Yet it was done, Rogers fumed as he sat alone at the counsel table, ignored by the chairman, by the members of the committee, even by the press. If you read the newspapers, Rogers thought, you wouldn't know there *was* a chief counsel to the committee, or if you did know, you would have thought it was Wright.

"Everything is right on schedule," Boxer responded when J.T. ignored Rogers's question.

"Thank you," Rogers replied, staring at Wright.

"You got your copy of this morning's transcript, didn't you?" Boxer added, to defuse the tension. Rogers was so obviously not in the chairman's or the committee's favor, Boxer went out of his way to be courteous to him. Sometimes Boxer would go over to Rogers, as he shuffled papers around his desk, to let him know what was going on, so he wouldn't be totally out in the cold.

"Yes, I did, Marty," Rogers replied. True, Boxer wasn't from his social stratum either, but he was a pleasant, intelligent young man. "I was sure you had left them for me."

"Marty," demanded Wright, turning in his seat two chairs to the right of Rogers. "Come here a minute, will you?"

"Excuse me a minute, Mr. Rogers."

"Come over to this side," Wright said, indicating that Boxer should come to his side away from Rogers. "Why are you talking to Rogers? I told you to stay away from him, didn't I?"

"I just asked if he had a transcript—"

"I don't give a damn what he has. He can't read anyway. I told you to ignore him, and that's what I want you to do."

Boxer said nothing. He always tried to be a buffer between the two men. He disliked neither of them, but he certainly disliked the tension and antagonism between them—particularly since J.T. usually maneuvered him right into the middle.

John Entrerri was dressed in an elegant, dark gray flannel suit and a crisp white shirt with gold cufflinks at the wrists. His tie was gray silk with a tiny polka-dot pattern. His shoes, custom made for Gentleman Johnny in Italy, were black, highly polished, and a touch pointed. He put a long, thin cigarette to his lips, and lit it with a gold lighter. He was looking out a window in the small witness room. George Russo, his lawyer from New York, was at his side, also facing the window.

"I don't give a good rap, George. I won't be put on television," Gentleman Johnny protested softly.

"I'll tell the committee counsel, and see—"

"Tell that little prick Wright that I won't be his patsy. He only subpoenaed me here to put on a show, to make a fool out of me. He knows I have nothing to do with anything he's investigating. The FBI knows that too. Do they have the right to take television pictures at these hearings?"

"That's tough to answer. They may have, they may not."

"George, tell Wright that I won't have my face on television, so people can recognize me, bother me in the streets. I'm not some Milton Berle. He's going to have to start contempt proceedings, because I won't testify if those television cameras are on me in there."

Several other witnesses and their lawyers were in the witness room, waiting to be called. None of the witnesses spoke to each other, although occasionally their eyes would meet for a moment and then slide away without a sign of recognition. Not that most of them didn't know one another. They didn't know everyone in the room, however, and they were sure that the FBI had planted a phony witness and a phony lawyer just to see who spoke to whom, who paid deference to whom, and what, if anything, could be overheard while the witnesses spoke among themselves. The waiting witnesses were, according to Wright's stories to the press, leaders and members of organized crime in America.

"I'll see what I can do," said Russo. "I'll talk to Wright. You'll be all right by yourself here, won't you?"

Johnny smiled. "Go ahead. I'll be all right."

Russo opened a side door and entered the hearing room. Immediately he was engulfed in a babel of sound and a sea of people as he threaded his way to the counsel table.

"May I interrupt you a moment?" Russo asked when he reached Wright.

"What is it, Mr. Russo? I'm very busy," Wright said curtly, looking up from his papers only for an instant.

"I'd like to discuss my client's reservations about—"

"The hearing's going to begin in a moment. You'd better get him ready." Wright didn't bother to look up.

"My client refuses to testify," Russo said flatly, annoyed at Wright's rudeness.

"What do you mean, he refuses to testify?" Wright demanded venomously. He suddenly became aware that several members of the press corps had turned to listen.

"What's happening?" Rogers asked, turning toward the commotion.

"I'll take care of it," Wright snapped. He stood and moved quickly to the side, motioning Russo to follow him. The media people hovered, straining to catch their conversation. Wright realized that John Entrerri's refusal to testify—even if he were cited for contempt—could be a major disruption of the hearings, could make them lose a great deal of force and drive, and that could make him look like a kid who'd tripped on his own shoelace. Over Russo's shoulder, he noticed the chairman motioning to him, asking if it was time to begin the proceedings. "Excuse me," Wright said, rushing forward, standing on tiptoe to whisper to the chairman, who leaned over the podium. Anders nodded gravely. Wright walked hurriedly back to Russo.

"What the hell do you mean, Entrerri refuses to testify? I'll have him tossed in jail so fast his head will swim."

"He'd prefer that to having his face spread all over the television screen."

"Is that it? The television cameras?"

"That's it."

Wright thought rapidly, his hand to his chin, ignoring Russo. The crowd in the room was getting restless. The noise was noticeably louder.

"My client realizes that you're putting on a sideshow here, and that he's one of the main attractions. He's not interested in being made a public exhibition. Even if that causes you to start contempt proceedings against him."

"You said that already," Wright said impatiently.

"Mr. Wright, I'm an attorney, just as much as you are. I—"

"Okay, okay, I'm sorry," Wright said impatiently. He thought silently for a moment, shrugged, then turned to Russo. "Listen, Mr. Russo, if your client's only worried about his face being on television, why don't we stipulate that during his testimony his face won't be shown?"

"What?"

"Let them televise the table top, his hands, his feet, the soles of his shoes, for all I care," Wright explained. Secretly, he was thinking of the tremendous dramatic effect of Entrerri's face *not* being televised.

"That's not what my client had in mind."

"Why not? His face won't be on television, and he won't be prosecuted for contempt. And more importantly, we get on with the proceedings."

"I think you took me a little too literally, Mr. Wright."

"We don't have time for semantics. Either he gets going now or we get going with contempt proceedings. Mr. Boxer—" Wright called to Marty.

"Yes, Mr. Wright," Marty answered, sensing the formality of the moment.

"Do you have those contempt papers I asked you to draw up in reference to John Entrerri?"

"Yes, sir." Marty walked back to the counsel table. He picked up a folder and began to leaf through documents inside. He selected one and came back to Wright. "Here they are."

Wright shoved the documents toward Russo. "Read these."

Russo took them and began to read.

"You see, we're ready for action this morning," said Wright, "and frankly I don't care whether the action is testimony or contempt."

Russo calmly read the proposed contempt application. He was impressed by the thoroughness with which Wright approached the hearings.

The hubbub in the room was more intense. J.T. looked toward the chairman, who was staring back at him, waiting to gavel the hearings to order.

"You can't bring a summary contempt proceeding before this committee now," said Russo calmly. Inwardly, he was anything but calm. "We'd be entitled to an opportunity to answer the allegations."

"I don't have time for all these legal niceties right now. Just get your client into that witness chair, or stay inside the witness room and watch the contempt proceedings on television. If I'm wrong, you'll have to prove it in an appeal court. Believe me, you won't win here." He turned toward the chairman, nodding, silently mouthing the word "okay."

Anders brought his gavel down resoundingly on the podium. "Ladies and gentlemen . . ."

J.T. resumed his seat, leaving Russo standing in the aisle, the contempt documents in hand.

"Mr. Wright—" said Russo, walking toward Wright.

"What, what? Jesus Christ, more?"

"If my client does testify, the camera will not focus on his face. Agreed?"

"Fine. Marty, go talk to the camera crews, you know who to talk to. Tell them that for legal reasons, when Entrerri testifies, they can't focus on his face."

"What?"

"Just listen to me, all right? Tell them the tabletop, the floor, his hands, anything but his face. Come on, Marty. We've been delayed enough already."

"Ladies and gentlemen . . ." the chairman repeated, his gavel sounding again.

George Russo walked back toward the witness room, where Gentleman Johnny waited. He carried the copies of the contempt papers that Wright had given him.

The noise in the room was changing now. It was quieter, yet more intense, swirling into the corners of the room, under the chairs, filtering to the floor.

"I saw you on television talking to that weasel. What did he have to say for himself?" Johnny asked.

On a high shelf to one side of the room, Russo saw a television monitor showing the proceedings. It displayed a miniature reproduction of everything he had just left in the hearing room. The chairman was still gavelling the chamber quiet.

"He said the television cameras won't focus on your face. They'll focus on the tabletop, on your hands."

"You're kidding."

"No, I'm not."

"My face, my hands? What the hell's the difference?"

"The difference is that he's ready to start contempt proceedings if you refuse to testify. Look." Russo handed Entrerri the papers. "He'd love you to refuse to testify. He'll start these hearings like a circus, with you as the featured attraction. What's the difference if you take the witness stand? You're not going to say anything anyway."

Entrerri read the papers.

The chairman began making his opening statement.

"I'm still going to take the Fifth?"

"That's right. They have the power to hold you in contempt if you don't appear, but they can't give you immunity, so you can still invoke the Fifth Amendment. Let's beat him at his own game."

"The little son of a bitch."

"Call your first witness, counselor," the chairman intoned at the end of his opening remarks. The television monitor showed a closeup of Anders's mountain-rough features. The camera panned to the counsel table and a closeup of Wright reading legal papers.

"That punk. I'd like to give him a punch in his mouth," Entrerri said as he watched the monitor.

"Let's do what we have to do," said Russo. "Do you have the paper I prepared for you?"

"Right here," Entrerri said, reaching into his inside breast pocket. He glanced over the page again. "I repeat this after each question?"

"Yes."

Boxer opened the door to the witness room and said, "Mr. Wright wants to know if you're ready for testimony."

"Tell that little—" started Gentleman Johnny.

"We're ready," Russo interrupted. "But the cameras are to stay off my client's face."

"I took care of the television situation myself," said Marty. "The television people assured me they would strictly follow counsel's instructions."

"You think you can trust that Wright? Maybe he'll double-cross us." Turning to Marty, Johnny said, "They can't take my picture as I walk in, either."

"I've instructed them to aim their cameras at you only when you're at the witness table, and never at your face."

"The first witness, Mr. Chairman, is John Entrerri of New York City," said the chief committee counsel, reading from notes on the table before him. The television screen showed the committee counsel table.

The television announcer's voice spoke in hushed tones from the monitor in the waiting room. Gentleman Johnny and Russo looked up at the screen.

". . . A most unusual situation is about to unfold here momentarily. John Entrerri—Gentleman Johnny, as he is better known—has refused to permit his face to be televised, for reasons that we do not now know. When Entrerri, the reputed head of gambling rackets in New York City and a high-echelon

member of organized crime, testifies before the committee, you will hear his voice, but you will see only his hands. We are trying to find . . ."

Johnny removed a diamond ring from the pinky of his left hand and unstrapped his watch, placing both items in his jacket pocket. He felt inside his pocket for the paper that Russo had given him, in case he needed it.

"Okay, let's get it over with," said Johnny.

George Russo walked first down the aisle toward the witness table, between rows of gawking spectators. He indicated a chair in front of several microphones for Johnny, and sat next to him.

"Are those things working?" said Johnny, pointing to the microphones.

"Assume they are," said Russo, putting his hand over the one closest to him.

"I can ask you a question if I want, can't I?"

"Certainly."

"What is your name, please?" the chairman began.

"John Entrerri."

"Where do you live?"

"Pound Ridge, New York."

"What line of business are you in, Mr. Entrerri?"

"Mr. Chairman, on the advice of my counsel," said Johnny, "I respectfully decline to answer that question on the grounds that my answer may tend to degrade or incriminate me."

On the television monitor, a pair of clasped hands appeared.

". . . This is really unusual, as you can imagine, ladies and gentlemen. The witness, whom you cannot see on your screen, is just sitting with folded hands, and we are only permitted to take pictures of those hands. In a moment we will flash a still picture of Mr. Entrerri from our files, so you will have some idea of what Entrerri looks like. But you will not be seeing any live coverage of Entrerri's face, or anything else except for his hands on the screen . . ."

"Mr. Entrerri," the chairman asked, "are you a citizen of the United States?"

"Mr. Chairman, upon the advice of my counsel I respectfully decline to answer that question on the grounds that my answer may tend to degrade or incriminate me."

Wright was watching Entrerri intently.

"Mr. Entrerri, are you married?"

"Mr. Chairman, upon the advice of counsel I respectfully decline to answer that question on the grounds that my answer may tend to degrade or incriminate me."

"Are you, sir, sometimes known as Gentleman Johnny?"

"Mr. Chairman, upon the advice of my counsel I respectfully decline to answer that question of the grounds that my answer may tend to degrade or incriminate me."

"Let me ask you this, Mr. Entrerri," Wright interrupted, leaning forward across the table. "Is there any question you *will* answer before this committee and the American public?"

"Most respectfully, sir, I refuse to answer that question on the grounds that my answer might tend to degrade or incriminate me."

"Is that on advice of counsel?" Wright prodded sarcastically.

Gentleman Johnny shot a stiletto look to Wright as he moved an inch closer to the microphone. "Most respectfully, on the advice of my counsel I refuse to answer that question, too, on the grounds that my answer might have a tendency to degrade or incriminate me."

"Do you have any children, Mr. Entrerri?" Wright snapped, staccato and hard, taunting Johnny.

"Most respectfully—"

"I know, I know," said Wright patronizingly, "you refuse to answer on the grounds that your . . ."

The rest of what Wright mimicked was lost in the audience's loud guffaws. Anders, fighting a smile, gavelled for silence.

The television cameras, passing from the chairman to Gentleman Johnny's hands, failed to pick up the menacing stare Johnny gave Wright.

"Mr. Chairman, Mr. Chairman," George Russo called loudly, to be heard over the crowd.

"Yes, Mr. . . ." The chairman's eyes searched his desk for the piece of paper with the lawyer's name.

"Mr. Chairman, I realize these hearings are public, are being televised on national hookup, and as such there is some theatrical aspect to the proceedings. However—"

"Just a minute, counselor," reprimanded the chairman, not wanting to lose face before millions. "These proceedings are most serious indeed, and I believe that your comments are intended to cast aspersions on the character of this committee."

"Mr. Chairman, neither my client nor I mean to be disrespectful of this committee. However, may I ask that your counsel—or should I say *junior* counsel—accord some respect to the Constitution of the United States."

"The Constitution?" Wright chimed in, his face screwed into a frown.

"As I understand the Constitution," said Russo, "my client enjoys certain rights and privileges, one of which is the Fifth Amendment prohibition against compelled selfincrimination. Now I'm not sure, but it seems your junior counsel is, by inflection and attitude, ridiculing the constitutional privileges of Mr. Entrerri."

"That's a scurrilous smokescreen," countered Wright, "fabricated to allow Mr. Entrerri to make a mockery of this committee and the very Constitution his lawyer is parading for television."

"Mr. Chairman," said Russo, "I've made an objection to the proceedings and I'd appreciate your advising me as to whether a witness before this committee, invoking lawfully and rightfully a constitutionally sanctioned privilege, must be subject to the taunts and derision of counsel?"

The chairman hesitated.

"He can hide behind it if he has to," Wright injected caustically.

"Mr. Chairman, are you conducting these proceedings according to American law or according to Mr. Wright's distasteful need for national publicity?"

"I advise you, counselor," the chairman said gravely, "not to mock these proceedings yourself. I think we'll all get along fine if everyone observes the usual protocol. Let's proceed."

The television audience saw Gentleman Johnny's hands calmly folded into each other, waiting for the next question. Nothing had happened that he hadn't expected. He and Russo had both known that Wright would try to make a production out of his invocation of the Fifth Amendment. They had discussed it together and agreed upon a strategy of passive repetition of the Fifth, regardless of Wright's antics. Russo sat back momentarily, the onslaught abating as the participants took a breath and a pause to reevaluate.

"We both got a little too involved," Russo whispered, leaning to Johnny, covering the microphone with his hand.

"I know. That—" Johnny hesitated, lest the microphone pick up what he was going to say about Wright, then went on, "He gets to you after a while."

"Mr. Entrerri, are you a member of an organized crime family known as the Pasquale Bedardo family?" J.T. hurled at Gentleman Johnny.

"Most respectfully, on the advice of counsel, I decline to answer on the grounds that my answer might tend to degrade or incriminate me."

"Is this Bedardo family one of five organized crime families in the New York City area?"

"Respectfully, on the advice of counsel, I refuse to answer on the grounds that my answer might tend to degrade or incriminate me."

"Excuse me, Mr. Wright," the chairman interrupted. "I'd like to ask Mr. Entrerri some questions, and I know my colleagues also have some questions they'd like to ask."

"Excuse me, Mr. Chairman," Russo said. "I'd like to confer with my client first."

Anders nodded.

"Now they're going to get down to specifics," Russo said to Gentleman Johnny, automatically covering the microphone with his hand.

"I know. Now they're going to parade out families and names and all that other garbage the newspapers write."

"Don't let it bother you. Just keep taking the Fifth," said Russo. "Their questioning may go on a long time."

"Let them go on forever, I'll sit here and repeat the same thing."

"In a couple of questions, answer by saying 'same answer,' instead of repeating the whole thing over and over."

"Just say 'same answer'?"

"Right. See if we can cut this short, not make it seem so long and drawn-out."

"Okay, counselor."

They both sat back, ready to proceed.

"Are you ready now, sir?" asked the chairman.

Gentleman Johnny did not reply.

"Very well. Mr. Entrerri, are you the *consigliere*"—he made a hill-billy singsong out of the attempted Italian pronunciation—"of the Bedardo crime family?"

"Most respectfully, Mr. Chairman, on the advice of my counsel, I decline to answer on the grounds that my answer might tend to degrade or incriminate me."

"Mr. Chairman?" asked Senator Carleton.

"The chair recognizes the distinguished senator from Louisiana."

"Thank you, Mr. Chairman. Mr. Entrerri"—Senator Carleton, although he tried, did hardly better with the Italian pronunciation—"are these crime families tied together in a national alliance, presided over by a central commission?"

"Most respectfully, Senator, on the advice of counsel, I decline to answer on the grounds that my answer may tend to degrade or incriminate me."

"Does this commission oversee all crime families in the United States, including the crime family of Francesco Venitello in my home state of Louisiana?"

"Same answer, Senator."

"Same answer as what?" countered J.T.

"I respectfully decline to answer that question on the advice of counsel, on the grounds that my answer might tend to degrade or incriminate me."

Wright folded his arms, a sour look on his face. He noticed that the little red on-the-air light was lit on a television camera pointed toward him. He leaned back in his chair with a look of disgust.

"Do you know Francesco Venitello personally, Mr. Entrerri?" Senator Carleton continued.

"Same answer, most respectfully, Senator."

"Perhaps you'll answer this question, Mr. Entrerri." He pronounced the name to rhyme with *dreary*.

"That's Entrerri, Senator," Gentleman Johnny corrected.

The Senator looked up from his notes. "My apologies, sir. Now. Mr. Witness . . ."

The crowd laughed. Even Gentleman Johnny was amused.

". . . does this organized crime family of Francesco Venitello—I hope I'm pronouncing that right . . ." He looked at Gentleman Johnny again.

Johnny said nothing.

". . . does this crime family control usury and gambling operations in New Orleans?"

"Same answer, Senator."

"Same answer as *what*?" J.T. said with feigned annoyance. "This committee is entitled to a complete answer to each question."

Gentleman Johnny said nothing.

"Senator Carleton," said the chairman, "may I interrupt you for a moment?"

"Certainly, Mr. Chairman."

"The chair recognizes Representative Wellman of Missouri."

"Mr. Witness"—the Missourian wasn't even going to bother to unscramble the name—"is it true that there are twenty-seven major crime families in the United States?"

"I refuse to answer that question on the grounds that my answer might tend to degrade or incriminate me."

"And that these groups are connected to crime families in Italy?"

Gentleman Johnny leaned over to his counsel.

"What's the matter?" Russo whispered.

"Nothing. I just wanted to take a breather. These questions are a lot of crap. They know I won't answer anything."

"That's why you're such a good witness. They can say anything they want, and you won't disprove them or disagree with them."

Gentleman Johnny shrugged.

"Same answer, most respectfully," he said into the microphone.

On the desk before Representative Wellman, and on those of all the other members of the committee, were pages of questions, general and specific questions about cities, families, names, and dates. They were all composed by Wright and the committee counsel staff, for the committee members to ask Entrerri. The Chairman called on each member in turn, and each asked his own questions, focusing particularly on an alleged crime or crime family in the member's home state. The session went on all morning, with the television cameras showing every questioner, and then cutting back to Gentleman Johnny's hands. About noon, the chairman announced a luncheon recess.

"Mr. Wright, may I see you for a moment?" asked the chairman as the committee made its way back to its side chamber. He guided Wright to a spot where they could speak privately. "Well, how do you think it went?"

"Perfectly."

"But that 'eye-tie' som-bitch didn't answer a single question!"

"That's exactly what we want, Senator. It shows how insidious this crime situation is, how it has a stranglehold on the entire nation, and there aren't adequate laws to cope with such a vast criminal conspiracy." Wright was priming Anders for the reporters, and the chairman listened intently. "That's why these hearings are essential, to let the nation know how badly we need the new legislation that the committee is going to propose at the end of the hearings."

The chairman nodded, looking up as he saw reporters starting to stream into the committee room.

"What's on this afternoon?" the chairman asked quickly. "Do we still have that Giono, Giordano . . . whatever his name is?"

"It might be better if we put Guardaci on tomorrow morning," said Wright. "More impact. You can build him up this afternoon as a surprise witness—be sure not to mention his name—who's going to break the code of silence. The media will play it up big. We'll have a bigger audience tomorrow."

"Are we on safe grounds to say all these things?"

"Of course, Senator," Wright lied, knowing there was no place anyone could go to verify the drama Wright was making up.

"This Guardaci is the surprise witness we have that entire script for, who testified before the committee in private session?"

"Exactly, Mr. Chairman," Wright replied. "In fact, I even had some extra copies of the transcript of his testimony made up. I'm going to slip them to our more important friends in the media. This way they can file an early and complete story of the upcoming proceedings."

The chairman looked at Wright and smiled. He had to admire this young snake from New York. He really knew his way around.

"Mr. Chairman," asked the first reporter to reach Wright and Anders, "doesn't this Entrerri's constant refusal to answer questions make this hearing rather pointless?"

"Quite the contrary, sir," said the chairman benignly. "It only points up more dramatically the need for the legislative reform that I and my committee are drafting. Such insidious criminal activity, if it exists in the proportions that we think it does, must be fought with new laws, out in the open, to protect the public from its strangling effects on our everyday life."

Wright grinned as he walked toward Boxer.

MAY 31, 1952

BIG JIM WRIGHT was six feet three inches tall, wide-shouldered, barrel-chested, lion-maned. His hands were large, roughened from hard work as a youth, when his father, a caretaker on local estates in Millville, New York, required Jim to work summers as a grounds keeper.

Big Jim stood now on one of the balconies of his large white house with black shutters on the top of a hill at the edge of Millville. Though it was early morning, the sun was already hot. In the south field, behind a white plank fence, his bay thoroughbred stallion, Mayday, grazed quietly. To the east of the house, behind the formal gardens and the swimming pool, was another paddock holding two bay mares. Big Jim felt pride and pleasure as he viewed his domain, the hills of Millville, and, beyond, the Catskill and Adirondack mountains. He didn't own all the hills or the mountains, but he owned the view. And more than that, he controlled the destiny of most of the people who lived on or owned those hills and mountains. For Big Jim was president of the local bank, the insurance company, the largest local construction company; he was the Republican county leader, and a representative to the Congress of the United States.

Big Jim turned as he heard the gravel in the driveway compressed beneath the wheels of a car. A dark Cadillac eased along the curved driveway and disappeared on the far side of the house. Big Jim went inside. The house was stately, with wood-paneled halls, five bedrooms, several guest rooms, a bar, even a small chapel.

"Good morning, darling," Big Jim said to his dark-haired wife waiting for him in the bright, flowery breakfast room.

"Good morning, James," said Angela. Angela was of Italian ancestry. Like Jim, she had been born in Millville. They had gone to Millville High together, had been childhood sweethearts, had married, and were raising four children: Andrea, Maria, Dana, and the youngest, their only son, John Thomas—usually called J.T.—named after Big Jim's now deceased father.

Big Jim sat at the breakfast table, even though he could see through the picture window of the breakfast room that someone from the car that had just stopped in the driveway was walking down through the banks of summer flowers toward the pool house. That was where he held court for political cronies or favor-seekers. He never permitted business in his home.

"I don't feel old, and you certainly don't look old, Angela," Big Jim said abruptly. "But with J.T. graduating high school today, it makes me feel older."

"You're not old, James," Angela soothed, her hand reaching out and touching his. "We started young."

"That's my girl. Always knows how to make me feel good." Big Jim smiled. In his mind, Angela was still the pretty young girl from Millville who had been his first date, his first and only love.

"You know, Angela, I can still picture you in the house over on Franklin Avenue, and how your father and mother gave you a hard time for going out with an American," Big Jim mused.

"And I remember you winning all those team letters, being the top athlete in school." Angela smiled at some silent recollection. "Your folks weren't too crazy about you going out with me, either," she added.

"Good thing your father and mine were both caretakers. That, at least, gave the families something in common."

Angela's father had worked on a local estate. He, as well as many of his relatives—Millville was stocked with Italians from Castellamare di

Stabia, near Naples—had turned to gardening and caretaking after the stonework that had brought them to America ran out. The stonework had been on a two-thousand-acre estate then under construction. The overseer of the construction of a main house, two large barns, a huge greenhouse, and other buildings, all of stone, had gone to the docks in New York City to hire Italian stoneworkers. When additional workers were needed, the foreman never had to go to the docks again. Those Castellamarese sent home for their brothers, uncles, and cousins, all of whom were stonemasons. There were, ultimately, over two hundred and fifty Castellamarese in and around Millville. When the construction ended, a majority of the emigrés settled in Millville, raised their families, worked on the estates as groundkeepers, opened businesses, and formed the nucleus of the staffs and shop owners who serviced the many estates and wealthy families, the fox hunts, the horses that set the grand life style of Millville. The working people, in turn, were well served by the estate dwellers—the "hilltoppers," so called because they settled as high as they could on the hilltops to catch whatever breezes were available in the dog days of August. Whenever anything was needed in the village, it was donated by one of the wealthy families. Millville became the first village for miles around to boast a modern library, a modern water and sewer system, a first-class post office, and shops featuring amenities not usually found in small villages.

Millville had also been the headquarters of John Morgan, the Republican county leader of Ulster County. Morgan, a baseball player in his earlier days, was a great sports enthusiast. No one ever played ball in Millville who impressed him as much as Big Jim Wright. Morgan saw a major-league career in Big Jim's future, and he decided to nurture that career. He introduced Big Jim to coaches and scouts, and arranged tryouts for him in Florida. Unfortunately, Big Jim's career was cut short by cartilage damage in the knees, late in his senior year of college. That injury ended the sports relationship but not the association between Big Jim Wright and John Morgan. It was thus that Big Jim, Morgan's right-hand man, became a lawyer, Morgan's law partner, and finally Ulster County Republican leader to succeed John Morgan.

"You have a visitor, James," Angela said, looking across the lawn to the man walking toward the pool house.

"Now that Eisenhower has decided to run, and our chances of taking over the presidency are so strong, everyone wants to be friendly. Contracts are popping up like dandelions."

Angela sipped her tea.

"After thirteen years with Roosevelt and seven with Truman, it's been a long starvation," Big Jim said with hungry enthusiasm. "Our time has come, though."

"Don't take too long with your visitor, dear," said Angela. "We have to be at J.T.'s graduation early."

"J.T. will be off to college in the fall," Big Jim mused. "We have no more babies, Angela."

"I know." She was quietly sad about that. "But at least J.T. won't be too far away. He'll only be at Browning."

"Now don't start. It'll be good for him to be away from home for a while. Make a man out of him." A certain disappointment always lurked at the back of Big Jim's mind when he thought of J.T.'s slight stature—he was five foot six, 135 pounds, too short and light even for a quarterback. J.T. had always resisted Big Jim's sport enthusiasm and encouragement. In his senior year, as a sop to his father, J.T. had become the manager of the varsity football team. Although Big Jim never told J.T., as far as he was concerned, becoming a team manager was salting the wound.

"J.T. *is* a man," Angela said firmly, knowing how Big Jim thought. "Just because he didn't win any letters doesn't mean he isn't a man."

"I know." Big Jim became quiet. It was still a vast disappointment.

"I'm proud that J.T. is going to go to Browning," Angela added. "Can you imagine? When we were going to college, someone from either of our families going to Browning was as unlikely as going to the moon."

There were footsteps on the stairs.

"Morning, Dad," J.T. said, walking past his father to the breakfast table. "Morning, Mother," he said, kissing Angela's cheek.

"Good morning, graduate."

J.T. sat down and began to butter some toast. "You know, Dad, I'm thinking I might go to law school when I get out of Browning. What do you think?"

Big Jim looked at Angela. She smiled.

"That'd be fine, son, just fine. You'll make a good lawyer," said Big Jim. And he meant it. Already he could seldom win an argument with J.T.

"That'll be just wonderful," said Angela, seeing that Big Jim was truly pleased with the idea. She had never given up hope that her husband and their only son would someday become close. But it had never happened. Big Jim was too sorely disappointed with J.T.'s aversion to sports, his dislike of competition, his retreat from anything physical. J.T., for his part, was excruciatingly aware of his father's disappointment. He was equally aware of his own physical limitations. He was small; he just couldn't run or throw or fight. Perhaps, though, he could compete with the big boys, the muscleheads, the strong backs, beat them where and when it really counted, in the real world. All he had to do was fight with the one weapon he had, his mind. He could compete there. He could outthink, outsmart, outmaneuver, out-connive the best of them, even his father. He just had to keep the game mental, not physical. And what better way of keeping the game mental than by becoming a lawyer, where the fierce competition was all cerebral. God, he was going to show the big people something; he'd tear them down to size, eat them alive, make them dance to his tune.

A lawyer would be perfect, thought Angela. Weren't all the people running the government lawyers? J.T. and his father would finally have something in common.

"That might work out really well," said Big Jim, giving the idea further thought.

"How's that, Dad?"

"Well, after you practice law awhile—in my office if you'd like—and with a little political know-how, perhaps you could run for the state legislature. With our name and the Republicans behind you, you'd be a shoo-in. After that, who knows? Maybe you can take my seat in Congress."

"Take it easy, Dad. You've already got me in Congress, and I'm not even out of high school yet."

"Think ahead, son. Think ahead."

AUGUST 7, 1954

MARTY BOXER lived with his mother and two sisters in an apartment that was part of a row of small buildings on Second Avenue in New York City, named, for whatever reason, the Florida Flats. He'd been the sole male in the family since his father was reported missing in action after his navy fighter plane trailed smoke down into the Pacific during the battle for Luzon. Marty had been seven years old then, and his sisters had been only two and three.

The prospect of Marty leaving for Browning College was bittersweet for Ann Boxer. A schoolteacher, Ann had always leaned toward intellectual pursuits, and she had always wanted Marty to go to college, to be a professional man. She had cherished the same hope for her husband, Steve, but the war had changed a lot of hopes and plans.

Stephen Boxer had come from a tough section of the Gas House district (in those days, New York City was a patchwork of neighborhoods, each with its own name). Avenue B and Seventeenth Street was made up of rows of dilapidated walkup tenements, cold-water flats, with communal toilets located in the public halls. Winters were cruel, people poor, life hard, and kids foraged in the street for bits of unburned coal from ash barrels to bring home to keep their families warm.

Ann Gannon was a young girl from a nice family who lived in the Florida Flats, and attended Epiphany Parochial School. Her father was a court clerk. Although their homes were separated by only a few city blocks, all part of the Gas House District, Ann lived on the right side of the district, and Steve Boxer on the wrong side. Not that Ann's family ever said much about that, nor openly proclaimed that their position in life was superior to that of the Boxers'; it was just a reality. The Boxers were poor, very poor. Steve's father was a street vendor, a trade he'd picked up in the Depression. When Steve was young, his father had a wagon with frankfurters and soda, which he pushed to busy streetcorners during the day.

Right from the start, Ann adored Steve Boxer. He was an older man, three years older than she, and in the early high school years, that seemed a lifetime of experience. Ann's one disappointment with Steve was that he had quit high school and was drifting from one dead-end job to another. The Gannon family tradition had always been to attend college. A high school dropout was a far cry from what Ann Gannon's father expected for her, and Ann felt no differently. Yet she knew that Steve was intelligent, decent, thoughtful. He just never had the chance to know anything better than the harsh world of Avenue B.

Steve was intrigued and pleased with this bright, pretty Irish girl from Second Avenue. When she started talking to him of finishing high school, getting a better job, going to college at night, she made it sound as though it could all really happen.

Steve had always had a talent for drawing. He would often go downtown on Sunday mornings—by himself and later with Ann—to walk through the deserted Wall Street area, studying and sketching the huge stone buildings, the statues, the lintels, the setbacks, the gargoyles. Steve and Ann began talking about his going to drafting school and later, perhaps, becoming an architect.

But the Japanese bombed Pearl Harbor before Steve got started, and a Japanese fighter shot down his plane, and all their dreams were over. And Ann and the three children were alone. They moved into the Florida Flats with Ann's parents, and later, when Ann started teaching, into their own apartment in the same building. Jim Fay, the Democratic leader from the Anawanda Club, on the next corner from the Florida Flats, talked to Monsignor O'Connell from Epiphany—Ann's father being an Irish Democrat, her late husband being a war hero—and Ann began to teach. When her children were old enough to go to school, they attended Epiphany.

Thus, Ann Gannon Boxer's world revolved around three blocks in the city of New York, and around three children. Her hopes were pinned primarily on Marty. He talked of becoming an architect, attending Cooper Union, fulfilling his father's ambitions and dreams.

Marty had always excelled in sports, first in the sandlot over by Bellevue Hospital, and then in Stuyvesant High School. And when a scholarship from the Veterans of Foreign Wars post on Twenty-third Street became available, and the trustees of Browning College accepted him, Ann Gannon Boxer was in God's own heaven.

But she and the girls would be all alone now. She had come to rely on Marty so much lately.

J.T. Wright was assigned to be Marty Boxer's Big Brother at Browning. That meant that J.T., then a junior in the college, had to get in touch with Marty at home, discuss his upcoming residency at Browning, explain the traditions, help to indoctrinate Little Brother into the upcoming world, what clothes he would need, what books, answer any questions about Browning, and in general, make the transition into the Browning world easier.

J.T. wasn't thrilled by the prospect of being anyone's Big Brother. He was far too shy to be as outgoing as he thought a Big Brother should be. He was sure, therefore, that he'd be too awkward to have any kind of rapport with a Little Brother—especially since his assigned Little Brother was attending Browning on an athletic scholarship. J.T. knew, from years of experience with his own father, that he had very little, if anything, in common with a football player. As he rode down to New York City on the railroad, J.T. kept thinking of what he would say, how he would greet Little Brother. They had spoken on the phone and somehow agreed that they should each spend a weekend at the other's home. He had agreed to go to the city first and Marty agreed to spend a weekend, two weeks hence, at J.T.'s home in Millville. J.T. was imagining, as the train bounced and clacked toward New York, a gruff, coarse, beer-swilling football player. The image made J.T. cringe. His palms began to sweat as he stood in the concourse of Grand Central Station, watching the information booth, looking for Marty Boxer. Actually, J.T. was supposed to be *at* the information booth to meet Marty. But he took a position well removed from the booth and waited. He wanted to see Marty first, wanted to see what this Little Brother looked like, size him up. Although how that would change anything, J.T. didn't know. He still had to meet Boxer, be with him, regardless of what he looked like when he first showed. But seeing him first would give J.T. a slight advantage, an edge, at least in his own mind, before he had to go over and introduce himself. And J.T. liked to have an edge.

Hundreds of people were streaming by J.T. each minute, some on the run, some ambling, some staring up at the train schedule on the wall. He didn't see anyone who looked like a football player waiting around. Then J.T. saw a tall, handsome young man in slacks and a sports jacket; the jacket looked new, as if it might have been bought for someone about to go off to college. The young man had a strong face and dark, curly hair. He was about as tall as J.T.'s father, and about as big through the shoulders and chest. But in that strength and size there was no sign of the beefy boor that J.T. was dreading. In fact, there was a delicate Botticelli quality to the youth's aquiline nose, and something sensitive in the dark eyes. J.T. took a few steps away from the side wall near the ticket counter where he pretended to be reading a timetable, circling slowly, like a shark, toward the young man at the information booth. The young man now started to study J.T. They looked away from each other, then each sneaked another look.

"J.T.?" said the tall young man cautiously.

"Marty?"

"Hi, J.T., I'm Marty Boxer."

"Hi, I'm J.T. Wright. Boy, that's one hell of a dumb introduction."

They laughed and shook hands.

"How was your trip?"

"How can trips on the Central be?"

"I guess you're right. Let me take your bag," Marty said, reaching down and lifting J.T.'s overnight bag.

"I'll take it. It's not heavy."

"I've got it. You're my guest," said Marty. They started to walk toward the exit. "I'm sure glad to meet you. I've been looking forward to it."

"You have?"

"Sure. I mean, going to Browning and all is quite a thing for me and my family." He saw the quizzical look on J.T.'s face. "Well, you see, my dad is dead, you know, and, well, my family can't afford to send me to college. My mom's a teacher. Don't let her bother you, by the way, if she plays you up like the big man on campus. I told her my Big Brother was coming down, and boy, she got all excited, got all the shopping done, cooked a big meal . . ."

J.T. was studying this handsome young man. His enthusiasm and openness was real and engaging.

"Anyway," Marty continued as they reached Lexington Avenue, "when I got this scholarship to Browning, well, wow, I mean that was it, you know. My mother was so proud. She's a schoolteacher, you know. I told you that already, didn't I?"

"That's okay."

They were weaving through a stream of people coursing into the station. The evening rush-hour return to the suburbs was beginning.

"Do you get to the city very often?" Marty asked.

"No, not really."

"Where are you from? Home, I mean?"

"Millville. I don't imagine you've heard of it. It's one of those quaint little towns in the country."

"Sounds nice. I love the country. Not that I get to it very often."

"Well, you're going to come up and spend the day, I mean the weekend, with us. And when you do, you'll have plenty of country. Of course, you'll have to watch out for my old man. I'll warn you about him now. He's a sports freak. Big guy, like you, and when he heard my Little Brother was going to Browning on an athletic scholarship, he got as enthusiastic as you say your mom did about me. Boy, he'll have your plate heaped to the ceiling every time you come over, and buy gallons of milk for you to drink. He wanted me to be a football player. I kind of disappointed him. I'm not exactly built like a fullback."

"Heck, with your courses and majors, my mom'll do the same thing to you. She'll probably talk your head off about school."

J.T. smiled as they stood on Lexington Avenue, surrounded by people rushing and bustling. They had struck up a friendship that welled up from somewhere inside of them, and hit just the right note.

MAY 10, 1956

"HURRY UP, GIRLS," urged Courtnay Crawford, standing on a ladder, as she strung a long roll of red crepe paper across the ceiling of the student dining room.

The large room, usually filled with the clatter of plates and the gossip and laughter of hundreds of college girls, was slowly being transformed with streamers, colored paper balls, and a mirror-faceted revolving globe, into a ballroom for the Junior Hop of Caldwell College, Class of '57.

"Do we have any more streamers, Courtnay?" asked Mary Sprain, who had just cleared a dance area.

Mary, like most of the other girls, wore a plaid skirt, a button-down shirt, and a blazer with leather elbow patches. Most of the girls wore dirty white buck shoes.

"If there are no more in the large cardboard box, then that's it," said Courtnay, who was chairman of the Dance Committee. She stretched to give more push to a thumbtack. She backed down the ladder, then looked around the room. A few girls were still placing candles, flowers, and ashtrays on the tables—the dean of women, with much misgiving, had relented about the ashtrays, but only for the girls' escorts to smoke, and then only if it was absolutely necessary.

"It certainly looks different now," said Sandy Shields, a member of the committee, walking over to Courtnay.

"I'll say," replied Courtnay.

"Well, are you ready?" called Grace Ann Upham as she entered the dining hall. "Hey, this place looks great. Are you finished?"

"Just about," said Sandy Shields.

"Well, then, let's get moving if we're going to watch rugby practice."

Grace Ann was eager to start out for their brother college, Benjamin Browning, an exclusive men's school about ten miles down the road on the Hudson, to watch the last rugby practice before the big Founder's Day game on Sunday. Founder's Day at Browning and the Junior Hop at Caldwell were always scheduled for the same weekend, toward the end of the school year, signaling the end of classes and the last cram before end-of-term exams.

"I'm ready," said Marguerite Stevens, who had been seated at one of the decorated tables. She picked up her books. "Anyone want a lift?"

"I do," said Sandy.

"Wait for me," said Ronnie duPont, who was standing on a chair, retying a fallen streamer.

Courtnay's car was a new Corvette, painted a custom shade of coral. Her father had given it to her as an advance graduation present.

"I'll go with Courtnay," Grace Ann called as the girls ran across the wide lawn.

Marguerite Stevens and three other girls piled into Marguerite's large, year-old Pontiac convertible. Marguerite pushed a lever and the top folded back behind the rear seat.

"Last one there is a rotten egg," yelled Grace Ann from the passenger seat in the Corvette.

"You're on," Marguerite responded as she backed out of her parking space with the top still descending. She was closer to the exit than Courtnay, and as she backed out, her car blocked Courtnay's.

"You rat!" Courtnay protested.

The girls laughed as the two cars, Courtnay's right behind Marguerite's, tore down the campus road. Courtnay tried to pass, but Marguerite's car solidly hogged the road.

"Hey, no fair." Grace Ann, holding on to the top of the windshield, stood up and shouted in the streaming wind.

The girls ahead waved goodbye to Courtnay and Grace Ann. They laughed as the cars accelerated along the road high on the west side of the Hudson. The surrounding hills were verdant, lush, bathed in warm spring sunlight as far as the eye could see.

Courtnay blew her horn at Marguerite. The girls in Marguerite's car turned around, their thumbs in their ears, wagging their hands and sticking out their tongues at Courtnay's frustrated attempts to pass them. Just before the two cars reached the turn that led to an iron gate and the narrow, tree-lined road to Browning, they passed a shopping plaza. Courtnay shifted into low gear and gunned her car into the entrance of the parking lot. Marguerite, seeing Courtnay's car in the rearview mirror, stepped on her accelerator. But the Pontiac was no match for the Corvette. Courtnay cut through an aisle of parked cars, aiming at the far exit. When she reached the exit, she was a car-length ahead of Marguerite and pulling away.

Now it was Grace Ann's turn, her hair flowing in the wind as she knelt on the seat, to stick out her tongue at Marguerite and her passengers. Courtnay slowed down almost to a crawl, hogging the center of the road, forcing Marguerite to follow at the same pace. Marguerite blew her horn. Courtnay retaliated, even louder, as the two cars made their way through the front gate of Browning.

Benjamin Browning College had been built high on a plateau above the Hudson River. The campus was picturesque. Tree-lined paths wound between old, ivy-clad brick buildings. Interspersed with the old buildings, and designed to blend in unobtrusively, were some recently added contemporary buildings such as the Harris Library, donated by the alumni Harris Brothers of the investment banking firm of the same name. There were new dorm facilities for underclassmen, donated by an anonymous alumnus. The athletic fields were along the bank of the river at the foot of a sweeping, grassy hill. Downriver, near the George Washington Bridge, this rise was called the Palisades. But here, at the edge of the Hudson Valley, the embankments bordering the river were not so steep or dramatic. That was the way everything was at Benjamin Browning College: underplayed, subtle. There was no great show of wealth, no ostentation. The moneyed families who had been sending their sons to Browning for decades were secure in their old, enormous wealth, wealth, which they never flaunted but merely used as the foundation for the future giants of industry and banking. There were also scholarship students at Browning whose athletic prowess or intellectual potential overrode considerations of their lack of blue blood or old green money, and students whose families were involved in government. The families of these last were not rich, but they were powerful, the front-runners for the wealthy patrons who furthered political ambitions in return for government influence on behalf of big business and high finance. It was unseemly for wealthy old families to dirty their hands in the world of politics. To finance it, to watch discreetly as others accepted their support and did their bidding, was sufficient. And to accept at Browning the sons of the most powerful of their political surrogates was to ensure continued fealty.

The girls parked the two cars at the top of the road that led down to the athletic field, where Browning's rugby team was involved in an inter-squad scrimmage.

"Is Marty playing?" Courtnay asked anxiously of no one in particular as she scanned the field. The girls walked toward the sidelines, where the substitutes and the coach were.

"I think I see him in the middle of that, that . . ." Marguerite tried to think of the word.

"It's a scrum," interjected Sandy, "which always sounds deliciously sexy to me."

Sandy's outspoken ways always shocked the other girls. Although it was a woman's secret, never revealed to men under any circumstances, the girls knew Sandy was physically passionate, sensual. Perhaps what shocked the other girls most was her candor. All the girls, whether or not they admitted it, were excited by the young men, their strong muscles, the touch of their rougher skin against their cheeks while they danced, their hard breathing in the dark, secluded paths leading back to the dorms. Sex had been quite a topic of conversation after Sandy came back one night, roused all her close chums, and revealed that she was the first of them to have had a man. The other girls had blushed with embarrassment, and then envy and curiosity set in. Sandy had to go into details many times to satisfy those who wanted to know just how it was done and how it felt.

"There he is!" cried Courtnay as the scrum seemed to burst apart. Marty Boxer ran with the ball, and the spectators screamed encouragement. Then he lateraled to Roderick McDowell Watson.

"He scored, he scored," the spectators began to shout.

"Hello, David," Sandy said to one of the substitute players, as the girls reached the sidelines. She was not very interested in the game.

"Hi, Sandy," said David, flushed with enthusiasm for the score, which broke the tie.

Sandy remained standing next to David, gazing casually out toward the playing field. There was a time-out now. The first-team players listened to the coach give instructions for defending their lead as the assistant managers distributed towels and water bottles.

Other substitutes stole glances at Sandy standing next to David; two of them nudged each other. They didn't know all, but they knew Sandy was as close to hot stuff as they could get, and they were curious and anxious.

Sandy studied Marty Boxer as he wiped his face with a towel. He was one of the best-looking men on campus. Besides, he was a curiosity—an athletic scholarship student from New York City who had no idea who or what the families of any of his classmates were or did. Marty was totally common. Sandy watched the biceps in Marty's arms flex and swell as he wiped his face and neck.

Marty looked over at the girls and smiled. But he wasn't looking at Sandy. It was Courtnay, wearing Marty's ring on a chain around her neck, who had all his attention.

"That was sensational, Marty," Sandy called enthusiastically.

Marty's eyes shifted to Sandy for a moment. He smiled, then turned his eyes back to Courtnay. Marty was a very straight young man, and Courtnay was his girl.

The coach called Marty to attention, and looked frowningly at the girls on the sidelines.

The scrimmage resumed as the coach and team managers

ran off the field. The head manager, a sallow-skinned senior in wrinkled chino pants and dirty white bucks, nodded a shy smile at Courtnay.

"How can you stand that little man?" Sandy shuddered. "What's his name again?"

"J.T. Wright," Courtnay replied, her eyes on Marty. "Truthfully, I can't stand him either. But he's Marty's Big Brother, and Marty thinks J.T. is really terrific. Marty insists I fix him up with dates."

"Who did you fix him up with for the Hop?"

"Margo Haupt."

"That cute blonde sophomore?" Sandy said. "Why would she go out with someone as drippy as Wright?"

J.T. heard his name mentioned. He didn't know what the girls had said, but he glanced at them in the shy, hangdog way he usually had around women.

"Because," Courtnay explained quietly, "Marty said that if J.T. didn't go, he didn't want to go either. Randy Haupt, Margo's brother, is on the team with Marty. That's how come J.T. is going to the dance with Margo."

"I can't imagine what Marty sees in J.T.," said Sandy. "He isn't attractive or rich or funny or fun, or anything."

"What's his father do?" asked Ronnie, who had been listening from Courtnay's other side.

"His father is a congressman and the Republican political boss of Ulster County, which is the county we're standing in right now."

"Ahh! The plot thickens," said Ronnie.

"His father also happens to be on that committee in Washington, whatever it's called, that has to do with finance and banking," Courtnay added.

Sandy nodded knowingly.

The final whistle sounded with the first-team players victorious. Marty, after getting slapped on his rear end a few times by his teammates, ran over to Courtnay.

"Marvelous, Marty," said Courtnay, kissing his cheek.

The rest of the girls were delighted to be surrounded by the other players.

J.T. Wright came over, directing a sheepish smile at Marty; then, self-consciously, the smile evaporated.

"Thanks, Otto," Marty grinned, reaching out and pulling J.T. into a kind of headlock. "You were right, you know that, Wright."

J.T. grimaced. "How could I be wrong? Otto Wright can't be wrong, can he?" That was a standing joke between Marty and J.T. Marty called him Otto because, backward or forward, Otto spelled Otto—and Otto Wright was, therefore, no matter which way you looked at him, always right.

"You said to tighten up the defense and you were right, as usual." Marty ran his hand quickly through J.T.'s slick hair.

"Hey, stop it," J.T. protested, breaking free of Marty's grip, smoothing his hair.

A car was driven quickly down the hill, dust billowing behind it. Mary Thorne coursed right up to them and jammed on her brakes. She looked worried.

"What's the matter?" asked Sandy.

"Courtnay, you just got a call from Lester Lanin's office."

"The band people for tonight?"

"Right."

"And?"

"The man on the phone, a Mr. Richards, started giving me double-talk. He said they were having trouble getting a bus or a band here tonight or something because of I don't know what."

"What?" Courtnay moaned.

"He left his number for you. I didn't really understand what he was talking about."

"What are we going to do?" asked Sandy. "It's too late to get another band now."

"We can always dance to records," said Grace Ann.

"In formals? Where's the number?" Courtnay asked, annoyed.

"There's a phone in the students' lounge," said Marty. "Call from there."

A crowd formed around the pay phone in the students' lounge now. The players were still in their blue and gray Rugby uniforms. Other Browning students, in chinos, button-down shirts, and school blazers, joined them. J.T. was on the phone, waiting to be connected.

Although he wasn't the most popular person in the senior class, everyone recognized that J.T. knew how to talk, knew how to handle serious matters. He had taken the phone, and immediately—reversing the charges—called his father's office. He wanted to place his calls through the switchboard there, so he wouldn't seem like some schoolboy talking business from a pay phone.

"Hello, Helen, this is J.T. Is my father in?" He listened for a moment. "All right, then, dial Superintendent Kennedy, at the state police barracks."

"What do the state police have to do with this?" asked a male voice between sips from a Coke bottle.

J.T. shut his eyes patiently as he waited.

"Superintendent Kennedy? Yes, J.T. Wright." He waited. "How are you?" he said with a smile. "He's fine, too, thanks . . . I sure will . . . I wanted to ask you a little favor if I could, Mr. Kennedy. Dad isn't in right now. But I thought maybe I could call you and ask anyway. I hope you don't mind."

The people in the lounge strained to catch whatever they could.

"I really appreciate that. Dad will too. You have offices down in the city too, don't you? Yes, New York City, sir." He raised his eyebrows and smiled at Marty when he said *sir*. "Well, I'm over at Browning and there's this big formal over at Caldwell tonight. Now, the school contracted with an orchestra from the city . . . I know this request is a little unusual . . . but this band is giving us a hard time, right at the last minute. Frankly, I doubt they actually intend to show up. And that'll really screw things up, if you'll pardon my expression, sir."

Everyone in the room got a kick out of that. J.T. covered the mouthpiece and made a face for people to keep quiet.

"I was wondering if someone in your office down there could call and let this band outfit know that certain people are interested in the dance up here coming off without a hitch."

J.T. listened, his eyes wandering over the crowd.

"Oh, I didn't mean for you to go out of your way and do this yourself, sir," J.T. protested. "I thought perhaps one of your men could take care of it . . . I know it's an imposition . . ." He listened. "I'll give you the name of the outfit." He made a hurried motion to Courtnay. Courtnay jotted something on the back of a notebook.

"The name of the orchestra outfit is Lester Lanin, and their address . . . oh, you already know them? Oh, I see. You have to have your troopers help them occasionally when they're playing at society affairs in Chappaqua and Millville and Saratoga. Well, then, that ought to make it even easier. Shall I call you back?" He paused. "No, I don't have a phone in my room. I'm in the student lounge right now. I'll have to ring you back. Oh, okay." He gave the number of the pay phone and thanked the superintendent effusively, then hung up.

The group looked at him eagerly.

"He's going to call back in a few minutes."

The group milled around the lounge, waiting for the phone to ring, sipping Cokes and horsing around. A sophomore came in, wanting to make a call. He was told to walk to another phone.

"I told you J.T. was really okay, didn't I?" Marty said to Courtnay privately.

"It'll be terrific if he gets this all straightened out. Although it probably won't help his personality. He already acts like he knows everything, or like he's just swallowed the canary or something."

"He's just shy."

"A lot of people are shy, Marty, but they don't act like he does."

"Well, try to be nice to him if we have a dance tonight. Don't make him feel uncomfortable."

"Don't make *him* feel uncomfortable? How about telling him that for me?"

"Come on, hon," said Marty. "What the heck, you're the most popular person in the school, the queen of the prom, the most beautiful . . ."

She smiled.

The phone rang. One of the rugby players answered. "Just a second," he said, "he's right here. It's Lester Lanin's office," he said, handing the phone to J.T.

"Hello," J.T. said curtly. "Yes, it is. Oh, really," he said, his eyes narrowing with concentration. "Yes, the superintendent is a good friend of ours too."

J.T. turned toward the crowd, nodding. "You will. Very well," he said smugly. "Miss Crawford, the dance chairman, is here. I think you should tell her that. I know she'll be relieved to hear it."

J.T. nodded his head vigorously, a big, satisfied smile on his face. He handed the phone to Courtnay.

"Otto Wright—are you right again?" Marty laughed, picking J.T. up in the air. J.T. grimaced in Marty's bear hug.

The crowd cheered wildly as Courtnay announced that Lester Lanin would indeed be playing at the Caldwell Hop.

MARCH 13, 1960

THE UPROAR THAT STARTED IN HER FAMILY when Courtnay Crawford announced that she and Marty were going to be married was not as loud or long as it might have been—nor nearly as great as the uproar had been in her sophomore year at Caldwell College, when she was dating Stan Warinski, one of the locals from the town where Caldwell was located. Stan was handsome and fun, and Courtnay, isolated and lonely in an all-girls school, had been delighted to have some pleasant male companionship. But when her family heard that she was steadily dating the son of a local plumber, a running battle ensued. And of course, the more the family downgraded her choice, the more resolute and loyal to Stan she became.

The family used every argument they could think of: the Warinskis had no social position, no money; Stan had no job, no future, no career; she'd have to get a job to support herself in a fashion that would be, at best, far shabbier than what she was used to; the living and spending habits she had grown up with would have to be abandoned.

The family even importuned family friends and retainers to speak to Courtnay about this totally impractical liaison. Her uncle, Howard Thorpe, then the attorney general of the State of New York, sent his personal lawyer, John Vogt, to speak to Stan several times. Vogt and Stan would meet, have a pleasant meal together, and when it was over, Vogt would explain to Stan that his continued dating of Courtnay could lead nowhere for either of them, and that it was unfair of Stan to tie Courtnay to his kind of life. Vogt, reluctantly but loyally, even offered Stan money on behalf of the family to stop seeing Courtnay. Stan told Vogt to go to hell for his efforts.

John Vogt grew to respect Stan, and ultimately had to report back to the family that, if anything, the meetings with Stan were making things worse.

The family seemed to resign themselves to the situation after that; or at least they played a waiting game, and in time, Courtnay and Stan did stop seeing each other, although Courtnay occasionally called Stan—even now—just to have a friendly chat. Stan, Courtnay thought, had an unfailing eye for the true value of a situation. When Courtnay was down, hurt, or lonely, she would telephone Stan to ask his advice. Stan could always see the problem far more clearly than Courtnay could, and in no time at all he would have her laughing. She even discussed her engagement to Marty with him, including the fact that Marty's family had no background, no money, and she was afraid that her family would start the same old arguments all over again. But Stan reasoned that her family would appreciate Marty's college education and his acceptance at Yale Law School—J.T. Wright was just finishing his law studies at Yale. At least she was engaged to a man with a future. Stan suggested that Courtnay should threaten to resume dating *him*, if the family gave her too hard a time about Marty.

It turned out that her family's resistance to Marty was mild, in comparison to its earlier resistance to Stan. Courtnay and Marty married just before he graduated third out of forty-two in Browning's class of 1958. Marty enrolled in the Yale Law School, partly on scholarship, partly on grant. The couple rented a three-room apartment in a private house on a tree-lined New Haven street within walking distance—if you liked long walks—of the law school.

J.T. Wright continued to be one of the major forces in Marty's life. It was he who counseled Marty to choose Yale. And it was J.T.'s tutoring that enabled Marty to achieve his fine marks at Browning. J.T. tutored

Marty in every subject for his four years at Browning. Even after J.T. had graduated from Browning, Marty would stay at J.T.'s house in Millville at least one weekend a month, and J.T. would come home from Yale to tutor him. And it was J.T. who had predicted accurately that the Yale background would set Marty well, not only in landing a good job with a Wall Street law firm, but with Courtnay's family.

Marty stood facing the bathroom door in their apartment. He could hear water beating on the shower curtains inside. "Come on, Courtnay, hurry out of the shower. Courtnay—can you hear me?"

The water stopped. "I'll be right out," she called back. "I just have to rinse my hair."

"We're supposed to meet J.T. in half an hour."

"J.T. can wait a little bit. He won't turn into a pumpkin, will he?" Courtnay opened the door, wrapped in a bath towel. Another towel was twisted into a turban on top of her head.

As much as J.T. and Courtnay saw each other because of Marty, they were never close or friendly. Whether J.T. made Courtnay defensive because of his attitude, or whether some attitude of Courtnay's made J.T. react poorly, neither could say. But Courtnay rarely had difficulty in getting along with other people. J.T., on the other hand, rarely had people around long enough to get along with them at all.

"Don't be hard on J.T. He just can't seem to let his hair down with you, the way he can with me."

"He's starting to lose it, did you notice?"

"Lose it?"

"His hair. Did you notice?"

"I didn't." Marty shrugged as he stepped into the bathroom. He turned the water on in the shower, then leaned toward the mirror in the medicine cabinet and looked at his hair.

"Will you love me if I get bald?" Marty asked.

"Of course I will, silly boy. But not J.T. I won't like him better one way or the other."

"I think you enjoy nurturing your dislike of J.T. Why?" Marty noticed that Courtnay's towel had slipped a bit. She had beautiful breasts.

"If you really want to know, it's because he's a user. Particularly, he uses you so he can have social contacts with people who otherwise would have nothing to do with him."

Courtnay noticed Marty staring at her bosom. She didn't bother to adjust the slipping towel.

"Use me? I use him. He tutors me, gives me his old term papers, everything. If it wasn't for J.T., I wouldn't have had the grades I had at Browning; I probably wouldn't be living here with you in New Haven. I'd probably not be living with you at all. The fact that he helped me get accepted to Yale didn't hurt my prospects with your family." Marty reached out and tugged at the end of Courtnay's towel. It came loose and fell to the floor.

"And I wouldn't miss living with you for anything." He moved closer to her and held her in his arms. She wrapped her arms gently around his back. Her soft breasts pressed warmly against his bare chest.

"I wouldn't want to miss that either," she said, kissing his neck. Her hand slid down his chest to his pants. She worked at the buttons. "I guess there is some good in J.T.—he helped bring us together." Their mouths fused, their tongues dancing together. She tugged at his pants and shorts—first at one hip, then the other—until they dropped down to his knees.

Courtnay kissed the midline of Marty's chest with her warm mouth. She reached down and slowly lifted his legs, one at a time, from his pants and shorts. Her tongue was in his navel, then it coursed hotly down his stomach. Courtnay pushed his legs into a wide stance, her tongue dancing lower on his stomach. She slowly eased herself onto her knees. Her mouth never left his body. Her arms wrapped around his lower body. She held him to herself as she kissed and ran her tongue along his thighs at each side of his swollen masculinity. Suddenly she grasped his buttocks and pulled him even closer, her mouth licking, kissing, rubbing, gently sucking, devouring every part of him.

He drew himself free of her mouth and dropped to his knees next to her on the floor, pulling her firmly until they lay next to each other, their bodies drawn into each other in a moaning, frenzied passion.

MARCH 28, 1960

LUCY ARNOLD WALKED QUIETLY into Senator Evard Anders's office. The senator was talking on the telephone, half twisted toward the large window behind his desk, which overlooked the Capitol building. He was speaking with General Skip Richardson, Chairman of the Joint Chiefs of Staff. Senator Anders was on the Senate Ways and Means Committee, as well as the Judiciary Committee, and several other of the most powerful committees in the Senate. His eighteen years in. the Senate, as well as his dominant position as leader of the Southern Democratic bloc, gave him influence and power beyond that of the ordinary senator. The members of President Eisenhower's staff were his errand boys; the President wanted it that way. The senior senator from North Carolina was able, if he so desired, to deliver votes that were crucial to the Republican President's legislative program. And the President wanted Senator Anders to deliver those votes. Despite rumors that Senator Anders had aspirations toward the Democratic presidential nomination in 1960, President Eisenhower still accorded the senator great deference and respect. He needed Anders more than he resented the senator's longing to joust with Eisenhower's hand-picked successor, Richard Nixon.

The senator twisted back to his desk. He noticed Lucy gazing over his head, out the window. It might be a terrific view of the Capitol, he thought, but what the heck business does my secretary have lolly-gagging out the window? The senator motioned to Lucy to speak. She mouthed her message silently. The senator couldn't understand her and listen to the Chairman of the Joint Chiefs at the same time. He motioned her to wait a moment.

"Okay, General, if you say all those tanks are still essential, even in the Atomic Age, I'll have to go along with you. But you're going to have to appear in front of the committee and explain why." He listened for a moment. "Of course I'm going to be with you. Christ, General, you know I'm a Keep-America-Strong man. I want you to have all the weaponry you need. But hell, I'm just one member of the committee. There are a bunch of New York liberals you'll have to convince." He paused again. "Well, sure, I'll try and convince them too. Do all I can. It's always good to hear from you, too. Right. Thanks for calling." The senator hung up the phone and looked to Lucy.

"It's J.T. Wright, for his three o'clock appointment," she said.

"Who?"

"The young lawyer that joined the counsel staff for your Judiciary Committee. Big Jim Wright's son."

"Oh, right, right. Put down on my list that I want to give Big Jim a call and chew some fat with him when I get a minute. What's the young man want?"

"I don't know, Senator. He called and asked for an appointment with the chairman of his committee. I told you about it, and you said to give him an appointment."

"I did? When was that?"

Lucy lifted a notebook she had been holding at her side, and thumbed through the pages. She always marked down the precise time and date of each instruction. The senator could never remember the instructions he gave, and sometimes denied giving them when they conflicted with something else he wanted to do.

"It was three-thirty on Thursday, March twenty-first. You were sitting at your desk. You had just dictated a letter to Congressman Kruger."

"All right, all right. You know," Anders said, smiling, "I hate that damn note-taking habit of yours. You always make me look bad."

The senator and Lucy had been together as employer and employee for a long time. They had also been together for other, more intimate reasons. But that had been a long time ago. Somehow their dalliance had been able to survive that well-known dictum in the political and business worlds, don't fool around with the people who work in your office. The senator's former personal relationship with Lucy never interfered with their working relationship. And now it was so many years ago that they each occasionally wondered if it had ever really happened.

"Shall I show him in, Senator?"

"I guess so. What else do I have on the schedule?"

"Just a massage at the athletic club."

"Just a massage! At my age, that's the closest I get to having a party." He laughed, mostly because Lucy knew that despite all his protestations of age and seniority, which sat well with his constituents, there was still plenty of the devil in him—particularly in regard to the wife of a certain representative on the Judiciary Committee. The representative didn't know, or didn't let on that he knew, that the reason he was so favored by the chairman with key assignments was that it gave the chairman more access to the representative's wife.

Lucy walked out of the large paneled office and returned with J.T. Wright.

The senator studied J.T. He knew J.T. was on staff. In fact, after Big Jim had called, the senator had personally directed J.T.'s appointment to the staff. Although he had seen J.T. in passing occasionally, the senator had never really taken a good look at the boy before. Must look like the mother, the senator thought to himself. Doesn't look a damn thing like Big Jim. J.T. was wearing a gray herringbone suit with black unshined penny loafers. He looked small, unmuscular.

"Well, well," the senator said jovially, "the linchpin of my committee's legal staff."

"Not quite, Senator," J.T. said diffidently, although he was sure the description was accurate.

"Sit down, sit down. How's your old daddy?"

"Really well, sir," said J.T. in his most respectful tone.

"What can I do for you, young man?"

"Well, sir, I have an idea that would be both beneficial to the American people and at the same time very advantageous to you personally."

"That sounds like one hell of an idea, son. What is it?" The senator winked at Lucy, who was standing back from the desk, silently taking notes.

"Well, I've been doing a lot of reading into the workings of past Senate committees . . ."

"That's very commendable. Very."

"Thank you, sir. Recently I've been studying the Committee on Un-American Activities. Those McCarthy hearings excited and engrossed the public at the time."

"Yes?" The senator wanted to get to his massage.

"And they made an unknown senator from Wisconsin a very famous man."

"You think I'm an unknown senator?"

"Not at all, sir. But I believe that the Judiciary Committee could conduct hearings that could have the same, or greater, impact on the public. And with network television coverage, which McCarthy didn't have at the beginning, such hearings could make the star of new hearings—yourself, sir—a household name."

"You're thinking that might help me if I were interested in the presidential candidacy, is that it?" The senator's eyes narrowed on J.T.

"I have no idea about the presidential candidacy, sir," J.T. lied. He knew the senator was jockeying every day to enhance his presidential field position. "But it certainly couldn't hurt your political reputation to be in everybody's home on television every day."

"Just what do you imagine will absorb the public's interest in such fashion?" the senator asked, trying to let an appearance of calm serenity mask his curiosity.

"A subcommittee to investigate organized crime. Full hearings, with all stops pulled out. Charts with the names of the major criminals in the United States, the cities they blight, the whole works."

The senator looked at Lucy, who in turn looked at J.T. Neither said anything. J.T. took this as his sign to continue.

"The committee has subpoena power. Big-name crime figures

would be dragged into the light to be exposed. No one's ever done it before. Everyone hears about the syndicate, the mob, the Mafia, but no one knows who or what it is. And no one has ever been able to bring it to light before. With these hearings, you, a man of integrity and courage, will be able to expose this diabolical organization to the American public."

"Let's say these criminals do respond to the subpoena. What makes you think the public will become involved in such hearings?" asked the senator.

"Humanity's perverse fascination with the unknown, with evil and immorality."

"The evil that men do lives after them, eh?"

"Exactly, sir. Why people have this perverse fascination, I don't know—but it's there. Another really important reason the public will be fascinated by the hearings is that these slimy characters will refuse to testify."

"They'll be awfully short hearings then, won't they?" the senator injected.

"Not at all, sir. See, the committee has subpoena power, but not the power to grant immunity from prosecution. The criminals we sub-poena will all hide behind the Fifth Amendment, just like in McCar-thy's hearings . . ."

"Where does that get you, if the witnesses refuse to answer questions?"

"Their refusals make this organized crime syndicate all the more sinister. The press will plaster them all over the front page and on the television screens. If a person knows his way around the newsmen—and, with all due modesty, sir, I made it my business to get to know the newspapermen in this town very personally—they'll write their stories well larded with the right important names, the right slant."

The senator looked at this young lawyer very keenly. "How'd you get to be so conniving, so young?"

"I learned from my daddy where the real power was," J.T. said in a kind of down-home way.

"That figures." The senator smiled.

"So, with the newspaper people ready to play ball with us, and with the right questions asked the right way, when some criminal refuses to answer, the American public will clearly see how dangerous these people really are."

"Listen, I have an appointment a few blocks from here. Why don't you walk with me and tell me more about this idea of yours?" the senator said, standing.

"My pleasure, sir."

"Lucy . . ." The senator started toward the door. "J.T. and I are going to walk a bit. If anyone needs me, you know where we'll be."

"Yes, Senator."

APRIL 10, 1960

THE DOOR TO THE LAVISH SUITE in Washington's Ambassador Hotel opened on a vestibule that led into two rooms: one was a bedroom, the other a sitting room with a convertible sofa and stuffed chairs. Loud talking and laughing escaped from the closed door to the suite. As guests arrived, and the door was opened, loudness, laughter, smoke, and the smell of booze flooded into the corridor.

"Who the hell is there now?" called a voice from the crowded sitting room as the door buzzer sounded.

"Hey, it's Jim Duneden," called another voice from the same room as J.T. opened the door.

A fully stocked folding bar was set up in the sitting room, with a bartender in a white jacket in attendance. Music drifted from a radio.

"Hello, Jim. I'm glad you could make it."

"Oh, yeah, J.T. Glad you asked me," Duneden said, gazing eagerly into the two rooms to see what was happening and who was there.

In the bedroom, a group of six or seven men and three women were drinking, exchanging gossip and dirty jokes. Duneden recognized Bill Crean from the *Washington Post*, as well as Joe Wasnak, a photographer from the same paper. He recognized some of the other men. He didn't know the women; he could see they were kind of flashy, overly made up, with tight clothes and good tits. Duneden stared at a young blonde girl who had her back—and a nice ass—to him. He started for the room with the bar.

"Hey, Jim, you son of a bitch, where the hell have you been?" called "Slats" Peabody, a city editor at CBS, from his perch at the bar. With Slats was Mac Baron from AP. A stunning older blonde woman stood with them. She looked like she could sing Wagner.

Duneden waded into the room enthusiastically, aiming right for Brunhilde.

J.T. didn't mind being left unceremoniously at the door. He wanted all his newly cultivated friends from the press and television world to enjoy the booze and women he provided at his monthly meeting of the Mountaineers' Club. J.T., in fact, had founded and funded the Mountaineers' Club singlehandedly, for the very purpose of entertaining members of of the Washington press corps. The first time he had come down on the train to Washington, to be interviewed for the associate counsel position, he had decided that an occasional party to entertain the guys in the press room would go a long way. J.T. even had cards printed up, with the name *Mountaineers' Club* imprinted over twin mountain peaks. Except, if one studied the vague mountains in the background of the membership cards, one realized they weren't mountains at all; they were a woman's breasts. The overt sexual tone of the Mountaineers wasn't exactly to J.T.'s taste, but he knew the guys in the press room would go for such things. There were only two requirements for membership in the club: you had to be connected with the news media in some capacity—mostly in reporting or editing—and you had to get a membership card from J.T. Wright.

"Boy, J.T., those three in there are something," said Joe Wasnak, coming out of the bedroom on his way to the bar for a refill.

"I'm glad you think so," said J.T., flicking him a smile. He stood in the vestibule, from which he could keep an eye on the activities.

Wasnak got his drink and started back to the bedroom. "Are there going to be more dames?"

"There may be, later," J.T. lied. "Aren't five enough for you?"

Wasnak laughed. "I guess you're right, J.T."

Of course I am, J.T. thought to himself. *Otto Wright is never wrong. What sophomoric shit*, J.T. silently reprimanded himself.

The blonde woman joined J.T. in the vestibule.

"I'm going to set up the phonograph in the bedroom," she said. "Is it okay to start now?"

"Whenever you say, Lana," J.T. replied. "I'll leave that stuff up to you."

"Say, J.T., why are you monopolizing the girls?" said Duneden, coming over to them, drink in hand. He was blatantly eyeing Lana. "That's not being a good host."

"Lana, in case you weren't introduced, this is my friend Jim," J.T. said, purposely not giving his friend's last name. "He's the fellow I told you about."

"Oh?" said Duneden with surprise.

"Don't worry, J.T. didn't say anything bad about you," Lana said coyly. "He just said I should be extra nice because you were a special friend of his. He didn't tell me you were good-looking too," she said with professional aplomb.

"Oh, hey. This Brunhilde's got a good line of you-know-what," said Duneden, laughing, putting his arm around Lana's waist. "Anybody ever tell you you were built like Brunhilde?"

"Is that something like a brick shithouse?" Lana shot back coyly.

Duneden laughed loudly. "I knew you were my kind of woman the moment—if you'll pardon the expression—I laid eyes on you."

"He's cute, J.T. You've got a good line yourself," Lana said to Duneden.

Duneden sipped his drink. "That I do, that I do," he said.

"Remember what they say about self-praise," Lana cautioned as she turned out of Duneden's arm and into the bedroom.

"What's that?" He followed her.

"Self-praise stinks."

J.T. winced at the banal repartee. He planned on leaving as soon as the festivities started. After all, he threw these parties for the others; that didn't mean he had to stay.

Lana set up a small portable phonograph on one of the night tables next to the bed. Duneden hovered around her, plugging the phonograph into the wall socket. She put a record on the turntable and set the needle down gently. Pounding striptease music blasted the room.

"Hey, hey," said one of the voices from the bar. "Sounds like a little action is starting in the bedroom."

Others cheered.

Everyone quickly drifted into the bedroom. Two of the girls, nodding to Lana, began to dance in place. The men moved back to give them room. The girls moved provocatively to the music. One began to work at the belt of her dress. The men cheered loudly. She unfastened it and threw it into a corner. She was the center of attention as she teasingly slid off her clothes and played to the leering men, coming close to them as she shook her bare breasts in their drinks. She actually wet one of her doorbell-button nipples in Joe Wasnak's Scotch.

Howls and cheers.

Another girl stripped down to a G-string, then danced through the room, making her way to the vestibule. J.T. pressed himself back into a corner as the girl passed him. A few men followed her into the sitting room, watching her teasingly sliding the G-string down, then up, then further down. Her companion soon followed.

A second pair of girls began a dance routine in the bedroom. The record ended, but the dancers kept bumping and grinding. Lana quietly turned the record over, then joined J.T. in the vestibule to watch her charges. Duneden followed Lana and stood in the vestibule, watching one room, then the other. Soon there were four nude women gyrating, teasing the cheering voyeurs.

"I'm going to take off," J.T. said to Duneden. "Lana knows how to take care of things."

"I bet she does," leered Duneden.

"Why don't you stay, J.T.? Have some fun," Lana suggested.

"I have an appointment with the chairman of the committee," J.T. lied. "Have to go over some material for the crime hearings."

"Right, right," Duneden said, putting his arm around Lana's waist.

The two girls in the bedroom evoked howls and cheers as they began to perform tricks. One balanced drinks on her breasts as she walked across the room. The other, not to be outdone, showed an amazing ability to pick up dollar bills between her legs. The men set up bills for her to pick up.

J.T. quickly slipped out of the doorway, delighted that this meeting of the Mountaineers' Club was coming off so successfully.

APRIL 30, 1960

Senator Anders was at his desk, hidden behind a newspaper he held widespread. J.T. waited quietly at the side of the desk as the senator read an interview of himself by the celebrated *Washington Post* columnist James C.R. Duneden. J.T. gazed absently out the window at the Capitol building, its dome alight in the gathering dusk. Spring had blossomed from winter's gray, and around the Capitol, cherry blossoms danced at the ends of delicate branches. J.T. felt great, felt that his life was in blossom too, ready to bloom in a big way. His name was spread across the front page of every newspaper.

"This is one hell of a column," the senator commented from behind the paper.

"Duneden's a good writer," said J.T.

"Very cooperative too. Didn't put in a thing we didn't discuss in advance." The senator lowered the paper. He was smiling. "Son, you can really deliver."

"Thank you, sir."

The senator put the newspaper up again, then lowered it. "Forgive me for being so rude, reading this here newspaper right in your face," he apologized.

J.T. laughed. "Don't worry about it, Senator. Coverage is what politics is all about, isn't it?"

"Right, right." The senator lifted the paper again.

The senator's secretary entered the office. "Senator?"

"Yes?" the senator said from behind the newspaper.

"It's almost time for the committee meeting."

"What time is it?"

"Four thirty. The meeting is at four forty-five."

"Thank you, Lucy. I'll be finished in a minute. You come along with me too, J.T.," the voice from behind the newspaper said.

"Yes, sir," J.T. answered.

"How'd you like the article?" the voice behind the paper said.

"Are you asking me, Senator?" asked Lucy.

"Well, of course I'm asking you." The senator put down the newspaper, folding it back to its original shape. "I know you've read it already. She reads everything before I do," he said in an aside to J.T., "even my personal mail. She knows what I'm doing, even before I do. Well, what did you think of the interview?"

"Very impressive." Lucy was standing near the door, her pencil and pad in hand.

"Well, for Christmas sake, Lucy, come on in and make like you're going to stay for a few minutes."

Lucy sat on a couch near the door.

"As long as you're going to sit all the way over there, why the hell don't you just sit in your office and leave the door open and we'll shout," the senator smiled. "Come on over here, will you?"

Lucy walked to the senator's desk and sat in the chair opposite J.T.

"You thought it was impressive?"

"Very. It did everything it should have, put you right into the national picture."

The senator looked at J.T. "That was J.T.'s doing. He arranged the interview. He and Duneden and I had lunch and discussed the subjects we would cover, like a dry run. And damned if Duneden didn't go for it all, and cooperate a hundred—and I mean a hundred—percent."

J.T. nodded.

"Now why don't we go to that committee meeting, J.T., and we'll get ourselves approval to hold the hearings. After the members read Duneden's article and see how interested the press and the American public are in organized crime, the vote will go like oil through a funnel."

"That's how you planned the article to break, isn't it, Senator?" said J.T. "Right before the vote?"

"You bet I did," Anders said, standing, walking around the desk toward J.T. "You bet I did." The senator put his arm around J.T.'s shoulder as they walked to the door. "J.T., you are one hell of a smart young man. Isn't he, Lucy?" he said over his shoulder.

Lucy smiled.

The senator and J.T. left for the committee meeting across the street in the Capitol building.

"That was some interview, Senator," Senator Carleton from Louisiana remarked as Senator Anders entered the hearing room.

"Thank you, Senator."

"I never realized you were so concerned about organized crime," Senator Carleton added.

"Well, I've been doing a lot of research into the subject, and damn, I said, this is a serious problem, serious enough to start some hearings and draft some new legislation. Fact is, that's what I'm going to propose today. I hope you'll go along with me on this, Senator?"

"Suppose I will. Especially with the kind of national concern that's indicated in this article."

"Believe me. I just happened to mention to Duneden over lunch last week that I intended to propose such a hearing. He immediately became as interested as could be. By the way, Senator, if we have such hearings, I'm going to propose that they be public hearings, nationally televised, so the people back home can see what a problem organized crime really is."

"National television coverage?" Senator Carleton was impressed. "These hearings sound right on the money to me."

Anders looked around the room. "Looks like most of us are here. Perhaps we should call the meeting to order. By the way, Senator, this subject matter might get under Senator Maggiacomo's skin, seeing that he's eye-talian."

"You think that Senator Maggiacomo is somehow going to try to protect those hoodlums because they're eye-talian too?"

"No, I wouldn't say that. But what the hell, you know, it's kind of like owning up to the fact that your blood kin are polecats. You know what I mean. He could be a mite sensitive about the subject."

"I get you."

"A lot of the members of the committee look up to him. So if he gets a little touchy, you and I are going to have to calm him down, get around him somehow, so he doesn't sidetrack the hearings. Oh, say, Senator Carleton, do you know our new associate counsel to the committee, J.T. Wright?" Anders said, motioning to J.T. to join them.

"No, can't say that I do."

"Senator Carleton, this here is J.T. Wright, one of the brightest young men to join us on Capitol Hill in a long time. You must know his daddy, Big Jim Wright."

"Big Jim? I sure enough do. A good friend of mine. How is your daddy, J.T.?"

"Very well, sir."

"You're the newest member of Craig Rogers's team, eh?" asked Senator Carleton.

"Yes, sir," J.T. acquiesced.

"Excuse me a moment, Senator Carleton," the chairman said. "I want to call the meeting to order."

"Very well, Senator. I'll be talking to you again, young man," Senator Carleton said to J.T. "And be sure to give my very best regards to your daddy, hear?"

"I will, sir."

The twenty-six members of the Joint Judiciary Committee were divided equally between senators and congressmen. The committee was further split along party lines in accordance with the ratio of Democrats to Republicans in each of the Houses of Congress. Since the Senate was Republican, there were more Republican senators. And the House, primarily Democratic, had sent more Democrats.

One of the functions of the committee was to investigate matters that required new legislation or a modification of old legislation, particularly in areas dealing with crime and the criminal justice system.

Organized crime, according to the chairman, fell into the category of new legislation.

The committee members stood throughout the room, conversing as they waited for the meeting to begin.

"Will the meeting please come to order," the chairman announced from his seat midway down the oval table.

The room began to quiet down.

J.T. sat at one end of the long oval table. There was an empty chair next to him. He was delighted to see that Rogers was not around.

"Thank you kindly, gentlemen," said the chairman after the members were all seated. "I have some information I want to share with you this afternoon concerning an area where there is a compelling need for new legislation."

Craig Rogers opened the door, peered in at the long table surrounded by the committee, hesitated, then walked quickly to his seat. J.T. frowned.

"Organized crime is a national contagion," the chairman announced dramatically. "It's like an octopus. Its tentacles reach into every city, every business, every home, wreaking havoc on everything it touches. Our committee counsel has, at my request, studied the subject and reported to me that there exists an incredible void of legislation to control this pestilence."

J.T. watched the committee members, making notes on their reactions to Ander's remarks.

"Organized crime is a vast organization, not unlike an underground government. It is nationwide, worldwide, with a committee-like board of directors as its governing body. It's composed of groups or gangs called families, in cities throughout the country. There is a family in Detroit, in Chicago, in Florida. There are families in New Orleans, in Philadelphia, in Arizona, in New Jersey, in New York. In fact, in New York there are five families. There are families in Rhode Island, in Connecticut, in Massachusetts, as well as many other states." Anders knew that a member of the committee came from each state and city that he had mentioned. "This thing is like a spreading cancer, gentlemen. And there are no laws with which to deal with this cancer. I am recommending that we investigate what legislation is necessary to cope with this plague. I am proposing that we conduct open, televised hearings."

A buzz of soft conversation filled the room.

"Yes, gentlemen," the chairman said loudly, to override the buzzing. "I have had our staff check with the media, with the public, with law enforcement. The public wants to know, the media is anxious to tell them, and the law enforcement agencies are ready to cooperate in every way possible. In other words, gentlemen, the time is ripe for such hearings; our people, our constituents, are waiting for us to act. I would like to hear some of your comments."

The chairman sat, looking around the table. He glanced at Senator Maggiacomo of Connecticut. Maggiacomo's face was pensive as he read some notes on a pad in front of him.

"Senator?" a young representative from New Mexico asked tentatively.

"Yes, Mr. Keller."

"My state is not one you've mentioned where there is a family of these people, but I've read various monographs on the subject, and I was formerly a special agent of the Federal Bureau of Investigation . . ."

That news intrigued several of the members, who looked more carefully in Keller's direction.

"Since there is a code of silence among the members of organized crime," Mr. Keller continued, "who will testify at these hearings other than law-enforcement officials? And, that being the case, what will these hearings reveal that we don't already know or can't easily ascertain from reading official reports and studies already accessible to this committee?"

"That's a very good question, which deserves a very good answer, Mr. Keller," said the chairman. "I think I'd like to have Mr. Wright, our associate counsel, answer that question. Mr. Wright."

J.T. braced himself, then stood. He nodded to the chairman. "Gentlemen, it's a great pleasure to be a member of this committee's legal staff, assisting Mr. Rogers in this study."

Rogers looked at J.T. and nodded slightly. He had no idea what studies had been made on this subject. But with true political aplomb, he rode the wave.

"What Mr. Keller has said is correct," J.T. continued. "There is a great deal of law-enforcement literature available to us. However, the point of these hearings is not to rehash some tired reports and studies, but to dramatically present the picture of this cancer, as the chairman has so aptly called it, to the American public. These hearings—broadcast throughout the country via radio and television—would awaken the public to the magnitude of the problem."

"How would the public's awareness via radio and television help us to formulate legislation, which, as I see it, is the only purpose of these hearings?" asked Representative Wicks from California.

"Shall I answer that question, Mr. Chairman?" J.T. asked.

"Why don't you," the Chairman said, shuffling the hot potato back to J.T.

"Just as the McCarthy hearings aroused the public to the menace of Communism, these hearings would arouse the public to the menace of organized crime."

There were murmurs around the table.

"Now, gentlemen," said the chairman, rising, "let me just suggest one thing. When Mr. Wright refers to the McCarthy hearings, he's referring only to the wide public dissemination of those hearings. However, let us not forget the ultimate fate of the late senator from Wisconsin. We must be careful not to make the same mistakes. This will be a search for the truth, as the lawyers put it, not a witch-hunt."

The murmurs quieted a bit.

"And if we can, by television, bring the menace home to the American public," the chairman continued, "then they, our constituents, can bring to our attention far more information about this menace than is presently in the hands of law enforcement. In other words, these televised hearings are intended not only to get information to the public, but to get some information back from them."

"And television and radio coverage into every corner of the country wouldn't hurt us with our voters, either," Senator Carleton threw in.

The committee members laughed.

"That would be a side effect we could all live with," chided the chairman. "Why don't you continue, Mr. Wright?"

"Thank you, Mr. Chairman. Senator Anders has mentioned the McCarthy hearings and possible abusive methods. The chairman has said that the proposed new hearings wouldn't be the same. That's not to say, however, that there would not be people who would appear at our proposed hearings who would try to hide behind the Fifth Amendment."

"Who would they be?" asked a voice from J.T.'s left. "Surely law-enforcement officials aren't going to take the Fifth."

"Certainly not," said the chairman, rising again. "Mr. Wright is referring to the crime figures. You all know we have the power to subpoena, and we'd subpoena these crime figures right out of their lairs, right out into the light of God's day, and ask them questions about all their activities. As Mr. Keller, who was in the FBI, has already said, there is a code of silence in these crime families. Thus, many of these crime figures would rely on the Fifth Amendment and refuse to answer our inquiries."

"Could we compel them to answer, or punish them for refusing to answer?" asked a representative from Iowa.

"Mr. Rogers, would you help us out with the legal technicalities?" the chairman said diplomatically.

Rogers was caught short. He removed his wire-framed glasses, polished their lenses, and replaced them carefully on his nose.

"Our committee does have subpoena power, gentlemen, but not the power to grant immunity from prosecution based on information uncovered by testimony. Since we cannot grant immunity from prosecution, a witness could claim possible incrimination, and invoke his absolute constitutional privilege against self-incrimination, the Fifth Amendment."

Rogers looked around. Everyone seemed to have understood his explanation. He sat.

"How could we accomplish anything by that?" asked Representative Whalen from the right side of the table. "If they won't answer the questions, what good is calling them in the first place?"

"May I answer that question, Mr. Chairman?" said Senator Maggiacomo, raising his hand.

"Yes, certainly," said the chairman warily.

"The purpose of subpoenaing people you know will refuse to answer questions is to dangle them in front of the American public. As we learned from the McCarthy hearings, people can be crucified for legitimately invoking their Fifth Amendment privilege. In those hearings, witnesses legitimately refused to answer questions about whether they had ever been members of the Communist Party, or a group sympathetic to the aims of Communism as an economic philosophy.

"Remember, back in the early thirties," Senator Maggiacomo continued, "in the middle of the Depression, it was fashionable to be a member of some leftist group trying to figure out how to put bread on the table. How could a person in a responsible job, twenty years later, a person who may have gone to one meeting and found out the whole socialist thing was a lot of baloney, how could that person answer yes to McCarthy's question? There would be no waiting for an explanation. McCarthy didn't want an explanation. He wanted yes or no. Yes was automatic ruin. And if the witness denied the accusation, McCarthy had proof that the witness had been a member for two weeks, or had attended one meeting of an organization long dead and buried.

"I can't imagine that our results would be much different," Senator Maggiacomo said, looking around the table. "What would we ask? 'Are you a member or an associate of members of an organized crime family?' If the witness denies it, we'll present proof that he associates with known or suspected criminals. That'll suffice to make the witness both a liar and a criminal. You all know, gentlemen, we already have laws dealing with perjury and actual crimes. So no new legislation is needed to deal with any person we can prove is either a liar or a criminal. Better yet, perhaps, the witness says, 'Yes, I am an associate of criminals; I was once a criminal, but I haven't committed any crime in twenty years.' What are we going to do, gentlemen? Create laws that banish people who haven't committed a crime—but might in the future? Perhaps, as a third alternative, the witness simply refuses to answer. Wonderful. Then we can crucify him, because obviously he has something to hide. These proposed hearings would merely be an exercise in sensationalism and publicity-gathering, rather than a true search for necessary, viable legislation."

The men around the table were silent as they considered Senator Maggiacomo's remarks.

"Are you saying, then, Senator, that we should forego hearings—just as some say McCarthy's hearings should have never taken place—because some people who only flirted with crime for a short time—just like the one-time Communists—will be embarrassed?" asked Senator Monrow from Georgia. "I say that the good American is *never* involved in crime, and *never* involved in Communism, not even for one day, and those that are, even just once, are *not* good Americans." Senator Monrow's face was flushed with American self-righteousness.

"Are *you* saying, then, Senator," asked Senator Maggiacomo softly, "that those privileges and rights written into our Constitution by very wise men a hundred and eighty years ago, to protect the American people from abuses, should now be ignored because life in the rest of the country isn't always as black and white as it is in Georgia?"

"Sir," said Senator Monrow indignantly, "I don't know what you mean by your reference to black and white, but if you intend to cast aspersions on the sovereign state of Georgia, which I so proudly represent, then I say—"

"Gentlemen, gentlemen," said the chairman.

"No, Mr. Chairman," said Senator Monrow, red as a beet, "I demand an apology from Senator Maggiacomo, who seems a little oversensitive because most of these hoodlums are eye-talians."

All eyes turned to Senator Maggiacomo.

Senator Maggiacomo pursed his lips. "I see many of my fellow members watching me expectantly, as if I should become infuriated by a remark calculated to achieve just that result. First of all, I can not be held responsible for the oversensitivity of my colleague at the use of a very common American—and I emphasize *American*—idiom. I don't know what the senator from Georgia refers to when he suggests that this idiom casts aspersions on the sovereign state of Georgia, but I do invite him to explain to the committee his indignation over my use of it. Perhaps the colors black and white offend him? I don't know. But I'd like to know. And surely, after such an explanation, if there is need for an apology, I shall indeed be delighted to give one. Senator Monrow, the floor is yours."

All eyes returned to Monrow.

"Gentlemen, our function is not to debate other issues," interrupted the chairman. "It is to decide whether the proposed hearings would be feasible and beneficial."

"I don't intend to be hoodwinked into a debate the subject of which was cause for a civil war," said Senator Monrow. "But Senator Maggiacomo should still explain to us *his* reluctance to bring all these hoodlums, whether they be eye-talian or not, out into the open."

"I am not overly reluctant, nor am I unaware that there are criminal elements in this country of Italian or Italian-American ancestry," said Senator Maggiacomo.

The chairman watched the thrusting and parrying with patient amusement. He had seen these two duel many times in the Senate.

"Perhaps I could sum up my position on the proposed hearings quite simply," continued Senator Maggiacomo, "by saying that although there are no alleged crime families in Georgia—Italian or otherwise—still there is unlawfulness, murder, rape, burglary, robbery, and every other crime committed in every other state, every other nation of the world. There are such crimes in Georgia, are there not, Senator Monrow?"

J.T. was getting nervous. The chairman was right, Maggiacomo was crafty.

"Are you waiting for an answer from me, Senator?" said Senator Monrow, aware that the others were looking at him. "You want to know whether there's crime in Georgia? Yes, the answer is yes. Does that in any fashion explain this organized crime problem?"

"Indeed it does," replied Senator Maggiacomo.

"Well, I for one fail to see it."

"Or refuse?" added Senator Maggiacomo.

"Now, Mr. Chairman, am I being baited or am I not? I ask that we conduct this meeting so that we have no undignified displays or insults that require further answer or debate."

"Or perhaps satisfaction," Senator Maggiacomo added. "Unfortunately, where I come from, we have no practice of dueling with our detractors."

"Let me explain the usefulness of these hearings, Senators," J.T. interrupted from the far end of the table.

All eyes turned to the junior counsel.

"We cannot deal with the entire problem of crime at one time with this committee. True, there are many crimes not committed or controlled by organized crime. However, we can, and hope to, address ourselves to this one area of crime at this time. The chairman indicated to me that there was already enough legislation on the books against murder, burglary, robbery, and rape to cope with those crimes. But there is a dearth of legislation to cope with this sophisticated new kind of organized criminality. And that's what our purpose is here: to find out the true dimensions of organized crime, and then figure out how to cope with it."

"If we could uncover something new, perhaps that would be beneficial," agreed Senator Maggiacomo. "But are we going to learn anything new? Or are we just going to have an open, televised rehash of what we already know, what we can already easily obtain from the FBI or the police? If we're just going to put on a show, then I question the purpose altogether. Is that unreasonable?"

"Senator, do you agree that if we could come up with new, never-before-revealed information, if we could bring this menace out into the open, these hearings would be worthwhile?"

"I think—no, I'm sure—I'm being led down the primrose path, but yes," Senator Maggiacomo smiled.

"Well, we have just such new information," J.T. said boldly.

"Somehow I knew that was next," Senator Maggiacomo countered.

"I was advised by the FBI that an informant has come to the surface, a member of organized crime, one marked for death by his criminal peers, who wishes security and protective custody in exchange for revealing to us the inner workings, the families, the names of individuals, the crimes, the whole story," said J.T. "I have interviewed this man already, and his knowledge of the workings of organized crime is quite impressive. He could testify at private executive hearings, so the committee would be satisfied that what this witness says is new, revealing, even shocking. Wouldn't that be the difference between a witch-hunt and a legitimate investigation, Senator?"

"So long as it's not a witch-hunt, I repeat, I am interested in it," the senator said, studying J.T. closely.

Anders smiled across the long table at J.T. "Well then," he said, "let's have an executive closed session to hear this informant give us his new and revealing information, and if he is what Mr. Wright says he is, then we'll have a vote on the hearings. Is that satisfactory, gentlemen?"

The murmurs were almost unanimously affirmative.

"What's the witness's name, Mr. Wright?"

"Joseph Guardaci."

NOVEMBER 21, 1960

COURTNAY SAT OPPOSITE MARTY. J.T. sat to Marty's right in a light blue suit that was in need of a pressing. J.T.'s rumpled appearance was not unusual, even under the best of conditions. He was so involved in moving quickly in so many directions, he never bothered with the frivolous world of style or fashion. And like a crowd around a gambler on a hot roll, people around J.T. weren't concerned about his clothes, they were too fascinated with the action. The suit J.T. was now wearing, for instance, was a slightly electric blue with a nubby shantung pattern. His tie—the most tasteful part of his ensemble—had creases near the knot from being pulled down so often in his office and up again for public appearances in the hearing chamber.

"How did you think the questioning of Gentleman Johnny went today?" J.T. asked Courtnay, putting the menu down. They were in the Jockey Club, one of Washington's most exclusive restaurants.

"It went rather well," she replied, knowing J.T. was really asking how his own performance had come across on television. Courtnay wouldn't dare tell J.T.—although she was sorely tempted—that what was very apparent on TV was his thinning hair.

"Why not just say it was nice?" J.T. joshed. "Come on, Court, you can say something besides 'it went rather well.' What did you think when Gentleman Johnny wasn't televised?" J.T. prodded.

"His part was really dramatic," Courtnay said.

"That's who was dramatic—Gentleman Johnny?" J.T. joshed with feigned annoyance. He was obviously feeling high, pleased with the hearings.

"She's just too shy to tell you to your face that you were rivetingly attractive, sartorially splendid, and all sorts of other terrific things," Marty chided.

J.T. looked down at his suit. "Now I know you're soft-soaping me." They all laughed.

The captain and the waiter silently came to the side of the table. The captain had his order pad at the ready. A busboy poured water and set down bread and butter.

"Have you decided, darling?" asked Marty.

"I'll have the steak Diane," Courtnay said.

"Yes, madam. And for the gentlemen?" said the captain, turning first to J.T.

"I don't know. What do you suggest?"

"May I recommend the frogs' legs, sir? They're exceptional today."

"Don't you dare eat frogs' legs at this table," said Courtnay.

J.T. shrugged to the captain, who was silent, patient. "What are you going to have, Marty?" he asked.

"I'm going to try the steak tartare."

"Very well, sir." The captain made a note.

"I'll just have a regular steak, medium," said J.T. "We ought to have a bottle of wine with this feast, too. The expense account can afford it."

"Oh . . . this is really a rare mood, I see." Marty grinned.

J.T. smiled back. His happiness seemed infectious. Even Courtnay was in a good mood, which was unusual when she was around J.T.

"Captain, will you bring the wine list?" Marty said enthusiastically.

"Certainly, sir. I'll send the sommelier over in a moment." He handed the waiter the order list, and they both retreated discreetly into the darker recesses of the restaurant.

"Are you through with Gentleman Johnny now?" Courtnay asked.

"I think we've gotten as little as we could have hoped for," J.T. said with a wry smile. "You agree, Marty?"

"That's for sure. And no one else could have done so much with so little. You got tremendous mileage out of his appearance."

"The very fact that he didn't answer made it seem all the more sinister," said Courtnay. "A vast criminal empire out there that no one would talk about."

"Where's that wine?" J.T. said with delight. "That calls for a toast."

"I hope you don't mind my saying this, J.T.," Courtnay said, "but you're in a rare mood tonight. Usually you're so quiet, so . . ."

Marty looked worried.

"So dramatically understated?" J.T. proffered. "Mysteriously withdrawn with the knowledge of some exotic secret?"

"That's close," Courtnay smiled.

Marty and J.T. laughed again.

The captain returned to the table, carrying a telephone.

"A call for you, Mr. Wright."

"Thank you," J.T. looked at Marty and shrugged.

The captain plugged the phone into a jack next to their table.

"Hello?" said J.T. He heard some clicks on the wire. "Hello?"

"Hello, J.T."

"Yes, Mr. Chairman," J.T. said purposely, so Marty and. Courtnay would know who was on the phone.

"Listen, son. These newspaper and television people are banging my door down, wanting to know what we have up our sleeves for tomorrow. I don't know if I should tell them anything about Guardaci. But at the same time, I don't want to antagonize any of our friends. What do you think? I hate to bother you in the middle of anything, but I didn't know what I ought to do."

"Who called?"

"The television stations, the newspapers. Everyone. Even Duneden."

"Mmmmm . . . well, perhaps we can tantalize them with a little morsel, although I don't know why they can't wait until the morning. They have enough of a story for today."

"Yes, that's what I think. But I didn't want to antagonize them, you know. What the heck, we need these fellows."

The sommelier, with tasting cup and wine cellar key on a chain around his neck, arrived with a leather-covered wine list. J.T. motioned to him to give the list to Marty.

"I'll tell you what, Mr. Chairman. I'll talk to them, or at least to Duneden. I'll take care of it, if you want me to."

"Sure, sure. Frankly, that's just what I had in mind. I hate to interrupt your evening, though. Is she pretty?"

"Who's that?"

"Why, the girl you're in the middle of, of course." He laughed.

"Oh, yes, she's quite beautiful," said J.T., looking at Courtnay.

"Hot damn, son. What shall I say to the reporters when they call?"

"Tell them—except for Duneden—that you're trying to get in touch with me, that you can't release anything without clearing it with me, because there are legal complications. Tell them you're tracking me down but haven't found me yet."

"Sounds good. What about Duneden?"

"Tell him where I am. He can call me here."

"Do you want his number?"

"I have his number, Mr. Chairman. If he's really interested in the story, he'll call back."

"Whatever you say."

"I'll check in with you later," said J.T.

"Don't call me at home. I won't be there. And I don't want the wife to get wind of the fact that we're not having an executive session tonight, understand, son?"

"Right, sir. Talk to you in the morning. Is she pretty?"

"You son of a gun. Don't you know Southern gentlemen never reveal that sort of thing?" Anders laughed again.

"Good night, sir."

J.T. put down the receiver.

"What was that all about?" asked Marty. Courtnay was watching avidly, caught up in the excitement of the political whirlwind.

"Chairman's having some trouble with the press. Told him I'd take care of it. Did you order the wine yet?"

"No." Marty began to study the list.

"May I say, sir," the sommelier said quietly to J.T., "you were very good on television today."

"You really thought so?" J.T. said, pleased.

"Yes, sir. Especially with that Gentleman Johnny from New York. You really showed him."

"You think we got to him?"

"Very much so. You had him tied up in knots."

"Make that two bottles of wine," J.T. said with a grin.

The sommelier, everyone, laughed. Marty ordered a red wine and the sommelier left.

The captain returned. "Mr. Wright, another call."

"Thank you." He looked at Marty and Courtnay and smiled. "When you're important, you're important."

"Hello?"

"Hello, J.T., Jim Duneden. Anders just called me and told me where I could contact you."

"Right, I told him to do that," J.T. said. "I want you to get whatever information you need on these hearings." J.T. silently mouthed Duneden's name to Marty and Courtnay.

"I appreciate that, J.T. Tell me what you have planned for tomorrow. I need something to spice up my column."

"Well, there's a secret informer I'd prefer you to call something like 'Mister X,' so that his erstwhile underworld friends won't rub him out."

"An informer? You think the boys won't know him the minute he appears on TV?"

"I've been thinking, Jim, perhaps I should have him testify the way Gentleman Johnny did, without his face being shown."

"I'd imagine they'll know who this guy is just from the way he talks and the things he talks about."

"I guess that's true. But it won't hurt if the public had a little spectacle."

"Have him testify with a mask on, then. Let him look like a real crook."

"That's great, Jim."

"I was just kidding, J.T."

"I wasn't."

"That's what I was afraid of."

"You can print something about our having a very dramatic informant witness, whose life is in danger, a hood who's breaking the code of silence, that sort of stuff."

"You know for sure that your witness is going to talk?"

"The committee's already been through his testimony in executive session. We've already got a script prepared for tomorrow."

"You do? You son of a bitch, where's my copy? That's my column for tonight."

"You can't print anything from the script, Jim. Not until the witness testifies."

"Yeah, but I can tantalize them with something about it. I can hint at things. Anybody else have a copy of the script?"

"Just the chairman and myself. Even the committee members won't have copies until tomorrow morning."

"Great. Let me have an exclusive. How do I get a copy?"

"I can get one to you later."

"You have one with you now?"

"Yes."

"I'm sending someone for it right now."

"You'll have to keep it strictly under wraps until he testifies," J.T. admonished.

"Beautiful, sweetheart. Talk to you later. I'll call you at home when I've finished reading it."

J.T. hung up the phone.

"What's this drama that's going to happen tomorrow?" Courtnay asked, consumed with curiosity.

"If you thought today's witness was something, wait until you see tomorrow's," said J.T. "Tomorrow we're going to have an informer, a stool pigeon from the syndicate, who's going to give the inside story about the mob on television, coast to coast—first time anywhere."

"How did you ever get someone to do that? I thought they never did that sort of thing."

"It was a stroke of luck," Marty chimed in.

"It wasn't luck at all, Marty. It was intensive research, investigation, and hard work by both of us, wasn't it?" J.T. said with a smile.

Courtnay looked at J.T. She had never liked the way Marty took a back seat to J.T., and how J.T. seemed purposely to keep Marty in that place. Even though the mood was jovial, Marty was J.T.'s foil. And Courtnay wished that it was different.

"Well, this witness, Joe Guardaci's his name, was a member of organized crime, and while he was in prison, the mob wanted him killed—part of a vendetta or something. He found out about it, and one day when he thought an inmate was going to try to kill him, he hit the other inmate in the head with a pipe first."

"Oh, my God," said Courtnay. "Did he kill him?"

"He did. Then he had a twofold problem. Having killed an inmate, he was subject to indictment and prosecution by the authorities. And with the mob still interested in killing him, he had no place to hide. So he did the best thing he could think of."

"What's that?" asked Courtnay.

"Why, he got in touch with Superman, of course," said Marty.

"Exactly right," smiled J.T.

"I take it you're Superman," said Courtnay.

"Right again—in the guise of a mild-mannered junior counsel . . ."

"Beneath whose rumpled suit," Marty added, "is a man of steel."

"Rumpled suit?" J.T. look down at his tie. "You know, Marty, I wasn't doing too badly until you started this Superman bit."

"A little comic relief never hurt Shakespeare any, Otto," replied Marty, reaching out and patting J.T.'s back.

"Take it easy now," J.T. kidded. "This guy is really the man of steel. Stronger, if that's possible, than my father."

"I know," said Courtnay.

"Have you been manhandling this lovely young woman?" asked J.T.

"Not at all, not at all."

"And even if he were, we'd never tell," Courtnay said coyly.

"Marty, listen to this. I got this idea just now, talking to Duneden. This Guardaci is so frightened of being rubbed out, of being killed by the boys, that he won't testify without wearing a mask."

"A mask?"

"Don't you see the drama of it? A man in a mask, looking like a crook, telling the public all about organized crime. He can't let the people he's testifying about know who he is, or he'll be killed. The public will eat it up."

"It's crazy," said Marty. "What kind of a mask?"

"Who cares, even if it's a flour sack with eye holes cut out. Hot damn, the television people, the papers'll eat it up."

"Has anything like that ever been done before?" Marty asked.

"No. That's exactly why we should do it. And listen to this. Day after tomorrow, Duneden will print another exclusive story. He's going to find out that the mob bosses got together after Mister X testified and put a fifty-thousand-dollar price on his head for breaking the code of silence."

"Won't a column like that in some way encourage someone to kill this Mister X?" said Courtnay. "Some nut might take it seriously."

J.T. smirked and shrugged. "No great loss. This thing is really coming together now. I've got to call Duneden and tell him about his story for tomorrow night." J.T. reached for the phone and dialed.

Courtnay looked at Marty in disbelief. She wasn't sure whether J.T. was vicious or merely callous. Whichever, she was shocked by his manipulations. Marty was more embarrassed than surprised.

"Probably not at home," J.T. said, after listening to the phone ring several times. "I'll call him later."

The sommelier returned to the table, carrying a bottle of wine in a silver cradle.

"Oh ho," said J.T., "we're having the full treatment tonight."

"I believe I ordered another wine," Marty said somberly as the sommelier displayed the label before uncorking the bottle.

"If you and your guests will be so kind, Mr. Wright, the manager has selected this wine for you, compliments of the house. It is an excellent wine, very rare, *magnifique*."

Courtnay and Marty looked at J.T. Despite their dismay at J.T.'s attitude, the surge of power that had just begun to flow was very heady.

"Thank the manager for me," said J.T., motioning for the sommelier to uncork the bottle.

The sommelier pulled the cork and sniffed it delicately, his eyes closing with delight. "An excellent wine for you, sir." He poured a little for J.T. to taste.

"Go ahead, it's all right," said J.T.

The sommelier shook his head, urging J.T. to taste his wine.

J.T. sipped and put his glass down. "Terrific. Go ahead."

The sommelier poured for Courtnay and Marty, then added to J.T.'s glass. They raised their glasses in a toast to success and drank the full-bodied wine.

The captain pushed a flaming serving cart to the edge of their table.

"Tell me," J.T. said to the captain, "did you see the crime hearings on TV today?"

"My wife had the TV on when I woke up, but I didn't watch, to tell you the truth. I wasn't too interested. Was there something special you were interested in, sir? Perhaps I can ask one of the waiters."

"No, no, never mind," said J.T.

The captain turned to a customer who signaled from the next table.

Courtnay held back a laugh, her hand to her mouth, as J.T. looked at them with feigned anger. Marty kept a chuckle inside until the captain was out of hearing.

"Marty, if you leave that lunkhead a tip, I'll cut you out of my will. Wasn't interested! The very idea," J.T. said, laughing now. "Here's to tomorrow." He picked up his wineglass.

"Tomorrow," said Marty.

They clinked their glasses together.

NOVEMBER 22, 1960

"NOW, MISTER X, does this organization you've told the committee about have a name?" J.T. asked.

The huge hearing room was tomb-silent, the attention of spectators and legislators alike riveted to the short, squat man who sat alone at the witness table, a black cloth hood over his head. The man's eyes showed through two holes cut in the hood.

"Yes, the name is *La Cosa Nostra*. That's Italian for 'our thing.'" The man's voice was rough, guttural, a voice of the slums.

"'Our thing'?"

"Yeah, that's what it's called."

"And is there some initiation ritual you have to go through in order to become a member of this Cosa Nostra?" J.T. continued, reading from the script before him.

Mister X's entire testimony had been reduced to a script with both questions and answers when he had testified before a closed session of the committee. After that, another closed session of the committee convened—without Mister X in attendance—so that the committee members could go over the transcript together and refine portions of it, until a final version emerged in the form of the script now on the desk before J.T. and the other committee members. The one detail that was changed at the last minute was Guardaci's name—to Mister X, so that, together with the hood, J.T.'s dramatic presentation would be complete.

Mister X also had a copy of the transcript before him. In fact, he had had the transcript for several days. J.T. had sent it to the army base where Mister X was being detained; Guardaci no longer had to live in a prison or eat prison food. He would serve the rest of his sentence at such a facility. That was part of the bargain Guardaci made with the government, through J.T., in exchange for his testimony.

J.T. had sent instructions with the transcript. Mister X and his guards—another part of Guardaci's deal was that special agents were to be with him around the clock—were to read the transcript aloud and rehearse questions and answers until Mister X was able to respond practically verbatim without referring to the transcript. J.T. wanted Mister X's testimony to look natural, spontaneous.

"Yeah, you have to stand in a room with all the other wise guys— that means guys who are already in 'our thing.'"

"Yes?"

"Then you all hold hands together, and the boss tells you to repeat an oath."

"What oath? Do you recall?" asked J.T.

"Well, yeah," he hesitated.

"What oath, Mister X?" J.T. pressed.

"Well, you take a knife and a gun, and you say things like, 'I will take up the knife and the gun and I will protect my friends, and die by the knife and the gun before I am *disonorata*.'"

"What does that mean, that last word? Is it Italian?"

"Yeah, that means a man without honor, a disgrace."

"Mister X, when did you begin your life of crime?"

"When I was borned was as good a time as any," Mister X said, looking directly at the little red light on the television camera that was taking a closeup of him.

J.T. watched Mister X, a smirk creasing his thin lips. The son of a bitch, J.T. thought. He had explained the workings of the TV cameras to Guardaci, and now he was playing to the cameras, even with a hood on his head. That'd be all right, J.T. thought, if Guardaci stuck to the script. But he had begun ad-libbing, first words, now little jokes. J.T. thought he might request a recess if Guardaci didn't get back in line.

"When did you start getting in trouble with the law, Mister X?" the chairman said, more insistently.

Mister X read the transcript before him silently. He nodded, then looked up. "When I was a kid, I was sent to reform school. I was about thirteen years old."

"What were the charges?"

"I robbed a candy store, got three dollars and change."

He was back on track now, thought J.T. If only the cretin would stay on it.

"And how long were you in reform school?" the chairman continued.

"A year, maybe, the first time. I was in and out until I was about eighteen."

"And then what did you do?"

"I got involved with a gang, and after that I became a member of La Cosa Nostra."

"Was that right after reform school?"

Mister X thought for a moment, his head cocked to one side. "Not exactly," he said unsurely.

"Can you think hard, Mister X? Try and refresh your recollection," J.T. interrupted. "Take your time and refresh your recollection."

Mister X looked down at the script. So did every member of the committee.

"Oh, I joined another gang—the Little Gang, we called it, and we used to go around and stick up stores. One guy would drive, and stay in the car, two others would run in the store, grab the money, and run."

"Is that how you did it, just grabbed the money and ran?" asked the chairman.

"Well, sometimes we had to persuade the people." Mister X said coyly to the camera.

"What does that mean?" asked the chairman, glancing down at J.T. momentarily. J.T. didn't look up, but he could feel the chairman's consternation—and his own annoyance. Guardaci wanted to play games with the television audience, be cute, say things that would bring a laugh. But the laughs weren't in the script.

"That means we had to use guns."

"So you didn't just walk into these stores and the people gave you their money voluntarily. You held the people up with knives or at gunpoint?" the chairman continued.

Now the chairman was ad-libbing, J.T. thought.

"That's correct," said Mister X. He had noticed the sour look on J.T.'s face and curbed his answers.

"I'd like at this time to turn over the questioning to my distinguished colleague, the senator from Louisiana," said the chairman.

"Thank you, Mr. Chairman," said Senator Carleton, sitting two seats to the left of the chairman. "This Little Gang, I take it, was not a part of organized crime?"

"That's correct."

"So it wasn't until later, then, that you became involved in organized crime?"

"That's correct."

"And did you personally go through this ritual with the knife and gun?"

"That's correct."

"As a full-fledged member of La Cosa Nostra, thereafter"—the senator from Louisiana's accent handled the Italian pronunciation no better than did the chairman's—"did you share in the proceeds of crimes you didn't commit yourself? And if you got in trouble, did La Cosa Nostra take care of your lawyer and bondsman, and if you went to jail, did it take care of your family?"

"That's not correct."

"What's not correct?" asked Senator Carleton.

"That I shared in the take from other crimes, or that anybody paid anything for me if I had troubles. I was on my own. I got in trouble, that was my problem. Oh, the guys'd help out, if they could kill a witness or put muscle on someone. But money? Forget it! I had to go for everything myself. The bosses, they shared in the action from guys like me. But not me from them."

"Can you name some of these bosses? Who are the higher-ups in organized crime?"

Mister X looked down at his script for a minute as he feigned reflection for the TV audience. "Well, like Gentleman Johnny Entrerri. He's a boss of one of the New York mobs. Not really the top boss. He's an underboss in the family of Pasquale Berdardo. In New Orleans, where you're from, Senator," he read from the script—the hearings were so well orchestrated that these answers were scheduled to be given to questions from the Senator from Louisiana—"there is an organized crime family. The boss there is Carmelo Torino."

"Carmelo Torino is the boss of organized crime in New Orleans right now as we sit here?"

"That's right, Senator."

The senator looked grave for the viewing audience back home.

"Senator," said the chairman, "I'd like to turn the questioning over to the representative from Arizona, Congressman Cole."

"Certainly, Mr. Chairman," said the still somber-looking Senator Carleton. He was going to milk his allotted time dry.

"Mister X," asked a bushy-haired young man sitting at one end of the podium, "can you name the various cities in which there are organized crime families?"

"Yeah, sure," said Mister X. "In fact, I prepared, with Mr. Wright, a chart of all those cities." J.T. had made sure that his name was liberally salted into the script, so that he was either visually or verbally in front of the audience nearly all the time. The camera now swung to J.T., who, with Marty Boxer, produced from under the counsel table a large pasteboard on which was drawn an outline of the United States. The map was dotted with stars representing the territory of crime families, under the stars were the names of the bosses of those families.

A Senate page placed the chart on an easel that could be seen by the committee members, counsel, Mister X, and—most importantly, of course—the television cameras.

"These are the crime families, Mr. Congressman," said Mister X after a television camera had an adequate opportunity to study the chart.

"How many of those families are there, Mister X?"

"Twenty-eight all together, Mr. Congressman."

"And I see there's a star in my home state of Arizona. Is that in Phoenix?"

"That's right, Mr. Congressman. Philly 'the Gimp' Bon Giorno moved there for his health. Actually, he left his family in Brooklyn and set up another family in Arizona. They got all the same rackets like in New York, only smaller."

"What are those rackets?" asked the congressman, already knowing the answer that would alarm the city fathers back in Phoenix. They could be consoled, however, by the fact that their congressman was right on top of the problem, stemming the catastrophe.

"Loan-sharking, gambling, protection, like that," Mister X replied.

"The chair recognizes the senator from Connecticut," said the chairman.

"Thank you, Senator," Senator Maggiacomo responded. He sat one seat away from the chairman. "Mister X, I see a star in my home state too. That's in Bridgeport, is it not?"

"That's correct."

Senator Maggiacomo was, in addition to a distinguished senator, a former history professor from Harvard and an expert on the Renaissance. He was revered in the Senate for his command of the English language; his oratory had mesmerized the Senate many times. And what most others were unaware of was that he spoke Italian, French, and Spanish with equal distinction.

Senator Maggiacomo had conflicting emotions as he began to question Mister X. Mister X indeed! He had objected vehemently to the circus atmosphere of the hood and the pseudonym. But he had been outvoted overwhelmingly. Guardaci represented everything Senator Maggiacomo despised. Guardaci brought ignominy and shame to Italians in the United States. It was because of him, and others like him, that when people heard an Italian name they thought not of the most glorious period in human history, the Renaissance, which had produced Michelangelo, da Vinci, and Dante, but of Prohibition, which had spawned the likes of Capone, Luciano, and Genovese. When the senator heard Guardaci use Italian words to give some Latin seasoning to the hearings—at the suggestion, there was no doubt in Senator

Maggiacomo's mind, of J.T. Wright—Guardaci spoke the way an illiterate hillbilly would speak English.

While Senator Maggiacomo despised Guardaci and his kind, he equally despised opportunists like Senator Anders and J.T. Wright, who were hungry for cheap publicity; the lazy law-enforcement people who needed a target to blame for their incompetence and impotence; the movie industry which catered to the public's willingness to buy tickets to their tawdry films. They all pandered to the image of Mister X for their own selfish glory. And Senator Maggiacomo hated participating in the farce.

"How many people—altogether—are in this organization, Mister X?" asked the senator.

"More or less, in the whole country, five thousand."

"You're saying that in the entire United States, forty-eight states, there are, altogether, only five thousand people involved in organized crime?" Senator Maggiacomo asked.

J.T. examined his script. He knew that question wasn't there, but he looked anyway. Senator Maggiacomo was an unknown quantity to J.T. He was not interested in publicity, and he was senior enough in the Senate to be independent, almost untouchable. And J.T. knew from executive hearings that Senator Maggiacomo could be trouble at these public hearings. He alone had bridled at the prepared script. Outvoted, he had had no choice but to accept the script. But now, before the press and the public, he began to depart from it. J.T. drew in his breath, half turning to view Senator Maggiacomo.

"That's correct, Senator," Mister X replied.

"That's less than one-thousandth of one percent of the Italian-Americans in this country, isn't it, Mr. Witness?"

"I can't say, Senator," Guardaci shrugged.

"That makes the Italian-American community purer than Ivory Snow, doesn't it?"

"I can't tell you that either, Senator."

"You can say, can't you, Mr. Witness, that these five thousand people, whether they're men or women—"

"All men, Senator," Mister X volunteered.

"Thank you. You can say that these five thousand *men* are not responsible for all the murders that took place in the United States last year, can't you?"

Guardaci shrugged. He didn't remember that question in the script. "I don't follow you, Senator," he finally said, confused.

"You're not saying these five thousand men are responsible for the twenty thousand rapes in the United States last year, are you?"

"Rape?" Guardaci looked around. He glanced at J.T., who stared straight at the desk before him, his body tensed with helpless anger.

"What's this rape? They don't do no rape. That's—that's—"

"That's a crime that takes place without the help of organized crime, correct?"

"That's correct."

"Is organized crime responsible for the one hundred thousand burglaries that took place last year?"

"What are you getting at, Senator?"

"Is this organization you are talking about responsible for every mugging in this country?" the senator sailed on, ignoring Guardaci's question.

"Mugging? They don't do no mugging, neither. That's for bums."

"Then the rapists and muggers aren't part of this organization you're a member of, correct?"

"That's correct." Guardaci drifted slowly through a fog, unfamiliar with the questions, where they were leading, or what he should answer.

J.T., however, knew quite clearly where Senator Maggiacomo was heading. What he didn't know was how far the senator would go. J.T. looked down at a script ripe with unpicked questions and answers.

"I don't think you answered my question concerning all the murders each year in our country. Several *thousand* murders last year alone. Are the members of your organization responsible for all these acts of violence?"

"Of course not, Senator . . ."

"You've told us about murders, rapes, assaults. How about burglaries? Is this organization of yours responsible for every second-story man in the nation? Do they all owe allegiance to your organization?"

"I don't get that, Your Honor—I mean Senator." Guardaci said with a chuckle, "I thought I was in court."

The spectators broke up in a roar of laughter.

Even Senator Maggiacomo had a crease of a smile. But the senator was smiling because he knew from a brief glance that J.T. didn't think Guardaci's performance was amusing.

"Is every burglar in this country a part of your organization, Mr. Witness? Is it as simple as that?"

"Most of them burglars are just junkies looking to make a score and get a fix. There ain't no junkies in Our Thing."

Now there was a point, thought Senator Maggiacomo, that J.T. Wright would certainly pounce upon as soon as the senator relinquished the floor. The members of organized crime were not junkies, but they were apparently quite involved in supplying the junk. Before he was bitten by Wright, Senator Maggiacomo decided to pull the tiger's teeth.

"Junkies, narcotics addicts, aren't members of organized crime, is that correct?"

"That's correct."

"Organized crime is responsible, however, for a great deal of the narcotics traffic in this country. Is it responsible for *all* the narcotics that are brought into this country?"

"All? No, not all, Senator. There are a lot of groups involved in junk."

"Would you say various ethnic groups participate in narcotics trafficking?"

"That's correct."

"Now, Mr. Witness, if I might summarize your testimony, I believe you have testified that all muggings, assaults, rapes, murders, burglaries, are not all committed by people in or affiliated with organized crime, correct?"

"That's correct, Senator."

"And all the laws this committee might pass concerning organized crime—even if we put every member of organized crime on an island, with no possible escape—would not eliminate crime in our nation's streets and homes, would it?"

"You mean would there still be crimes, even without La Cosa Nostra?"

"That's correct," the senator mimicked.

The crowd roared their laughter and approval. The newspapermen could hardly make notes.

Guardaci was chuckling too. Even J.T. Wright surrendered a quick smile.

"Nothing would change, Senator. Nothing."

"Thank you, Mr. Witness," said the senator, turning to the chairman.

"Thank you, Senator," the chairman said with relief. "Now, the representative from the state of Missouri."

"Mister X, you've told us about the different families. Can you tell us more about the people who run these families?" asked the Missourian, following the script precisely. The members, as well as counsel for the committee, and those in the press corps who had copies of the transcript, felt more secure.

"Yes, sir." Guardaci felt more secure now, too. "Like I said, in the New York area there are five families. One of them has an underboss named John Entrerri, who you had here already. That gang is headed by Pasquale Bedardo. Another—"

"Maggiacomo wasn't as bad as he might have been," J.T. whispered to Marty.

"He's a brilliant man," Marty replied.

"Who, Mister X?"

Marty smiled momentarily.

"Maggiacomo's a goddamn fool," J.T. whispered harshly. "Does he think the American public knew, or even cared about what the hell he had to say?"

In the background, in response to the Missourian's questions, Mister X meticulously followed the script, naming the bosses of families throughout the country. Another chart was placed on the easel, which showed the names of family bosses, their underbosses, and *consiglieri* or advisors. This chart had been compiled through the joint efforts of an FBI-police task force. Guardaci had never met or heard of most of the people named. But he had dutifully memorized the chart and now recited his vast knowledge of the nationwide crime organization.

"Maggiacomo made a valid point, I thought," Marty commented.

J.T.'s face soured. "Follow the goddamn script."

Marty, chastened, looked down at the script. Inside, he was stung with humiliation.

At thirty-one, Gerald Wynans, a representative from New Jersey, was the youngest man on the podium. He was also the congressman with the least time in office; this was his freshman year in Congress. His father had been the congressman from his home district for twenty-five years. Like a true feudal lord, Wynans's father had passed his fiefdom of the provinces lying west of the Raritan River to his son. J.T. disliked Gerald Wynans. Perhaps it was because Wynans was so young, although J.T. was younger. Perhaps it was because Wynans was short and had a nonathletic pudginess tending toward the pear-shaped; although J.T. wasn't any taller nor much more muscular. Perhaps it was because Wynans's father had broken the ground for him, and he was participating in the hearings because of family influence. Big Jim had inportuned the chairman to hire J.T. as the junior—or, as J.T. insisted, the deputy chief-counsel of the committee. Perhaps it was because Gerald Wynans seemed hesitant, unsure. J.T. wasn't that. And if he were, he'd never let it show. That was it, J.T. knew, the openly displayed diffidence he saw in Wynans that accounted for J.T.'s dislike of him. J.T. was the one who first called Wynans "Fat Ass." Anders had used it without thinking one day, and then it stuck. Not openly, not to his face, not that he even knew, but Wynans was now known to the members of the committee and the staff as Fat Ass.

"I hope this idiot can read the goddamn script," J.T. said sarcastically when the chairman called upon Wynans.

Marty said nothing. He happened to like Wynans. He was young, recently out of college, unassuming and friendly enough to be able to relate easily to Marty. He was trying to do a job, and do it well. He took his responsibility seriously. And behind that appearance of uncertainty was a determination to learn everything there was to know about being a representative, and do a real job for his constituency. Marty and Wynans spoke occasionally, and, perhaps to make up for the curtness J.T. always displayed, Marty was always courteous and pleasant to Wynans.

"Mister X., would you describe how organized crime infiltrates legitimate business?" asked Wynans.

"Well, let's say we're talking about restaurants. Sometimes, when a good fellow—that's another way we call another guy in the mob, a 'good fellow'—if he sees a good place, and it don't belong to nobody—"

"How could it not belong to anyone?" Wynans interjected.

"That means that the restaurant isn't already connected to a good fellow, nobody is speaking up for it, in other words."

"Go ahead."

"So the good fellow will make a move on the place. That means," Mister X explained quickly, "that maybe he'll send some of his guys to start some trouble. They start fights and arguments at the bar, walk out without paying the tab. When the owner grabs them at the door or out in the street, they threaten to break his head, and he's too scared to do anything. A few nights of this kind of aggravation, and no wise guys show up to protect him, the good fellow shows up and says to the owner, 'Hey, this sort of thing shouldn't be happening in a nice place like this. Maybe I can help you out.'"

"Go ahead, Mister X," said Wynans.

The crowd was fascinated by Mister X's testimony.

"So then the wise guy who's playing Good Samaritan arranges to have the bad guys stop the trouble. Of course, they're all in it together in the first place, but the owner don't know that. He thinks the good fellow is doing a terrific job. The good fellow comes around every once in a while, has a drink, has dinner. Now he's there, he's in, he already made his move. Only it's not just him. It's also his gang."

"Would you explain that, please?" said Wynans.

"Certainly, Mr. Representative. Whenever a wise guy takes over something, that's his own. If a wise guy's got the smarts to get himself something, it belongs to him, and it don't belong to the others in the gang, except that he kicks in a piece of the action to the boss every week. When the boss gets his piece, that's his. He don't give nothing to the other guys in the gang. Wise guys are really on their own."

"Then the gangs are made up of independent factors, is that it?" asked Representative Wynans.

"I don't get the question."

Representative Wynans saw a signal of request from Senator Maggiacomo. "Mr. Chairman, may I yield the questioning to Senator Maggiacomo for a moment?" he asked.

"Yes, certainly," said the chairman.

"Are you saying that every gang member is on his own to earn his legitimate or illegitimate living, Mr. Witness?"

"That's correct," Guardaci said lightly.

"And the only one who benefits from all of this is the boss?"

"Sometimes the boss shares with the underboss or the *consigliere*, but that's about it."

"Is that the way the gangs are with each other?"

"Correct."

"Can you elaborate?"

"The gangs don't really work with each other. They are out to earn as much as they can for themselves. But they cooperate with each other. If a wise guy makes a move on a restaurant or some other business, and finds that there's another wise guy, either from his own mob or some other mob, already in there, he leaves the place alone and goes to the next place. He don't take a place from another wise guy. It's the same with the families. If one family makes a move and they find there's some other family already there, they'll go look for something else. In other words, with all the suckers there are in the world, why step on another wise guy's or another family's toes? You get what I mean, Senator?"

"Indeed I do," replied Maggiacomo. "The gangs don't work together under one roof, one national set of rules, one head, one treasury, one set of goals?"

"That's correct. Lucky—that's Lucky Luciano—got rid of the boss of all bosses. There ain't been one since. The bosses are just bosses of their own mobs."

"Is there a central commission in charge of all the mobs?"

"In charge? No. Not in charge, Senator. But if there's a beef, then some guys have been appointed to the commission to iron out the beef."

"Like arbitrators?"

"Exactly correct, Senator."

"This organized crime doesn't work together all the time, then?"

"Correct."

"Mr. Chairman, may I return the questioning to Representative Wynans?"

"Certainly."

Representative Wynans found his place in the script.

"What does this 'good fellow,' as you call yourselves, do after starting and then ending trouble in the business he intends to invade?" asked Wynans.

"Well, his first move is to tell the owner that it'd be a good idea if he could put one of his men on the payroll, to work, not just to show up, in case trouble starts. Now when the mob guy gives the job to somebody, he's giving the guy a chance to earn, a chance to put bread on his table. This worker is then *with* the wise guy, is obligated to the wise guy, owes him some allegiance. You get what I mean?"

"Does that mean that each mob member may have his own smaller gang?" asked Wynans.

"Correct."

"And when he gives work or favors, the people to whom he gives out this work or these favors become obligated to him?"

"Now you got it."

"May I ask Mister X something at this point?" said J.T.

The chairman looked at Wynans, who nodded. "Go ahead, Mr. Wright."

"Are these smaller gangs made up of people who are also part of La Cosa Nostra?"

"Yes and no. I mean, they ain't necessarily 'made' guys."

"What does that mean, 'made' guys?"

"That means an official member of Our Thing."

"So that there are many more people involved in this life of crime than are officially members of your organization, is that correct?"

"Correct."

"Do you know how many people are involved, whether or, not they're made?"

"Not exactly. But there are a lot."

"Thank you," said J.T. He felt a surge of victory. He wanted to turn and look right at Maggiacomo, but he resisted, staring down at his script instead, scratching with a pencil as if he were making some notes.

"Does this mob member get any kickback from the person to whom he gives the job?" Representative Wynans asked.

"Yeah, probably. Not always."

"Does the mob member ever get further involved in this legitimate enterprise, further than, say, just getting some work with which he can expand his gang?"

"Sure. First he muscles in on the owner. Then, as time goes by, he gets a little bigger piece, then bigger. The guy is too afraid to do anything, and before you know it, they're partners."

The chairman looked at the clock on the wall. "Would this be an appropriate time to recess?" he suggested to Representative Wynans.

"Certainly, Mr. Chairman."

"This session is now in recess," said the chairman. "We will resume at two o'clock sharp."

The audience shuffled to its feet. Mister X was immediately flanked by his guards, who stood around his table as the crowd moved out of the hearing chamber.

JANUARY 15, 1961

THE CRAWFORD PALM BEACH COTTAGE—if twenty-five rooms over-looking the ocean, with servants' quarters, a gate house, tennis courts, and a pool surrounded by cabanas could be called a cottage—was spectacular. Tall French doors opened onto a manicured lawn, which swept down to a turquoise pool surrounded by stone cherubs pouring water from flowers and seashells into the pool. Beyond the pool, the rolling surf, flecked with white foam, glistened in the soft light of the January half moon. The fragrance of the tropics—a combination of salt air, sand, palm, and sea grape, blended with the deep perfume of gardenia bushes—surrounded the main house.

Courtnay's family was having its annual party. J.T. had been invited. His invitation, however, was not Courtnay's idea; in fact, she was not in favor of such an invitation. Cici Crawford, Courtnay's mother, had invited J.T. for the weekend, because J.T. was now a celebrity, and thus he helped make the party more sensational and newsworthy.

Cici, always a clever woman, had also invited Dana Reynolds. Dana was Courtnay's age, and single. Her family were the major stockhold-ers of RBM, Reynolds Business Machines. Her grandfather, in fact, had founded that international company. The Reynoldses and Crawfords had known each other, socially and commercially, for years. Dana had also graduated from Caldwell, two years behind Courtnay. Yet the two girls had never been very close. In fact, Dana had very few friends. She was intelligent, with a shrewd business mind, athletically tall, quite buxom, nicely proportioned; but she was also completely independent, reserved to the point of being aloof. Cici thought it would be great fun to throw the cool, blue-blooded Dana into the mix with the parvenu J.T. Wright. When Courtnay found out her mother was playing matchmaker again, and had even asked J.T. to be particularly nice to Dana, a chill descended on the Crawford house. Not that Cici cared. She was too busy arranging the gala. J.T., well aware that Dana was a Reynolds of the RBM Reynoldses, said he'd indeed try to be a pleasant escort.

Palm Beach is magnificent, dug out of the Florida coast with gold-plated shovels. In the peaceful beauty of the tropic dawn, black men in trucks drive along the main roads, cutting down the dead or browning palm leaves and trimming the grass along the edge of the road. When the folks in the mansions rouse themselves languidly from bed to breakfast beneath striped canopies overlooking their pools and the ocean, at tables set with linen, crystal, and silver, they see no blade of grass out of place, no limp palm leaf, not even black men working in their paradise. It is a playground for the wealthy, the bailiwick of corporate presidents and chairmen of boards, who have devoted a lifetime to more assets. The average age of the moguls is beyond what might be called spry. Some are in wheelchairs, their faces paralyzed from strokes that are an occupational hazard, part of the cost of doing big business. But their clothes are elegant, the gowns and jewels of their wives beyond the imagination, in style or price, of ordinary mortals.

J.T. had now been on the front page of every major newspaper, on every television screen, for months. He appeared there as a flame, a consuming conflagration, searing the criminals with withering questions which they couldn't or would n't answer. And the less they answered, the more he questioned, hounded, pounded. With such publicity, J.T. became a "must" for the guest lists of clever hostesses. Celebrity guests are still an exclusive preserve cherished by hostesses, guests, and notables alike. These parties reassure them all that they are truly different, important, very special.

In the glass-domed conservatory-turned-cocktail lounge with J.T. and the other guests were the Duke and Duchess of Ansbury, the perennial society party guests, the most prestigious of the "musts." They would not accept invitations to just any party. It had to be exclusive and very chic, and of course, their traveling and living expenses had to be covered while they stayed, even if they remained until the next invitation was not only received but approved.

J.T. knew how Courtnay felt about him. If nothing else, he was perceptive. And he knew Marty didn't have enough influence with Courtnay's family to get him invited. He was quite aware, therefore, that he had been invited to amuse the other guests with anecdotes about the criminals he questioned, the feeling of looking across a flimsy desk at murderers, cutthroats, and the like. *But they won't get as much out of me as I will out of them*, J.T. thought as he looked around the guests. *This is where the dough is, and where I intend my future to be.*

"Do you know J.T. Wright?" asked Cici Crawford, introducing Anthony and Margo Kent. They shook hands.

"I've seen you on television," said Margo through lips that hardly moved. Perhaps years of directing servants had influenced her everyday speech. "Those characters you question would terrify me. Some of them are so sinister and swarthy. I don't know how you do it."

"I try not to think about it," replied J.T., sipping ginger ale from his glass. No one—except his bartender—knew what he drank. He didn't want anything to interfere with his thinking. "If I did, I'd be a lot more frightened than you are when you watch it on TV. I'm sitting right in the same room with them."

They laughed. Cici looked around at the room, which was filling up with guests.

"Let me steal J.T. for a few minutes, darlings," said Cici. "I want to introduce him to my other guests."

"Certainly, darling," said Margo.

"They're from *the* Brewster-Kent family," Cici whispered to J.T. He made careful mental note.

J.T. watched the Duke and Duchess hold court just ahead of them. He was fascinated. Here were the Duke and Duchess of Ansbury, in person, looking just like their photographs, she beautifully coiffed, he sitting erectly, a drink in hand. J.T. felt a little giddy—not because he was now inside the bakery against the window of which his nose had so often longingly been pressed, but because he was now one of the pastries everyone else was pressing their noses against the window to see. He was not just there. He was there because he was somebody, because people wanted to meet *him*, talk to *him*. He was one of the attractions.

"Your Highness, Duchess," Cici said to the royal couple, "may I introduce J.T. Wright?"

The Duke reached out his hand. The Duchess nodded with a tight, toothy smile.

"Mr. Wright is an attorney with the American Congress. He's been on television every day for months. He's like my morning Bloody Mary; as soon as I get up, I turn on the hearings and have my breakfast with J.T. and Mary."

"Mary who?" asked the Duke.

"Bloody Mary, darling," said the Duchess.

"Ah. What sort of hearings are these, Cici?" asked the Duke. Other people milled about, waiting to greet the royalty. The Duke or Duchess would smile or wave occasionally to others around the room.

"Why don't you tell the Duke and Duchess about your hearings, J.T.," urged Cici.

"We are investigating organized crime in America," said J.T. "We're conducting hearings to determine what new legislation might be useful to combat it."

"Crime is a problem the world over," the Duke mused. "Just the other day we had a bag—a small bag, but it was quite lovely—taken from our things at the airport in Naples on our way here. Suddenly it wasn't there and that was that. But you know how it is in Naples. We were coming from Capri, of course."

"I'll ask at our hearings if anyone's seen your bag," said J.T. humorously.

"Oh, I don't think—ah, I see, you're joking."

The Duchess still smiled that same smile, as if it were painted on her, except, occasionally, her eyes widened as she greeted another guest over J.T.'s shoulder.

"Darling," someone said loudly from behind J.T., drawing it out into an entire sentence. A woman in a multicolored silk Pucci moved past J.T. and embraced the Duchess.

"Look who's here, darling," the Duchess said to the Duke. "Frannie."

"Why, it's dear Frannie," said the Duke.

J.T. didn't know whether to stay in the midst of their new conversation or leave. He stood awkwardly a moment. He spied Marty across the room and stepped back two steps, then turned, making his way toward Marty.

"Where's Courtnay?" J.T. asked.

"She went upstairs with Dana Reynolds for a few minutes. They'll be right down."

"Oh, brother. How bad can this Dana be that Cici fixed me up to be her escort? Why did I say yes to this detail?"

"Because Cici asked you to, and you're such a nice guy. Have you been meeting people?" Marty asked.

"I've never met more counts and no-accounts, dukes and the like in my life."

"Impressed?"

"No question."

"You see that tall thin man over there, with the mustache?" said Marty.

"Sure, Count Claude-somebody-somebody de Fabisson, right?"

"Do you know what he does?"

"You mean in general, in a closet, in front of mirrors?"

"Making a living."

"Haven't the faintest idea," said J.T.

"He's a jewelry salesman. In Tiffany's, right here on Worth Avenue. During the season, New York sends him down here. Out of season, he's in New York. These people would much rather buy their jewelry from a count."

"Is he really a count?"

"Definitely. And when you read about this party in the papers or in the magazines next month, they'll be sure to mention the Duke, the Duchess, the Count, and all the notables."

"Is it always this much bull?"

"I beg your pardon," Marty feigned offense. "Ah, here's Courtnay and Dana."

Courtnay entered the room with statuesque Dana. Not bad at all, thought J.T.

"Marty," said Courtnay, "you know Dana. J.T., this is Dana Reynolds."

J.T. studied Dana as she was turned toward Marty. She had large features, and was heavily made up. Her hair was thick, shoulder-length, and blonde. She wore a strapless, sequined cocktail dress. *What a set of lungs*, J.T. thought as Dana turned to face him. Her eyes caught him gazing at her bosom, and she was not offended.

"Don't tell me, I already know," Dana said to J.T. Her voice was deep, a bit raspy. "You're J.T. Wright, the gang buster. I've caught you on TV many times."

J.T. was waiting for her to finish. Apparently she already had.

"Thank you."

The conversation evaporated.

"You remember meeting Dana before, don't you, Marty? At East Hampton," said Courtnay.

"Certainly."

"That was ages ago."

J.T.'s eyes wandered to Dana's bosom again. Dana caught him staring again, and her eyes were bright with amusement.

"J.T., how would you like to buy me a drink?" Dana smiled. "And you can tell me all about your hearings. I'm a great listener." She took J.T.'s arm and aimed him toward a waiter with a tray of drinks.

Marty and Courtnay watched the two of them walk away. J.T. looked back over his shoulder with a little smile on his face.

"Now he's met his match," said Courtnay. "Dana's a real whirlwind. Plays football on the beach with the men, a whiz in business."

"I know a lot of lawyers," Dana said to J.T., passing up a waiter with the tray of champagne. "Let's get something else to drink." They walked through the doors opening on to the lawn overlooking the pool. The soft rush of the ocean, scented with gardenias, filled the air. "Come on, there's a bar in the pool tent."

Just to the side of the pool was a large striped Arab-style tent. Inside, a bartender stood behind a small bar. Several men and women were seated outside the tent on white wicker chairs. Music from the orchestra playing in the main house was piped over loudspeakers to the tent. Two couples were dancing.

"Vodka martini," Dana said, "but just swirl the vermouth in the glass and throw it away."

"Yes, ma'am. Sir, would you care for a drink?"

"I've had several. I think I'll just cool it with a ginger ale for the moment."

"Very well, sir."

"Ginger ale? Aren't you overdoing it a tad?"

"If I don't, I might fall right into the pool."

"Don't worry. If you do, I'll carry you back to the house."

"That's different, then," J.T. kidded.

The bartender put two drinks in front of them.

"Let's walk over to the ocean wall," said Dana.

The two of them stood atop the concrete bulkhead, watching the waves break about a hundred yards out from the wall. The rollers lifted and curled into white foam, then slithered into thin sheets along the beach.

"I just love it down here. The water's so clean, so blue. Do you like the ocean, J.T.?"

"Not really. It's too rough. I don't swim."

"I can teach you, if you like."

"Are you a swimming instructor too?"

"As a matter of fact, I was the AAU hundred-yard breaststroke champion when I was fourteen."

"Now that sounds like my kind of activity."

"Very cute, dear boy. When do you want to start your swimming lessons?"

"I'm just going to be down for a couple of days, Dana."

"Me too. Then I'm heading back to New York. But we have a pool at Locust Valley. You could come there and I'll teach you."

"Won't it be too cold for swimming in a pool?"

"It's indoors, dear boy. Do give Dana a little credit for brains."

"Indoors. Wonderful." Good God, J.T. thought, that really costs money.

They both looked out over the ocean again. J.T. didn't know what to do now. His experience with women was quite limited.

"You say you know a lot of lawyers," he said, just not to be standing, looking foolish.

"Yes, there's always some litigation going on with Daddy's business. And my uncle is a partner in Stevenson & Stetinius. They represent RBM."

"That's a high-powered firm," said J.T. "One of the biggest on Wall Street."

"It's fifth largest in the United States. Have you ever been in private practice, J.T., or did you go right into government?"

"Right into government." J.T. sipped his ginger ale.

"Thinking about going into private practice when you're finished?"

"Sure. When the right situation comes along. Which I hope will be soon. There's just so much I can get out of being associate counsel to a Senate committee."

"What kind of law are you interested in?"

"I haven't quite made up my mind."

"You ought to talk to my uncle. He's been a lawyer forever. Why don't we all meet some day in New York for lunch at '21' or someplace?"

"I'm always in Washington," replied J.T.

"You must be able to get one day off. Surely all those crooks can get along without you."

"Probably a lot better than they're doing right now in front of the committee."

Dana laughed. "Come on, silly boy, let's go inside," she said, taking his hand in hers. "You've got to promise to come to New York to meet me. Do you promise?"

Dana's hand was very warm and very strong in his. An RBM Reynolds, built like gangbusters, holding his hand as if she meant it, J.T. marveled.

"Do you promise?" Dana repeated as they made their, way to the house.

"Yes, sure."

"Great."

They were again enveloped in the music and talk and gaiety of the party.

MARCH 19, 1961

J.T. STEPPED CAUTIOUSLY down the steps to the "21" Club. He had never been inside before; even the heft of the glass door was intimidating. A slick-haired young man at the reception desk looked inquiringly at J.T.

"I'm supposed to meet Mr. Delafield and Miss Reynolds for lunch," replied J.T.

"Neither Mr. Delafield nor Miss Reynolds has arrived. I do have Mr. Delafield's reservation. Perhaps you'd care to wait in the lounge, sir?" the young man said, indicating a sitting room to the rear of his desk. "Or perhaps at the bar?" He pointed to a doorway beyond a cigar-and-magazine counter.

"I think I'll wait in the bar."

Two striking women, wearing luxurious mink coats and flashes of gold at their wrists, entered the restaurant.

"Hello, Steve."

"Mrs. Whitney," Slick Steve said enthusiastically. "I haven't seen you in ages!" He completely forgot J.T.

J.T. wandered slowly toward the bar. He could now see the dining room, straight ahead of him.

"21" is a watering hole for the rich and famous, those who want to be rich or famous, and those who want others to think they are. J.T. stopped at the cigar counter to give himself a chance to absorb the layout before proceeding to the dining room. He bought a package of Wint-O-Green Life Savers.

"We were away for the holidays," J.T. overheard Mrs. Whitney explaining to Slick Steve, who accompanied the women to the dining room.

"Oh? Where did you go?"

"Our place in the islands."

"Of course. By the way, your horses did marvelously at Saratoga last year."

"Yes, didn't they?"

The women and Slick Steve laughed pleasantly.

"Mario, Mrs. Whitney's table," Steve said to a short, gray-haired man in a tuxedo standing at the entrance to the dining room.

J.T. turned toward the dining area, hoping he didn't look as out of place as he felt. Slick Steve had done all he could to heighten J.T.'s discomfort.

"I'm sorry, madame, your table will be five minutes more," Mario explained with a pained expression. "Everyone is going so slowly today."

"Damn," complained the other woman, looking at her gold watch. "We'll be late for the theater."

"I do have a table in the next section," Mario apologized, looking toward other tables separated from the first section by a beamed arch. Beyond the second section was yet a third, where several tables were empty.

"Darling," said the woman with the gold watch, "there's only one place we sit. You know that."

"Of course," said Mario.

"Of course," Slick Steve agreed. A couple had just entered through the glass portal. He had to return to his post.

J.T., waiting halfway between the cigar counter and nowhere, turned toward the front, hoping to see Dana Reynolds. It wasn't Dana.

"Perhaps," Slick Steve said as he started for the door, "you could squeeze in another table for the ladies."

"Yes," said Mrs. Whitney. "Mario, do see if you could set up another table."

"Very well, madame." Mario bowed, motioning to a man in a red jacket. "It will be only a few moments, ladies. Would you care to wait by the bar?"

"Yes, let's," said the other woman. "I could kill for a Bloody Mary."

Slick Steve directed the couple that had just entered up a staircase opposite the cigar counter. There were several dining rooms upstairs, but nobody who was anybody sat there.

J.T. walked casually toward the bar.

"May I help you?" asked Mario, looking curiously at J.T., trying to place his face.

"Just going to wait at the bar."

"May I ask who you are waiting for, Mr. Wright?" Mario said, delighted with himself for having recognized J.T. "I'll let you know as soon as they arrive."

J.T. was also—although silently—delighted to be recognized. To stand out in a crowd of people like those at "21" was a special pleasure. He felt a great deal better already.

Mario's satisfaction was less amorphous; he had long ago realized that recognizing people and making them feel important was all part of his service, and a significant factor in the computation of gratuities.

"I'm waiting for Mr. Delafield, Chauncey Delafield," J.T. replied. "And Miss Reynolds."

"My pleasure, Mr. Wright," Mario said enthusiastically. "I hope they don't arrive for a few minutes." He shrugged, looking at all the filled tables.

The dining room was wood-paneled. The banquettes along the wall and the small tables in the center were all covered with red checked cloths. The other two dining sections were exactly the same as the first.

J.T. watched as one red-jacketed waiter carried a small tabletop over his head, while another carried the base.

"Excuse me," Mario said to J.T., moving to assist the waiters. He spoke to people seated at a nearby table. They rose. The waiters pulled their chairs back, moved their table slightly, and the new table was set in the small opening. A cloth, plates, and glasses were set in place, and Mrs. Whitney and her friend were ushered to their table.

J.T. made his way to the long bar.

"Yes, sir?" the bartender asked.

"Scotch with a splash of branch water," said J.T. He hated the taste of Scotch, but he had heard someone order that drink in a restaurant in Washington, and it sounded sophisticated enough for "21."

"Yes, sir."

The new table having been put in operation without a ripple of difficulty, Mario returned to his post at the door. J.T., at the edge of the bar, leaned toward Mario.

"Mario, is there something special about this section that people don't want to eat in the other areas?"

"My customers are special customers, Mr. Wright," Mario whispered confidentially. "I know what they need. I can take care of them. Every place where Mario is not, Mr. Wright, is Siberia."

"I get it," J.T. said, venturing a sip of his Scotch. He watched the luncheon activity for a while. The room was filled with animated conversations. Some people paid their bill and left.

"Ah, Mr. Delafield," Mario said to a man just entering the dining room. "Mr. Wright is waiting for you at the bar."

Chauncey Delafield was dressed elegantly and immaculately, with a stiff white collar and a solid-colored silk tie. His complexion was pale, his skin smooth. He had a thin white mustache and slick gray hair. He looked the epitome of the successful businessman.

"Mr. Wright," said Chauncey Delafield, walking over to J.T., extending his hand.

"Hello, Mr. Delafield." J.T. shook his hand.

"Your table will be ready in a minute, gentlemen."

"That's fine, Mario. I'll get a little libation at the bar while I'm waiting. When my niece arrives, let me know."

"Of course."

"Hello, Mr. Delafield," said the bartender. He began putting ice in a glass. "How are you today?"

The bartender poured gin over the ice and set the glass before Delafield.

"Give Mr. Wright a fresh drink, Rudy."

"I have one right here," said J.T.

"Let Rudy freshen it up for you."

Rudy placed another drink on the bar in front of J.T., discarding the hardly touched first drink.

"Cheers," said Delafield, raising his glass.

"Cheers," replied J.T., lifting his glass and letting the Scotch touch his lips. This drink may sound elegant but it tastes lousy, J.T. thought.

Model airplanes hung from wires over the bar. So did beer tankards and steins, and bats and balls and a myriad of curiosities which hung in bars of every stripe. In "21," however, they seemed *objets d'art*.

Delafield downed his drink with dispatch.

"Rudy." He motioned to the two glasses.

Rudy dutifully made fresh drinks, placing J.T.'s on the bar directly behind the one he was already trying to ignore.

An elegantly dressed man walked toward the door.

"Carmine, how are you?" Delafield said happily.

J.T. turned to face Carmine DeSapio, the Democratic power in New York State. He was more impressive in person than in newspaper pictures, with his handsome features, his Roman nose, and the smoked glasses he always wore because he had some eye ailment. The public thought he wore dark glasses because he was sinister, and he never dispelled that idea.

"Carmine, this is J.T. Wright, a friend of my niece Dana. J.T., Carmine DeSapio."

"You and Senator Anders are making quite a show down in Washington," said DeSapio.

"I'm delighted you think so," said J.T.

"Have a drink, Carmine?"

"No, thanks, Chauncey. I'm just waiting for some people. We'll probably be coming to talk to you about some fund-raising in a little bit."

"How do you think the gubernatorial picture is shaping up?" Delafield asked.

"Rockefeller—no question about it."

"You think so? Interesting." Delafield drank. "What did you think of the Kennedy-Nixon squeaker?"

"It was the Catholic question that made it close," said DeSapio. "I thought Nixon might sneak in through the split. But the Kennedys are smart—especially Bobby. They even got your Senator Anders to support them in the end," he said to J.T. "Reluctantly, but he supported them. He's probably already oiling his guns for the rematch."

"Carmine knows everything there is about politics—wrote the book," Delafield said to J.T. "You think Kennedy is going to be able to control the Congress?"

"No question. He'll take the primaries and be reelected too."

Delafield nodded respectfully.

So there it was, all analyzed and red-ribboned, the kiss of death for Senator Anders's presidential quest.

"Sure you won't have a drink, Carmine?"

"Thanks, no, Chauncey."

"What you say is very interesting, Carmine," said Delafield. "I've been getting financial feelers from a lot of people for Nixon already. You know, at RBM they send anything that smacks of politics to me. I'm Archie's utility outfielder."

"That's as it should be, Chauncey. You're the most knowledgable one in the whole setup when it comes to politics."

"Carmine, we go back too many campaigns for you to have to soft-soap me. You know the company is willing to support whatever candidates you have as well as the Republicans. We play both sides of the street and make no bones about it. That's just good business sense to me."

"I'm glad to hear you say that, Chauncey. We still have a heck of a fight on our hands. And it'll be expensive."

"I imagine it will. I'm ready to talk when you are, Carmine."

"You're a good friend, Chauncey. Have been a long time. We need more like Chauncey," DeSapio said to J.T.

"That's awfully kind of you to say, Carmine."

"Here's my party now," said DeSapio. "Good seeing you, Chauncey. Call you next week. Nice meeting you, J.T."

They all shook hands, and J.T. watched DeSapio being shown to a table.

"He's probably going to have a good financial pep talk with some-body," Delafield said as he turned back to the bar. "We give to both the Democrats and Republicans. What the hell do we care who's elected, as long as our business has friends where it counts."

J.T. was intrigued.

"Dana tells me you're interested in getting into private practice, J.T.—I hope you don't mind my calling you J.T."

"Not at all, sir."

"Well, that's where the money is. You can't make a dime in govern-ment. Of course, the experience that you're getting with those hear-ings, and the connections you're making, are certainly going to be valuable assets."

"Yes, sir," J.T. agreed.

"Mr. Delafield, your table is ready for you now," said Mario.

"Thank you, Mario," said Delafield, raising his glass and draining the colorless liquid.

Mario guided them to a corner banquette and pulled the table out so they could sit.

"Two more drinks," Delafield said to Mario.

J.T.'s insides wrenched at the thought of another drink, but he said nothing.

"Yes, sir. Do you care for a menu?"

"We'll wait for my niece, Mario. We'll have our drinks in the meantime."

"Very well, sir." Mario walked away.

"What would you like to do in the private sector, J.T.?" Delafield asked.

"I'm really not sure, sir. I haven't had much experience with any particular kind of law that I'd be more inclined to one than any other."

Delafield nodded understandingly. A waiter arrived with their drinks.

J.T. lifted his glass dutifully. He was getting to hate the Scotch more with each sip.

"I think I'd like to be involved in litigation, the give-and-take of trial work," J.T. continued.

"I can understand that," said Delafield. "Not that I do any trial work myself. Haven't been in a courtroom in ages. Hope not to be for ages more," he laughed.

"Hello, Chauncey," interrupted a portly man in a dark blue suit, who stopped at the edge of their table.

"Mr. Ambassador," said Delafield enthusiastically. "How are you? May I present J.T. Wright. J.T., Ambassador Smith, United States Ambassador to India. How are all the Indians these days, Richard?"

J.T. rose to shake hands with the ambassador.

"Stay where you are, Mr. Wright, stay where you are. India is fine, Chauncey. A lot you give a damn anyway. I've enjoyed your committee hearings, Mr. Wright. Think you're doing a great job."

"Thank you very much, Mr. Ambassador," J.T. said, flattered.

"Are the hearings finished now?" the ambassador asked.

"No, sir. I just came up for the day to meet Mr. Delafield. I'll be going back to Washington this evening."

Delafield worked at his drink assiduously. He lifted a finger to the waiter and pointed to J.T.'s and his glasses.

"Want a drink, Richard?"

"Thanks, no Chauncey. I'm having one at my table."

"So what? Have another. Waiter, send a drink on my tab to Ambassador Smith's table."

"You're a true madman, Chauncey. A delightful one, I must add. If you want a lift to the airport in my car, J.T., I'm going to be leaving right after lunch. Have a meeting with the President this evening."

"Oh?" said Delafield.

"My master's voice."

"Now you don't believe that, Richard. You never have taken a back seat to anyone."

"I'd like that very much, Mr. Ambassador," said J.T., delighted.

"Didn't Dana say something about having dinner together this evening?" Delafield asked.

"Don't let me interfere with true love," the ambassador said lightly.

"It's not like that at all, Mr. Ambassador," said J.T. "I do have to get back for meetings with the chairman myself this evening."

"Well, let me know." The ambassador went to his table.

The new drinks arrived. The waiter took J.T.'s old drink and placed a fresh one before him.

"Don't drink much, eh?" said Delafield.

"I didn't think you noticed," smiled J.T.

"Hell, man, you've hardly touched any of the drinks you've had."

"I'm really not much of a drinker."

"Good. Don't trust a man who drinks too much. Except for myself, of course. Not so sure I trust myself, either." Delafield laughed. "Seriously, I can understand your liking for trial work, J.T.," Delafield said, continuing a conversation that J.T. had almost forgotten. "All the give-and-take you're used to at the hearings, thinking on your feet, questioning, that's very much like trial work."

"Yes, sir, that's exactly what I mean."

"Cheers," Delafield said, raising his glass. "You don't have to drink if you don't want to, J.T. I'm on a liquid diet."

"Oh, there's Dana," J.T. said, seeing Dana at the entrance of the dining room. She looked great in a tailored suit.

Mario spied Dana at the same time. He walked over to her quickly, bowed, and led her to the table.

"Hi, everyone," she smiled.

Mario pulled out the table and Dana slid onto the banquette. She kissed Delafield on the cheek.

"Hi, J.T.," she said happily. "How've you been?"

"Really fine," he said, smiling back.

"Mario, bring me a Manhattan, please."

"Of course, Miss Reynolds."

"We were just talking about trial work," said Delafield. "J.T. seems interested in that. I think that is one terrifically exciting kind of law. Except, of course, J.T., the firm I'm with tries like hell to keep its clients out of court."

"Does it always succeed?"

"No, unfortunately. Most of the time it does, but not always."

"Well, then," Dana said, "doesn't that mean that firms like yours need some trial people? Maybe you need someone on the staff to handle the RBM matters?"

"No, I don't think so," said Delafield. "I head up the law staff that handles the RBM account," he explained to J.T. "Although . . ." Delafield sipped his drink pensively.

"What are you thinking, Uncle Chauncey?" Dana asked.

"Well, you know, I'm just thinking that the kind of experience that you're having, J.T., the trial kind of experience, and your contacts in Washington, could be valuable assets to a law firm."

"To Stevenson & Stetinius, for instance?" Dana asked hopefully.

Delafield smiled. The waiter brought Dana's Manhattan.

"Here's good luck on the prospects of a new career on Wall Street," said Dana.

"Aren't you jumping the gun just a little?" said Delafield.

"Not at all," she said. "J.T.'s going to be terrific when he gets to New York."

"Say, Chauncey," a man called from two tables over, "did you talk to Marge about dinner this Thursday?"

"Damn, I forgot, Frank," Delafield rose. "Excuse me just a minute," he whispered. "I have to gracefully extricate myself from a boring dinner party. Dana, why don't you show J.T. the speakeasy?"

"What's the speakea y?" J.T. asked Dana.

"Come on," Dana said.

They walked through the swinging doors to the kitchen. "What's the speakeasy?" J.T. asked again.

"Hold your horses," Dana said, touching his arm. "I'm glad you decided to take me up on the suggestion to meet Uncle Chauncey."

"My pleasure."

She looked at him with serious, sincere eyes. He looked away.

An assistant maitre d' came over to them. "Miss Reynolds, Mario asked me to show you downstairs."

"Thank you."

The man went ahead of them, down a stairway to a cellar. The floor was concrete, and the walls were of cinderblock, all painted battleship gray and white.

"You see, sir," the maitre d' expounded like a tour guide, "when this place first went into business, Prohibition was the law in this country."

They walked along a cinderblock corridor.

"However, some people liked to drink anyway. The owners of '21' tried to figure out how to provide for the pleasure of their customers without being closed down. You will notice that the walls in this cellar are very thick." He pounded his fist against the wall. "Try them."

Dana looked at J.T. expectantly.

He pounded his fist lightly against the wall. "Solid?" he said.

"If the police came down here to check whether anyone was drinking on the premises, they'd be greeted with these solid stone walls. However . . ." The maitre d' took a long piece of thick, stiff wire from behind an overhead pipe. ". . . there was this tiny hole in this one block," he said, fitting the stiff wire into the hole. "And then . . ." Suddenly the wall itself swung inward. ". . . inside," he said, walking ahead of J.T. and Dana into a small room complete with booths, bar, and liquor. "Voila!"

J.T. was very impressed. Now he pounded his fist earnestly against the cinderbock wall that had swung open to permit them access to this hidden oasis.

"The wall is eighteen inches thick," said the maitre d', "and it swivels, just as it did during Prohibition, on special hinges that can each support over a thousand pounds."

"Just think of it, people actually sat down here in the bowels of the earth, just to have a drink," J.T. marveled.

"Uncle Chauncey would," Dana said. "Speaking of Uncle Chauncey, we'd better go up. He must have gotten out of that dinner date by now. Thank you," she said to their guide.

When they returned, Delafield was sitting at the table by himself, sipping a drink.

"Ahha," he said, rising. His face was quite flushed now. "Did you gain access to the interior world?"

"We did."

"Excellent. Do you care to order now, Mr. Delafield?" asked Mario.

"Sure. What'll it be, kids?"

They ordered, and Mario left to place their orders.

"Now, you were saying, Uncle Chauncey, that you thought that someone in J.T.'s position, with his experience and contacts in Washington, would be just the kind of man you could use at your firm."

"I did? I don't remember that." He sipped his drink and smiled brightly. His teeth were very white and straight. "But then I don't remember much that happens after my fifth lunch drink."

"Does that mean you think J.T. might find a place at your firm?"

"J.T.'s still involved in the Washington hearings. Perhaps someday, when he's finished with them and the committee, we could talk?"

"Oh, that's wonderful, Uncle Chauncey. Isn't it, J.T.?"

"It sure is."

"And I thought I was being noncommittal."

The waiter arrived with the lunch order.

"You're going to stay for dinner, aren't you, J.T.?" Dana asked.

"I don't think so," said J.T. "I have to get back early for a committee meeting. Ambassador Smith said he'd give me a ride to the airport."

"Oh, no," said Dana unhappily.

"I really have to get back. If I stay for dinner, I'll miss my appointment. The last plane leaves at seven o'clock."

"Make him stay, Uncle Chauncey."

"I can't make you stay, young man, but your best supporter is going to be awfully unhappy if you don't."

"I'm sorry," he said to Dana, "but how will I get back?"

"There's always the company plane. It's sitting out at Butler Aviation. We could fly you back to Washington after dinner."

It would have been quite a coup for him to go back to Washington with the Ambassador, J.T. thought. But going back in RBM's private plane wasn't a kick in the stomach either.

"Okay, I'll stay. I'll call the chairman and tell him I'm going to be late."

Dana smiled. "Thanks, Uncle Chauncey."

"Cheers," said Delafield, lifting his glass.

MARCH 20, 1961

"IS THE SENATOR IN?" J.T. ASKED.

Lucy, who was sitting behind her desk, reading the page on which she was typing, looked up momentarily. "He is." She continued to read.

J.T. walked directly into Senator Anders's office. The senator was on the phone. J.T. sat on a couch, hunching forward to read a copy of the *Congressional Record* on the coffee table.

"That's right, Nat, we've still got a lot of strength in the South and West." The senator winked at J.T. "And we have to keep it that way."

J.T. nodded and smiled.

"Yes, I've been in touch with the people from Illinois. I think we can muster even more strength there the next time." He listened. "That's right. Keep a low profile for the time being. But there are still a lot of people who can't get over having a Catholic in the White House. That's his Achilles' heel." Pause. "I know he's the President now. But he's still an Irish Catholic President, and we know a lot of people who aren't happy with a papist. We'll have to stir up more of that kind of sentiment, that's all."

J.T., despite his appearance of total absorption in reading the *Record*, was listening intently to the senator's conversation. He knew from Carmine DeSapio's comments in New York that the senator's hopes for the presidency were dead. Anders would be too old to be a serious contender after two Kennedy terms.

J.T. had also realized during his hop in the private RBM plane last night—God, he had felt like a ruler of the civilized world; Dana rode down with him and returned with the plane to New York—that the answer to his quest for money, fame, and power wasn't going to be found as junior counsel to a congressional committee, or on the salary that went with it. He realized that the time and opportunity to set a new course had arrived. The tide was with him, and Dana Reynolds was trying her damnedest to ease his passage. He might as well take advantage of it, J.T. thought as he waited for the senator to finish on the phone. After all, how long would Dana be rooting in his corner before she felt that they were a serious duo and would expect him to do something serious about their relationship? Dana was as nice a girl—woman—as he'd ever known. But he didn't feel like getting married, getting tied down, not with Dana, not with anybody, not right now. There were worlds to conquer, and he'd travel faster if he was lighter—and that meant no family dragging him down. Yes, he'd better take advantage of Dana's contacts and get as high up the mountain as he could before Dana demanded commitments he didn't intend to undertake—not now, not ever.

"All right now, Nat, you keep on top of it, and let me know what's going on out there, hear?" He hung up the phone. "Morning, J.T. How was your trip to New York to see the folks? Did you give my regards to your daddy?"

"Yes I did, Senator. How did everything go here?"

"Very smoothly, thank you. I was more involved in politics than anything else. I guess you can tell that it's still pretty hectic from my conversation just now."

"How's your campaign going?" J.T. asked to be polite.

"Damn well, J.T., damn well! We're starting to pick up more support now than we had before the election. Particularly in the South and West, where people, frankly, aren't happy with a Roman Catholic president. Those people are entitled to a president of their choice, too."

"You think that prejudice is strong enough to defeat Kennedy the next time?"

"That prejudice has been strong enough to beat everyone before, except Kennedy. I'm inclined to think it was just a weak moment in history, one that can be turned around."

"I don't know, sir. These political things are a little beyond me."

"They're not really that complicated, once you get the hang of it," the senator observed. "But these campaigns are really like working in the salt mines."

"I can see that," J.T. commented, again politely.

"What's on your mind this morning, J.T.?"

"I was just wondering, sir, how much longer you think these hearings should continue."

"Why, until we root out every crook in the country, parade them before the folks at home in their slimy splendor. Frankly, J.T., I wouldn't mind if these hearings continued all the way to the next election. Why do you ask?"

"Well, sir, quite candidly, I was just thinking that the hearings can't last forever, and with you on your way to bigger and better things, I was wondering where I'd go from here."

"The future, you mean? Well, hell, son, there's always room in the White House for a bright young man. Maybe as counsel to the president, something like that. There'll be a spot for you—if we get there, that is," the senator added quickly, to give the conversation a balance of humility.

"That's very kind of you, Senator, and I certainly appreciate the confidence you have in me."

"Even if we don't make it, there's always a place on one of the staffs, chief counsel to a committee. I don't think you'll have to start looking for a job, J.T. No, sir. You've won your spurs already."

"Thank you again, Senator. It's just that I was thinking about getting back to New York, going into practice with my father, maybe running for something myself. This political fever is catching, I'm sure you know that, Senator."

"I've known that for years, J.T. That's how I got here myself. Started out knocking on doors, getting out voters for other candidates. And one thing led to another—alderman, supervisor, commissioner. It's something that gets in your blood. The excitement, the action." The senator smiled. He seemed just about to fall into another folksy reminiscence. But J.T. didn't want to be sidetracked.

"That's why I was wondering how far you wanted to go with the hearings," J.T. pressed.

"I guess we'll just have to keep at them until we're finished. The coverage hasn't hurt either one of us too much, eh?"

"That's certainly true."

"I think there's still a lot more mileage to the hearings, isn't there?"

"I'm not so sure, Senator," J.T. said slowly, thoughtfully. "I mean, we've had a lot of witnesses who took the Fifth Amendment. We've had the charts, the names of the families, the personnel of organized crime paraded before the committee. We've had our inside informant, complete with bag over his head. What else is there to go into that we can justify as necessary in order to start drafting legislation?"

The senator pursed his lips. "Well, I've been relying on you so far. And I'm going to leave it that way. If you tell me there's not much more we can get out of the hearings, then there isn't. How much longer do *you* think they can run?"

"Let me put it this way, Senator. I'm not running out on you. I'm staying with the committee as long as the hearings go on. But after that, I'd like to try the private sector."

The senator thought for a moment.

"Tell you frankly what's involved, so you understand the true picture, J.T.," said the senator. "I've been trying like one son of a bitch to raise enough money to get a presidential campaign going. It's tough, I don't mind telling you. Going to parties, talking to people, trying to sell myself. That's not easy. I can sell banana oil in the Senate. But to go out and sell yourself, tell people how wonderful you are, ask them for money, that's tough. Frankly, I don't expect I'll be able to raise enough money to go the long haul. So my plan has to work out in the next couple of months or I'll run out of steam. And if that happens, I'll look like some fool with egg on his face. That won't happen, though, J.T. I mean my looking like a fool. I'll walk out gracefully before then."

"What is your plan, Senator?" J.T. was listening carefully.

"To make a long story short—if it's not already too late—it's this. I know I can't maintain a presidential campaign. I know that as well as anyone. But I also know the political game pretty well. Kennedy will buy me off with some kind of high position—Supreme Court, ambassador, something—before my purported presidential campaign catches the fancy of some sugar daddy who wants to fight the papists to the death. Kennedy can't afford to let my steamroller build up steam. Understand, son?"

"Yes, sir, I do." J.T. liked the senator's craftiness. "If there's anything I can do . . ."

"I know that, son. I know that. And don't think I don't appreciate it. Or all the other things that you've been doing. The hearings are the only things that got me this far, I'll tell you that. And I appreciate it. More than you know, believe me."

"You carried the ball, sir. I just inflated it."

"Hogwash, J.T. You did the whole goddamn thing yourself."

J.T. smiled appreciatively.

"Can we keep the ball rolling until something breaks, one way or the other?" asked the senator. "I mean, let me tell you. I know I've got a tough shot. But it's a real shot at immortality, son. Supreme Court of the United States, ambassador to Spain, something. I've got to go for it. It's the culmination of a dream. Even if it doesn't work out, I'll have come a hell of a lot closer than most people. You see the picture I'm drawing for you, J.T.?"

"Yes, sir, I sure do."

"If it doesn't work out, I still have my Senate seat. But if I can just hold on long enough to become a thorn in somebody's side . . . you get me, J.T.?"

"I understand perfectly, sir."

"Will you stay with the hearings? I mean, keep the hearings going until then?"

"I will."

"And then, son, you'll have one powerful friend in me. I mean that. One powerful friend."

"I can use all the friends I can get," said J.T., smiling.

The senator grinned. J.T. was his kind of folks.

SEPTEMBER 12, 1961

THE DRIVEWAY OF THE REYNOLDS FAMILY ESTATE in Locust Valley was a long tunnel of huge, closely planted fir trees. Near the house, the stand of trees ended, replaced by wide, manicured lawns. A circular driveway cut perfectly into that lawn, led to a huge Tudor mansion.

"This is quite a place—for a weekend, that is," J.T. kidded.

"It's not a bad way to live, Otto," replied Marty.

"It is one of the nicer estates," said Courtnay. "You should see their apartment in New York. It's really wonderful. On Gracie Square, just over the river. A triplex."

"Lovely, lovely," J.T. said softly. He was indeed quite impressed.

Marty stopped the car at the front entrance. A uniformed police officer in a short leather coat pointed to the car. Marty rolled down the window.

"I'll take it, sir," the officer said. Most small-town constabularies will keep the traffic flowing at big parties. In the Reynoldses' case, this was choice duty.

"Thank you," said Marty, getting out from behind the wheel.

The front of the house was illuminated with spotlights, and planted with trimmed shrubs and bushes. Fall leaves had all been carefully removed by the groundskeeper. J.T. thought back to another season, the year before, as he'd sat at the desk of Senator Anders's, when spring and his career were dawning on the Capitol. That seemed so long ago; so much had happened since then. The hearings, his days in Washington, all had come and gone. J.T. smiled inwardly at the thought of all the progress he had made in those eighteen months. A servant in black livery opened the door to the Reynolds mansion.

"Good evening," said the servant.

"Mr. Wright and Mr. and Mrs. Boxer," announced. J.T. Marty helped Courtnay off with her coat. The servant took it, then took Marty's and J.T.'s coats.

"Cocktails are in the library," said the servant.

"Thank you." Courtnay led the way across the marble floor of the large, two-storied foyer complete with winding staircase. Another servant in livery opened the door to a huge room warmed by an enormous fireplace.

J.T. scanned the room discreetly. He recognized Chauncey Delafield first; then, sweeping the room, over the fifteen or so guests, he saw Dana in a chair near the fire, talking to a couple on a small loveseat. The room was decorated as if it were in Palm Beach, with green rug and white furniture with flowered upholstery.

Dana saw her three friends, and rose and walked toward them. She greeted Courtnay, kissing her on both cheeks, and then did the same to Marty. She wore an exotic perfume, J.T. thought as Dana touched his right cheek with her cheek. It was actually not a kiss, it was more the brushing of his cheek and the sounding of a kiss.

"I'm glad you three finally got here," Dana said warmly, leading them into the mainstream of people. She began introducing J.T. to the other guests. He made careful note of each name and face. There were faces he had seen at the party in the Crawfords' Palm Beach cottage. Courtnay's mother and father were there, as were Frannie and the Count. He met Chauncey Delafield's wife, a rather thin, austere-looking woman wearing little makeup on her angular face. She was drinking a martini, straight up.

"Dad, this is J.T. Wright," said Dana.

Archibald Reynolds was heavyset, with dark hair; he wore a mustache that was waxed to points at the ends, and a tuxedo with an impressive set of diamond studs.

"Pleasure to meet you, J.T. Dana speaks of you often." Reynolds placed a proud, fatherly arm around Dana's shoulders.

"Care for a drink, J.T.?" Reynolds asked, signaling to a servant, who moved silently through the room carrying a silver tray.

"You can get him all the Scotches with a splash of branch water that you want, Archie," said Uncle Chauncey, joining the group, "but he doesn't drink worth a damn. Hello, J.T."

"Hello, Mr. Delafield."

"You made it just in time," Dana said to J.T. "Angelo was starting to go into one of his frantic states," she said as an aside to her father.

"Angelo is our magnificent chef," explained Reynolds. "He goes into hysterics, however, if his magnificent creations aren't served exactly on time. And, God knows, we don't want our chef to get frantic. Did you want that Scotch with a splash, J.T.?"

"I'd rather have a Perfect Rob Roy." That was the latest fancy-sounding drink that J.T. was willing to try.

Reynolds sent the waiter to fetch J.T. a drink. Marty and Courtnay drifted off to speak with other guests.

"So you're starting in private practice with Stevenson & Stetinius on Monday, eh, J.T.?" said Reynolds.

"Yes, sir, thanks to Mr. Delafield."

"It was really Dana," said Delafield. "She was your biggest supporter."

Dana looked pleased.

Reynolds looked admiringly at Dana again. There was no question she was the apple of his eye.

"They probably won't pay you what you're worth," Reynolds said to J.T. "But I'm not sure that's bad."

"Don't you have that a little mixed up, Archie?" said Delafield.

"The hell I do. Nothing better for a young man starting out in the world of business—and the law can be considered a business—than to work hard and not make enough money. Forces you to learn how to work harder, be independent, self-sufficient. That's the trouble with kids these days—they don't know or even *want* to know how to work. They want it all given to them. World's all mixed up."

"Before you get into all of this, Archie, can I get myself another drink?" Delafield said lightly.

"Kid all you want, Chauncey, but our way of life is finished. You wait and see what's going to happen. I mean it."

The servant returned with J.T.'s drink.

"Get me another of these," said Delafield. "And make sure that Mrs. Delafield gets a refill too."

J.T. sipped. Christ! he thought to himself. Scotch was mother's milk compared to this concoction.

"You were saying, Archie?" said Delafield, a mischievous grin on his face.

"Kid all you want, Chauncey. But people nowadays don't want to work. Can't get people to take on jobs on which people just a few years ago raised entire families, sent kids to college—bootblacks, gardeners, factory workers, field workers. You can't get them. You can't get anybody who wants to be a domestic—"

"Aha, there's the rub. Probably lost a couple of housemaids and can't get anybody to replace them. Is that it, Archie?"

Reynolds grinned. "Well, that just happens to be true, but it doesn't change any of the things I'm saying. If people refuse to work, yet want even higher salaries for less work, if we can't produce goods at competitive prices, what do you think is going to happen to the economy?"

"You'll retire and live off your coupons and stock options, Archie," said Delafield.

"Hell, Chauncey, stocks will be worthless. So will money. Inflation is going to be a major problem."

"Shall we announce dinner, dear?" asked a tall woman, her hair pulled back into a French twist.

"Margaret, did you meet J.T. Wright?" asked Reynolds.

"How do you do?" Mrs. Reynolds allowed without a smile. "Shall we go in to dinner now?"

That wasn't exactly a warm welcome, J.T. thought to himself as he placed his almost untouched drink on the nearest servant's tray.

The guests were ushered into a large dining room with three separate large tables, each adorned with vases of tall flowers, each set with a different exquisite pattern of china. A place card held by a small golden cherub stood before each plate.

"J.T., you sit here." Dana indicated a table where her father was seated. She sat to her father's left, J.T. to his right. Mrs. Reynolds sat at the head of the second table. And Chauncey Delafield headed the third.

The guests all found their places and the servants brought out the first course. It tasted something like raw fish, but J.T. had no idea what it really was. He watched the others to make sure that he picked up the correct fork, waiting to see that the others eating this creation didn't die.

"How does it feel now that you're not in the government?" Reynolds asked J.T.

"Fabulous, sir."

"Those hearings must have been thrilling," said a woman seated two seats away. "Those sinister people and everything." She, too, spoke through her teeth, hardly moving her lips.

"It was exciting at times," J.T. replied.

"Which times were those?" asked a man sitting next to the woman who spoke through her teeth.

Reynolds was looking at J.T.

"Tell us about Gentleman Johnny," urged another woman sitting on the opposite side of the table.

"Gentleman Johnny was right at the beginning of the hearings," said J.T. as a servant took his appetizer away. *At least I didn't have to eat whatever it was*, he thought. "And he was quite impressive."

"He seemed rather suave, in a greasy sort of way," slid through the first woman's teeth.

"I don't know if *suave* is really the right word, darling," slid from the second woman. "Wasn't it more like *sinister*?"

Dana glanced at J.T. with a hint of amusement on her face. I'm glad she thinks this is funny, he thought.

"Well, I did say greasy."

"Perhaps greasy suave *is* sinister," said a man sitting next to the first woman. He was thin, with glasses.

"*Tres amusant*, Booth," said the second woman.

A servant approached Reynolds's left side with a plate that held an entire fish, head and all, on a bed of rice, mushrooms, and parsley. Two large silver utensils were on the plate next to the fish. Reynolds took a portion and the servant moved toward J.T. He watched the servant's approach with dread, then looked at the fish. Its glassy eye was staring up at him.

J.T. picked up the silver utensils and put a portion on his plate.

The servant moved silently on.

Strolling violinists came into the room and began to play. J.T. saw Marty and Courtnay at the table with Chauncey Delafield. The servants brought out bottles of white wine in silver ice buckets. They poured for everyone except Delafield, who discreetly ordered a gin martini.

The servants then brought out vegetables, each in a silver serving plate. There was some sort of asparagus and potatoes in a thick, creamy sauce.

Reynolds leaned over to J.T. "Sometimes I wish one of these guys would bring out a nice steak sandwich, you know what I mean?"

"Yes, sir," J.T. said smiling.

Dana was smiling too. She heard that.

"Have you put any of these men in jail by now?" asked the second woman. She sat back from her plate, finished eating, although the plate was virtually untouched. She lit a cigarette.

"The hearings were intended to find out what legislation was needed to put them in jail," replied J.T.

"We don't have laws to put these slimy people in jail?" asked another man at the end of the table.

"Now they're slimy, you notice," said the man with the second woman.

"*Tres amusant, encore*, Booth," said the second woman.

Oh, brother! thought J.T. as he looked at Dana. She was enjoying J.T.'s reaction to all these goings-on.

"May I propose a toast?" said Delafield, standing at the head of his table. "Actually, it's a double toast."

"Then you'll need two glasses of wine," said Reynolds.

"Don't worry, Archie, I've already drunk them," replied Delafield.

Everyone laughed.

"The first part of my toast," he said—he was glowing a little; he felt good—"is to our host and hostess for a wonderful dinner party . . ."

The guests raised their glasses.

"Hear, hear," a few of the men rejoined.

"And, as an aside, to their wonderful chef for having prepared the same. And second, to J.T. Wright, who'll be the newest associate in my firm starting Monday morning. Welcome."

The guests drank.

Delafield sat down and motioned to the servant to bring him another special drink.

The woman with the cigarette at J.T.'s table doused the remainder of her lit cigarette in the creamed potatoes on her dish.

The violinists played at each table. The servants cleared the plates and brought out small fingerbowls set on doilies on small plates. J.T. watched the others take the fingerbowl and doily and place them to the side. He followed suit.

Suddenly the music rose into a crescendo as three servants marched into the room carrying trays of animals sculpted out of ice cream and sugar, illuminated from below. The guests *ahhed* and clapped to the beat of the music as the confections were marched around all the tables. One of the glowing confections was placed on each table, so the guests could enjoy it at close range.

Corks were popped from bottles of Dom Perignon, and toasts were made again to the host and the hostess. This time the chef was called from the kitchen in his floppy white hat to bathe in the glow of the guests' applause for a magnificent dinner. The chef grinned triumphantly, then returned to his kitchen.

The women, mentioning something about diets, hardly touched the dessert. Neither did anyone else, for that matter. The animals melted elegantly in the middle of the tables.

"Chauncey, are you ready for cognac and cigars?" Reynolds asked.

"I'm not much of a drinking man," said Delafield softly. "However, to be sociable, perhaps I could go a touch."

J.T. thought to himself that he had never been any place before where the people were so *amusant*.

The guests moved to the sitting room. The men were served cognac and cigars; the women, after-dinner cordials, except for Mrs. Delafield, who had a martini, straight up. She too must have been getting some of those special drinks during the meal. She seemed ossified, sitting stone-silent and motionless, her eyes barely focused.

"Glad to have you aboard," Reynolds said to J.T. "I'm sure that you'll be quite an addition to the law firm. And while hard work is good for you, don't let them abuse you down there. Remember, men think, machines work. You know what that means, don't you?"

"I believe so, sir."

Reynolds drank heartily from his snifter.

"J.T.," Delafield called.

J.T. turned. Delafield was standing with an elegant, somewhat effete-looking man who had been sitting at his table during dinner. J.T. remembered being introduced to him by Dana at the beginning of the evening. "This is George DeValen, a client of ours." The man's face was slightly flushed.

"How do you do," DeValen said. He had a British accent.

"Hello," said J.T.

Marty joined the group. Dana and Courtnay were chatting on the loveseat by the fire.

"This is Marty Boxer," J.T. said.

"Very glad to meet you."

"I tell you, Chauncey, I'm delighted to be a client of your firm and not with the opposition, now that J.T. is joining you."

"That's splendid," said Delafield.

"Oh, yes. I've seen Mr. Wright in action on television. I wouldn't want him working against me."

It was J.T.'s moment to flush.

"George, darling," called a dark-haired young woman with exotic eye makeup and a neckline sliced down almost to her waist; her dress was backless, and the halter was loose around her fulsome and apparently magnetic breasts. The eyeballs of the men could almost be heard clicking to attention. "Come, darling, we have to get to Le Club for Oleg and Gigi's party."

"Right. Right. Sorry, old chap," he said to J.T. "I'll probably see you at the shop, eh?"

DeValen was towed out by the woman with the magnetic breasts.

"What was that?" J.T. said, to no one in particular.

"Why, those were tits, son," said Delafield. He laughed.

"Chauncey, for Christ's sake," reprimanded Reynolds. "Besides, they were bazooms."

"Knockers," countered Delafield, looking around to be sure the ladies couldn't hear.

"Boobs," Reynolds laughed.

"Melons."

"Jugs."

All the men were laughing now.

Reynolds thought for a moment his eyes to the ceiling. "You've got me, you son of a gun. I can't think of another thing . . . except cantaloupes."

"Honeydews."

The women turned to see what was causing the uproar.

Reynolds and Delafield stifled their laughter as best they could, although it surfaced and sputtered.

"Casaba," Reynolds whispered. He and Delafield turned and shook with laughter.

The women turned back to their own conversations.

The servant in charge of the cognac came by with the decanter again. Reynolds and Delafield didn't mind if they did. J.T. declined. Marty passed.

"DeValen is a high roller," Delafield, now composed, said to J.T. "He's a financial genius."

J.T. looked toward the door through which DeValen had disappeared.

"Has a strange way of doing business," Delafield continued. "But he's a sensation, a powerhouse. He's been taking over one corporation after another."

"Excuse me for a moment, Chauncey," said Marty. "I think the girls are looking for us."

"Scott Fitzgerald was right," said J.T. as they walked toward Dana and Courtnay, who were standing by the fireplace, looking in their direction. "Rich people are different."

"That they are, Otto."

"We were just going to come over and rescue you," said Dana. "My father and Uncle Chauncey can chew your ear off when they're on Remy Martin."

"What time is it now, Marty?" Courtnay asked.

"Ten forty-five."

"You're not going to go?" said Dana unhappily, looking at J.T.

"We must in a little while," said Courtnay. "We have to drive back to the city. And Marty and I have commitments tomorrow we just can't miss."

"Oh, that's a shame. Are you going to stay the evening, J.T.? You can use one of the guest rooms."

"No, I don't think so," he replied. "I've got to start getting my apartment into shape. I just sublet this little place in the Village a couple of days ago, and everything is still in cartons."

Dana frowned.

J.T. leaned close to Dana. "Can we talk alone for a few minutes?"

"Of course," she said happily. "Let's go this way."

J.T. followed Dana out of the room, looking at the others to see if anyone noticed him leaving.

Reynolds had.

Dana led J.T. to a small den across the hall from the sitting room. There was a polar bear rug on the floor, leather chairs, a fire in the fireplace.

"Sit down, J.T.," said Dana, sitting on a tufted couch. Dana smiled, waiting.

J.T. felt ill at ease, as he always had, with women. "I guess I just wanted to say thanks for all the things you've done for me so far. I mean, all the things you've done for me, period," he corrected himself, feeling more awkward.

"That's not necessary, J.T. If you weren't as terrific as everyone thinks you are, they wouldn't have hired you, no matter what I said. So it wasn't anything I did."

"I just wanted to say thanks, anyway."

"You're sweet to say so, J.T.," Dana said, kissing him on the cheek.

"No I'm not," he said frankly. "I think I'd like to be, but I'm really not."

"Of course you are."

"Dana, I always seem to either hurt people or disappoint them. Especially people who care about me. I don't know why, but that's the way it usually turns out."

"That's ridiculous."

"But that *is* the way it is. And I just want you to know—not that you care very much about me, or I about you, but—Jesus Christ, I really put my foot in it now."

"Relax, J.T. You don't owe me a thing. And I don't expect a thing."

"I didn't mean that."

"Hush now, and listen, and I'll tell you why I did it."

J.T. sat quietly.

"I know you're not in love with me. That doesn't matter. I just decided, this time, that I was going to do something I felt like doing—"

"Dana—"

"No, let me finish this, because this is tough enough as it is. J.T., you've become special to me. Men usually think I come on too strong, too independent, whatever. Don't ask me why, but you make me feel comfortable, happy—oh, I don't know, you make me feel something that no one else has. Irrational, isn't it, to love someone who doesn't love you?" She laughed softly. "But I do. And I don't want you to feel obligated to me in any way. I'd hate for you to feel that. What I did, I did selfishly. It made me happy. Promise you won't feel obligated or even mention it again."

She looked at J.T. silently. He was staring at the fire. He turned; Dana quickly glanced away.

"I don't know what to say to all that, except—"

"You don't have to say anything."

"Can I say thanks?"

"You already have."

J.T. studied Dana as she watched the fire. Despite what she had said, J.T. knew human nature, knew that you get what you pay for, and you pay for what you get in this world. He wondered if Dana didn't really believe he owed her something.

Dana looked at him, surprised by the appraising look in his eye.

"Can you come to the city one of these days soon?" he asked coolly. "You can help me decorate my apartment. We'll have dinner, go to a movie?"

"Yes to all three," she smiled.

NOVEMBER 20, 1961

THE OFFICES OF STEVENSON & STETINIUS occupied the twenty-fourth, twenty-fifth, and half of the twenty-sixth floors of a Wall Street tower overlooking Broad Street and the New York Stock Exchange. At the main entrance, on the twenty-sixth floor, a receptionist sat before a small console switchboard from which she could announce calls and clients. A large glass wall behind the reception desk revealed a two-storied library with a wide wooden staircase winding down to the main reading and research area.

One hundred and fifty-eight lawyers staffed Stevenson & Stetinius. It was one of the largest law firms in the United States. Most of the offices of the young lawyers who were not partners or members were small, cramped squares on the twenty-fourth floor. These cubicles were large enough to accommodate a desk and a chair. On the wall outside each office were small horizontal tracks in which a plastic name plaque was inserted. The plaques, of course, could be easily removed. So, too, the occupants. When the standards for starting salaries in the legal profession were set, they were set against the mythical salaries paid to the young men who sat in these small rooms at Stevenson & Stetinius and other prestigious Wall Street firms. The 1961 starting salary on

Wall Street was ten thousand dollars, and young law-school graduates attacked the bar exam with visions of such salaries in mind. The figure was misleading, of course. That salary was paid to perhaps twenty-five or fifty of the top people out of many thousands of graduates in the entire country. And no one said that the Wall Street firms were above hiring several of the potentially top men, maintaining them on payroll for a year or so, and then, after testing the crop, weeding out the excess baggage. So, in reality, a mere handful of young people out of the entire United States were paid the high salary, and the rest of the young legal fraternity were deluded into dreams of grandeur.

Of course, none of that had anything to do with J.T. Wright. He neither had one of the cubbyhole offices on the twenty-fourth floor, nor was he paid the salary of a neophyte out of law school. If one thought about it, which no one had so far, J.T. Wright *was* a neophyte out of law school. True, he had had one previous position as a lawyer, that of deputy counsel to the Judiciary Committee, where he had shown that he was a dogged pursuer who could run down the sleekest and fleetest enemy. Yet, in truth, he had obtained no real or practical legal experience on the committee. Hadn't his interrogations been exercises in asking questions of witnesses who gave no answers? The hearings weren't struggles in which truth was the quest. They were staged productions, where every question and answer had been ground and reground into a fine *paté*. If truth were important rather than trouble, then it would be known that J.T. Wright had never been in a courtroom in any official capacity, not even to drop off papers for a clerk to file. He had never even drawn pleadings—not even a stipulation for a two-week adjournment in an actual court case. But no one spoke of that. In fact, no one even thought of that. For when J.T. Wright came onto the law-office scene, there was a special aura about him that derived, of course, from his co-workers having first seen him on the magical television screen—that enchanted glass which transports individuals from the realm of the merely mortal to a special category of humankind. And when J.T. had appeared on the magic glass, he had been seen grappling, or so it seemed, with all sorts of sinister, frightening characters out of the netherworld. As in days of yore, when what was seen in print was revered and accepted as the primal truth, in the age of television, the medium of truth had changed; and what was seen on the magic glass was truth, more acceptable and revered than print. For didn't the viewer see reality with his own eyes? Surely, if J.T. could cope, as he had appeared to, with such denizens of perdition and abomination as he did on television, he could go into court on a breach of contract, an infringement of patent, a corporate merger, and tackle the vested, eyeglassed lawyer-adversaries sent in by the opposition. And so it was that in the world of the Wall Street lawyer, most of whom never have seen, never shall see, and never want to see a courtroom—although court is the sometimes unavoidable arbiter of their labors—J.T. was a warlord, a samurai, a champion. Of course, such was not a truly respected lot, not in peacetime. Only if the level of negotiations was so reduced as to be totally fruitless, was the leg chain of the champion pulled. For the courtroom practitioners seemed as barroom brawlers to the cool, calm negotiators of the conference room.

Because he didn't fit into any of the normal pigeonhole categories of the firm, and because Chauncey Delafield—and, inferentially, RBM—had personally sponsored his joining the firm, J.T. was made a Member. That was the middle of the hierarchy, higher than an associate of the firm, lower than an august partner. And J.T.'s salary wasn't bad, he thought: twenty-two thousand five hundred a year.

J.T. was behind the desk of his new office when Joan Hines, his secretary, entered.

"Mr. Wright, would you like some coffee?" she asked.

On the members' and lesser partners' floor, the twenty-fifth, the offices were commodious and the corridors were wide. Secretaries were posted at desks just outside the attorneys' doors. On the executive floor, the twenty-sixth, the lordly senior partners were ensconced in ornate, huge offices. Delafield's office was on twenty-six.

"No, thanks," J.T. said curtly.

God, Joan thought, *what a sourpuss.* She was going to ask Personnel for a change.

J.T. knew he was not the model of a pleasant, affable boss. *So what?* he thought. He displayed exactly the kind of personality people expected of him, one for which he was hired. Besides, he didn't want to enter the Boss of the Year contest.

"Do you want me to do anything?" she asked.

J.T. perused a document on his desk. *Yes,* he thought to himself, *get the hell out of here.* "No, not right now," he answered, not looking up.

Miss Hines went back to her desk, shared a frown with the secretary at the next desk, then began rereading *Catch-22.* She had run out of books in her desk, and had forgotten to bring something new from home. J.T. gave her so little work, and dictated so rarely, that she was bored to death.

Paul Cooper, another member of the firm, came into J.T.'s office. Cooper's office was directly next to J.T.'s. He, too, specialized in handling suits, or potential suits, relating to RBM products.

"J.T.," he said, "I'm going to have a conference this afternoon with the lawyer from Poughkeepsie who represents the several plaintiffs who claim that the design defects in RBM typewriters injured each of their plaintiffs at one time or another—even one girl whose fingers were severed."

"Yes?"

"Well, inasmuch as it is a potential court case, and that would be in your ballpark, I thought it would be a good idea if you were present. Besides, it would really strike them where they breathe, psychologically, to see you involved in this case, to realize that this isn't a kid's game we're playing."

The contrast between Cooper and J.T. was striking. Cooper was the epitome of how a Wall Street lawyer should look: dark blue pinstriped suit, metal-frame glasses, rep tie, plain brown shoes. And the coat and hat Cooper wore in the street were superb examples of eclat: a black Chesterfield with velvet collar and an aged, wrinkled fedora. Those battered fedoras were really the badge, the panache of the Wall Street law-firm denizens. If you could handle wearing a hat that didn't match your coat, and appeared literally to have been run over by a car, then you passed the first test. You really looked Wall Street. J.T., on the other hand, didn't look Wall Street at all. He wore no-style, odd-colored suits, penny loafers that he never shined from date of purchase, and a trench coat in winter snow or summer rain, belted with a knot around his waist.

In addition to the sartorial difference, J.T. and Cooper were a physical contrast. Cooper had pale, almost transparent skin, slicked-down hair parted close to the center of his head, thin slices of lips. He would have looked a Wall Streeter in the nude. J.T. never could resolve, in his own mind, whether Wall Street lawyers looked as they did because they thought this appearance marked them apart from everyone else, or because they were so out of touch with the real world that they didn't realize how other people looked and behaved. Either way, J.T. figured, they were pure phony. He learned in a very short while that he didn't much enjoy the company or style on Wall Street.

"Can you sit in on the conference?" Cooper asked.

J.T. shrugged. "I'm working on this other matter, the one out of Syracuse. The infringement of a dictating-equipment patent."

This work was tedious bullshit, J.T. thought. Contracts, patents, claims against RBM, all requiring him to read masses of paper. That was another thing J.T. discovered. Law firms here on Wall Street buried each other in paper like pigs burying each other in mud. Not all the work the young lawyers produced was brilliant or even clever, but there was a lot of it, all heavily documented. Everything that happened had a memo and a time bill attached to it. And this procedure was slow, ponderous. The pace was entirely too slow for J.T. He wanted action, not papers, not memos.

"Perhaps you could sit in for a minute or two," suggested Cooper. "It would really be stunning. If the other side realizes that *you* are going to try the case against them, they'll choke."

"What time?"

"About two thirty."

"I'll try to make it," J.T. said to Cooper.

"Splendid."

J.T. watched the empty door frame after Cooper left. He wondered how, in so short a time, he could find this work so totally bland and boring. He just had to get used to it, he said to himself, looking down and beginning to read a memo for the fourth time, a memo by one of the junior members of the firm about a meeting with attorneys from Cadwallader, Wickersham & Taft, who represented Taylor Aluminum. The two companies had an ongoing disagreement over a contract that required Taylor to supply metals for RBM's manufacturing needs. The cost of manufacturing and raw material had risen dramatically, and Taylor wanted to pass the increase on to RBM. Naturally, RBM didn't want to pay the increase.

J.T. yawned and stretched as he rose to his feet. He walked out of his office, along the corridor that led to the elevator to heaven, as the twenty-sixth floor was known.

The decor became noticeably plusher as J.T. walked past the more expensive secretaries at more expensive desks, past larger, more impressive offices. He was walking through the private preserve of the senior partners, the ones who shared the substantial booty remaining after all the members, associates, lawyers, clerks, secretaries, and librarians were paid. J.T. stopped at Chauncey Delafield's office. Delafield's secretary, an older woman with glasses, buzzed Delafield, then told J.T. he could go in.

"Hello, J.T.," said Delafield. He had a copy of *The New York Times* spread before him on the desk. "What brings you to these parts?"

"Had to take a break from the reading."

"Got you poring over many a volume of forgotten law, eh?"

"I wish somebody had forgotten some of these contracts," said J.T. "I've been here a couple of months and have yet to get off the chair at my desk except to go to the men's room. My eyes, my rear end, and my brain are all going soft."

"I know exactly what you mean," Delafield laughed.

"I'm starting to feel like I'm a copy editor instead of a lawyer. I'm just reading RBM contracts."

"Don't bite the hand that feeds us," Delafield said mockingly.

"I know, I know. But any law-school student could do what I'm doing. Remember what Mr. Reynolds told me?"

"What's that?"

"'Men think, machines work.'"

"Ah, yes. I get it." Delafield looked at his watch. "To tell you the truth, the reading bores the bejesus out of me too. How about an early lunch?"

"I have to be back about two fifteen to pound my chest like King Kong in front of some adversaries."

"We'll make it," Delafield said. "Let's go to the Lawyers Club. This way we won't have to fight the traffic all the way to '21.' We'll drink fast." They walked toward the door. "Of course, I should know better than to talk drinking to you. I have to tell you honestly, J.T., you are the most boring drinking partner I ever met in my life."

J.T. laughed.

"I'm going to lunch," Delafield said to his secretary.

"Yes, sir. Don't forget that you have an appointment at two thirty with Mr. DeValen."

"Very well." They walked toward the elevators. "DeValen was asking for you, J.T. Do you know him?"

"Don't you remember? We met the night of the dinner party at the Reynoldses."

"Of course. How could I forget?" Delafield laughed. "The woman with the . . ." Delafield made a discreet motion toward his own bosom. "Archie and I got a little smashed," he said just as an empty elevator arrived. "DeValen was asking for you, saying how delighted he was that you were with the firm now, and that if possible, he'd like you to work on his matters."

"That was kind of him."

"He's involved in some new corporate machination, taking over other companies, paying them with their own stock. I don't know exactly how he does it, but whatever it is, it works."

The elevator reached the ground level.

"Perhaps it might be more interesting for you to work on some of his matters. It isn't court work, but it might be a change of pace."

"Sounds interesting. I'd like to try it," said J.T.

"I think we can arrange to have some of his work transferred to you."

They walked along Broad Street, past the old Treasury Building with the bronze statue of George Washington on its steps, in the spot where he had taken the oath of office as president. At Broadway, St. Paul's dark bell-tower overlooked an ancient graveyard; Alexander Hamilton was buried there.

The Lawyers Club was just north of St. Paul's.

"Do you think there'll be much court work for me, sir?" J.T. asked as the elevator rose toward the dining room.

"I'm sure there will be. Fact is. " The elevator door opened and they were greeted by a maitre d' who escorted them to a table. Delafield ordered his usual drink. J.T. ordered a vermouth cassis.

"Vermouth cassis? By God, J.T., you're a pisser."

J.T. just grinned, with a little shrug. "You were saying about the court cases."

"Oh, yes. You have already saved us from a couple of cases in court. You didn't even know about it. But our adversaries know that you're with the firm. And threatening them, with you as our tomahawk, has worked quite well."

The drinks arrived, and J.T. and Delafield placed their lunch orders.

"Cheers," said Delafield, hoisting his glass. J.T. sipped at the vermouth cassis. It wasn't too bad, he thought.

"Of course, that probably doesn't satisfy your thirst for blood, I know. But you've only been here two months. We'll have some court for you."

"Does DeValen's work have to do with court?"

"Not at the moment. It's mostly stock . . . I guess the word is 'manipulation,' but I don't want it to sound sinister. He thinks up high-finance schemes that put ten or twelve companies together under one roof—his, of course. That's what he's doing now. Getting more companies."

Delafield ordered another drink. He looked to see if J.T. wanted another, saw J.T.'s glass practically untouched, and frowned.

"I never asked this before," said J.T., "but if I were to get some cases, clients who came to me because they know me or know of me, would I be able to handle them in the office?"

"Perhaps. It would depend."

"Depend on what?"

"On how much the fee was. If the fee was substantial, then I imagine you could. Of course, the fee would be paid to the firm. You would be recompensed for having brought the business to the firm by way of a bonus or raise in salary."

J.T. nodded.

"You have some prospective clients?"

"No. Just wondering. Now that I'm out in private practice, perhaps people who saw me and were impressed might look me up."

"Sounds reasonable."

Delafield had two more drinks. By the end of lunch, he was robust, red-cheeked, and quite affable. They walked back to the office.

The lunch crowds were gone, but the sidewalks were still quite crowded with messengers, salesmen, brokers, buyers, sellers, all kinds of people hustling and bustling to get somewhere before the market closed. Lawyers, clients, and clerks rushing to get to or from court. This area was always filled with people during the work day.

"When you finish pounding your chest, J.T.," said Delafield as they rode up in the elevator, "come to my office. DeValen will be there."

"Great," said J.T., envisioning corporate empires as the elevator door closed. His vision disappeared as he walked back to his office. All those dreary documents were still piled on his desk.

NOVEMBER 20, 1961

DEVALEN'S BLUE LIMOUSINE COURSED SLOWLY, languidly through the blaring, hectic canyon of Park Avenue. The sound and confusion outside, however, could not penetrate the thick glass windows. The car was opulent—actually ostentatious—complete with a telephone, a built-in bar with cut-crystal glasses and decanters, and a chauffeur. The DeValen coat of arms was discreetly painted on the rear doors. J.T. had a ginger ale as DeValen sipped a Scotch and water.

"I'm glad Chauncey had you in on the conference this afternoon," DeValen said. He wore a two-button suit of silk mohair, and a diamond pinky ring. "I liked your style on television, and when I met you I knew that you'd be right for the kind of work I'm doing."

"You only talked with me for a minute, then rushed off to Le Club," said J.T.

"Wonderful. You have a superior memory as well."

"I'd never heard of Le Club before your wife mentioned it. I asked Dana about it."

DeValen frowned. "That wasn't my wife. But you remembered, that's the point." He sipped at his drink. "No, that's not really it, actually. Not your memory. It's your drive, your intensity . . . I hope you don't mind my being frank?"

J.T. shook his head.

"You see, I'm rather down-to-earth. Brought up the hard way. My father was a rather ordinary Methodist minister, and we were naturally as poor as the proverbial church mice. I wasn't born with a silver spoon in my mouth, like some people you and I know. And Dad didn't leave me a million dollars to play around with. I made my own millions. And I've become bloody bored with these pantywaist lawyers you usually meet on Wall Street. Chauncey's quite a guy, though. I like him . . ."

J.T. nodded.

"But he doesn't want to—isn't able to, actually—handle all my legal matters by himself. And I know this is your kind of action."

"That's the thing I really miss right now, action."

"That's exactly what I thought. You're a real street fighter. You aren't afraid to get your hands dirty. That's why I want you to work on my legal matters. Those other twits Chauncey recommended, I tell them what I want to do and they tell me we'll have to check this statute, that regulation. By the time they stop worrying about every little detail and writing me a memo . . . Good Lord, the memos . . . I must have some fifty thousand dollars worth of memos that say absolutely nothing. Then another fifty thousand dollars worth that tell me I received the first batch."

J.T. laughed.

"You can laugh, you wretch," DeValen kidded, "but I'm the one who has to pay. I don't really give a damn about the money. What the hell? No sense being greedy. As long as I get something in return for paying. But after all the memos, I'm still where I was when I started. I need someone who can move fast on his feet without worrying about picky legal niceties. When I move, sometimes I've got to move fast."

J.T. liked the sound of DeValen's approach.

"Sometimes I'm working on a takeover of a corporation, for instance, and management drops its guard for a moment. That's the time to strike. But I can't. Not with the lawyers I have working for me now. They fudge around this way, then that. And by the time they're finished, I'm lucky I haven't lost my deal. I can't afford that anymore."

"I understand," said J.T. "But there are several lawyers handling your matters right now. I couldn't very well just walk in and tell them that I'm in charge."

"Of course not. I will. That might be stepping on their egos, I know, but I don't give a good damn. They already think I'm some kind of madman because I have no reverence for money. Most people worship at the altar of money. I like the money, of course, but I like the action more."

"I know there's something wrong with me, too. Because I understand what you're saying."

"Good. Chauncey does too, by the way. But he's got a little red wagon. He reveres neither money nor work."

"He and I can't handle your account alone, either," said J.T.

"You'll supervise the others."

The limousine stopped in traffic.

"Where are we?" asked J.T.

"Around Forty-sixth Street. Where are you headed?"

"I'm just taking a ride with you," J.T. replied. "I live down in Greenwich Village.,"

"I like the Village. First apartment I had in New York was in the Village. It was different then. No weirdos. There were plenty of writers and artists, and a lot of nuts. But not the kind of weirdos who go out of their way to make themselves weird. Do you want to stop for a drink?"

"I really don't drink."

"I thought all lawyers drank. Jesus . . . did you ever see anyone in your life who could drink the way Chauncey can? But he never gets sloppy or mean. Just mellow. I don't drink either," DeValen reflected. "Well, on occasion," he said, looking at the glass in his hand. "I have to have my wits about me all the time. When the opportune moments arrive, you can't be out to lunch."

J.T.'s credo was reaffirmed from on high.

DeValen pushed a button and lowered the window that separated them from the chauffeur. "Frank, after you drop me off, drive Mr. Wright wherever he's going."

"Yes, sir."

The partition slid up again.

"Frank is an ex-cop. He's very good. Carries a gun, has a lot of friends still on the force."

"It isn't necessary for the car to take me downtown."

"Of course it is. I don't need it anyway. I have a meeting, and Frank will be sitting doing nothing."

The traffic began to move a bit.

"I was just thinking . . ." J.T. began.

"What's that?"

"If we really want to get things done, I know this young lawyer who's really on the ball. We worked together in Washington. He's great at taking care of details, seeing that people get things done. You must know him. His name is Marty Boxer. He's married to Courtnay Crawford."

"You want him to work on my account?"

"Yes."

"I'll talk to Chauncey. Does Chauncey know him?"

"I'm sure he does."

"I'll get Chauncey to put him on the payroll. After all, I'll end up paying for him in the end, won't I?"

"That's true."

"Everything costs me down there. I think they charge rent for the time I sit in their chairs."

The limousine made its way through the ramps beneath the Grand Central Building, emerging on the other side of Park Avenue.

"I've got a meeting now, I'm trying to get control of Horn & Hardart."

"The Automat?"

"Right. That's the first thing I want you to work on. It's a sweet deal. Horn & Hardart owns the real estate on which most of their restaurants are located. Some of that is prime. Fifty-seventh Street, Times Square, Lexington and Forty-fifth. The real estate alone is worth around fifteen million dollars. The company's stock is selling today for about seven dollars a share. There are just a little over a million shares outstanding. That means the whole company is theoretically worth under eight million dollars."

"I don't understand," said J.T. "If the real estate is worth fifteen million dollars, how can the company be bought for less than eight million?"

"Management. One of the things that you can rely on in this world, J.T., is the inefficiency of other people. You think Horn & Hardart is running efficiently? Wrong. General Motors? Wrong. The United States government? Wrong. Always take inefficiency into consideration—don't bank on it, but take it into consideration when you're trying to accomplish something, and when you're evaluating the other side. When you ask how could a company with assets in real estate of over fifteen million dollars be selling for only eight million on the market, the answer is management. But what do I care? That's what makes the deal so sweet. What do you think is the first thing I'll do if I get hold of this company?"

"Put in an efficient system."

"Wrong. Sell the real estate! I'll lease back all the stores to myself first, of course. Ninety-nine-year leases. Then sell the real estate. I'll make ten million dollars on that. Then I'll sell the restaurant chain for another, say, five million dollars. How's that?"

"That sounds like my kind of business."

"That's what you work on first, then. Help me put it together."

"You bet." J.T. was excited at the prospect.

The car turned on Fifth Avenue and stopped in front of Rockefeller Center.

"I'll get out here. You keep the car, tell Frank where you want to go. If you pick up any girls, save a pretty one for me."

"That's a deal."

"I'm glad to have you working for me," said DeValen. He patted J.T.'s knee, his hand rested there.

"I am too."

"And don't worry about Boxer—it is Boxer, isn't it?"

"Yes."

"Good memory, very important. See what I mean?"

DeValen walked next to the huge statue of Atlas toward the entrance. The chauffeur remained at the curb until he saw him disappear inside the revolving door.

J.T. sat back in the soft, thickly upholstered seat, admiring, luxuriating in all the accoutrements of wealth. He pushed one of the chrome buttons. The partition lowered slowly.

"Frank, the next stop will be Grove Court in Greenwich Village. Do you know where that is?"

"Basically."

"Just head down Fifth Avenue until you get to Washington Square Park. I'll direct you the rest of the way."

"Yes, sir."

J.T. felt like a king. This was the way to go. And goddamn, wasn't everything falling right into place? He pressed the chrome button again.

"Frank, how do I use this phone?" he asked authoritatively. *If you speak as if you know what you're talking about, people figure that you do*, he thought to himself. "I have to make a phone call for Mr. DeValen." *Why did I make an excuse to the driver?* he chastised himself. No more making excuses to underlings, he admonished himself. Ever!

"Just pick up the phone and the operator will answer. Give her the call number, and then the number you want."

"What's the call number?"

"New York, 4396."

J.T. closed the partition. *Don't thank him*, he directed himself. *He's getting paid to do this. That's the only way to treat servants.* He picked up the phone, gave the call number, and then the number of the Judiciary Committee offices in Washington.

J.T. heard some interference noise on the phone as they passed between the tall buildings. The phone rang at the other end.

"Judiciary Committee."

"This is J.T. Wright. Can you find Marty Boxer for me?"

"I'll try, sir."

Try hard, he thought to himself.

There were a few moments of silence.

"Hello?"

"Hello, Otto. This is Otto."

"J.T. How the hell are you?" Marty said happily. "Where are you?

How's everything going? You sound funny." Marty's voice resounded in the phone like an echo after each sentence.

"I'm in the back of my limousine, talking on the phone." J.T. could hear his own voice echoing.

"The back of a *what? Whose* limousine?"

"No time for questions now. I just wanted to tell you to pack your bags, you and Courtnay. There's a job waiting for you here at Stevenson & Stetinius."

"Are you kidding?"

"Is Otto Wright ever wrong?"

"How did this happen?"

Marty sounded happy. *So am I*, J.T. thought. He realized he had a big grin on his face. "I'll call you tonight and explain everything. Just hurry up and get your bags packed. The hell with the furniture. Courtnay can arrange for that later. You can bunk with me. I can't wait for us to work together again."

"I can't hear you . . ."

"I said I can't . . . oh, forget it. I'll call you tonight."

J.T. pressed the phone back onto its receiver. They were passing the Empire State Building. He thought about taking one of the crystal glasses from the bar and having a drink. That seemed the thing to do. It wasn't exactly chic to pour ginger ale into cut crystal. *But, if that's what Otto wants, that's what Otto gets.* He took a glass, put in ice cubes with silver tongs, and poured his ginger ale. He leaned back in his seat, saluted himself, and sipped. Never tasted better!

He picked up the phone again, and went through the same procedure.

Squawks and squeaks, and the number began to ring.

"Reynolds residence."

"Dana, please."

"Who shall I say is calling?"

"J.T. Wright."

After a few moments, Dana picked up a phone. "Hi," she said warmly.

"How are you?"

"I'm fine. Where've you been?" she said happily. "I haven't heard from you in two days."

"Uncle Chauncey is working my butt off."

"Uncle Chauncey doesn't know what it means to work a butt off, his or anyone else's. Where are you? You sound funny."

"I'm in the back of DeValen's car." He downplayed it now. Dana wouldn't be impressed by a limousine and a car phone.

"What are you doing there?"

"Just working out an arrangement. He wants me to handle all his work in the firm."

"That's wonderful."

"It is pretty wonderful." He sipped his ginger ale and gazed out the window. It was delicious watching people stare into the limousine at a man on the phone, sipping what looked like champagne from a crystal glass. This was the way to live.

"Maybe we should celebrate over a little dinner?" Dana suggested.

"Sounds good. We should go someplace fancy. Maybe '21.'"

"I thought I'd come over to your place and cook."

"You know how to cook?"

"I'm going to experiment on you. Call me when you get home. We'll discuss it without the whole world listening."

"What do you mean?" J.T. asked.

"That phone you're on is like a ship-to-shore radio. Anyone can listen to us on their shortwave radios."

"I'll call you when I get home," J.T. said hastily, wincing. He hung up.

NOVEMBER 20, 1961

DANA LOOKED AROUND J.T.'S APARTMENT WITH CURIOSITY. He was far from a neat housekeeper, she thought. In fact, his apartment was a. mess. Clothes were strewn on the only chair in the little living room; books and papers were on the floor; empty glasses were on the TV. Other than the chair, the living room contained a small sofa, an end table with a lamp, and a small television set on the floor. There were no pictures on the walls. The bedroom, even smaller, had an unmade studio bed, and a dresser on top of which lay a myriad of papers, loose change, an empty cough-drop box, and a broken shoelace. There were no pictures on these walls either. This was J.T.'s entire apartment, except for a pullman kitchen, where the only cupboard was practically bare. A quart of milk, a bottle of ketchup, a jar of pickles, and a lonely can of tuna fish sat in the refrigerator.

On the counter next to the sink was the bag of groceries Dana had just bought to make dinner.

"I'm going to straighten up the kitchen first," said Dana as she took off her jacket. "Then we'll make dinner together, okay?"

"Sure."

"You don't cook much, do you?"

"Not too much." J.T. looked around the kitchen. It seemed all right to him. He was quite content to go around the corner to the deli and buy a hero sandwich; that and a can of soda was as good a solo dinner as any. More important than being good, it was fast. J.T. caught Dana looking around the apartment, perhaps surprised that he hadn't added neat, elegant, well-appointed decor. He didn't have time for all that fancy stuff. This apartment was just a place to rest as he struggled furiously up the mountain. Furniture, cooking, eating, all that would only delay his ascent.

"Tonight I'm going to make something special. Different, anyway," Dana said cheerily. She was happy to be doing something domestic, particularly for J.T. At home, the only thing she did in the kitchen was raid the cupboards occasionally at night. Angelo ran the kitchen with such efficiency, the refrigerators were usually locked.

"What did we buy, anyway?" J.T. asked.

"I'm going to make a recipe I found in a magazine. Have you ever had beef Wellington?"

"No."

"Well, you're not going to have it tonight, either."

"Oh?" He laughed. They laughed together.

"This is the recipe for poor man's beef Wellington. It's much easier and quicker. It's made with a loaf of Italian bread, chopped meat, and spices and things."

"Sounds good to me," said J.T. "I'm half Italian."

"You are?"

"My mother's Italian."

"I didn't know that."

"Not too many people do, except those who are close to me."

"Does that mean I'm close to you?" She looked into his eyes.

"I guess it does." He began taking the groceries out of the bag.

"You have to help, J.T.," Dana said, starting to sort the used dishes and glasses left in the sink. "We'll wash these first."

Dana washed and J.T. dried with his only dish towel. Then Dana sponged off the tops of the counters and searched about for a frying pan. She found a never-used one in the cupboard.

"What do you want me to do?" J.T. asked.

"Slice the bread down the middle like you were going to make a hero sandwhich."

"I'm an expert at that."

"You mean because you're Italian? I didn't mean anything like that."

"I didn't either. I meant because I buy hero sandwiches at the deli all the time."

"Oh. And then set the table."

"What table?"

"Oh, dear. Where do you usually eat?"

"Sitting on the couch, watching TV. I use the little table next to the couch when I have to. I put the lamp on the floor."

"All right," she said, smiling. This dinner was becoming an adventure. "Put the table in front of the couch."

J.T. began to arrange his sparse furniture for dining. "Shall I put the chair up to the table, so one of us can sit on the couch and the other on the chair?"

"Terrific."

J.T. tossed the clothes that had been on the chair onto the unmade bed. The unusual aroma of cooking filled the apartment.

"That smells great," said J.T., joining Dana in the kitchen.

"Oh, come on . . ."

"When the only smell of food around here is usually milk wetting the Rice Krispies, anything'd smell great."

They both laughed again.

"I don't know about you, J.T., but I'm having a grand time. I feel very comfortable with you."

"I know what you mean. Not about you, I mean about me."

"Oh, my, the meat," said Dana, turning quickly to the stove, stirring. "I almost burned the main course."

"I probably couldn't tell the difference—not that your cooking is always burnt. I mean—"

"I know what you meant," she said, smiling. "I don't know why, but somehow I feel we understand each other, everything about each other, even before it happens. As if we've know each other a long time."

"I know what you mean."

The meal was prepared. J.T. even helped make a salad—iceburg lettuce with a bottled dressing poured over it. Despite the fact that there was no salt, the meal tasted terrific. J.T. turned the television on and they watched *For Whom the Bell Tolls*, with Gary Cooper and Ingrid Bergman. There wasn't too much conversation during dinner, but then Gary Cooper never did say much.

When they had finished, they cleared the dishes away and returned the furniture to its original places.

"Where do you want to go to now?" J.T. said as they stood in the kitchen.

"Why not see the end of the movie?"

They sat next to each other on the love seat. J.T. could feel the touch of Dana's hip against his. He did not dare to look at her. His eyes were riveted on the TV.

"Tell me about your new situation at the office," Dana suggested, turning to J.T.

"I told you all I know about it already. DeValen wants me to handle whatever he has in the office. He said he's sure I'll handle it well."

"I'm sure you will. You'd handle anything well."

J.T. began to feel a flush, a warmth, his chest felt tight, his breath heavy. He noticed that Dana, too, was breathing in a deep, labored kind of way.

"Are you okay?" he asked.

"Fine."

Their hands were beside each other. J.T. glanced down. Like two spiders, their hands moved slowly, painfully toward each other; during a commercial, they finally touched fingers.

"When do you start this new job—I mean, assignment?" Dana said, ignoring the fact that their fingers intertwined.

"Right away, I guess."

J.T. didn't know what else to do. Their breathing was slower, heavier. He was galvanized by fright and ignorance into a state of immobility. *What should I do next?* he thought to himself frantically. They pursued an aimless, wandering conversation, each of them murmuring meaningless words as they sparred for time to contemplate, to think about what was to happen next.

"It sounds very exciting," Dana said.

"It does sound excited—exciting, doesn't it?"

J.T. decided he'd reach his arm along the top of the couch and drop it around her shoulder. The arm, however, just wouldn't lift. It was like cement. Dana wanted to do, to say something that might encourage J.T. But she couldn't think of any words. Her mouth couldn't make the slightest sound of encouragement.

"Will you be getting a new office?" she asked, her mouth so dry she could hardly speak.

"I don't know. I don't think so. Maybe." *God, what a fool, what a helpless, hopeless failure I am*, J.T. thought. His throat felt as if it were lined with sandpaper. He thought that instead of putting his arm up over her shoulder, he'd slide it across her waist and pull her closer. *I can't do it*, he screamed angrily inside himself. *Goddamn it. I can't do it*. He felt like running from the room and banging his head into a wall.

I wish J.T. would do something, thought Dana. I can't even move.

The two of them just sat there, holding each other's hands, wondering what the next move should be, who should make it. The more they thought about doing something, anything, the less they could do.

Come on, come on, J.T. urged himself. Make a move. It'll all fall into place. But he couldn't. He just couldn't.

"Do you want to go out to a movie?" he finally said.

"If you do."

"Why not? There nothing on TV."

They both smiled nervously as they got their things together and went off to the Greenwich Theater to see whatever was playing there.

MARCH 16, 1962

"I COULDN'T GET YOU AN OFFICE ON MY FLOOR," J.T. explained as he and Marty inspected the small cubicle the office manager had assigned to Marty. "I'm on the Members' floor. That sort of thing is really a big deal around here, who sits where, who has a corner office. A very chicken-shit outfit."

"I understand."

"By God, it took long enough, but it's good to have someone here that I can talk to," J.T. said happily.

"How could I refuse? A good firm, a good salary, and last but by no means least, our old team is back in action. Anyway, Courtnay was really anxious to get back to New York, even before you called about the job."

"Then it worked out just right."

"Otto, I'd better tell you something."

"About what?"

"Courtnay."

"Having trouble?"

"No. She's pregnant."

"A baby? You're kidding."

"No. She's due in November."

J.T. was dumbfounded. His pal's wife was having a baby. Funny, thought J.T., here was a great announcement, and no bands played, no crowds cheered. J.T. searched for something appropriate to say. But all he could muster was, "That's really terrific, Otto."

"Yeah."

They stood silently, awkwardly for a minute.

"Anyway, I'm sure glad you're here. Our team can outthink these Wall Street preppies three to one."

"You really think so?"

"Absolutely. These Wall Streeters are real stiffs," he said softly. "Jee-sus, they're boring. Come on, let's go up to my office."

They walked through the corridor to the stairway.

Although J.T. had already been associated with the firm for almost a year, he was such a recluse that people in the lower strata of the firm rarely saw him and were still awed by the recollection of him at the hearings, on television, a pseudo-celebrity. The girls at the desks, even the other attorneys, hesitated momentarily when they saw him walking, stared discreetly, then went about their business.

"Your office will be finished in a day or so," J.T. assured Marty. "If there's anything you want that they don't issue you, just let me know. We're on special assignment, and I'm in charge. After Delafield, of course."

They arrived at J.T.'s office. His new secretary looked up and smiled, mainly at Marty.

"Where do I begin?" asked Marty.

"DeValen's got so many projects going right now, I don't know what you should tackle first."

"I thought you were concentrating on that restaurant chain takeover."

"That's still in the works. We've made our offering, eight dollars per share. We're waiting for the stockholders to decide whether they want to accept it. We've already cornered twenty-two percent of the stock, but it's not enough to control the corporation. The majority holdings are held closely by the Hardart family. And they won't sell. They feel it's a family operation, and it should stay that way."

"What other projects are in the works?"

"He's buying gas and oil rights on land in Alaska. He wants to start drilling. We formed a new company for exploration."

"That costs a lot of money, doesn't it?"

"Millions. But the holdings of all his companies are intertwined, all the funds are pooled into the drilling operation. When the oil starts flowing, we'll use dollar bills for toilet paper."

"Just as an aside, what happens if this oil and gas doesn't prove out?" Marty asked. "Are the stockholders of the various companies in a position to beef about misuse of corporation assets?"

"When DeValen took them over and their stock ran all the way up, nobody was heard to complain. As long as they keep making money, why should anyone start?"

The phone on J.T.'s desk buzzed. He picked it up. "Yes?"

"There's someone on the phone for you, Mr. Wright. He said his name is Jim."

"Jim who?"

"I asked him. He said it was personal."

J.T. pushed another button on the phone. "Hello?"

"Hello, counselor. My name is Jim. I'm a friend of Patsy Bedardo. He asked me to call." The voice was raspy and low.

"Patsy Bedardo?" said J.T., his mind seeing flashes of the committee charts of organized crime families.

"Patsy's been indicted, arrested this morning. He's over at the Southern District magistrate's. He wanted me to pick you up and take you over there."

"Hold on a moment." J.T. put the phone on hold. He looked at Marty, his eyes wide. "Somebody says he's calling for Patsy Bedardo, who's been arrested. Wants to pick me up to take me to court. What do you think?"

"I think you should be careful. You know how these people are."

"You think it could be somebody trying to rub me out because of the hearings?"

"Would you put it past them?"

J.T. thought a moment longer. "They wouldn't do something like that at the courthouse," he said to Marty. "They'd want to meet me someplace where there wouldn't be other people."

"Maybe this is a new method."

"Thanks a lot."

"Hello," J.T. said into the phone again. "I didn't even know he was arrested. I didn't hear anything on the radio or see anything in the papers."

"It just happened."

"Perhaps he can come to my office."

"Can't do that until he gets bailed out, counselor."

"Hold on. I have another call." He pushed the hold button. "This guy sounds like an enforcer," J.T. said to Marty. "You really think they want to bump me off?"

"Why would Bedardo call *you* to represent him?"

"Don't worry, you're not scaring me, Marty. This guy on the phone already used up all my scare. Maybe I should call the police?"

"Tell the enforcer to call back in ten minutes. That'll give us a chance to talk about it."

J.T. pressed the phone button. "Can you call back in ten minutes? I have something I must finish before I go to court."

"Sure, counselor. Ten minutes." He hung up.

"What could I tell the police?" J.T. said to Marty. "That someone called and wanted me to represent Bedardo?"

"Let's see if Bedardo's really been indicted. Then we'll know if this is a ruse to set you up."

"I'll call one of the FBI agents who worked on the hearings," J.T. said. "They ought to know." J.T. took a small personal phone book from the drawer of his desk. His hands were trembling.

"Take it easy, Otto."

"Shut the door, Marty." His voice was starting to rise. "Jesus Christ. These animals don't fool around when they get going." He dialed the phone.

"It may very well be a legitimate situation."

"What do we do, assuming there is no indictment?"

The number he dialed began to ring. "Federal Bureau of Investigation."

"Let me speak to Special Agent Howard Leighton, please."

"One moment."

"What do we do, assuming there is no indictment?" J.T. pressed Marty.

"Ask Howard. He's in the FBI."

"Leighton," said a familiar voice on the other end of the line.

"Howard, am I glad to talk to you. This is J.T. Wright."

"Hey, J.T. How's it going?"

"I just got a call from someone who said he was calling for Patsy Bedardo . . ."

"You're going to be handling Patsy's case, J.T.? Congratulations."

J.T. looked at Marty and nodded, grinning. "When was he arrested, Howard?"

Marty blew out the breath he had been holding.

"There was a sealed indictment that was unsealed today. We're rounding up a whole bunch of people in New York. It's a major narcotics bust. It's already hit the papers. Bedardo's got to pay a big fee, J.T. Now I know you're in the chips."

"I wasn't sure it was a legitimate call," said J.T.

"Nothing involving Bedardo is legitimate, J.T.," Leighton remarked.

"Howard, I'm going to send someone to get me a newspaper. Thanks for the information. Sorry to bother you."

"I'm glad to hear you're doing so well, J.T. Don't be such a stranger."

"Take care, Howard." J.T. hung up the phone quickly. "Bedardo's been indicted," he told Marty, happy and relieved.

"That still doesn't mean it isn't a ruse, using a good moment to get you."

"Holy cow, you're a pleasant soul. Now what?"

"I don't know. Call Howard back and ask him."

"I'd seem like some kind of frightened fool, jumping at shadows."

"You are frightened."

"I don't want Howard to know that. He was congratulating me on all the money I was going to make."

"Did he say what kind of case it is?"

"A major narcotics arrest. Rounding up a bunch of people here in New York."

Marty turned on a small radio J.T. had on a bookshelf. He hunted the stations for a news report.

". . . the latest arrest brings the total to thirteen in this case. We repeat, the Federal Bureau of Investigation has made arrests—including Patsy Bedardo, reputed head of an organized crime family here in New York. More details at eleven twenty-five . . ."

"I still don't know who called me," said J.T.

"Let's assume that Bedardo wants you to represent him. Are you going to take the case? And, more important, are the powers around here going to let you take it?"

J.T. mused. "It would be some case, wouldn't it? Front-page publicity every day of the trial, coverage everywhere. Just like the old days. Couldn't do any harm, could it?"

"That'd make it worse, from the firm's point of view."

"I discussed with Delafield the possibility of handling my own cases in the office. He said, basically, that the name of the game is making money. So . . . if Bedardo pays a high enough fee, we ought to be able to convince them around here that he's sufficiently respectable to be represented by counsel."

The phone on the desk buzzed again. J.T. picked it up.

"Yes."

"A Mr. Entrerri for you."

J.T. looked at Marty. "It's Gentleman Johnny!"

Marty sat on the edge of his seat.

J.T. picked up the phone. "Hello?"

"Hello, counselor," said the familiar voice.

"Hello, Mr. Entrerri," J.T. said coolly.

"I can understand you might have been somewhat skeptical after the first call," Gentleman Johnny said. "Patsy sent word that he wants to have you represent him. He never stopped talking about the way you took on all comers at those hearings. Said if he ever picked up an indictment, he'd want you. Can you handle his bail application?"

"The bail applications?" J.T. said calmly, wondering how one handled a bail application.

"He's already told the U.S. Attorney he wanted to wait for his lawyer. So they're all waiting, and not too patiently."

"Is there a number where I can reach you?" J.T. asked. He wanted a bit more time.

"I'm on the outside right now, counselor. I'd very much appreciate it if you could handle the case. If it's a question of fee, either Patsy or I will straighten it out with you this afternoon, or maybe tonight over dinner."

"I only see clients in my office," J.T. said firmly. He looked at Marty. Marty winked.

"Does that mean you'll go to court?"

"I'll call the magistrate right now and arrange to go over there."

"Terrific, counselor."

J.T. hung up the phone. Marty was staring at him with curiosity. "Well?"

"Right now, we have to handle a bail application for Bedardo. He's at the magistrate's office."

"Shouldn't you talk to Delafield first?"

"Maybe I should," said J.T. He dialed Delafield's intercom number.

"Mr. Delafield's office," said the secretary.

"This is J.T. Wright. Does Mr. Delafield have anyone with him right now?"

"Not right now. Shall I buzz him?"

"No, I'll come right up." He hung up the phone. "You get to the library, Marty. Check out the statutes, so we handle this thing properly. I'll pick you up there."

"Okay."

J.T. walked quickly through the corridor toward Delafield's office.

"Yes, J.T., what can I do for you?" asked Delafield.

"I've just received a phone call asking me to represent Pasquale Bedardo," J.T. started. "It's a criminal case."

"Oh?"

"It won't interfere with anything I'm already handling. And I'm sure he can pay a substantial fee."

"What kind of criminal case? Well, what's the difference, I wouldn't know what you were talking about if you told me. I'm not sure, frankly, J.T., how the other partners are going to react to your handling a criminal case in the firm name."

"Perhaps I could handle it in my own name?"

"That'll present a problem too. I'm going to have to ask around."

"What should I do meanwhile? This man's over in court right now."

"You could go over there to see what's going on. But I wouldn't get too involved in the situation until we find out what the reaction is over here."

"What's your reaction, sir? The only reason I even entertained this matter was that you said you thought I might be able to handle cases of my own, so long as the fee was appropriate."

"Yes, I remember that, J.T. I have no reaction to speak of. A criminal case should be like any other court case. Go over and see what the lay of the land is, and meanwhile I'll make some inquiries here."

"Thank you, sir."

MARCH 16, 1962

J.T. WALKED QUICKLY UP THE STEPS of the Federal District Courthouse on Foley Square. The building was a tall, thin tower with a pointed, gold-leafed roof set amid a variety of other government buildings. Next to the Federal Court building on the north was the New York State Supreme Court, and next to that was the State Office Building, and next to that was the Criminal Court for New York County. On the south side of the Federal Court was the giant Municipal building, with an archway cut through the bottom; cars exiting the Manhattan side of the Brooklyn Bridge drove right through the building into Chambers Street.

Because traffic was so heavy, J.T. and Marty had left the taxicab a couple of blocks away from the courthouse and begun to walk. People in this legal community immediately recognized J.T. Wright from television. He smiled or nodded to some. They smiled back.

"I guess a lot of people look at television around here," said Marty.

"How could they forget a face like this?" J.T. whispered lightly.

"That's true too," Marty laughed.

They pushed through the revolving door and entered the courthouse. "Excuse me, where is the magistrate's courtroom?" Marty asked a guard.

"Straight through those bronze doors at the back of the lobby, and all the way to the back."

"Thanks."

They walked along a narrow, angled corridor to the very back of the building. The small courtroom was filled with standing people, all talking in small groups. At the front of the room was a judge's bench and, next to the bench, a lectern. The young man who stood at the lectern looked just like someone who might work in J.T.'s office: wire-framed glasses, dark blue suit, brown shoes. When J.T. entered, there was a marked silence.

"Can I help you?" asked a young woman standing in a doorway to the side of the judge's bench.

"We're here for the Bedardo arraignment," said J.T.

A buzz of conversation filled the air. The newspapermen in the room rushed over to J.T.

"Are you going to represent Bedardo, J.T.?" asked a reporter familiarly.

"Are you going to the other side now, J.T.? Representing criminal cases?" asked another.

"Who called you?"

"How does it feel on the other side?"

"Are you going to be able to get him bail?"

"What kind of bail do you think the magistrate will set?"

J.T. was against the wall, fielding the reporters' questions coolly.

The young woman came back to the doorway. "Would you gentlemen come this way, please?" She spoke to the young assistant U.S. attorney at the lectern, as well as to J.T. "Magistrate Bishop would like to see you."

"No one else in the magistrate's office now," she said as the newsmen tucked in right behind the prosecuter.

The magistrate, an old, thin man with gray hair, sat behind a large desk.

"How do you do, Mr. Wright? I'm Magistrate Bishop. Do you know Mr. Keating?"

"No, sir, I don't," said J.T., turning to nod at the prosecutor. Keating nodded back coolly.

"Haven't seen you around here before," said the magistrate. "Except on television, of course." He smiled. "Are you going to represent Mr. Bedardo?" The magistrate was making notes on a piece of paper.

"I received a phone call that Mr. Bedardo had been arrested and was going to be arraigned," said J.T. "I'm going to represent him, at least for the arraignment."

"There's no need to discuss the matter, then," said Keating, "unless you're actually going to file a notice of appearance on behalf of Bedardo." There was obvious hostility in Keating's attitude.

"There's no question about that," said J.T. in kind. "I'd like to talk to Mr. Bedardo."

"Perhaps the marshal can bring Bedardo up from the pen so Mr. Wright can talk to him," said Keating. "We've been waiting almost an hour already."

"It might be better if you went down to the pen to talk to Mr. Bedardo for a few minutes," said the magistrate. "Especially with this crowd up here."

"I think that might delay us even further, Your Honor," said Keating.

"There are many people waiting," Bishop wavered.

"I came as soon as I was notified, Your Honor. I have no idea when Mr. Bedardo was arrested, or how long these people have been here, or even what they have to do with this case."

"These are the arresting agents, newspaper people, other assistant United States attorneys," replied the magistrate, sitting back in relaxed fashion. There was something accommodating about him, as if he not only recognized J.T. but extended him a friendliness and familiarity ordinarily reserved for longtime acquaintances.

"I think I should at least speak to Bedardo before the arraignment," said J.T. The more hostile Keating was, the firmer became J.T.'s resolve to get into the case. "How can I make a bail application on his behalf without talking to him?"

"That's quite true, of course. I don't think a few more minutes are going to make any difference, Mr. Keating. Why don't you show Mr. Wright and his associate down to the marshal's office," the magistrate said to his secretary. "I'll call and advise them you're coming down."

"Thank you, sir," said J.T. "I'll be as quick as possible."

Keating was clearly displeased by the magistrate's obliging attitude. His mouth grew tighter and thinner.

"Come this way," said the secretary as she led J.T. and Marty out to the corridor, down a stairwell, and into the marshal's office. Just inside was a large cage that formed a reception area. Beyond the cage was a large office.

"Can I help you?" a marshal asked. As he looked at J.T., recognition spread across his face. "How are you, Mr. Wright?"

"Fine, thanks. The magistrate said I might see Mr. Bedardo."

"Right, he just called down. He didn't say *you* were his lawyer."

The marshal turned a large key in a lock on the inside of the cage. "Is this counselor with you, Mr. Wright?"

"Yes."

"Okay. Sign in, and then I'll take you to the pen." He pointed to a large book on his desk.

"I'm going back upstairs," said the secretary. "Call when they're on their way back up, Bernie?"

"Right, Sally."

The marshal led J.T. and Marty across the large office. Conversations had become subdued as people studied J.T. The marshal opened the door, beyond which J.T. saw cells on both sides of a wide corridor. Another cage door barred their entry.

"Okay, open it up," the first marshal said to a guard inside the cell area. He opened the barred door and J.T. and Marty entered the pen.

"Which cell is it?" asked J.T.

"Second one on the left."

"Right here, counselor," said a thickset bald man with a stub of a cigar in his mouth. Bedardo reached his hand through the bars to shake J.T.'s hand. His grip was very strong. His eyes were so dark they looked black. He studied Marty with suspicion.

"This is Marty Boxer, my associate."

"How are you?" Bedardo said coldly. He studied the two lawyers as they looked at him with equal curiosity.

If someone saw Bedardo on the street, J.T. thought, and didn't know who he was, he would just see a short old man with dark eyes.

Yet here, in this atmosphere, knowing who the man was, there was something electric, something powerful, something sinister.

"What do you think?" Bedardo finally said.

"About what?" asked J.T.

"About bail? Can you get me out to the street? Listen," he said, motioning J.T. closer to the cell door. Bedardo looked over his shoulder. There was another man in the cell, a young man sitting silently on a bench against the far back wall. He knew who Bedardo was, and didn't want to appear too curious about what was going on.

"Look, counselor," Bedardo whispered through the bars, "I know you don't handle too many criminal cases, but I know what you can do. And I know you still have connections with the feds, you know? You take care of this situation for me, fight like a son of a bitch, and don't worry about money."

"Tell me about yourself. I need some information for the bail application."

"I got a misdemeanor, disorderly conduct, when I was a kid, maybe thirty-five years ago. Other than that, I ain't got a sheet for nothing. I got a wife, three kids, and I own my own trucking business. This case here, it's a frame. See, I know they have me right here," he said, touching the tip of his nose, "and I know that when they have you there and they want to get you, they get you. So I know the case is going to be a ball-breaker. But you're one guy who can neutralize the ball-breaking. Do the best you can for me, that's all I'm asking."

"What's your home address and telephone number?" J.T. said, signaling to Marty to take down the information. Marty already had a pad in hand.

"First get me out, then we'll have a nice dinner and you'll get everything you want, you get me?"

"Let me give you my card," said J.T., looking in his wallet. He didn't have any cards. Marty gave Bedardo one of J.T.'s cards. "I don't conduct business anyplace but in my office," J.T. added.

Bedardo chomped a little tighter on his cigar. "Whatever you say, counselor. You're the doctor, I'm the patient." He smiled a little around the cigar. But his eyes didn't warm up at all.

J.T. and Marty went back upstairs and reentered the magistrate's office. The magistrate was on the phone, his back to the door.

"Yes, that's right, the one from television," he said just as he swiveled to see J.T. He flushed a bit. "I'll call you later, dear," the magistrate said quickly into the phone. "Yes, right after I finish." He hung up. "Are you all set?" he asked J.T.

Newsmen, spotting J.T., began to edge into the magistrate's office.

"No, no, not in here, please," said the magistrate, raising his hands. "Sally, see where Mr. Keating is, so we can get this arraignment over with."

The secretary went into the courtroom.

"Can't we just talk to Mr. Wright a minute, Your Honor?" asked one of the newsmen, moving another tentative step into the office.

"Not now, we have to finish this arraignment."

"Only a minute," the newsman repeated, taking another step. "We have a deadline." Other newsmen advanced in the first newsman's wake.

J.T. realized why Keating wanted to speed up Bedardo's arraignment. If the story didn't make today's afternoon editions and broadcasts, the morning papers would beat the horse to death, and by tomorrow evening it would no longer be a hot news story. Evening press coverage would be lost, and the U.S. attorney in this district wasn't allergic to all the coverage he could get.

J.T. had conflicting emotions. He wanted to thwart the U.S. Attorney's appetite for news—especially at his client's expense. On the other hand, the stories would prominently display J.T.'s name as well.

"I agree we ought to move this right along, Your Honor," J.T. said loudly to the magistrate. The newsmen stayed where they were, writing on their pads. "After all, my client has been detained for a substantial period of time now on rather flimsy charges." J.T. decided he was not only going to help the newsmen get their stories filed on time, he was going to give them something interesting to file.

"Have you spoken to your client?" one of the newsmen asked from the doorway.

Keating entered the magistrate's office. "You wanted me, Your Honor?" He looked with hostility at the newsmen hovering around J.T.

"Yes, I was wondering . . . perhaps we should shut this door?" he said to his secretary, seeing the newsmen hanging on his every word.

Several of the reporters groaned.

"Sorry, sorry, we'll be right out and you can report everything that we do on the record." His secretary shut the door. "I was wondering, Mr. Keating," the magistrate said, "if you and Mr. Wright could agree on a bail amount, so that we don't have a long dispute on the record?"

"Your Honor," said Keating, "there *are* substantial reasons why Mr. Bedardo should have no bail. I'd prefer to do all of this once, on the record."

"Very well. I just thought there might be some agreement. After all, everyone's entitled to reasonable bail. Go ahead out to the courtroom," said the magistrate. "We'll do everything on the record."

J.T. was the first to open the door. Immediately the newshounds descended—as he'd known they would.

"What's going to happen, J.T.?"

"Is your client going to make bail?"

"How does it feel to be a defense counsel representing people who were the subject of your investigations in Washington?"

"Let me answer the last question first, if you don't mind," J.T. said. "I approach both situations the same way, as a professional, and I do whatever task I have with the same determination to do the best job I know how."

J.T. and Marty had already foreseen the likelihood that such a question would be asked by newsmen. And they had formulated the answer J.T. had just given. Sounded pretty good, J.T. thought.

The magistrate came out of his office and sat behind the bench. "Come to order, gentlemen. Mr. Keating, you have an arraignment."

"Yes, sir. United States against Pasquale Bedardo."

The magistrate made some handwritten notes. He looked around. "Is the prisoner here?"

"He's on his way up," said a marshal standing next to the bench.

"Please, get him immediately."

"Are you going to be taking on more criminal cases?" a reporter whispered to J.T., moving closer to him.

"I have to decide that on a case-by-case basis," he replied.

Other reporters moved in quickly. Keating's mouth contracted perceptibly as he read from some papers on his lectern.

"Is there any conflict of interest involved in the fact that you were at one time investigating organized crime figures and now you're representing them?" another reporter asked softly.

Two marshals entered with Bedardo, whose hands were manacled. Everyone in the room was silent as they viewed the crime boss, who looked every inch as he should have, defiant, the unlit stub of a cigar—Bedardo must keep a supply of half-smoked cigars, thought J.T.—still in his mouth.

"Can you take those handcuffs off my client?" asked J.T.

"I'm not going to jump out the window," said Bedardo. "The truck with the 'x' marks the spot didn't get outside yet."

One of the marshals silently unlocked Bedardo's manacles. Bedardo rubbed his wrists.

"Let's proceed," said the magistrate.

The room began to quiet again.

"Go ahead, Mr. Keating," said the magistrate.

"Your Honor, you have before you Pasquale Bedardo, on indictment 62 CR 579, charging the defendant and twelve others with the crime of conspiracy to import a narcotic substance with various substantive counts of possession with intent to distribute and sell same substance."

"What is the plea to be, Mr. Wright?" asked the magistrate.

"Not guilty, Your Honor."

Bedardo, standing next to J.T., was totally silent.

The reporters listened and wrote on their pads.

"Very well, not guilty." The magistrate made a note on the paper before him. "What is the government's position on bail?"

"The government is recommending no bail in this case, Your Honor. The basis for this recommendation is the fact that Mr. Bedardo is a kingpin in organized crime. He is the head of a crime family in the New York area. His presence on the street denigrates law and lawful authority. In addition, the defendant is charged with the importation—I really should say control of the importation—of most of the narcotics sold and distributed in the New York area. It is a multimillion-dollar operation with international connections and importation routes. This is a vast scheme, which shall continue to flourish so long as this man is at liberty in the street. The government submits that Mr. Bedardo is a menace to the community, a clear and present danger, who should remain in jail pending his trial."

The magistrate nodded and turned to J.T., who said, "Your Honor, I hope that the constitutional system of justice that we've been enjoying in this country hasn't changed without my hearing about it. Under that system, people accused of crimes are presumed to be innocent until proven guilty.

"If presumption of innocence *is* still the law, however, then I can't imagine how the government—charged with upholding and enforcing that very law—now takes the position that Mr. Bedardo should be punished either for this crime, of which he is presumed innocent, or of some other unknown and unnamed misdeed for which he hasn't even been charged. Mr. Bedardo has had one misdemeanor conviction, approximately thirty-five years ago. Other than that, he has never been arrested, charged with a crime, or anything else relating to the penal law. If the government claims that something Mr. Bedardo has done is or was illegal, then he should have been charged with those other crimes and prosecuted for them."

J.T. glanced over at the newsmen. They were writing at full speed.

"Surely, Your Honor," J.T. continued, a bit more timbre in his voice, "such a nonprosecutable past cannot be sufficiently grave to be considered by you as a basis to deny my client bail. Moreover, my client has roots in this community going back almost sixty years, owns a business, and is a law-abiding member of the community." J.T. looked over to the newsmen again. They were enjoying the whole show.

"Mr. Prosecutor, I'll hear you."

"Your Honor, the government is in possession of significant information that the government does not wish to publicly reveal at this time, in order not to jeopardize the source, that this defendant is a boss of an organized crime family and is at the head of the narcotics trafficking in this area. His very presence on the street ensures the continued flow of narcotics. We shall reveal such information to the court at the appropriate time."

The magistrate looked back to J.T.

"Your Honor, I wish I had a flag and an apple pie right now. I'd lend them to my brother at the bar, Mr. Keating, so that he might wave the one and offer a piece of the other to all here present. What I told you about lack of evidence against my client has now been proven certainly true. The government doesn't present a single fact for you to consider, even in light of my statements. The prosecutor merely waves the flag and asks you to punish Mr. Bedardo on the basis of nothing. Such application is an outrageous attempt to visit punishment on this defendant for the ills of mankind, the addiction of dope fiends, and the inability of the police to cope with the flow of narcotics. Surely, if you think it will accomplish anything, we can all agree to have a scapegoat. Let's fool the public into believing that the absence from the street of this one man will cure a multitude of ills that have plagued civilization from time immemorial."

"I don't intend to be fooled," the magistrate said slowly. "I think that the government is sincere in its suggestion that it possesses certain information which must be kept confidential. However, I cannot detain this defendant without some proof of actual crimes, actual danger to the community, or a belief that he will flee the jurisdiction."

"The government is willing to reveal the same to Your Honor alone *in camera*," said the prosecutor.

"I protest such secret proceedings," J.T. shot back.

"Mr. Prosecutor, have you reason to believe that this defendant will not answer the charges against him? That he will flee the jurisdiction?"

"Yes, Your Honor."

"May I know what the reasons are?"

"This defendant still has family in Italy, and it would be easy indeed for him to go back there and avoid prosecution. Particularly, Your Honor, where the charges allege the defendant to be the head of an international narcotics conspiracy. It would be quite simple for the defendant to flee to Europe without any impairment in his life style or interruption of his narcotics trafficking."

"If it would make things simpler," said J.T., "I offer to hold, as an officer of this court, the defendant's passport, so that he would have no means to leave the country. As an alternative, Your Honor, if this court feels that my holding of the passport would not be satisfactory, I would be willing to have the same held by Your Honor, sealed from the prosecutor, of course, so that Your Honor would be assured that the defendant is not going to flee the jurisdiction."

"It's quite easy to have a false passport made, especially for a man in a position of the defendant," said Keating.

"I am amazed that the government is now ascribing another baseless accusation against this defendant in order to have you keep him in custody."

"I think I've heard enough," said the magistrate. "I'm going to set bail at one hundred thousand dollars cash or surety bond."

The murmur of the courtroom grew louder.

"Will your client be able to post such bail?" the magistrate asked.

J.T. turned to Bedardo.

Bedardo leaned toward J.T. to whisper. "Good work, counselor. I got a bondsman already here," he looked into the crowd for a moment. "He's in the back there."

"Yes, Your Honor," J.T. answered the magistrate.

"When do you think he might be able to do that?"

"Here I am, Your Honor," said a small man with tight, curly hair as he made his way through the crowd. "I have been authorized to post bond on behalf of Mr. Bedardo."

The magistrate arched an eyebrow. "Very well, come into my office." The magistrate rose. "The judge to whom this case is assigned, Mr. Prosecutor, can reconsider your bail application if you have better information or believe that I am in error."

Keating, silent with anger, watched the reporters hovering around J.T. again.

"Excuse me for a few minutes, gentlemen," said J.T., turning to his client. "I'm going to go back to my office," he whispered to Bedardo. "Call me there when you get out of here."

Bedardo studied J.T. for a few minutes, then smiled. "Okay, counselor. You did good. I'll see you in an hour or so. I never been to a Wall Street law firm anyways."

MARCH 17, 1962

"DID YOU SEE WHO JUST WALKED BY?" Jeremy Thorne said with disbelief to Roger Munro, another associate whose office was close to J.T.'s. Thorne had been walking toward the washroom when he recognized Patsy Bedardo.

"Who?" replied Munro, looking out to an empty corridor.

"Benardo, Benito, something . . . the crime boss that Wright's representing on a criminal charge."

"No kidding. Where?"

"Just walking down the corridor as big as you please." He signaled Munro to come to the door.

The two men stood in the doorway, peeking out at the short, stocky figure walking with another, taller man who carried an attache case. A receptionist coursed along ahead of them toward J.T.'s office.

"Did you ever believe you'd see that in this office?" asked Thorne.

Marty Boxer emerged from the elevator and walked toward J.T.'s office. Thorne and Munro pulled their heads in quickly at Marty's approach.

"This is Mr. Wright's secretary," said the receptionist who was guiding Bedardo and his companion.

"Thank you, miss," said Bedardo.

J.T.'s secretary, who had been involved in reading a Philip Roth novel, stood and ushered the two men into J.T.'s office.

J.T. was a study in concentration as he perused some papers on his desk. He had taken these documents out of a random file in his room when the receptionist announced Bedardo.

"Ah, good morning," said J.T., rising. "I expected you yesterday afternoon."

"Well, those rats over in the courthouse delayed me." Bedardo shook J.T.'s hand with healthy vigor. "And then I had some things to do last night. I was tied up. Somebody was supposed to call and tell you that. Did they?"

"Yes. No problem."

"Say hello to Joey," Bedardo said, indicating a full shouldered man with no neck and dark, thick hair. His hand, which J.T. now shook was large and meaty.

Marty entered J.T.'s office.

"You know Marty Boxer."

"We met at the court."

"Sit down," said J.T. "We received a call from the court a short while ago. The case has been assigned to Judge Laird Morgan."

"Morgan? I hear he's a crazy Texan."

"He's not going to be that crazy with us," J.T. said without concern.

"I like to hear you say that," said Bedardo. "But I understood he was a real crazy son-of-a-bitch. A prosecution man through and through."

"Our information is that he's not so bad."

"That's good news, counselor." Bedardo winked slowly at J.T.

"Anyhow, the government has requested a bail review in front of Morgan tomorrow morning."

"What do you think he'll do?"

"I'm not quite sure," J.T. said. "He might raise the bail somewhat—to placate the government. Keating was very upset that I was able, to get you any bail at all."

"I could see that," Bedardo said with pleasure at the thought. "He'd like to see me in some dungeon. These bastards have no souls, you know what I mean? No feelings. They don't even know they're dealing with human beings. And you're supposed to put your tail between your legs when they look down their noses at you. He'll be in hell before I dog it for him or any other som-n-a-bitch." He looked at Joey, who nodded. "What do we do now?"

"Between now and tomorrow morning, you have to do nothing. We have to do some legal research here at the office," J.T. said, looking from Bedardo to Marty. He already had Marty hard at work on the law books, so he would have citations ready for Morgan.

"In addition, I want to get my investigators working, talking to everyone who will talk to me, taking statements from them, the whole works."

Bedardo pursed his lips and nodded approval. "Excuse us a minute," he said to Joey.

Wordlessly, Joey walked out of J.T.'s office.

Bedardo looked at Marty. "Forgive me, counselor, but I have something personal I want to discuss alone with Mr. Wright for a moment. Is that all right?" Bedardo said, turning to J.T.

"Marty is going to be working on this case right down the line. In fact, if I'm not here, he's the man you should talk to; it's the same thing as talking to me."

"I understand that, don't get me wrong. I just have something that I want to discuss with you personally."

"Marty, would you mind for a moment?" J.T. asked.

Marty nodded and stepped out of J.T.'s office, closing the door behind him.

"I wanted to talk to you about your fee," Bedardo said, taking the attaché case that Joey had left next to his chair. "What is your fee, anyway?"

"I don't know yet. I have to see just what's involved in this case, and then I have to talk to the senior partners. Of course, whatever fee is set doesn't include expenses or investigators, or an appeal if that's ever necessary."

"Counselor, I don't intend to argue with you about money," he said, putting the attache case on J.T.'s desk and opening it. It was filled with packets of bills in wrappers: tens, twenties, fifties, hundreds. J.T. had never seen so much cash in one place.

"What's this?"

"I brought a retainer. Lawyers have to be paid."

"As I said," J.T. spoke a bit breathlessly, "I don't know yet what the fee should be, or just how the senior partners want it handled." J.T. couldn't take his eyes off the contents of the attache case. "I'll have to ask what they want to do about cash. I guess cash, check, doesn't make much difference."

"What I'll do is give you this, and then I'll make out a check. That is my daughter will make out the check. Her husband is an accountant. They'll make a loan to me and I'll give you the check. That you put in the bank. That'll be the fee, in case the Internal Revenue people come nosing around. Another check I'll give you myself. The rest, whatever it is, I'll give you like this, and you make it go south, you know what I mean?"

"South? You mean not report it to the Internal Revenue?"

He nodded, automatically looking over his shoulder at the empty room.

"And if the Internal Revenue comes here to inquire about the fee you paid?"

"Counselor, I don't have to tell you what to do, do I? You do whatever you think is best. The people around here'll go along with whatever you say, I'm sure."

"I don't know about that."

"You've got nice ways about you, counselor. I know you can talk to them. You keep this meanwhile," he said, closing the attache case.

"I can't keep this kind of money around."

"You keep it here," Bedardo said with a gesture of finality. "You don't have to say anything to me about what you do, who you know, what kind of arrangements you make, counselor. Maybe some of your friends want something, the judge wants a vacation." He winked at J.T. "You need more, I'll get it. Just give me a couple of days."

"I don't think the firm is going to go for any of this. And I don't particularly go for the idea that you think I'm a fixer. If that's the reason that you've come to me to represent you, I think you've come to the wrong man."

"Counselor, don't get offended. I came because you have a good mouthpiece. I saw you use it in court yesterday, just like I thought you would. That was great, you know? That's what I want, okay? But if there's something you have to do, do it. Okay? Investigators, expenses, whatever. I'm not going to question you, you know what I mean? And if, as it happens, because we're living in the real world, somebody is on the take, give him a taste. If not, it's okay too. You get me?"

"I guess.so. I just want you to know I'm not here to bribe people."

"That's not what I'm here for, either."

"The firm is certainly not going to get involved with covering up whether or not they received a fee. Frankly, there are too many people involved for that. The whole situation is unwieldy."

"Unwieldy. That's a good word. You think good, counselor. Good thing you weren't a wise guy, with that head of yours. The world would be in for a lot of trouble. You're right. There are too many people involved. Why don't you just keep the money for yourself; don't say nothing to the firm."

"I can't do that."

"Why not? It's a nice amount of money to have in your back pocket to start your own practice with, you know what I mean?"

J.T. studied Bedardo. "I'll meet you in court tomorrow morning, at nine thirty," he said. "By that time I'll know how the firm wants to handle this."

"Okay, counselor. Don't let the bastards in that U.S. attorney's office get away with a thing."

J.T. and Bedardo rose at the same time, J.T. walking around the desk to open the door. Marty and Joey were still in the corridor outside.

"Come on," Bedardo said, walking briskly toward the elevator. Joey followed silently.

"Come on in, Marty. I want to discuss something with you," J.T. said.

Marty entered the office. J.T. shut the door, walked to his desk, and picked up the attache case.

"Look at this," he said, opening the case.

Marty's eyes widened. "Holy shit."

APRIL 1, 1962

THE BANDLEADER'S BATON guided the usual, syncopated rinkytink rhythm as dancers in a fantasy of costumes foxtrotted. J.T. was not in costume, although the tuxedo he wore was so unorthodox for this crowd that it might as well have been one. It was a dark tuxedo, not exactly black, its satin lapels faced with a quilted design. He wore a ruffled shirt with a clip-on bow tie, one side of which occasionally lost its grip on his collar. Dana refastened his tie each time it lost its purchase, thinking J.T. was cute, his lost-little-boy quality appealing to her.

The Grand Ballroom of the Waldorf was ablaze with crystal chandeliers, candles at the tables. Laughter filled the air.

Dana and J.T. moved with the dancing traffic, passing George Washington, Captain Hook, Napoleon, and Henry VIII, who were dancing with Pierrette, Hester Prynne, Madame Pompadour, and someone who looked like Isadora Duncan. There were also Cleopatra and Robin Hood, Alice in Wonderland with the Lone Ranger.

Dana herself wore a costume that she had told J.T. represented Pocahontas. To J.T., she looked like any Indian squaw.

Chauncey Delafield wore the costume—except for the martini

glass—of someone from the court of Louis XIV, or maybe he was Louis XIV himself. J.T. wasn't up on the intricacies of the court of the Sun King.

Delafield's wife wore a Quaker woman's outfit. Archie Reynolds seemed to be a French moving man, horizontally striped sweater, beret, and all. Mrs. Reynolds was a French apache dancer.

"And what else did Uncle Chauncey say?" Dana asked J.T. as they stepped slowly to a beat that was only in J.T.'s head, the one to which he always danced, regardless of the music.

"He said that the senior partners were very disturbed that I would suggest a client like Bedardo to the firm for any reason, considering all the other clients and business that it might jeopardize. He also said the situation with the money was utterly preposterous."

"And what did you say to him?"

"I told him I didn't do anything to purposely upset anyone, but since it was Bedardo's idea, not mine, I didn't see what all the fuss was about either."

"You didn't tell him that you thought they were wrong, the partners?"

"No, I said they were entitled to run the office and to represent any clients they wanted to or didn't want to."

They danced next to a couple who looked like the Grim Reaper dancing with a bedsheet.

Adults in silly costumes always bemused J.T. He was befuddled, really, by the exhilaration of adults in children's fantasy, perhaps because he had no images dancing in his head, waiting to leap out full-blown in costume.

"What did he say then?"

"He said that was a good attitude, because that's exactly what the partners had in mind. To run their own office their own way, handling the clients they want."

"He wasn't angry with you or anything, was he?"

"I don't think Uncle Chauncey cared one way or the other. He was just telling me what the others thought. I imagine he went along with their thinking, but he wasn't angry."

"And then what?"

They passed another Robin Hood and a woman dressed in

brown burlap. J.T. imagined she too was supposed to be an Indian maiden—if you were willing to accept a five-foot-two-inch, one-hundred-eighty-pound Indian maiden with several inner tubes of fat around the waist.

"I said I understood. I should have said that I thought it would be a bit more interesting handling Bedardo's case rather than the day-in, day-out drudge paperwork of their kind of lawyering."

"I'm glad you didn't say that. Not to Uncle Chauncey. He's so nice. That would only hurt his feelings. He really likes you, you know?"

"I really like him too. He's not like the rest of those Ivy League drones down there."

"You were graduated from the same kind of school they were."

"Somehow. I can't understand that, either."

They repassed Marie Antoinette, who was now dancing with Captain Hook. The Captain's sword hit J.T. in the legs.

"Sorry," said the Captain in a feminine sort of way.

A fag interior decorator dancing with one of his customers, thought J.T. The bitchy personalities of some of the gay crowd seemed to fascinate the lady socialites. J.T. figured that the boredom of having money and leisure, with no challenge of survival, caused the wealthy to drift toward the unusual, the different, sometimes the perverse and self-destructive.

"Do you think you'd be happier somewhere else?"

"Perhaps. That's why I asked Uncle Chauncey if I could get a leave of absence."

Dana stopped dancing.

"I really want to handle this case. At least I'll find out if it's the kind of thing I enjoy. Besides, it's exciting. And there's a big fee," J.T. whispered softly, his mouth close to Dana's ear. He started her moving to his imaginary beat again. "There'd be publicity too. Good publicity. Perhaps it could lead to my own office. I told Uncle Chauncey that I really wanted to stay with the firm, that I didn't want to do anything that would jeopardize my position there. If I took a leave of absence, I wouldn't embarrass the firm and wouldn't be severing my ties with it, either."

Dana listened carefully. She thought J.T. was about the cleverest person there ever was.

"I told him that the experience and the trial work would ultimately benefit the firm. By handling cases like this, I would build my big bad reputation even bigger and tougher."

"What did Uncle Chauncey say?"

"He said I was a clever son of a bitch."

Dana laughed as they passed Napoleon and Hester Prynne.

NOVEMBER 23, 1963

MARTY AND COURTNAY'S DAUGHTER, STEPHANIE, was a fine, robust girl, eight pounds when born on November 23, 1962. Her first year had been fairly uneventful, except that her parents and grandparents took to calling her Muffy. During that time, Marty didn't see her as often as he'd have liked to, but then he was busy with J.T. on the Bedardo case. He too had obtained a leave of absence from the firm.

That circus of a trial—which lasted three months—was now behind them. Bedardo and twelve others were convicted on all counts, but not before the judge had to gag several of the defendants and have them tied in their chairs for disrupting the court proceedings.

Bedardo was sentenced to fifteen years and was awaiting the outcome of his appeal in Atlanta Federal Penitentiary. Despite the conviction, Bedardo was satisfied with J.T. as his defense lawyer. The telephone taps of others had yielded a wealth of incriminating evidence, and since Bedardo was charged in the common scheme of a conspiracy, answerable for all the acts and words of the coconspirators, his conviction was virtually inevitable and not at all a poor reflection on J.T.'s ability. Bedardo, convinced that J.T.'s contacts could be helpful with the Parole Commission, asked J.T. to continue to represent him on the appeal. He had even sent another attaché case to J.T. J.T. had to importune the firm to extend his and Marty's leaves of absence at least another six months until the appellate procedures, which were going slowly, were complete. There were partners in the firm who openly preferred that Wright never return.

Muffy's first birthday party, which had been scheduled to take place at the Crawford's cooperative on Park Avenue, turned into a very somber affair. The television in the den was turned on, and everyone sat silent as they watched the newscasts of the day following the assassination of President Kennedy.

"God, this is awful," said Dana, sitting on the floor in front of the couch.

Some of the women had tears rolling down their faces. So did Chauncey Delafield. So did Marty Boxer, sitting next to Chauncey.

J.T. was on the phone in another room.

"Yes, yes, well, the court hasn't decided the appeal yet," J.T. said into the phone. "That's about all I can tell you. I know Patsy is sitting in the can waiting. Tell him the judges are sitting on their big fat butts and there's nothing I can do to speed them up."

J.T. had returned the call of Fat Augie, one of Patsy Bedardo's men, who had made the weekly inquiry: when would the Second Circuit Court of Appeals decide whether Patsy would get a new trial. Surely J.T. had no objection to Patsy having a new trail. A third attache case would be forthcoming.

"Yes, yes, it's awful," J.T. said phlegmatically, his mind racing with other things. "Yes, I have the television on here, too. I've been glued to it all day," he lied. "Tell him when you go down to see him—" An interruption. "All right, when his wife goes down to see him, tell him that no news is good news. That's right, no news is good news. The court must be bogged down on some point and they're arguing among the three judges. That's good, because that means that something about the convictions is bothering them. Right . . . right. I hope so too. Okay then, give me a call in a week. If I hear something before then, I'll call you."

J.T. hung up the phone and looked at the list of calls from his answering service. Most of them could wait until tomorrow. He decided to answer one more. He dialed the number and waited.

"Hello, Mrs. Morris Steinfeld, please. J.T. Wright. Yes. I'll hold."

J.T. had read in the papers that Morris Steinfeld, the president of the vast Blackstone hotel chain, and his wife were on the verge of a divorce. This call might bring a lucrative matrimonial case.

"Hello, Mrs. Steinfeld. This is J.T. Wright." He listened. "Yes, my office does handle matrimonial cases." J.T. wasn't exactly talking about Stevenson & Stetinius now. In fact, it had been so long, and so much had happened on his leave of absence, that he often forgot that he was only on his own temporarily. "I certainly would represent you if you wanted me to," J.T. said. "My experience is that these things should be explored and the initiative taken at the first opportunity."

J.T. was actually thinking that Mrs. Steinfeld should come to his office and retain him before she changed her mind or was sold a bill of goods by some shark of a matrimonial lawyer.

"How about first thing in the morning? If there's anything that needs to be done, we'll do it tomorrow. Is nine thirty too early? Well, make it ten o'clock. Tonight? That's a little unusual. Where are you located? Eighty-third and Park? Well, the first steps *are* very important. Very well. In about forty-five minutes."

J.T. hung up the phone, quite delighted. Handling Mrs. Steinfeld's divorce proceedings meant a big chunk of money. Marty came into the room.

"What are you doing here all by yourself?" Marty had taken J.T.'s seclusion as private grief.

"Just thinking."

"About what?" asked Marty.

"About going back to the firm."

Marty looked puzzled. "What do you have in mind?"

"Staying out. Doing what we're doing now—permanently."

"I don't know much about the finances of it all," said Marty, "but there would be a lot of expenses involved—a library, secretaries, furniture, copying machines, all kinds of things."

"I know. That's why I'm just thinking about it. If we could generate enough fees during our leaves of absence, maybe we could afford to make it permanent. If not, we go back."

"Where do all these new clients come from?"

"Different places."

"What are you two doing in here?" Dana asked, coming into the bedroom.

J.T. looked up at her blankly. Lately he had felt a kind of pressure from her. Whenever they were together, she seemed to be on top of him, following him, standing next to him, wanting to listen to each word he spoke. He was starting to feel smothered.

"We're just talking," J.T. said flatly.

"Courtnay wants everyone to come into the dining room. We're going to cut the cake now."

J.T. rose. Marty walked out of the bedroom, toward the dining room. Dana let Marty pass, waiting to take J.T.'s arm.

"Go ahead, Dana," J.T. said chivalrously, wanting her to go through the door ahead of him.

She smiled, waiting for him on the other side of the door. "What's the matter, J.T.?" she asked, finally taking his arm as they walked toward the dining room.

"Wrong? Nothing's wrong."

"There is something wrong, J.T. I know it, and so do you. What is it?"

"Nothing. Nothing at all. I've just been very busy lately."

"I know that. It's not just that we rarely see each other anymore"—there was a reprimand in her voice—"but when we do get together, there's something between us, some kind of barrier."

"I haven't noticed that," said J.T.

"Happy birthday to you, Happy birthday to you," everyone was singing to the little girl in the high chair. *"Happy birthday, dear Muffy, Happy birthday to you."*

Plates of cake were passed around by a black woman in a white serving apron and matching lace tiara. After a couple of forkfuls, the guests, plates in hand, drifted back to the den. The television was turned on again, and the guests sat holding their birthday plates, tears beginning to roll down their cheeks again.

"J.T., I'd like to have a little talk with you," said Delafield, walking to where J.T. stood by the dining room table.

"Sure, Mr. Delafield," J.T. said, putting his plate down.

"Let's go inside, so I can get myself a drink."

"Sure," said J.T., knowing this had to do either with the firm or with Dana.

They entered the den. Delafield went to the bar and fixed a drink for himself, watching the reflection of the TV in the mirror. Somehow, between the television and the mixing of the drink, Delafield forgot about J.T. He sat on the couch again and began to watch a speech being made by the new President.

"I have to leave for a while," J.T. whispered to Marty, who was standing back against a wall.

"Where are you going?"

"I have to interview one of our new clients."

"Now?"

"We don't have so many clients that we can be independent."

"Since when?"

"Since this is Mrs. Steinfeld and we're going to handle her divorce. I think it could be a very lucrative source of new clients. Matrimonial lawyers are usually assholes."

"Isn't everybody?" Marty asked sarcastically.

"Now that you mention it, yes." J.T. smiled.

"Aren't you going to say something to Dana, or take her home?"

"You explain to her."

"Explain what?"

"You can do it."

"Thanks a lot, Otto."

J.T. opened the door and slipped silently out.

JANUARY 13, 1964

"IT'S GOOD TO HAVE YOU BOTH BACK," Delafield said with satisfaction to J.T. and Marty. "Is that Bedardo situation all finished now?"

"Not exactly finished, sir," said J.T.

"What does that mean?" Delafield said with a tinge of concern. "I thought you had returned to the firm all ready to go to work full time."

"We have," said Marty. "There's technically still a writ of certiori for the United States Supreme Court to hear the case. But there's virtually no hope of that being granted."

"Oh," said Delafield, relieved. "Well, we certainly missed your shock power around here, J.T., and your way of keeping things out of the newspapers."

J.T. grinned. His return to the firm was bittersweet. His stab at being independent had not been overwhelmingly successful, not by his own standards. True, he had handled a couple of matrimonials while on leave of absence, but the number of clients, the flow of excitement, was not sufficient to satisfy J.T. He didn't seem to have the patience for slowly building success. The instant he walked into Delafield's office, he was sure Stevenson & Stetinius wasn't the answer either.

"In fact," said Delafield, not aware of J.T.'s distracted thoughts, "we have a situation right now with Worldwide Films. We represent the company against some dissident stockholders who have brought a stockholders' suit for mismanagement and misfeasance against the officers and directors. They say they have proof the board made investments outside the regular business purposes of the company. They claim that Worldwide has been brought to the brink of financial disaster as a result of diversification into some hotels in Hawaii, which have turned out to be bad investments."

"*Are* the hotels bad investments?" asked J.T.

"I don't know if I would classify them as lemons," said Delafield, amusement glowing in his eyes. "However, the hotels are not filled to capacity. There were supposed to be new roads built, but the federal funds have been held up. When the roads are finished—if ever—the hotels should boom. But right now they're getting deeper in the red every day. There's a little spice to this stew. Several of the members of the Worldwide board owned the land on which the hotels were built. They sold it, through a dummy corporation, to Worldwide."

"Other than that, is there any merit to the stockholders' suit?" J.T. chided.

"I told you we needed some help on this one," Delafield smiled.

"What's the status of the suit?" asked J.T.

"They've served the board with a summons and complaint. Now the most desirable thing we can do for our client is to keep the suit buttoned up until after Worldwide's merger with CRA. CRA owns a lot of the film and TV stars and their contracts, and it also has a substantial amount of liquid capital. If the merger goes through, it will put the company in a financial position to be able to make some decent pictures."

"What's the status of the merger?" asked J.T.

"It's in the serious negotiation stage. I needn't tell you that if CRA gets wind of some lawsuit that alleges misappropriation of funds by Worldwide's directors, it wouldn't be the soundest position from which to negotiate. We have to keep this lawsuit under wraps. Which is where you come in, J.T."

"You want me to handle the suit?"

"Some of our men are already on it. But I suggest that you be the attorney out in front, the one who deals exclusively with the opposition. We just got their summons and complaint about a week ago, and we haven't put in an answer yet. What we intend to do is to make some motions, based on legal technicalities, to dismiss their suit. I think it would be advantageous if your name appeared on the affidavits in support of the motion. Let the other side know, right at the outset, what we have in store for them. And no adjournments, no time delays of any sort, no professional courtesy. We really have to play hardball on this one."

"Who's handling the papers now?"

"It's with one of the young fellows downstairs for research at the moment. But the case is really being handled by Prentiss."

"Marty," said J.T., "why don't you talk to Prentiss, see if you can get copies of all the papers."

"Already been taken care of, J.T.," said Delafield. "Copies of all the papers are on both your desks right now."

"That's organization for you," said J.T.

"Marty, will you excuse us for a couple of minutes? I want to talk to J.T. privately."

"I'll start looking over the Worldwide papers. Buzz me when you're finished, J.T. You want this door closed, Mr. Delafield?"

"Please."

Delafield selected a cigar from a humidor on the credenza behind his desk. He delicately sliced off the end of the cigar with a gold cutter.

"J.T.," he began tentatively, lighting the cigar, blowing smoke to the ceiling, "forgive me for butting into your personal life, but this matter does have just a little something to do with me, and I just wanted to have a chat with you about it."

"About what?"

"You and Dana."

J.T. nodded, studying Delafield, whose head disappeared momentarily behind a cloud of smoke.

"You two young folks have known each other a substantial period now . . . oh, hell, that's not exactly the right way to put it. You two have seen each other for, oh, say a year and a half, two years?"

"A little more than that, sir. About two and a half years. I was still in Washington at the time."

Delafield nodded. "You've always had an excellent power of retention, J.T. Recently I understand you've not been seeing each other very much. And I understand she's rather upset about that. Fact is, she's started to cause her parents some concern."

"I'm sorry to hear that, sir."

"Hell, man, I'm really sorry I even have to have this conversation with you, but the family—well, Archie, anyway, you know how he is with Dana—he asked me to talk with you."

"I understand, sir."

"I hope so. Hell, I think people ought to be able to do what they feel like, without anyone else interfering. I'd be as annoyed as all get-out if I were you sitting there. By the way, would you like a drink, J.T.?"

"No, thanks, sir."

Delafield swiveled in his chair and opened his credenza. He poured some straight vodka into a glass and filled the glass with ice he took from a little refrigerator.

"You don't mind if I do, do you?"

"No, sir."

"J.T., if you don't want to see Dana any longer, I can understand that. I know these things happen. But if you do want to stop seeing her, then do just that. Stop seeing her." Delafield sipped his drink, which was by now sufficiently chilled.

"On the other hand," he continued, "if you want to continue seeing her, then do so. But please try and get yourself out of this middle ground, where you're still seeing her but not very often and then not very . . . what's the word?"

"Attentively."

"*Exactement.*" Delafield raised his glass to J.T. and then sipped.

"You've just made me curious about my position with this firm, sir," said J.T. "Does it depend upon my amorous entanglements with your niece?"

"Now you've hit a nerve."

"I'm trying to."

"That's what I like most about you, J.T. You're right out in the open, no fuzzing around the bush. Not fuzzing . . ."

"Beating, sir."

"Beating it is. I should like to think that your amorous entanglements have nothing whatever to do with anything here. However, Archie is a powerful client of this firm. And I'm not able to control him all the time. If it came to any showdown around here, Archie's the one who would prevail."

"I understand, sir."

Delafield just nodded and sipped his drink. "That's the way it is, J.T. As a person who admires you, who thinks you have a lot on the ball, even if you are hump as a drinking companion, let me suggest that you get this thing with Dana straightened out one way or another. For my sake as well as yours."

"Yes, sir, I will."

"Good." Delafield sat back and puffed on his cigar. He attempted to blow a smoke ring toward the ceiling, but it spiraled out of shape the moment it left his mouth. "Never could blow the damn things. I'd like to mention another thing, J.T."

"Yes, sir?"

"The firm, as you know, was rather perturbed by your representing Mr. Benzadrino—"

"Bedardo."

"Whatever. And while we're having this heart-to-heart, let me just suggest that I'm only one of a lot of people around here. By the way, they also know about the fact you've been handling other cases, matrimonials and all."

"They don't object to that too, do they?"

"If I were you and I wanted to stay around here, I would not upset too many more applecarts." Delafield sipped from his glass.

FEBRUARY 17, 1964

"JESUS CHRIST, J.T.," groaned Delafield, his back to the young lawyer on the leather couch in his office. "What the hell is this now?" he asked, turning with a copy of the *New York Mirror* in his hand, opened to Lee Mortimer's gossip column, "New York Confidential."

"You mean the item about Margo Saperstein and me at El Morocco?"

Delafield read aloud, ignoring J.T.'s question.

"'Hot shot lawyer-around-town J.T. Wright, of Organized Crime Investigation Hearing fame, was whispering romantically into buxom blonde beauty Margo Saperstein's ear at swelegant El Morocco. Rumors say Margo and hubby are splitsville. Is Mr. Wright Mr. Right for Margo?'"

"Don't even tell me what it's all about, J.T.," Delafield said, looking up. "I don't really want to get involved in all of this, I've told you that before. But I have no choice when an item appears in the columns about you and dames. Every time you step out on Dana, she tells her father, and he tells me."

"I'm sorry, sir—I mean about the fact that you get into the middle of this. I'm not really stepping out. It's strictly professional."

"Not only that, J.T.," Delafield continued, not really listening. It was after lunchtime, J.T. figured. Delafield already had a couple of drinks. "I even have to listen to the other partners around here about you. They feel these items and the notoriety that you garner from them reflects poorly on the firm."

"How so?" asked J.T. "The article is about me, not the firm. And certainly the firm can't object to a fee of a hundred thousand dollars."

"A hundred thousand?"

"When it's all totaled up, that's what the divorce is going to cost Mr. Saperstein in legal fees by the time I—we—get finished with him."

"You mean you're going to represent this Margo Saperstein?"

"The firm is, sir. If it's all right with the rest of the partners, of course," J.T. said innocently. "I can't imagine why they would object. After all, it's a matrimonial, not a criminal case."

Delafield nodded without conviction. "Yes, but it's going to be somewhat sensational, from what I've read in the papers. A little seamy. This prospective client of ours isn't exactly a sit-at-home type."

"I think I can keep the matter very quiet. It definitely will not get to court."

"You're sure about that, J.T.?"

"I'll make sure of it."

Delafield shrugged. "Well, of course, your explanation is a bit better than what this gossip column implies, but I'm still not sure that some of the more conservative partners will be thrilled by the prospect of handling a hotly contested matrimonial."

"The firm has handled matrimonials before."

"Not scandalous ones."

"It won't take long to wrap the entire thing up. I've got Marty Boxer doing a draft of a basic separation agreement, one that we can use with a little modification in all our cases."

"All our cases? What does that mean?"

"That means that this is an easy way to make big fees, and I'd like to bring as many of these cases as I can into the firm."

"I'm not sure the partners are going to be happy with the idea that they're running a divorce mill."

"Matrimonials like these aren't the run of the mill. Our clients will be society folks, people who can pay substantial fees and want no mudslinging court fights."

Delafield frowned thoughtfully.

"When you see my name in the paper in the future, sir, you'll know that I'm out in the vineyards, harvesting the crop. You can tell that to people who put you in the middle."

Delafield leaned back in his chair, his eyes closed, a smile playing on his lips. "You're clever, J.T., really clever. Remember me when you get to your kingdom."

J.T. smiled.

MARCH 20, 1964

IT WAS SPRING AGAIN IN NEW YORK. The warm smell of the earth and budding trees filled the air with a promise of life. Bright sunlight glinted from the windows of midtown skyscrapers as J.T. and Aloysius R. Murphy, special counsel to the Governor, walked slowly west on Fifty-fifth Street. They had just lunched at "21" and were headed back toward the Governor's New York City office.

Murphy had called J.T. to "talk." About what, J.T. had had no idea. It had been mysterious and exhilarating—greatly exhilarating—to know that the Governor of New York State was even aware of him, and, better yet, that he wanted one of his special emissaries to "talk" with him.

"Frankly, we can't sit still with all this bad press spilling over the top about corruption and scandal in the criminal justice system. Cops on the take, judges accepting bribes—I don't buy the stuff about the judges, by the way, J.T. Oh, sure, there may be a few venal judges with whom you can still put in a contract, but my opinion is that the judiciary is pretty clean."

Traffic was stalled all the way back to Fifth Avenue. Horns blared and cab drivers cursed out their windows. But J.T. was so caught up in the excitement of this meeting he hardly heard the cacophony around them.

"The media is on the Governor's back about appointing a special prosecutor to investigate our criminal justice system," Murphy continued. "So the Governor tells me, 'Al, look around for somebody who can stand up to the pressure—somebody clean, without political affiliations, who can run the grafters down.' That's why I thought I'd talk to you, J.T. You have the right credentials."

J.T. was flattered. "It sounds very interesting," was all he allowed, although his mind was racing with thoughts of the power and prestige that would go with such a position. If the power wasn't built into the job, he'd make sure it got there before long. He'd make sure he was the terror of the state judiciary and the justice system. The Mountaineers' Club would have to rise higher than ever, he thought.

"I realize that the money couldn't compare to those big fees you're pulling down on Wall Street, J.T. I've seen the articles in the papers about you and the divorcees you've been representing lately. But then, you've worked in government before. You know what's involved in budgets and that sort of thing. The Governor has earmarked a budget of only a million to run the whole office. I know it's not much to get an entire staff, but it's a start."

"How many people do you anticipate on staff?" J.T. asked.

"That'd be up to you."

"Do all the personnel have to be lawyers or ancillary personnel?"

"I don't get you, J.T. What do you mean?"

"I think the problem of venality in official circles could be curbed significantly if there was enough press about all the indictments being handed down, the harshness of the penalties imposed for getting caught with your hand in the cookie jar. I'd say a press officer would be a significant part of the operations of such a special prosecutor's office."

"Sounds right on the money to me," said Murphy with keen interest. "I don't see any problem with that."

They continued to walk.

What a hell of a vehicle to get away from Wall Street and the stuffed shirts and the preppies, thought J.T. And although Delafield was the greatest guy in the world, J.T. didn't want him looking over his shoulder, keeping tabs on how often he saw Dana, and if not, why not. At the same time, the Special Prosecutor's job would be a fantastic springboard to getting into private practice. Once he got enough publicity as a fearsome shark, clients, especially women who wanted to get their pound of flesh from wandering husbands, would pour in. And so would the money.

"I'd say I'd be available for further consideration," J.T. said carefully. "That's not final. I have to talk it over with some close advisors, of course, but I'm interested."

"Excellent," said Murphy, stopping in front of his office building. "The Governor will be pleased. I'll get back to you." They shook hands.

J.T. turned back toward Fifth Avenue. As he walked quickly, glancing occasionally into shop windows, dodging between people strolling in the warm sunlight, he was hardly conscious of his surroundings. His mind was already soaring with visions of the heights to which such a prestigious job could carry him—Special Prosecutor of the State of New York. A blast of a horn right next to him, as a cab screeched to a stop, brought J.T. back instantly.

"You jerk! Watch where you're going!" yelled the cab driver.

MARCH 21, 1964

"**WHAT AN OPPORTUNITY**," J.T. crowed enthusiastically to Marty. The two were sitting in the living room of Marty's apartment, having a drink before dinner. Courtnay was in the kitchen, getting some cheese and crackers. Muffy was already asleep in bed.

"It's wild. Right out of the blue like that," said Marty. "It's something you dream about—the chance to do something about the cops, the judges, lawyers who are on the take every time some crook is let go with a slap on the wrist."

"When you start to analyze it, as you're doing right now, do you really know if it's true that there's a lot of corruption out there?" said Courtnay, placing a cutting board with two kinds of cheese on the cocktail table.

J.T.'s eyes shifted cautiously to Courtnay. "What do you think, Courtnay?" he asked.

"I think it's a wonderful opportunity to get to the bottom of things."

"That's it," agreed Marty. "A chance to get something worthwhile done. You dream about such opportunities."

J.T. was pensive. He nodded slowly, his glance shifting from Courtnay to Marty as they spoke. "It's out there all right," J.T. said firmly. "I've been thinking ever since Murphy suggested the position. I can think of a million areas to investigate. Judges giving criminals an easy ride for a price, calling up other judges, saying, "That's a friend of mine, go easy on him." It happens all the time. One guy commits a crime and gets a cakewalk. Another commits the same crime and gets the book thrown at him."

"You could do a great deal to eliminate such disparities," Marty reflected.

"I don't see the job as a way to heal social wounds," J.T. said abruptly. "I see it as a rat trap. From now on, the rats are going to shake in their boots anytime they put their hand out. They'll know the rat catcher is on the prowl."

Marty and Courtnay both looked at J.T., then exchanged glances.

"If you don't mind my saying so," Courtnay said, "I don't agree with that approach, J.T. I don't see this just as an opportunity to set loose a horde of vigilantes."

"Vigilantes?" J.T. said impatiently. "What does that mean?"

"What I think Courtnay is saying, J.T., is that this is an opportunity to do some good, not just to crush the bones of evildoers."

"It's the same thing. If you crush the crumbs, the only people that'll be left are the ones who will do the job wonderfully."

"I guess it's just a matter of emphasis," said Marty.

"It won't be my job to select the good officials, just to root out the evil ones. And I guarantee we'll find so much venality that we won't have time to work on setting the system right. But that'll take care of itself."

Neither Marty nor Courtnay spoke.

J.T. sat forward, stuffing a wedge of cheese in his mouth. "I have a great idea. We hire detectives, take the best bloodhounds the police have, get them on a leave of absence. We'll have them pose as criminals and let them try to bribe their way out of the system. What an angle! First we'll bribe the jailers, then the cops, then the lawyers, and finally the judges." J.T. devoured another wedge of cheese.

"Want a refill?" asked Marty.

"Yeah, another ginger ale," J.T. laughed.

"Good people fighting for good causes can't resort to evil, J.T. That's a conflict in terms," said Courtnay.

"Nonsense, Courtnay," J.T. said immediately. "You fight evil with whatever means there are, good, bad, or indifferent. That's probably been the trouble up to this point. The establishment fights by Marquis of Queensbury rules while the rats are sticking fingers in their eyes. No, we're not going to fight by *the* rules. We're going to fight by *my* rules."

"That's not eliminating evil, then," said Marty, handing J.T. a glass. "Substituting your evil for someone else's isn't eliminating evil, just displacing it."

"I see we're in the midst of Philosophy II here," J.T. said, with relish for the challenge. "The only problem is that the bums never took philosophy and aren't concerned with how many angels can fit on the head of a pin. Besides, how can something that we would do to catch evildoers, something not done with evil intent, be evil?"

"But there must be respect for the rule of law," said Marty. "That's the problem to be corrected, lack of respect for the law. And doesn't that start with the people charged with enforcing the law?"

"I agree completely," said J.T. "And if certain law-enforcement people have no respect for the law, then we'll weed them out and destroy them. How can that be bad?"

"It's not, as long as we don't break the law ourselves," said Marty.

"Breaking the law is a matter of intent. They intend to commit a crime. We won't. Our investigators will only seem to commit crimes, in order to flush out the rats. It's going to be glorious," J.T. exulted. "They're going to be jumping off every part of the ship." J.T. sipped his ginger ale. "If things go right, when we crush one slimy rat, ten others will be so shaken by the news reports of our merciless juggernaut that they'll give up their venality out of sheer terror. That's important, deterring rats from committing further evil acts. I want them afraid that every phone is tapped, every room is bugged, everybody they're doing business with is an undercover agent. They won't dare make a wrong move when we're operating at peak efficiency."

"Isn't that the Gestapo that you're describing?"

"Very cute, Courtnay."

Courtnay went back to the kitchen.

"Courtnay sure doesn't like the idea of our taking on the Special Prosecutor's office," J.T. said softly to Marty.

"She just sees it from a different angle. The overall objective is something no one could complain about."

"That's the way I see it." J.T. shrugged. "All's fair in love and war."

"Let's sit at the table, dinner's ready," said Courtnay, coming out of the kitchen with a tray. The two men rose. "Speaking of love and war, J.T., have you been seeing Dana much?"

J.T. set his jaw sullenly. "Off and on," he said as he sat at the table. "That's another thing. If we take this job, we can get out of Wall Street and make a name for ourselves. And then," he said more softly, "maybe people will stop asking me about my private life. For Christ's sake, everybody inside and outside the firm is giving me grief about Dana. I'm tired of the whole damn situation."

"What exactly is the situation?" Courtnay asked.

"Come on, Court," said Marty, "it *is* their private business."

"I'm not prying . . ."

"You may not be prying, but you are asking a lot of questions about something that doesn't really concern either of us."

"It really doesn't concern me, except that my mother introduced the two of them, and since J.T. is your friend and Dana's family and mine have known each other so long, in my mother's eyes, I'm in the middle. Not only in my mother's eyes, but Dana's, her family's. I don't enjoy the position I'm in any more than you do, but I'm in it. You understand? Don't you realize that I've been brought into every crisis situation all the way down the line? Just like Uncle Chauncey, I get flak too."

"I didn't realize you were in that position," said J.T. "Dana's a little too serious about this."

"And you?"

"Serious? I'm serious in the sense that I surely am not in this to fool Dana or hurt her," J.T. said with quiet sincerity. Courtnay was suspicious. "But I doubt seriously that anything's going to lead anywhere, if that's what the ultimate question is."

"Look, J.T., I don't care what you do when it comes to your private life. I'd just like to know what I'm going to be in for from Dana. For one thing, maybe I can turn the girl off the path of feeling there's something in the situation if there isn't."

J.T. was pensive for many seconds, then looked at Courtnay. "I'm not interested in getting married, that's for sure. Frankly, I've never given getting married a thought, not with Dana, not with anybody, not yet."

Courtnay poked at her food with her fork.

"Why has what I've said disturbed you if you're not involved in a partisan way?" J.T. asked.

"I'm not disturbed."

"Oh, come on. I can see it in your face."

"Well, since you're telling me the facts as you see them, I'll tell you the facts as I see them."

"Okay."

"Why didn't you tell Dana the way you feel about her a long time ago? You would have saved all of us a lot of grief."

"I never said anything to make her think it was any other way. I never said a word to her about the future, us, marriage, kids, a white picket fence, anything like that. Not one word."

"Didn't it ever occur to you that maybe she was thinking there was a future in your seeing each other? Don't you realize all the time and effort she's devoted to your relationship?"

"Not any more than I have! And I don't expect anything else out of the situation."

"Anything else is right." Courtnay stopped speaking suddenly. "We really should drop this right here. We're only going to end up arguing."

"Wait a minute," J.T. said angrily. "Dana may have first spoken to Chauncey, and he may have been instrumental in talking to the firm. But if I didn't have what it takes, just like if Marty didn't have what it took when I spoke up for him, the firm wouldn't keep either of us around for one minute. So Dana said a kind word. Does that mean I've become her indentured servant?"

"Of course not."

"So what's the problem? I don't want to get married right now. I don't know if I want to get married *ever*. And I'm not going to be pushed into it by Dana, Chauncey, Archie, or anyone else."

"I understand what you're saying, J.T. I'm only saying that you should have told her that."

"I never told her anything different. How am I supposed to know what she assumed?"

"Because it's obvious."

"Not to me."

Courtnay nodded silently, contemplatively. "Maybe that's the way it is," she said.

"That *is* the way it is."

"I don't mean about Dana."

"What *do* you mean, Courtnay?" Marty asked.

"I mean that's the way it is with J.T. He doesn't have the same drives or ambitions or feelings that other people have. And he doesn't understand how other people might be hurt or affected by the things he does."

"What are you saying?"

"I'm saying that someone close to you has to be very careful, because you don't have the same feelings of loyalty, love, concern, friendship that others do. Am I making myself clear?"

"Not really."

"J.T., you use people. Other people go along with it because they're your friends, lovers, pals, whatever. Most people get along in the world by giving and taking. But you don't give. You have no feelings of loyalty or warmth. And that frightens me, because our lives, Marty's career, are all wound up in you. Everywhere you go, we go. And when Marty's usefulness ends, you'll dump him. Just like Dana."

"That's not true, and it's not fair."

"Fair? I didn't know you knew the word, J.T."

"Let's drop it," J.T. said coldly. "I'm really not up for psychoanalysis tonight." He put his napkin on the table. No one was hungry anymore.

"Will you tell us the truth about your feelings for us before its gets to the end of the road?" said Courtnay.

"Oh, come on, will you?"

"I'm really serious, J.T. Will you? Will you be able to face up to that when the time comes?"

"It never will," J.T. protested.

"But if it did, could you?"

"Of course I could."

"Then tell Dana how you feel now. Can you do that?"
"If I wanted to."
Both Marty and Courtnay were studying J.T.
"Will you do it?" Courtnay pressed.
"Courtnay!"
"Will you do it?"
"Why don't you, Otto?" Marty asked.
"All right, all right."

MAY 10, 1964

"HOLD IT A SECOND, GOVERNOR," a photographer urged, aiming his camera at J.T. and the Governor.

"Sure thing," said the Governor with a crinkle-eyed, wide smile. J.T. grinned lopsidedly as strobe lights flashed about the two of them. His father and mother and Marty, Courtnay, and Dana stood proudly to the side.

"Did you appoint Mr. Wright to be a kind of watchdog over the judiciary and the justice system?" a reporter asked, shoving a microphone at the Governor.

"I have instituted this special deputy attorney general's post—special prosecutor, as you call it—to put to rest once and for all questions about the integrity of our justice system. No system can continue to perform its obligations if confidence in that system is undermined. I want Mr. Wright to investigate every aspect of the justice system and root out any corruption he finds, flush out any wrongdoers, until our justice system is again the finest justice system in America."

"Mr. Wright, how long do you think it will take you to carry out the Governor's mandate?" another reporter asked.

"Truthfully, there is no way to predict how long it will take. What I must do first is investigate and find the problem areas, and then prosecute the culprits to the limit of the law."

"You have no actual prosecutorial experience. Despite that, do you feel that you will be able to accomplish all that the Governor wants?" asked another reporter, pointing a microphone at J.T.

The lights were hot. J.T. felt beads of perspiration on his forehead.

"Let me just say that Mr. Wright's overall qualifications are second to none. That's why I appointed him," the Governor said, grinning.

The reporters laughed.

"And let me say that I will not rest, day or night, until I have accomplished everything that the Governor expects of my office," said J.T. "I've had plenty of experience ferreting out vermin in the public's midst. If there are vermin in the justice system, I'll find them and exterminate them."

The Governor smiled widely, nodding approval. "I have every confidence in Mr. Wright," he said. "I'm sure that as special prosecutor he will have our justice system cleaner than it's ever been—in as short a period as possible. I think the people of this state can rest easy now that Mr. Wright has accepted this post."

"When do you expect to have a fully operational staff, Mr. Wright?" asked a reporter.

J.T. already had a briefing session with Dan Mastretta, the Governor's press secretary, at which the anticipated questions of the media were covered and appropriate answers devised.

"I've already put a substantial staff together. I have no time to waste," J.T. said.

"How many people are already on staff?"

"I don't want to reveal a great deal about my staff. Much of it is going to be undercover, conducting covert operations. I intend to get to the bottom of the problem quickly, and I don't intend to be thwarted by the guile of the criminal element at the fringe—and only that, mind you, the fringe—of our justice system. I have no doubt that I am going to find that the vast majority of the people involved in our justice system are honest, hardworking, public-spirited individuals. And I promise this to the criminal fringe of which I've spoken: I'm going to get you, and I'm going to get you soon," he said, looking hard and straight into the cameras.

"I sure wouldn't want him after me," the Governor laughed, clapping J.T. on the back. "Any other questions, fellows?"

"Are there any areas of the system that you do not want the special prosecutor to investigate, any special consideration given to people whom you've appointed?"

"None whatsoever. Mr. Wright and I spoke at length before he even accepted this position, and I made it clear to him that he would have free rein, total independence of my office, to function anywhere he thought necessary."

Dan Mastretta was standing just outside the flare of the lights, watching patiently. He moved forward slowly toward the media people, waiting as the last questions were asked, the last pictures taken, and raised his hands.

"Okay, thank you," Mastretta said to the reporters.

"Thanks, fellows," the Governor said with his usual grin.

The reporters started to pack their equipment and file out of the conference room.

"We have to get going now, Governor," said Mastretta. "We have an appointment with the Board of Trade in fifteen minutes."

"Hey, hiya, fella," the Governor said, smiling widely at Big Jim Wright. Mastretta had done his usual precise job of briefing the Governor on the attending dignitaries. The Governor, a consummate politician, did not want to snub anyone. "You can be real proud of this young man," he said, turning to put his arm around J.T.

J.T.'s mother's eyes glistened. She held on to Big Jim's arm tightly.

"This is Mrs. Wright," Big Jim said.

"A real pleasure."

"And Mr. and Mrs. Marty Boxer," J.T. said. "Marty is going to be my chief of staff."

"Oh, great."

"This is Miss Dana Reynolds."

"Dana, of course. You're Archie's daughter, aren't you?"

"Yes."

"Give my regards to your swell dad, will you?"

"Yes, I will,"

"A couple of pictures with Mr. Wright and his family, Governor?" Mastretta asked. Mastretta's staff photographer stood at the ready.

"Oh, sure." He shook hands with J.T. as they looked at each other, surrounded by family. The photographer took a few shots, some with just J.T. and the Governor, the last one of J.T. and his family.

"We'd better go now, Governor," Mastretta urged.

The Governor started for his office. "Oh, J.T. Talk to Al Murphy or Frank Smith to iron out any problems—office space, funds, whatever. They'll help you along until everything is running smoothly."

"Yes, sir."

"Congratulations, son. I'm proud of you," said Big Jim when the Governor had left.

"Thanks, Dad."

His mother embraced J.T.

Over his mother's shoulder, J.T. saw Dana, and next to her Courtnay, looking at him expectantly. The time for his heart-to-heart chat with Dana was obviously at hand. He had to steel himself for the unpleasant task, he thought. He didn't want to hurt her. But at the same time he didn't want to falter, to weaken. He had been upbraided, called on the carpet, interrogated, and scrutinized about Dana for the last time. He might have had to tolerate the intrusions and the pushiness while his job and career hung in the balance. But now he was on a new flight to glory. *And that's a solo flight*, he reminded himself. No unnecessary baggage was going to be carried.

MAY 12, 1964

CHAUNCEY DELAFIELD STOOD AT THE BAR in the library of the Reynolds home, nervously mixing another drink for himself.

"All right now, Dana, take it easy, take it easy," urged Archie Reynolds, sitting on the couch next to his daughter.

Dana, red-eyed, was tearing a tissue to shreds as she spoke.

"Just calm down. We can't understand you if you're talking and crying at the same time."

"I can't help that," Dana said impatiently.

Delafield leaned against the fireplace.

"Tell us the story once again, all the way through," urged her father. He was having difficulty controlling his anger.

"After the ceremony he said he wanted to have lunch and a chat. We went to Edward's. That's a little place on Sixty-first and Lexington where we go occasionally . . ."

"Yes?"

"We were having a hamburger, and he was talking about his new career, his plans to be in every paper, every day, and about how the Governor was going to be so pleased he wouldn't know how he ever got along without J.T. Did I tell you the Governor sent you his best regards?"

"If I had known about this before he was sworn in, the Governor wouldn't have been quite so friendly to him, I assure you! In fact, Wright wouldn't have been sworn in as dogcatcher."

"That's probably why he waited until after he was sworn in to tell Dana," Chauncey said.

"The sniveling sneak. Go ahead, darling, tell us the rest of what happened."

"Do I have to? I've been through it all already."

"I'm sorry this upsets you, baby," said Archie, "but I want to hear exactly what happened, so I know what I have to do."

"Do about what?" Dana said impatiently. "The fact is that J.T. doesn't think we should see each other anymore because our relationship isn't going anywhere and he doesn't want to waste my time. Getting J.T. to want to see me is a little beyond even your influence, Daddy."

"There is something to be said, at least, for his upfront honesty," said Delafield.

"Don't start temporizing," Archie said sharply. "After seeing Dana steadily for . . . how long is it?"

"Not steadily, Daddy."

"How long have you been seeing him?"

"Three years."

"And after all the things we've done for him, all of which he was delighted to accept, now he realizes that your relationship isn't going anywhere? Why didn't he realize it before we moved the world around so he'd have a bigger space in it?"

"I don't know, Daddy."

"Why didn't he realize it before you brought him into the firm, Chauncey?"

Delafield had no answer.

"And you can bet he knows the Governor isn't able to un-appoint him now. The Governor would have egg on his face if he did. This little Mr. J.T. Wright is one conniving piece of work." Reynolds was furious.

"I don't know that all of this was calculated like that, Daddy."

"I agree with Dana, Archie. You judge him too harshly."

"I've been around this world a bit, and I know a hustler when I see one. I'm going to call the Governor at home anyway. Even if nothing can be done, at least the Governor will know he's got a snake working for him."

"Don't you dare, Daddy. Does everybody in the world have to know I've been dumped?"

"There's something in what Dana says, Archie."

"If he wanted to just use me for our family's influence, he could just keep stringing me along, couldn't he? Maybe it was—even if it hurts—an act of honesty and, actually, kindness."

"That's right, Archie."

"Don't give me that," Reynolds lashed out. "After all Dana's done for him, all the time and affection she's lavished on him, that's what she gets? A kick in the teeth? How dare he do this to a Reynolds?" He seethed, pacing the floor. "He must be a faggot," Reynolds snapped angrily. "That's what it must all be about."

Delafield thought back, trying to see if he had overlooked something.

"He's a faggot," Reynolds repeated flatly, pacing the room again.

"Oh, Daddy. That can't be."

Reynolds turned. "Why not?"

"It just can't. I mean—"

"He's pretty chummy with DeValen, isn't he, Chauncey? Why do you suppose DeValen has been so insistent about J.T. handling his affairs? Think about that." His eyes narrowed.

"Daddy, I can't believe—"

"Why else do you suppose that he told you all this—that he doesn't want to see you, marry you, inherit a life of absolute luxury. How could anyone pass all this up—except if he's a faggot?"

"You really think so?" Dana asked thoughtfully.

"Of course."

"No, it can't be that, Daddy," Dana said. "He's just more interested in himself and his idea of success."

"Don't be defending this pansy to me," Reynolds said angrily.

"Do you think Daddy's right, Uncle Chauncey?" Dana asked, turning to Delafield.

"I couldn't say. He never seemed to be a pansy to me."

"Taking advantage of a girl like Dana, as good and pure as a girl could be. Don't worry, Dana darling, your uncle and I will take good care of this debaucher of our family name."

"Daddy. J.T. didn't do anything like that to me. Truly. He really didn't."

Reynolds studied Dana. "Well! Doesn't that tell you what I've been saying is true? Ask yourself, Dana, in light of what you now know. Isn't he a queer?"

Reynolds fixed a drink for himself at the bar.

"Don't mind if I do," said Delafield.

Dana was silent, pensive.

"Want a little vermouth or something, darling?"

"Vodka on the rocks would be fine."

Reynolds looked at Delafield and raised his eyebrows.

"I guess you could be right, Daddy," said Dana, still thinking, brooding. "A pansy? God! How disgusting!"

MAY 31, 1964

ALL THE NEWS MEDIA carried the story of J.T.'s first staff appointments. Martin Boxer was appointed chief of staff. The next highest paid member of the staff was Fred Balzano, a columnist from the New York *Daily News* who had taken a leave of absence to join the special prosecutor's staff as communications officer.

J.T. sat at his desk on the twentieth floor of 270 Broadway, reading the *New York Times* account of the appointments.

Marty Boxer and Fred Balzano were on the couch, each reading a different paper.

"Did you read the *Times* profile on me?" J.T. asked.

"That's not a bad picture of you," Marty remarked.

J.T. looked up momentarily and smiled at Balzano, whose head was buried in the *News*.

J.T. had picked a man from the *News* as his communications officer because the *News* had the largest circulation of any paper in the country. He wanted Balzano's former fellow workers at the city desk to be friendly when stories started to pour in from the special prosecutor's office.

"The *News* didn't run a bad spread either," said Balzano, pleased with the first day's outing.

"They'd better not."

Balzano was tall, thin, with dark-rimmed glasses.

"Fred, I want you to keep the flow of stories in the media up until we get our first indictments. Marty, let's really get going, show the Governor and the people of the State of New York that we really mean business."

"Why don't we first hire the detectives and other personnel to staff the office?" said Marty. "Who's going to be doing the hiring, by the way, J.T.?"

"The chief of staff."

"Me?"

"Of course. The personnel people at the police department said they'd help you out on that. There's a pool from the state police and other law-enforcement organizations you can start with."

"That'll be a help," said Marty. "Are we going to have administrative staff soon?"

"Today. That's all set up," said J.T. "But Marty, don't waste too much time with that sort of thing. Get somebody else to handle that administrative crap. I want you to jump right on top of the investigations. I want us to do the most thorough, bloodcurdling job possible on the justice system. Let's get some indictments. We can start with this thing you told me about—what did you call it, the sergeants' club?—where the police sergeants were picking up payoffs from construction jobs, restaurants, small businesses, that sort of thing, and then sharing the take?"

"That's right," replied Marty. "It was very organized. The money was split up among all the sergeants in a precinct. And there were many precincts that had such an enterprise. We could indict perhaps twenty-five sergeants at one shot."

"Fabulous," said J.T. enthusiastically. "After you get that going, I'd like our boys to really dig for our own cases. Especially go after big names, the high and mighty. Judges, commissioners, the police commissioner himself. Show that we have no ties to politics or politicians."

"How about the Governor?" Balzano joked.

"That would be fantastic, really fantastic," said J.T.

"You have anybody particular in mind to start with, J.T.?" asked Marty.

"How about the Honorable S. Samuel DiFalco?"

"The surrogate?"

"Sure," J.T. said eagerly. "He has more money passing through his court than probably any other court in the United States. Every probated will and estate in New York County goes through there."

"There've been stories about him and his court in the papers for years," said Balzano. "But nothing's ever been proven."

"Nobody came up with anything because they weren't me. Look, he has to appoint guardians for minors and incompetents who inherit money. Hundreds of them every year, maybe thousands. Multiply thousands times thousands and what have you got?"

"Millions," said Marty.

"Wrong! Patronage, influence, kickbacks, graft, all kinds of possible goodies," J.T. gloated.

"Do you have anything specific, J.T.?" Marty asked.

"No. But we can have our investigators check into it. Where there's smoke, there's fire, especially if we blow our hot breath on it. How about it, Fred? Would DiFalco be a story?"

"A great story, no question," said Balzano.

"There may be nothing there except sour grapes from lawyers he doesn't appoint. I think we ought to go easy," Marty said hesitantly.

"Forget easy," said J.T. "If there's anything there, or anywhere else, I'm coming down on it like a ton of bricks. Put your first investigators on the Surrogate's Court, Otto."

Balzano looked quizzically from J.T. to Marty.

Marty nodded.

"One of the ways we can get some fast leads," said J.T., "is to squeeze information from people who've been caught, people we already have in our nets."

"Informers?" asked Balzano.

"Exactly," said J.T.

"Who?" asked Marty.

"Let's go back to the sergeants' club," J.T. said slyly. "About twenty-five sergeants in precincts all over the city, right? In addition to the construction jobs and the restaurants in their precincts, I'm sure they know a lot of things that happen in court, between their men and court officers, lawyers, judges. Now remember, these sergeants have been on the force, I would assume, for a substantial amount of time. They all have pensions coming up, and they all have a lot to lose if we prosecute them."

The others were listening carefully.

"So, we bring them in, one at a time, let them know that we can do something for them, help them retain their pensions, retire rather than be fired. We'll let them leave the police department with some dignity. All they have to do is make cases for us."

"They'd certainly be in a position to know things," said Balzano. "The sergeant is the hub of the precinct."

"Isn't that a better way to use those sergeants than prosecuting them?" said J.T. "Another approach could be to have our investigators pose as defendants who have to retain lawyers. They push their lawyers to bribe people in the court system. Then we grab the lawyers, offer them a deal to save their shingles, if they give us judges and DAs."

Marty listened, alarmed at J.T.'s remarks. There was a need for their work, but there was no need to be bloodthirsty. This was the time to voice his opposition, to protest, Marty thought, but he said nothing. *Maybe Courtnay's right, I follow J.T. like a puppy dog—without a murmur. But what's the use? He's not going to change anything, no matter what I say.*

"I have to get back to my office," said Marty, rising. "I have to conduct an interview."

"Who are you interviewing?" J.T. asked.

"An ex-detective named Carl Stern. He's interested in an investigator's job."

"Let's talk to him together," suggested J.T.

"All right." Marty walked to J.T.'s desk and picked up the phone. "Show Mr. Stern—he's in the waiting room—into Mr. Wright's office."

A young girl with frizzy hair opened the door and showed a stocky man with slick black hair and ruddy complexion into J.T.'s office.

"I'm Marty Boxer," said Marty, extending his hand. "This is Fred Balzano, and this is J.T. Wright."

Stern shook each of their hands. He had a double-pump kind of handshake. The first was a real finger-crusher; then he lifted his hand up with yours in it, like a handle on a well pump, and gave it another pump. J.T. thought his finger bones were going to break.

"Sit down, sit down," said J.T. He rubbed his hand unobtrusively behind the desk.

"What kind of work are you doing now?" asked Marty.

"Private detective. I follow people, investigate commercial crime, that sort of thing. It's a little boring, frankly. Not enough action."

"What kind of action are you looking for?" asked J.T.

"Something where I can get into the old harness, investigation, interrogation, making cases."

"You have experience doing that?" asked J.T.

"Twenty years on the force. I retired a second-grade detective."

"Why did you leave?" asked Marty.

"The job's not the same anymore. It's become a chicken-you-know-what kind of job now. All these punks running around in the street, tearing the city apart, and the commissioner tells you, don't take out your gun, don't raise a hand, be passive. So I tossed in my papers."

"We aren't promoting violence here," said Marty.

"Yeah, but this is different. We wouldn't be dealing with street crime, muggers, rapists, niggers, and punks like that." Stern rolled his left fist in his right palm as he spoke.

"There could be some violence," mused J.T. "People resisting arrest, trying to escape."

"Nobody escapes," said Stern. He pulled open the right side of his jacket to reveal a massive, long-barreled revolver. On his belt was a leather case containing handcuffs. "Just to show you, I was coming into this building before, and I'm down in the concourse. Some little punks, eighteen, nineteen years old, you know, try to panhandle me. I tell them get a job. And they make some remarks I ain't too crazy about. I told them so. One guy in particular comes on a little stronger. You know how these loudmouth niggers are. The louder they talk, the more chicken they are. *Bango,*" Stern said, reaching under the left side of his jacket for a small flat leather-covered blackjack. "I let him have this on the side of his head so fast he didn't know he was hit till he was on his knees. The others took off like deer. Punks like these are the ones botherin' women and old folks that can't take care of themselves."

Marty was repulsed by Stern; he seemed to enjoy his weapons too much.

"By the way," said Stern confidentially, "being on the job for so long, I know where there are a lot of bones buried."

"Oh?" said J.T.

"And if I don't know exactly where they are," Stern said, nodding, "I can sniff them out right quick."

"Mr. Stern, I don't approve of violence," said J.T. "But having someone on staff with your detective experience, your knowledge of the police department, could be helpful. You know, since we began this project, a kind of nagging thought has been in the back of my mind," J.T. confided to all in the room. "Perhaps someone might resent the job we're doing and come up here with a gun, or a knife. Someone staring at a blank wall, having nothing to lose, might come up here looking for a pound of flesh."

"They come up here looking for a pound of flesh, and they'll get it—their own," said Stern fiercely. "You could put in a buzzer. You press the buzzer, it rings where I'm sitting, and I'll be here with a machine gun. I have one, by the way."

"One what?"

"A machine gun. You should see the thing. What a beautiful piece of ordnance. Snap a twenty-shot clip on that thing, forty-five caliber, and you take half this building down."

"Marty, talk to Mr. Stern. I have a meeting uptown with the Governor's people in a few minutes. See if you two can come to a conclusion on salary."

"Thanks, Mr. Wright," said Stern, walking over to J.T and extending his hand.

"Get out of here with that meat crusher," said J.T.

Stern laughed heartily.

MAY 31, 1964

J.T. **WALKED CONFIDENTLY INTO "21,"** past Slick Steve, who gave him an enthusiastic welcome, past the cigar counter, to the bar. The bartender who had served him that first drink with Chauncey Delafield was behind the bar. How the world had changed from that time to this, J.T. thought.

DeValen, who was waiting for J.T. at the bar, smiled broadly when he saw him.

"J.T., how are you?" he greeted J.T. enthusiastically.

"Good, good."

"Your table is ready, Mr. DeValen," Mario said. "Good to see you again, Mr. Wright," he added with a flourish as he ushered them to their table. "Cocktails, gentlemen?"

"A double vodka over ice for me," said DeValen.

"I'll have a light, very light, Lilet and water," said J.T.

"How's the new job going?"

"No problems," said J.T. "How's your empire?"

"Fantastic. I've taken over another restaurant chain, and turned them into those places where you get all the salad you can eat and a steak or lobster tails."

"I've seen them."

The two of them took up the drinks the waiter served.

"Congratulations," said DeValen, looking into J.T.'s eyes as they clinked glasses.

"Thanks." J.T. sipped the Lilet. No matter what drink he tried, it always tasted like medicine.

"You can't imagine how unhappy I am that you've left the firm for this special prosecutor's office."

"Oh?"

"Not unhappy for you, of course," he said, touching J.T.'s shoulder. "Just that I was delighted having you working on my things, rather than those twits with the brown shoes."

"This isn't forever. I'm only going to do this until I build up my reputation. Then I'll open my own office. Right now the State of New York is paying for my advertising and publicity. I'll reap the results myself later on."

"Aha. Then there is method in your madness. I couldn't imagine why you'd want to go into government work when you could get rich just handling my affairs." DeValen tapped J.T.'s leg twice for emphasis.

"I can still give you the benefit of my ideas if you'd like, even though Stevenson & Stetinius are on the job."

"That would be excellent."

"When they tell you what action they want to take, you bounce it on me and I'll tell you what I think."

"Super," said DeValen. "I like that. And later on, when you have your own firm, we'll sit down and work out some kind of retainer or percentage—anything that'll help us come together better." He winked at J.T.

J.T. didn't like DeValen's touching and winking. But he certainly liked the sound of his business proposition.

Mario approached the table. "Excuse me, Mr. DeValen," he said, "but Mr. Chandler would like to buy drinks for you and Mr. Wright."

DeValen looked across the room to a table where a portly man with dark-rimmed glasses sat with a stunning blonde woman of voluptuous proportions. DeValen smiled and waved.

"Tell Mr. Chandler he bought us a nice bottle of red wine for our lunch," said DeValen. "And then select something for us that is dry and light, Mario. I'll leave it to you."

"Excellent, sir."

"Chandler's a big butter-and-egg man from out of town," DeValen explained to J.T. "He's got a company I'm looking to buy in Dayton. Makes superb batteries for cars. There's enormous profit in the after-purchase car market."

"What's an after-purchase market?"

"The car manufacturers sell their cars with mediocre equipment or accessories. After purchase, the buyer replaces the barely adequate battery, tires, wiper blades, with finer-quality merchandise. I'm getting into that market now. Confidentially, the real bigwigs from Detroit are in with me."

"You mean to say that the manufacturers purposely provide cheap batteries so they can sell better ones later on?" asked J.T.

"Not really. They put in the battery and other items the consumer is willing to pay for. If the manufacturer installed all top-of-the-line equipment, the car would have a price tag the average consumer would balk at. To keep the initial price down, they put in less expensive equipment. Later on, the dope who thought he had a bargain when he bought the car pays more to add the quality accessories than they would have cost as original equipment. But if John Q. Public thinks that's a better deal, we're certainly willing to accommodate him."

Mario brought the menus and handed one to each of them. "The hash is excellent today, Mr. DeValen," said Mario.

"That's for me. I recommend it, J.T."

"I'll try it."

The sommelier brought a bottle of red wine. He opened the bottle, smelled the cork, then poured a small amount in DeValen's glass.

DeValen's sniffed the wine in his glass with delight, then sipped. "Ahh, excellent, excellent."

"Thank you, *monsieur*," said the sommelier, serving J.T., then DeValen.

DeValen looked across the room, caught Chandler's eye, and lifted his glass to him.

Chandler lifted his glass in return.

"Who's the tomato?" asked J.T. "She's gorgeous."

"If you want to meet her," DeValen said blandly, "I'll introduce you to the little tart. She works for me."

"She works for you?"

"I have three or four girls, all equally attractive, working for me all the time. I pay for their apartments and clothes and they entertain my butter-and-egg men from out of town when they come to New York. I do business much more easily when a man's having a good time. Anytime you want to meet the girl, J.T., let me know," DeValen said indifferently, looking at J.T.'s face.

"No, I'm not interested," said J.T. He knew instantly he had said the right thing from the look on DeValen's face.

"I like you, J.T. You're an intelligent young man. The tarts are attractive, but a dime a dozen."

J.T. said nothing.

"We can make a lot of money together, J.T.," DeValen continued.

"I'm for that."

"We'll make a couple of million together the first six months you're in private practice."

"Sounds better all the time."

"Making a million is a lead-pipe cinch."

"Really?"

"Absolutely. Finding compatible people is far more difficult. That's why it's important we get along so well."

They clinked their wineglasses in a toast.

"We should have these lunches at least once a week, J.T. just to follow up on your idea of discussing my legal affairs, don't you think? I'll pay you a consultant's fee, of course."

"I couldn't accept any fee while I'm the special prosecutor," said J.T. "I'd have to start investigating myself."

DeValen laughed. "You've got a grand sense of humor, too." He patted J.T.'s leg under the table again.

FEBRUARY 10, 1965

J.T.'S INTERCOM SOUNDED. He was behind his desk, scouring newspapers for the latest stories about his office. Fred Balzano sat opposite J.T., idly blowing the smoke from his cigar into rings.

"Yes?" J.T. asked, pushing the button on the intercom as he continued to read.

"Mr. Stern is here. He wants to see you if you have a minute," J.T.'s secretary responded.

"Send him in," J.T. said, idly releasing the intercom button. "This is pretty good," he said now to Balzano, indicating the newspaper.

"Thanks, J.T. I thought you'd like it. A few months getting this show staffed and together made a hell of a difference. Now it's a lot easier to place articles. The reporters are really receptive."

"Have you given them the latest on the sergeants' club?"

"Not yet. I've been waiting for us to finish the investigation before releasing the balance of the story."

"It's already finished," J.T. said impatiently.

Stern entered the room. He was wearing a sports jacket over dark pants.

"Carl, aren't we finished with that sergeants' club investigation?" asked J.T.

"Just about."

"What does 'just about' mean?"

"We still have some odds and ends to clear up. I checked with Marty, and we're convinced that this Sergeant Lewis can give us a lot more. He seems to be involved in something we can't quite put a finger on. But we're almost there."

"Jesus," J.T. exploded. "Fred has terrific stories the media is dying for, and we're held up by one man?" J.T. pressed the button on the intercom anxiously. "Will you ask Marty Boxer to step in here?"

"That's what I came in to tell you, chief. I think this Lewis is on the ropes now. I have him in the other office. It wouldn't hurt if he saw you. The pressure would fold him."

Marty Boxer came into the room.

"Marty," said J.T., "why aren't we finished with the sergeants' club investigation?"

"We are, basically. I—"

"Good, then break it, Fred, break it. Why do I have to ask fifteen people around here, to get one straight answer? Christ, I have to kick ass all day just to keep people from falling asleep."

"What's this all about?" asked Marty.

"It's about a story I was holding back on the sergeants' club investigation."

"I told Fred to hold it until we complete the rest of the investigation," Marty explained, turning to J.T.

Balzano's face changed from fear to relief.

"What for?" J.T. blasted. "It's been on the fire six or so months. Let this part of the story go now. Jesus H. Christ, we need a new story every week! Every week!" J.T. looked at each of them. "Is it too late for today's deadlines?" he asked Balzano.

Balzano checked his watch. "Yeah. It's too late for the early people. We'd lose out on a lot of good coverage. Best thing is to hold it until tomorrow morning."

"God damn it!" J.T. shouted, picking up a book from his desk and hurling it against the wall. His jaw muscles tensed until they hurt. He stared out of his twentieth-floor window, trying to calm himself.

The others in the room stood silently.

J.T. blew out his breath and smiled a tight smile. "Let's try to salvage it tomorrow morning, first thing."

"Right."

"Maybe that'll work out better, anyway. Carl, you say this Sergeant Lewis is ready to fold? If he does before tomorrow morning, he might just save himself and help us out. Think you can make him understand the time element here?"

"Let me try again, boss. Maybe this'll be just the thing to open him up."

"Once these indictments are filed tomorrow morning, that's the end of him," said Marty. "Make him understand that."

"I've told him that. I told him we could help him save his pension, his job, we'd let him retire instead of being bounced, if he gave us some information."

"Bring him in here," J.T. said flatly.

Stern left the room.

"You sit over on the couch, Marty," said J.T. "Give him the feeling he's surrounded."

J.T. had arranged his office in the way he'd heard Mussolini had arranged his: his back was to the curtainless windows, causing bright afternoon sunlight to glare uncomfortably in the eyes of anyone approaching the desk. All of J.T.'s office appointments were set in the afternoon.

Stern came back into the office, followed by an ashen-faced man with thinning blond hair.

"This is Sergeant Lewis," said Stern.

Lewis nodded, looking around the room. No one acknowledged him. This was part of the routine: make sure the suspect feels invisible, ineffectual.

"Sit down, *Mister* Lewis," J.T. said.

Lewis sat in an isolated chair in front of J.T.'s desk.

"Investigator Stern tells me that you're not a bad fellow," J.T. started.

"You're in serious trouble, and we'd like to help you. But you have to help us help you."

"There's nothing I can help you with."

"Marty, hand me that file, please. This is your file, Mr. Lewis. Inside is an indictment. Here, look at it." J.T. handed an indictment to Lewis. "You see your name there, along with the others?"

Lewis read the document. Beads of perspiration glistened on his forehead.

"That document was supposed to have been filed two hours ago. But Investigator Stern asked that we hold it up until tomorrow morning. He thought that maybe you had enough sense to save yourself."

"I don't know anything about the sergeants' club."

"Stop bullshitting," Stern said harshly.

"You don't have to tell us anything about the sergeants' club," said J.T. "We know all about it already. How do you think we got this indictment?"

Lewis said nothing.

"We don't want you to do anything for us. Do something for yourself, for your wife, Marge," J.T. said, reading Lewis's pedigree from the file. "Your kids."

"You sons of bitches have this routine down pat."

"Take it easy, Sergeant Lewis. You're not going to do yourself any good that way," said Marty, who was to Lewis's left.

"Look, you do something for us, whatever you can," J.T. said smoothly, "and maybe we can have a secretary stay late, retype this indictment without your name on it. We have the authority to talk to the commissioner and let you retire from the job with vested rights to your pension. How many years do you have in already?"

"Seventeen," Lewis admitted resignedly.

"How can you waste seventeen years of your life, Lewis?" J.T. wondered. "Don't you owe a little something to your wife, your kids?"

"Leave them out of it."

"You're the one leaving them out of it," said Stern. "You're leaving them out in the cold when you get indicted. We have you by the balls." Stern cupped his hand.

"Make some cases for us," urged J.T. "Jesus, what do we have to do to help you help yourself?"

"What'll you do for me?" Lewis mumbled.

There's the first crack, J.T. thought.

"Hold it, Lewis, hold it right there. You've got this all wrong," J.T. said harshly. "It's not what we're going to do for you. It's what *you're* going to do for *us*. We don't need you. You need us to keep your job, your badge, your gun, your pension."

"I don't know anything that can help you," Lewis retreated again.

"Carl, you were wrong," J.T. said disgustedly. "You said this man had brains and was interested in helping himself. Marty, file those indictments first thing in the morning. And, Mr. Lewis, leave your badge and revolver on my desk."

"Leave them now?"

"When the hell did you think?" said Stern coldly.

J.T. watched Lewis. He knew he'd hit a nerve with that; a cop can't handle being asked for his badge and gun. It's like taking his balls off. He's afraid to become an ordinary mortal again, after tasting life with the gods of authority.

"Look, maybe I can think it over?"

"We've been at this for weeks now," Stern said angrily. "You've had plenty of time to think it over."

"What the hell can I give you?" asked Lewis.

"You've been on the force seventeen years. You've been in court. Somebody must have offered you dough, some court clerk must have done things for you, some judge, some DA. Come on, man, think," J.T. prodded. "We've got to do this now!"

"I really don't know anything. I've been inside for the last eight years."

"If you can't help yourself, you can't help yourself," J.T. shrugged. "Leave the badge and gun on my desk."

"You'll let me retire?" Lewis said slowly.

"If your information is good enough," said Stern. "Just because you give somebody up doesn't mean that information is going to get us a conviction."

"You'll have to testify, too," said Marty.

"No, not testimony."

"Say, Carl, will you be kind enough to get Mr. Lewis out of my office so I can go back to work? You're wasting my time."

"Maybe I know something about a judge, but . . ."

"What judge?" J.T. asked eagerly.

Now Lewis had touched a nerve.

"I'm not saying I can give you a judge. I'm just thinking out loud." Lewis shook his head slowly. "I can't give people up. It's against my nature."

"Is it your nature to leave your wife and kids out in the cold while you go to the can?" asked J.T.

Lewis looked down at his shoes.

Stern looked at J.T. and winked.

"I didn't have nothing to do with the judge personally, you know. But I remember, a couple of years ago . . . ahh, shit," said Lewis, stopping abruptly.

"Don't stop now," urged J.T.

"One of my cops collared a guy on a gun possession. I wasn't in court, but the cop told me that the lawyer told his punk client that he could work something out with the judge, but that it would cost a couple of large . . ."

"That's a couple thousand," translated Stern.

"What happened? asked Marty.

"I don't know what the lawyer did with the judge. I know the guy got a walk, though."

"Who was the judge?" J.T. asked.

"Tauber."

"Harry Tauber? In the Supreme Court?" J.T. asked gleefully.

"Yeah, only he was in the criminal court at the time."

Marty was making notes.

"Who was the lawyer whose client got the walk from Tauber?" asked J.T.

"Seymour Fine."

"Anybody know him?" asked J.T., looking around.

"Sure, he's one of those nickel-and-dime guys that hang around in the courthouse picking up cases," said Stern.

"Probably gives that 'talk to the judge' crap to all his clients, just so he can beat them for a few extra bucks."

"We don't know that for sure, do we?" said J.T.

"No . . ."

"But we're sure going to find out. We should talk to this Seymour Fine. He doesn't want to lose his sheepskin any more than Mr. Lewis here wants to lose his badge and gun."

"What's going to happen now?" asked Lewis.

"Take Sergeant Lewis's name off the indictment before you file it tomorrow," J.T. said to Marty. "We can always indict you again, Sergeant, if this information isn't on the level. Meanwhile, you can keep your badge and pistol."

Lewis sighed with relief.

"It's only temporary," cautioned Stern.

"Go ahead back to the job," said J.T. "Don't say anything to anybody, you understand?"

"I'm going to keep my job?"

"Do you think this is your birthday?"

"What do you mean?"

"We told you you could retire, if the commissioner approves, which he probably will. You don't think you can stay on the job after being a member of the sergeants' club? The police department isn't an old-age home for thieves."

"You are one son of a bitch, Mr. Wright."

"That's what I'm paid for."

"You mean to say I'm off the job even though I'm giving people up?"

"I mean to say it's better than going to jail. Show Sergeant Lewis out, will you, Carl?"

"You want me to debrief him first?"

"Yes, I guess that would be a good idea."

MAY 19, 1965

RHODA FINE drove slowly along the winding, tree-lined road back to her home in Chappaqua. She had just bought a brisket of beef for Seymour's dinner. That was his favorite meal, and Rhoda wanted to cheer Seymour up. He had been so depressed lately, picking on her and the kids, sometimes bursting into tears. But they understood he was under a lot of pressure because of the bribery investigation by Special Prosecutor Wright's office.

Rhoda still didn't understand how it all had happened. The only thing she knew was that Seymour had not been himself since he received a subpoena from Wright.

And then, all Seymour had told her was that this Wright son of a bitch wanted him to admit that he had bribed Judge Tauber. Seymour told Wright that he never bribed the judge, that he had just made up that story about fixing the judge to ream a few more dollars from his client. But Wright refused to believe him. Wright told Seymour he'd be indicted for bribing a policeman; that the policeman was ready to testify against him. And still Seymour refused to admit he'd bribed the judge. There was no bribe, Seymour screamed to Rhoda as he paced their bedroom night after night, pondering what to do.

Now Seymour faced not only losing his license, but disgrace and imprisonment. In addition, he was almost broke—they had always lived right up to the hilt of their means—and Seymour wasn't making any fees now. On top of that, the lawyer representing Seymour wanted six thousand dollars. And that was a professional courtesy, less than half the normal fee. Some courtesy, Rhoda thought bitterly.

A car came out of a narrow side road and Rhoda had to swerve to avoid it. She thought she'd better concentrate on her driving rather than on thinking and rethinking Seymour's plight as she had done every day and night for the last three months.

Seymour had gone to see his lawyer today, to prepare for the trial. What an ordeal that was going to be. They had already contacted their rabbi and friends, to see whom they could use as character witnesses. Seymour was so humiliated, he had already lost fifteen pounds, and was constantly tired and irritable. That was why Rhoda wanted to get Seymour's mood off the floor, at least for tonight.

As she turned into the long gravel driveway leading to their house, she saw Seymour's car in front of the garage. He had returned earlier than he thought he would. The house was a beautiful colonial, about fourteen rooms, with a barn where Debbie, their youngest daughter, kept her pony. Would they be able to stay here if Seymour lost his license, she wondered. She hoped they wouldn't have to give it up. It had taken so many years for them to be able to live in Chappaqua. How awful it would be, she thought, if they had to move back to an apartment in the Bronx.

Rhoda parked her car next to Seymour's and walked to the front entrance, wrestling her key from her bag as she juggled the bundles in her arms. The carved front door had solid brass trimmings. Just inside that door, in the now-dark foyer, a crystal chandelier her mother had given them as a housewarming present hung majestically in the center of a graceful circular staircase.

Debbie probably wasn't home from volleyball practice yet. All their other kids were at college, so she, Seymour, and Debbie would have a lovely dinner, and try to forget the heartache that Wright creature had brought them.

Rhoda turned the key in the front lock, still juggling her bundles.

She eased the door open with her foot, bracing the packages against her body so they wouldn't fall. The door swung open. There was a light on in the den to the left, but no light in the foyer. She didn't have a free hand to flip the switch, but she knew the way to the kitchen in the dark.

"Seymour," she called as she walked slowly. "I'm home."

There was no answer.

Suddenly Rhoda bumped into a heavy object that shouldn't have been in the middle of the foyer. What was that, she thought to herself, reeling backwards. She peered into the dark to see what it was. She heard a noise, a creaking from the landing above.

"Oh, my God!" she thought, burglars.

Suddenly, whatever it was that she had bumped into now bumped into her again. What was this? She reached a few fingers out and touched something that felt like . . . a shoe. A shoe . . . in the middle of the air . . . ?

Rhoda screamed. She ran in terror to the light switch 'and flipped it on.

"Oh, Seymour . . . oh, Seymour . . . oh, Seymour . . ." she screamed, moaned, cried as she sank to the floor. "You son of a bitch, J.T. Wright, you should have cancer everywhere in your body! Oh, Seymour, Seymour. . . ." she sobbed as the body of her husband swung lazily on the end of the rope attached to the landing above. "You son of a bitch, Wright! You motherless, soulless son of a bitch . . ."

NOVEMBER 23, 1967

MUFFY WAS A HAPPY CHILD at her fifth birthday party. And since this was the second party she had had that day, the first in nursery school, this one with her parents, grandparents, uncles, and aunts, she was socially exhausted but happy.

"Where does the time go?" asked Mrs. Crawford, turning to J.T. "Remember, it seems just yesterday that we had her first birthday party. That was when Kennedy was shot. That was in the Crawford's apartment, wasn't it, Courtnay?"

"Yes, Mother."

Courtnay and Marty had moved from the little three-room apartment they had rented when they came up from Washington to a luxurious six-room duplex cooperative that Courtnay's parents had purchased for them on Park Avenue and Eighty-third Street. Marty hadn't been too happy about his in-laws buying them the apartment; but Courtnay wasn't happy living in cramped quarters. On state salary, it was hard for Marty to afford anything larger. So when Courtnay came home with the news that her mother and father wanted to give her an apartment as a fifth-anniversary gift, he resisted—but not vehemently. After all, it was one thing to want to be independent, but, he thought, it was yet another thing to let that quest for independence stand in the way of Courtnay's family being able to do for their daughter what they ordinarily would have, what gave them pleasure, what made her happy. Since Courtnay was now expecting their second child, Marty wanted to do everything possible to make her happy.

In the meantime, J.T., too, had found new living quarters. The little flat in Greenwich Village had been all right when he first came to New York, first began working on Wall Street. But now he had a certain image to project. He arranged, through DeValen, to take a lease—with an option to buy later—on a small brownstone in the Chelsea area. It was a lovely house on a charming street—but it didn't change J.T.'s slovenly living habits. Now, however, with a larger apartment, there was more to be unkempt.

"Been reading about you in the papers, J.T.," said Mrs. Crawford.

"We have been rather busy," J.T. crowed softly.

"Who are you after these days?"

"The usual," he shrugged. "Nothing outstanding. We've pretty much decimated the grafters. The remaining ones are too scared to make a move."

"Do you want a big piece or a little piece, Uncle J.T.?" asked dark-haired Muffy.

"A little piece, Muffy."

Muffy very seriously cut the cake and Courtnay helped place it on the plate. Later, when all the guests had departed, Marty and J.T. sat in the library having a nightcap—a beer for Marty and a ginger ale for J.T.

"I'm not sure that's a sound idea, J.T.," said Marty. "I realize we've been on the trail of Judge Tauber for quite some time now without result, but I think your idea is a little off the wall."

"Why?"

"Because you want to manufacture a case where none exists. Frankly, what you're proposing is illegal."

"Look, all we do is have one of our undercover men indicted by the grand jury. We won't even let the DA know he's undercover. Let him go through the system as if it's a real case. Then he'll retain Tauber's son—what's his name?"

"Randolph Tauber."

"Randolph Tauber! What kind of a name is that anyway? The undercover man will retain young Tauber and tell him he's looking for a fix, a guarantee, for which he's willing to pay exceptionally well. We'll see if Randolph asks his father to influence the judge before whom the case is tried. What's wrong with that?"

"For starters," said Marty, "you'd have to get a phony complainant to swear in front of a grand jury that he or she has been the victim of a fictitious crime perpetrated by our undercover investigator. Now, to have our undercover man indicted for a phony crime is to subvert the entire function of the grand jury—not to mention that our office will be suborning perjury. Our investigator—the alleged victim—will have to swear he was the victim of a crime that never actually took place, won't he?"

J.T. nodded.

"So far you have the following crimes: the phony complainant, perjury, a class D felony punishable by seven years. We put him up to it. Subornation of perjury. Another D felony, subjecting *us* to seven years. Not to mention, of course, obstruction of, or interference with, governmental function. You can't abuse the legal process to catch people who are abusing the legal process, J.T. We've been over this ground before."

"We're not actually abusing the legal process. We don't intend to commit a criminal act. We're doing this specifically to uncover people who have violated their oaths of office."

"But we'd be violating the law ourselves."

"We *are* the law."

"No, we're not. We're just administering the law. We're just people. We're not the law. We're torch-bearers, conduits."

"Can you figure another way that we can catch Judge Tauber?"

"We've been trying for years now. Maybe he's really straight."

"Horseshit. I've seen the smoke myself. Now I want the fire."

"What smoke, Seymour Fine?"

"Let's not talk about that," J.T. said. He never liked discussing what had happened to Fine.

"What smoke has there been about Judge Tauber?"

"It's a hunch, all right? A hunch. I know we can get this guy. And God damn it, Marty, whose side are you on, anyway? We need some big cases. All we've been getting lately are cops taking bribes for not giving traffic tickets. We're putting ourselves out of business."

"Maybe it's about time. This was only supposed to be temporary."

"That's true. The time has come to move. But we can't just yet. We've got to go out in a blaze of glory. One big case, publicity week after week for, say, six months, so when we go out we'll have to beat clients away with a stick."

"Where are we going to get these phenomenal cases?"

"That's exactly what I'm trying to tell you," said J.T. emphatically. "We need a sitting Supreme Court judge on the griddle. Maybe a lot of them." J.T. leaned back pensively. "Maybe we could go after DiFalco again."

"Again? They threw out our first case against him. I told you not to—"

"Don't tell me you told me, okay?"

Marty nodded unhappily. This was another area about which he and J.T. constantly disagreed. "I don't mind trying to indict a Supreme Court judge if he's done something wrong. But let's not manufacture a case just to keep up publicity."

"I don't intend to manufacture a case. We're just putting all the ingredients together to see if we can have someone make a cake. Let's see what kind of baker Judge Tauber is."

"What makes you think young Tauber would involve his father?"

"If he doesn't, and goes out and does something on his own, we'll still nail him. The newspapers will beat the drums almost as big when we have the lawyer son of a Supreme Court judge on the fire. If young Tauber goes around bribing people, I'm going to get him. If his father helps him, I'll get him too. That's the way it is, Marty. This isn't necessarily a job for the fainthearted."

"Let me ask you this. If someone went into one of our grand juries and perjured himself about a phony case, would we prosecute?"

"Damn right."

"Then what's the difference when we send someone in to perjure himself? Just because we know in advance that it's going to happen doesn't change the fact that a person who takes an oath and lies in front of the grand jury is guilty of perjury. You know, in ancient times the punishment for perjury was death."

"When we know about it and it's for a specific purpose, it isn't perjury."

"Will the witness have his fingers crossed?"

"Stop busting my onions, Marty."

JANUARY 11, 1968

THE AUDITORIUM OF ST. BERNADETTE'S CHURCH in Bay Ridge, Brooklyn was set up with rows of long tables covered with paper tablecloths. A dais festooned with American-flag bunting stood on a stage at the front of the hall. American flags were arranged in stands behind the dais. Miniature flags were in the center of every table in the audience.

Pitchers of orange juice were distributed to each table as the young men and their fathers began to arrive for the Seventeenth Annual Father-Son Communion Breakfast of St. Bernadette's Parish. The sons scrambled between the rows of tables to snare chairs so they could sit with their friends and fathers. The moderator-priest grabbed a couple of overexuberant boys by their ears to calm them down. He was an Italian priest, and most of the fathers and sons of St. Bernadette's were also Italian, so a little ear-grabbing for discipline incurred no protest.

Carl Stern lived in St. Bernadette's parish and was on the breakfast committee that coordinated the annual affair. The German-American Stern family had blended immediately into the St. Bernadette parish activities when they moved into Bay Ridge fourteen months before. Several things accounted for the easy blending of the new German stock into the Italian enclave. Stern found many policemen and ex-policemen living in Bay Ridge. Only the stereotypical movie police department is still dominated by Irishmen; the major ethnic group in the New York Police Department is Italian, which makes up more than a third of the force. Those parishioners who were not policemen themselves were police buffs and supporters, conservatives who quickly accepted Stern and his tough stance on law and order.

Stern's close work with J.T. Wright did not affect him adversely in his neighbors' eyes. To the people of Bay Ridge, J.T. Wright was a crusader, a knight astride the white steed of righteousness, whose every skirmish in the press was met with vociferous support. The lambasting that Wright received from what were considered the liberal, pinko, double-dome Jews in the *Times* were met with rank outrage in Bay Ridge.

When Stern reported to the breakfast planning committee that J.T. Wright had agreed to be the guest speaker at this year's affair, they were ecstatic. Tickets sold out immediately. Extra tables had to be squeezed in to accommodate the record crowd.

Minutes before the breakfast was to begin, Carl Stern was in the rectory, a phone to his ear, listening to it ring at J.T.'s house. Monsignor Bonacci, short and heavyset in his crimson-trimmed cassock, hovered anxiously nearby.

"No answer," said Stern, putting the phone down.

"Are you sure he's coming?" asked Eddie Cardone, the president of the Parish Council.

Monsignor Bonacci looked very serious as he listened.

"I reminded him verbally and I left a note for him. I don't know what else I could have done," replied Stern. He was getting nervous.

"All right, everyone find places. There are plenty of empty chairs all around the auditorium. We're not going to set up any new tables while there are still places open," announced Jim DeFranco, vice-president of the Parish Council, as he stood behind the microphone on the dais, watching stragglers from the church wander around the auditorium.

"Are you sure he knows how to get here?" asked the Monsignor.

"Sure," replied Stern. "Besides, his driver can look up the address in the phone book."

"I thought you drove for him," said Cardone.

"Not on weekends." Stern was feeling queasy. He knew how unreliable J.T. was, how he could never get anywhere on time. Why had he put himself on the line like this? The Parish Council would drum him out of the neighborhood if J.T. ruined this breakfast.

"I'll start the breakfast. He should be here by then," the Monsignor said threateningly.

"No question," Stern assured him nervously.

There was a big cheer from the kids, who were in high spirits, when the Monsignor came into the hall. He waddled up to the dais, where the officials of the Parish Council and the honored guests waited. Everyone looked past the Monsignor for J.T. Wright.

"Good morning," said the Monsignor, walking directly to the microphone. He had to lower the mike head so he could reach it. He couldn't tighten the mike to stay at one height. Jim DeFranco fixed it for him.

"Good morning," he repeated into the mike. A deafening feedback whistle seared the room. The kids laughed. The Monsignor, annoyed, looked toward the control box just behind the curtain. One of the men hastily lowered the volume.

"Good morning," the Monsignor said again. "Let's all say grace so we can begin our Seventeenth Annual St. Bernadette's Communion Breakfast."

Steve Russo was crestfallen as the Monsignor started grace. He was the perennial MC, and had prepared a punchy speech, peppered with a few new jokes, to open the proceedings. After that, the Monsignor was supposed to be introduced to say grace.

The Monsignor gave one of his rambling graces, talking about all the things in the parish that God had blessed, and that He should continue to bless, as well as the food they were about to eat. When he finished, there was a big cheer as the young guests grabbed for their chairs and the cornflakes.

Stern and Cardone waited at the front window of the rectory, watching for J.T.'s car. Stern was becoming pale.

"Is he always like this?" asked Cardone.

"Most of the time."

"Christ."

A few minutes passed.

"Is that his car?" Cardone asked suddenly.

Stern stretched to look. "No. Shit."

A few people were on their way to the ten o'clock mass. Others were walking to Thirteenth Avenue to buy bread and pastries in the corner store, which stayed open until after the last mass.

J.T., who knew nothing whatever about Brooklyn, and his driver, who knew little more, had wandered about the streets for three-quarters of an hour. They finally arrived, leaving the car in the no-parking zone in front of the church. The head usher moved toward them officiously until he saw who it was. He smiled and told the driver to leave the car there; the ushers would watch it. J.T. was led down a stairway from the rear vestibule of the church to the back of the auditorium.

J.T. poked his head out from the stairwell. He saw a mass of people sitting at the tables, their flashing spoons in the cornflakes. He pulled back, but not before someone had seen him.

"Hey, he's here!" a boy shouted.

"Where?"

"In the backstairs."

The message flashed across the room instantly.

J.T. nodded to countless smiling faces as he walked across the auditorium to a standing ovation, picking up an entourage of well-wishers and handshakers. Men reached over to pat his back and shake his hand.

"Wright's here," an usher shouted to Cardone and Stern.

"Where?"

"Downstairs."

The two men raced downstairs, arriving at the dais just after J.T.

"God, am I glad to see you," Stern said as he took his place next to J.T., trying to catch his breath. "This is Eddie Cardone, our president."

J.T. shook Cardone's hand.

"A pleasure," said Cardone.

"Oh, and this is Monsignor Bonacci," said Stern.

"A very great pleasure to meet you," the Monsignor said.

"Thank you, Father."

"Monsignor," the Monsignor corrected.

"Thank you, Monsignor."

The milling around on the dais subsided and J.T. took his chair. As the others began to eat, J.T. wrote some notes on the back of a program, putting together a few remarks for the gathering.

"You're very popular around here," the Monsignor whispered to J.T.

"Really?"

"Absolutely. You stand for law and order, and we support that wholeheartedly."

"Oh?"

"Eddie," the Monsignor said to Cardone, who was sitting next to him, "Mr. Wright doesn't know how popular he is in our parish."

"Are you kidding, Mr. Wright? We appreciate the stand you're taking against crime, against permissiveness. We're from the old school around here, where people believe criminals have to pay. Around here there's right and wrong, and no in-between."

"Except Purgatory," added the Monsignor.

"Yeah," Cardone chuckled. "You're our kind of people, Mr. Wright. In fact, we were talking about you the other night at the Parish Council. You're the kind of man who should be in office to do something about crime."

"That's why we invited you here," added another voice near Cardone. "We like your style."

"You have our endorsement," Monsignor Bonacci said. "And in an Italian parish, that goes a long way."

"And now, fathers and sons," said Steve Russo from behind the lectern, "we have an exciting program this morning, some football Giants films . . ." The kids cheered. "We have our own Rocky Marchette . . ." They cheered again. Marchette was a minor-league ball player from the neighborhood. "And we have Special Prosecutor J.T. Wright." The youngsters were unimpressed, but their fathers were on their feet, cheering and whistling. They loved him. J.T. felt a surge of exhilaration.

APRIL 15, 1968

"FRED, THE STORIES YOU'RE GIVING THE MEDIA LATELY ARE REALLY POOR," J.T. snapped as he gazed out of his office window.

"I just place stories in the paper, J.T. I don't create them," Balzano replied. He was on the couch, looking at J.T.'s back.

"What's that supposed to mean?" demanded J.T., wheeling around. "Besides the fact you can't do your job?"

"I've had to spend more time lately keeping people from using bad press about this office in the media than I have getting our stories in. You know that as well as I do, J.T., so don't start pissing on me!" Balzano stared back angrily at J.T.

"Look, Fred," J.T. said soothingly, "I know there are lots of bleeding hearts in the editorial departments and on the bench, who start quaking in their boots when somebody comes along, like I have, and really starts making waves. They can't stand the sight of blood. But I tell you, Fred"—he started pacing, launching into a speech—"there are far more people out there, grassroots people, who are tired of the criminals running things, of corrupt politicians, of the police spending more time counting their money than keeping the streets safe. You've seen the letters we get every day from the working people. They're glad that somebody is finally doing something. You've seen the letters inviting me to speak at their dinners and meetings, haven't you?"

"I've had my staff cataloging and filing them just like you wanted," Balzano replied.

"Three speeches in Queens just this week," J.T. said, reassuring himself. "The people love us, which is another reason the politicians and the people at the papers are getting nervous. Our grassroots movement is beginning to shake their applecarts."

Balzano listened quietly. He had heard this all before.

"That's why, Fred, we really have to have some positive stories in the papers, to counteract accusations that we're coming down too hard with improper methods. We also need good press to fuse our people out there together, to give them something positive to talk about, to recruit new troops."

"Give me the stories, I'll get them in the papers."

J.T. walked over to Balzano. "You're right, Fred. We have to give you some positive news to print. It's critical right now if we want to keep our momentum going."

J.T. pressed his intercom button.

"Yes?" said his secretary.

"Tell Philip Levine to come into my office."

"Will do."

In a moment, a runt of a man appeared at the door. "You wanted to see me?" he piped in a high voice.

Philip Levine, who pronounced his name to rhyme with devine, wore round glasses that he constantly pushed higher onto the bridge of his nose. He waddled when he walked and had an unkempt shock of dark hair. He reminded J.T. of a mole. He was not at all the type of person J.T. would ordinarily tolerate. But Levine was unscrupulous, unfeeling, with an obsessive drive always to be right, to show everyone how clever he was. With such a personality, it was really little surprise that Levine had been personally signed on by J.T. to assist in his purge of the justice system.

Marty Boxer thought Levine was obnoxious, and had told J.T. exactly that many times. But J.T. kept Levine on staff to do those things that he couldn't ask Marty to do, or that he knew Marty would refuse to do.

"Yes," said J.T., "Fred and I were having a talk and we've agreed that our activity is not what it should be. He has no stories to send out."

"We've had several indictments lately."

"Which ones?" asked Balzano.

"The tax official who was skimming the cream in Staten Island," Levine replied.

"Diddlyshit," said J.T. impatiently. "I'm talking about some real indictments, something significant."

Levine thought. "There's that Judge Tauber story you wanted me to work on."

"Yes, of course. What's happening with that?"

"Well, I went to Judge Moriarty just the way you asked, and laid out the entire plan. He saw nothing wrong with it."

"That's what I told Marty," J.T. interjected. "Go ahead."

"One of our undercover people went to the DA's office in Brooklyn. I wanted the case to be processed in front of Moriarty, not Poster in New York."

"Poster's too goddamn liberal," said J.T.

"Our man complained that he was robbed by another of our men. Only the DA doesn't know that. The grand jury is going to vote on the indictment shortly."

"You lost me," said Balzano. "Give me a rundown from the top."

J.T. took over. "One of our undercover men is a complainant who has testified to a Brooklyn grand jury that he was robbed by another of our undercover men, Wolkofsky. And Wolkofsky is going to be indicted for robbery."

"Wolkofsky's going to be indicted under the name Rainone—just for a little color," Levine added.

Balzano looked at J.T. "What kind of shit is that? Does the defendant have to be Italian to be credible?"

"I don't know why an Italian name was picked," said J.T.

"I do," replied Balzano, "and I think it sucks."

"We'll have to get you a membership in the Italian-American Civil Rights League."

"Apparently you better."

"Come on, it's done already. We can't do anything about it now."

Levine continued, "We even pumped a phony old criminal record with two convictions for Rainone into the Albany computers. Similar crimes for authenticity."

"Did the Brooklyn DA know what was happening?" asked J.T.

"Not at all," Levine said with glee. "It's totally our operation. No one else is in on it to spill the beans."

"You advised Moriarty about that?"

"Sure."

J.T. nodded approval. "Go ahead."

"Anyway, Rainone went to Judge Tauber to ask for advice."

"Just like that, out of the blue, he went to Tauber?" Balzano said quizzically. "A judge can't represent a defendant in a criminal case. Even I know that."

J.T. looked a little worried as he turned to Levine.

Levine shook his head. "No, no. We got this woman, a Mrs. Mastrangelo—that's why we picked the Rainone name—who had tried to bribe a cop who stopped her for driving drunk the wrong way on a one-way street. During the processing at the station house, she mentioned she knew Judge Tauber really well."

"Aha," said J.T., rubbing his hands together, "the plot thickens."

"Right." Levine smiled his thin, weasel smile. "We told her we wouldn't prosecute her if she cooperated and introduced Rainone to Judge Tauber."

"Pretty move," J.T. said happily. "Go ahead."

"The judge tells Rainone he needs somebody who knows his way around the criminal courts, and sends Rainone to see his son."

"All of this is tape-recorded, isn't it?" J.T. pressed.

"Naturally. Anyone who talked to Judge Tauber was wearing a body tape, even Mrs. Mastrangelo."

"Fantastic," said J.T.

"Rainone told Randolph Tauber—that's the judge's son—that he wants a guarantee the case will be tossed out of court, or at least a guarantee of no jail. Whatever it costs."

Balzano nodded. "Where does the case go now?"

"After Rainone is indicted in Brooklyn, he and Mrs. Mastrangelo will testify in front of our Special Corruption Grand Jury about Judge

Tauber and about Randolph concocting a phony defense for Rainone; one where he charges he didn't assault and rob the complainant. He just hit him when the complainant made homosexual advances."

"Did young Tauber concoct a phony defense?" asked Balzano.

"Wait, I'm not finished. Next we're going to have the judge and his son testify in front of our grand jury. I'll bag them on perjury when they deny the story."

"What if they don't perjure themselves? How can I make a story out of that?" Balzano asked J.T. "You don't even know which way it's going to fall."

"It'll fall the right way," Levine said firmly.

"How do you know that?"

"I've had preliminary informal discussions with the Taubers in my office," said Levine, "and their stories differ significantly from the testimony of Rainone and Mrs. Mastrangelo."

"What do you think?" J.T. asked Balzano.

"Sensational stuff, if we can deliver."

"I'll deliver," Levine said proudly, looking for J.T.'s approval.

J.T. was all smiles. "Let's get it. Let's really get it," he exhorted Levine. "We need a big one right now. Fred, start pounding your typewriter."

"Right, J.T."

J.T. was delighted as Balzano left the room. Levine started to follow. "Phil," J.T. said slowly, seeing the door close behind Balzano, "are you sure this thing will happen the way you say?"

"Absolutely. I told you I already have the tapes. And the judge and Randolph have already told me their version. I know I'm going to have them indicted for perjury."

"Fantastic, simply fantastic." J.T. pushed back his chair, lifting his feet up on the desk. Levine stood, grinning. "Well, why are you still here?" J.T. said with feigned anger. "Go get me those indictments."

"Right, chief."

"And, Phil, this is important to me right now. But don't say anything to Marty Boxer. He said it couldn't come off."

"That's all the more reason for me to get it for you."

J.T. laughed as Levine rushed out of the office.

JULY 14, 1968

"NOW *THOSE* ARE HEADLINES," J.T. exulted, holding up a copy of *The New York Times* to Balzano and Marty. "The only thing that'd make me happier is a jury saying guilty. By God." J.T. read the headline again: WRIGHT INDICTS JUDGE TAUBER AND SON FOR PERJURY.

The Governor was in shirt sleeves, sitting comfortably in his private plane headed from Albany to New York City. Dan Mastretta sat on a nearby couch, skimming the morning newspapers for items that would interest the Governor.

"Have you seen the story about Judge Tauber?" Mastretta asked.

"I didn't read it, but I know about it. I received a telephone call from Chief Judge Borden at eight o'clock this morning. The judge was rather disturbed."

"About one of his judges getting indicted?" Mastretta asked.

"No, not at all. About the tactics of the special prosecutor. Judge Borden said that it was all well and good that corrupt officials are indicted and tried, but not in the newspapers. Borden also complained that Wright shows as much disrespect for the law as any person who's been indicted."

"Isn't perjury perjury?"

"That's what I said to Borden. I said, 'A grand jury heard evidence and indicted, what's wrong with that?'"

The plane bounced on an air pocket. The Governor felt a queasiness in the pit of his stomach.

"What did he say?"

"He said that he had been a DA for a substantial period of time, in Dewey's office, and a DA could have a grand jury return an indictment against anyone he wanted it to."

"Did he say there's something wrong with the Tauber case?"

"He said that Wright's methods in general have been so abusive that many of his cases have been thrown out of court. He said that subjecting officials like Judge Tauber to trial in the newspapers before Wright's dubious indictment is examined is outrageous. He said it's about time Wright's romance with the media is curtailed."

"Wright sure gets a lot of people worked up, doesn't he?"

"That he does," said the Governor, looking out the window. They were over Yonkers. "He's got everyone in the criminal justice system hopping. And that's exactly what he was supposed to do. But, hell, Dan, he can't recklessly indict people, using illegal methods."

"You think that's what he's doing?"

"I asked Judge Borden the same question, and he said he would speak to the administrative judge in Kings County, where Judge Tauber's case is going to be tried, and ask that this case be handled as expeditiously as possible. Borden felt that the surest way to get to the bottom of what Wright is doing is to let the system work, let the defense lawyers pore over the case, cross-examine the witnesses who testified at the Grand Jury. A trial would get everything out in the open."

"How long will all of that take?" asked Mastretta.

"Not more than a few months. If Wright's doing his job right, terrific. But if he isn't—well, we ought to know that too."

Mastretta grimaced as the plane hit another wave of turbulence.

Joseph E. Brill was one of the most respected criminal defense lawyers in the city. He was bald—actually shaved what little hair he had left—and wore a Vandyke beard; he was the epitome of a criminal trial lawyer of the old school. Judge Tauber retained Brill to represent him on the indictment.

"What do you think, Joe?" the judge asked, pale as he sat in Brill's private office.

Brill, his half-glasses low on his angular nose, read the indictment on his desk.

"I think the son of a bitch set you up." Brill, too, had been a DA in Dewey's famous office.

Randolph Tauber and his attorney, Peter L. F. Sabbatino, were also in Brill's office. Sabbatino, too, was one of the city's best defense lawyers. At seventy-five years of age, he had not forgotten anything. He still knew it all, and then some. Sabbatino and Brill both had their offices in the Woolworth Building, and had known and respected each other for a long time.

"What do you think, Peter?"

"No question about it," Sabbatino replied in his soft voice.

"How can you both tell that?" asked the judge.

"How else could Wright get a purported defendant to wire himself up and tape conversations with his own lawyer?" said Brill.

"A defendant worrying about his own health and welfare," added Sabbatino, "would not likely be working with the special prosecutor against his own lawyer, unless he didn't have any case to worry about in the first place."

"That's the way I see it, Peter," Brill agreed.

"We'll have to get the tapes and any other material they have," said Sabbatino. "I wouldn't even waste time asking Wright's people if they'll give it to us. We'll make formal motions."

"I want to get this thing brought to trial as quickly as possible," said the judge. "I'm being pilloried. So is my son, my entire family."

"They say they have tapes to prove the charges," said Brill carefully. "We can complain all we want about unfair tactics, set-up and the like, and I do not minimize that for a moment, but lying in front of a grand jury is perjury, no matter how you slice it. Is there anything to these charges?"

"They're a goddamn lie!" Tauber's son said vehemently. "They accuse me of concocting a phony defense for Rainone and lying about it before the grand jury. It's not true. I told this Rainone, or whatever his real name is, that he had a long rap sheet. He couldn't take the stand with that kind of record. I'm not in either of your leagues, but I know that. So why would I concoct a defense for him to testify to, that the complainant made homosexual advances? I told him he couldn't even take the stand. If they've got tapes, that's what'll be on the tapes."

"Unless they doctor the tapes," Sabbatino pointed out.

"You think Wright'd go that far?" asked the judge.

"Why not?" replied Brill. "If he's capable of doing what you say, why couldn't he doctor tapes too?"

"Jesus Christ," the judge said, leaning back in his chair.

"I never concocted any phony defense with Rainone," the judge's son repeated. "In fact, I told him that I wouldn't represent him, that he had to get another lawyer, because all he wanted me to do was make a fix for him. I didn't trust him. All he wanted was a fix, a fix. I told him he was reading too many comic books, and that he'd have to get somebody else."

"We've got to get our hands on those tapes, then, Peter. That's where the case lies."

"I already have one of my associates working on the motion papers."

"It's going to be great working with you again, Peter," said Brill. "And don't worry, judge, we'll hoist the son of a bitch on his own petard."

"It's difficult being a defendant, Joe," the judge replied wearily. "We sit and watch this sort of thing day in, day out. And then suddenly you're the defendant, and your stomach takes a different turn, and it turns and it turns. My whole life is in your hands."

"We'll do everything possible, judge," Brill said, looking at Sabbatino. "And then some."

"What is this Tauber situation all about?" Marty demanded angrily of J.T. They were alone in J.T.'s office. It was after ordinary working hours, although many staff lawyers were in their offices poring over books and papers.

"What do you mean, Marty?" J.T. asked, looking Marty straight in the eye.

"You know what I mean, J.T. How did all this come about without my knowing anything about it? Why did Levine handle it directly with you, and not with me? I *am* still chief of staff around here, am I not?"

"That doesn't mean that everything has to go through you, does it?" J.T. replied. He swiveled in his chair to look out at the skyline.

"No. But it just seems odd that you didn't let me in on any of it, particularly since the Tauber situation is very similar to discussions we've had many times about making a phony case to get an official. Is that what this is?"

"Certainly not, Otto," J.T. said, trying to stir up some of the old joviality. He didn't turn to face Marty.

"You're not convincing me, J.T.," Marty said sternly. "I smell something wrong in this case—especially where Levine handled it. He's a very dangerous little man."

"He's all right. A little ambitious, perhaps. But aren't we all?"

"Not all, J.T. Have you read the grand jury minutes in the Tauber case yet? Have you seen the evidence?"

"No, have you?" J.T. said anxiously, turning to face Marty.

"Not yet. But I'm going to take the file home with me this evening."

"I was thinking of doing the same thing myself. Perhaps you can take it tomorrow night?"

"I already have the file with me." Marty indicated a file on the couch next to him.

"Let me have it, will you?" J.T. tried to say casually.

"No problem, J.T. I'll just photostat it. This way we'll both be able to discuss the file tomorrow."

"I'd rather you didn't do that."

"Is there something in there you don't want me to see? Ordinarily you don't even bother to look in the files. What's the difference with this one?"

"No difference."

"Good. Then there'll be no problem if I photostat it."

J.T.'s jaw muscles set hard as he looked at the folder in Marty's hand. "I'd rather you didn't do that, Marty," he said firmly, "until I look it over myself. If Levine did something wrong, I want to know about it first. Particularly because, as you say, he was working directly with me."

"Here's the file," said Marty, handing the folder to J.T. "But if you don't have sufficient confidence in me to let me photostat the file and study it at the same time you do, then you can take this job and my title and shove them you know where." Marty's fists were clenched tightly.

"Take it easy, Marty, take it easy. What's come over you?" J.T. asked, smiling now, coming out from behind his desk. "Hell, Marty, it's only a file."

"And from the way you're acting, I know just what to expect in it."

"I think you're wrong. Unless Levine did something I don't know about."

"I see. If there's anything unethical or illegal in there, you'll lay it off on Levine."

"That's not what I mean at all. As far as I know, there's nothing amiss in the Tauber file."

"I'll find that out for myself. Unless, of course, you tell me right now that you don't want me to look at this file at all."

J.T. studied Marty carefully. He was in dead earnest, and looked angrier than J.T. had ever seen him. "I guess you can look at it, if it's that important. Take it."

"Fine. I hope you're right about what's in here, J.T."

J.T. looked at Marty, his face betraying nothing.

JULY 14, 1968

"WHAT'S THE MATTER, DARLING?" Courtnay asked Marty as they sat at the dining room table. Marty's face was darkly serious.

"Nothing much, just thinking."

"Thinking something terrible, from the looks of you. Come on, Marty, tell me what it is."

Marty placed his napkin next to his plate. He leaned back in his chair and crossed his arms across his chest. "I think J.T. is starting to let his hunger for publicity go a bit too far."

"*Starting* to go too far? From what I read in the papers, there are people who think J.T. and your office went too far a long time ago. What happened now?"

"The Tauber indictment."

"You think there's something wrong with the indictment?"

"You remember how many times J.T. has spoken about having one of our men pose as a criminal and then try to bribe his way out of court? Well, I think he's finally gone and done it."

"The Tauber case is based on a faked case?"

"I found out today that J.T. has had Levine doing his dirty work, and I blew my stack. I demanded to see the file."

"And what's in the file?"

"On the surface, the indictment seems well founded. Not against the judge so much, but against the son."

"That's a different situation then, isn't it?" said Courtnay. "If the son really did commit perjury, there's no excuse for that, regardless of J.T.'s actions."

"But there's something more to this, something I haven't quite figured out yet. I have to hear the tapes our undercover man made when he was talking to Randolph Tauber."

"Why don't you ask J.T. for them?"

"When I do, he's going to tell me that he hasn't heard the tapes himself. He's going to lay the whole thing off on Levine. I know him."

"Finally. It's been a long time, Marty."

"What really burns me is that he did all this without my knowing about it. I'm the chief of staff, and here he is conniving with other assistants behind my back, making me look the fool to the rest of the staff. When the public lambasts the office, the newspapers accuse us of raking people's rights over the coals, then I'll be a public fool, despite the fact that in some instances, like this one, I don't even know what's going on."

Courtnay walked over to Marty and put her arm around his shoulder. "Marty, I love you."

"What's all this about?" he asked blankly.

"You're finally seeing the light. J.T. is treacherous and self-concerned—and that's giving him all the best of it."

"I don't want to say you're right, but J.T. has changed lately. He's hungrier and hungrier for publicity and recognition. When we go through a dry period, when no really sensational stories are being pumped out by our press agent—that's what Balzano is, a press agent—J.T. gets frantic. And the time between J.T.'s need for publicity fixes is getting shorter and shorter. He's like a junkie now."

"Maybe it's time to start considering whether following J.T. around any longer is worthwhile. Maybe it's time to go out and do something on your own."

"There's nothing wrong with the purpose of the office, darling. Making the justice system more responsive is a really important task.

And with these crazy bastards that J.T. has attracted, and that he seems attracted to, I'm the only voice of sanity in bedlam. I have to stay right now."

"But you have to consider your own career, not just cleaning up J.T.'s mess."

"I'm not just cleaning up after him."

"Oh, yes you are. You've been saving him for years. And from what you tell me, that's getting harder to do. J.T. is getting more dangerous."

Marty frowned. "Dangerous?"

"Perhaps desperate is a better word. I've always warned you that J.T. wouldn't think twice about hurting even you if it suited his purpose. From what you tell me, his need for publicity is squeezing him to do desperate things. You can see it in this Tauber situation."

Marty thought silently for a few moments. "I'm going to call J.T.," he said, rising. "This thing is going to come to a head right now." He went to the phone in the den and dialed J.T.'s number.

"Hello?"

"J.T., this is Marty. I've looked over the Tauber file, and there's something wrong."

"I haven't had a chance to go over it yet, Marty. I'm a little tied up right now. We can go over it in the morning."

"It's not quite as easy as that, J.T. I don't want to be brushed off."

"You sound a little overwrought, Marty. I'm not brushing you off. It's just a case. We can discuss it tomorrow."

"It's not just the case, J.T. It's the fact that you went and pulled off this entrapment scheme, even though we'd discussed it many times and you knew I disapproved of it."

"Marty, there are some decisions I have to make on my own."

"That's not the point, J.T. It goes deeper than that."

"What *is* the point, then?"

"You've made a damn fool of me. You can make all the decisions in the office if you want. But as long as I'm chief of staff, I should know what's going on. It's humiliating to have people on my staff working on cases I don't even know about."

"That's not true at all, Marty."

"It sure as hell is," Marty said loudly.

"Marty, we can't discuss this over the phone."

"Fine. I'll come over."

"No, not now. I've got some people here. This is important business. It has to do with getting out of the special prosecutor's office."

"Getting out?"

"Right. There are people here who think I might have a political future. And frankly"—J.T. started to whisper—"they're willing to put up money to get me going."

"Don't change the subject, J.T." Marty's annoyance was not lessened in the least by J.T.'s plans of future glory.

"Well, if, as you tell me, the office is getting out of hand and I'm looking for a way to get the two of us out of it, then what's still bugging you?"

"I don't know if there's going to *be* the two of us anymore."

"What does that mean? Listen, if that little toad Levine has done something wrong, then fire his ass. You're still top man. I told him to get permission from Judge Moriarty, so everything would be absolutely approved in advance. For Christ's sake, Marty, you think I'm a crazy man, that I'd let something go on that wasn't legal? That I'd let something like this come between you and me?"

"I don't know anymore, J.T. Did Levine get Moriarty's approval?"

"I love your attitude, Marty. After all these years, you tell me you don't know if I'd do something that would come between us."

"It's not all these years, J.T. It's right now. You're getting publicity-mad. These people who write to you and tell you you're cleaning up the city and that you're a savior—they're the lunatic fringe. And you believe them."

"Can't we discuss this tomorrow morning, Marty? I'm telling you, I had nothing but the best intentions."

"All right, we can talk in the morning—early!"

"First thing. When Stern picks me up, we'll drive right over to your place."

"Eight fifteen."

"Eight fifteen it is."

Marty hung up the phone, still upset, feeling that he had just been conned again.

"What was that all about?" George DeValen asked as J.T. walked back into the living room. DeValen was sitting on the couch, a drink in hand.

"Nothing much," J.T. said pensively. "Just a little office problem. I'll take care of it tomorrow."

"Good. Shall we go out to dinner, or do you want to order something in?"

"I don't care." J.T. was disturbed that Marty was so angry. He'd have a lot of talking to do in the morning to calm Marty down out of this tree.

"Good, let's order in, dear boy. There's so much that we have to get settled."

JULY 15, 1968

"MARTY, MARTY, stop carrying on about a single case," J.T. urged. "Especially until we have a look at the rest of the file and see what it's really about."

They were in the back of J.T.'s car. Stern was driving.

"It couldn't have happened the way you're saying, J.T. Levine couldn't have done all this on his own."

"I told him to handle the matter, and to get Judge Moriarty's approval in advance for anything that might be the slightest bit questionable. He said he did. What's wrong with that?"

"Moriarty would approve anything, even drawing and quartering suspects."

"Well, what can we do about that? He's the judge presiding over all our cases in Kings County. If we went to him and he gave us his approval in advance, what did we do wrong?"

"Technically, nothing."

"The law is a technical thing, Marty. Everything we do is technical."

"What about the fact that you didn't tell me anything that was going on, approval or not?" Marty asked.

"Do you want to handle the entire case, just to make sure I'm not pulling anything sneaky here?"

"That's not necessary."

"Sure it is. I insist on it. You're assigned to handle the case personally, as of right now. Especially since it's right out in front of everyone's nose right now. Fred has to get on top of the press coverage, and you get on top of the case. The papers have been kicking us all over the place, and we sure don't need any more of that. Particularly now."

Stern stopped the car in front of 270 Broadway. "Park the car and then come upstairs," J.T. told him.

Marty and J.T. got out and entered the building. As they rode an otherwise empty elevator up to the twentieth floor, J.T. turned to Marty and said enthusiastically, "Wait till you hear about the new project I have on the boards."

"We haven't cleared up the old project," Marty pointed out.

"That's small potatoes," J.T. said. "This is something really exciting, and may get us out of the dreary prosecution business altogether."

"Okay, I'm curious. What is it?"

"Last night when you called, George DeValen was at the house. We were having a private talk."

"Yes?"

"Well, DeValen has always been interested in my career. He and I get together once or twice a week to go over his legal matters and to talk. When we're finished in the special prosecutor's office, he's going to give us a big fat retainer so we can start our own office."

"He said that years ago. Is that the big news?"

"Not all of it. The big news is that DeValen thinks we might be able to do very well in the Republican mayoral primary."

"You're not serious."

"I am serious. The Republicans have no one to run against Livingston, now that he's running on a Democratic line. And DeValen feels the city is getting a conservative bent. Law and order. The private citizens are tired of hiding in their homes while the criminals roam free in the streets. He wants to start a 'Draft Wright for Mayor' campaign. What do you think?"

Marty stared at J.T. The elevator stopped at their floor. "I can't believe it," he said as they entered the office.

"Good morning," said the receptionist, peeking up from her magazine.

"Good morning," said Marty.

"Why, what's wrong with the idea?" J.T. asked anxiously.

"You mean other than its being insane?"

"Why insane?"

"What happens with the special prosecutor's office? You couldn't keep the job and run for mayor, could you?"

"We'd resign. You're tired of it anyway, aren't you?"

"When did you decide that for me?"

"Well, *I* am, I know that. There aren't too many big cases now. With this one against Tauber, maybe we can finish in a blaze of glory, start our own practice with DeValen's fat retainer, and then enter the primary races. What do you think?"

"Open a practice with DeValen as our only client?"

"It'll be a really big initial retainer. This way it's a tax-deductible legal fee for DeValen, rather than an outright political contribution to our mayoral campaign."

"That man doesn't stop for a minute, does he?"

"He's clever, isn't he?"

"You two make a good match."

"However, clever as DeValen is, I'm one step ahead of him," J.T. scoffed. "Even if the mayoral thing doesn't work out, the publicity, together with the publicity we've gotten from this job, will help us draw clients in private practice. And DeValen's retainer will pay the nut."

Marty shook his head. "I don't like being too involved with DeValen. He's too slick."

"As long as he wants to foot the bills to get us going, what's the difference?"

"Well, I wouldn't want to get out on that private-practice limb and then have it cut out from under me because DeValen becomes disenchanted with the boy wonder. It'll take time to get an office going, you know."

"I don't like being at anyone's mercy either. But it's a springboard out of here. Besides, when I'm the mayor, we'll be on top of the world. Mayor of the greatest city in the world, the Emerald City . . ."

"And you'll be the Wizard of Oz?"
"No, the Wizard of Otto."
They both laughed.
"You're not mad anymore, are you?" J.T. asked Marty cautiously.
"You're something else, Otto, you really are."
"As long as I'm not wrong, I'm okay. Am I still right?"
"You're always Wright. But I don't know if you're right."

SEPTEMBER 12, 1968

"ARCHIE, DID YOU SEE THIS ARTICLE in today's *Times*?" Chauncey Delafield asked as they sat in the den of Reynolds's Gracie Square apartment. Fall was particularly cold. Inside, the fireplace was crackling warmly, a fine cognac was in the snifters, and the Sunday *Times* had been dismantled into the family's favorite sections.

"Which article, Chauncey?"

"An article about next year's mayoralty. Seems someone has started a movement to draft J.T. Wright."

"Let me see that."

Dana, who had been absorbed in the *Times* magazine rose and stood behind her father's large leather easy chair as he took the paper from Delafield. She read over his shoulder.

"This is very interesting," said Reynolds, absorbed by every word in the article. Dana read silently. "He's going to run in the Republican primary, is he?" Reynolds said to no one in particular. His face was streaked with displeasure. "Oh ho, listen to this. He says he will resign his position as deputy attorney general in order to make the run."

"Must have someone backing him," said Delafield. "He couldn't be doing this on his own money."

"Nor would he," Dana added acidly.

"Is Joe Albanese still the Republican Chairman?" Reynolds asked.

"Just in New York County. This mayoral primary is citywide."

"I know. But Joe is involved, isn't he?"

"Yes, of course, Archie."

"Fine," Reynolds said, putting the paper down in his lap. "I want you to get in touch with Joe, find out who he's backing."

"It's not Wright, I'm sure of that. Wright's running against the regular party choice."

"I read that," said Reynolds. "Tell Joe Albanese that he can have as much money as he needs to help the man he's backing."

"Okay."

Dana's hand moved from her father's shoulder to rub the back of his neck.

"But tell Joe that I want his candidate to run one hell of a campaign against Wright. If Joe doesn't have a dynamic candidate, tell him to get one. I want Wright humuliated. Humiliated!"

"Any amount, Archie?"

"Exactly. *Any* amount."

SEPTEMBER 20, 1968

JUDGE J. JAMES MORIARTY looked down at the lawyers at the defense table, his lips creased in their perpetual thin sneer; his black robes, buttoned up to the neck, contrasted with his white hair. Had he been a Jesuit, he would be a strict Prefect of Discipline, he was that strait-laced and unforgiving. He took pleasure in making people conform to his personal idea of righteousness. To add another ingredient to that volatile mix, Judge Moriarty was incompetent. He was not well versed in the law. And he masked this lack with a veneer of arrogance and hostility. Thus, any trial in front of Judge Moriarty was an adventure, leading, usually, into strange territory and ending with rulings distinguished by their tortuous illogic. When in doubt, which was often, he favored the prosecutor. In the criminal justice system, there are certainly good judges. But there are also many chosen because—and only because—they can be expected to align themselves with the old club, favor the prosecutor, lean toward conviction. Many of these prosecution-leaning judges are former DAs, and in their minds, the change from prosecutor to judge is merely a physical shift in the place they sit in the courtroom.

"Which is the next case?" the judge asked the court clerk. He saw

Judge Tauber sitting in the audience, and knew very well, from the calendar on his bench, that the Tauber case was next. But Judge Moriarty relished twisting the knife in Judge Tauber's gut. He watched Tauber's expression with morbid delight as the clerk replied.

"People against Tauber, Your Honor."

"Very well. Call it."

Marty, who had been sitting at the prosecutor's table, rose to his feet. Joe Brill and Peter Sabbatino rose and walked with their clients to the defense counsel's table.

Judge Moriarty looked down at Judge Tauber with contempt.

"Good morning, Your Honor," said Sabbatino, smiling. He felt nothing but loathing for the sanctimonious Moriarty. Everyone in the courtroom knew their mutual feelings, and all expected some acrimony before the proceeding was over.

"May the record reflect that I am handing each counsel answering papers to their motions for a Bill of Particulars and Discovery," said Marty.

"I acknowledge their receipt," said Brill. "I have not seen these documents before and, under the circumstances, am going to request an adjournment to determine if any reply is necessary."

"We move cases in this part. We cannot tolerate adjournments merely to read documents. Read them in the jury box, and make whatever reply you want to make orally, this morning. Then you won't need an adjournment." A gloating grin covered the judge's face.

"Even if I did that, Your Honor," piped in Sabbatino, "and were subjected to having to read these fourteen pages in the jury box, I would prefer to have written reply papers to better protect the record. It would seem more appropriate, particularly since this is the first time the case is on Your Honor's calendar, to have an adjournment."

"I would like to know what defense counsel's applications are before I commit myself to waiving written papers, Your Honor," said Marty. "I might want our law department to do some research."

"Mr. Sabbatino's points won't require much legal research, I'm sure. He just wants to scatter gun spurious arguments against the wall in the hope that some thing sticks. I'm fully aware of defense counsel tactics."

"Your Honor is very kind," said Sabbatino pleasantly. Lawyers in the front row snickered at his sarcasm. "However, Your Honor cannot seriously be referring to me. Your Honor well knows that I do not present spurious or frivolous arguments. The last two cases I've tried before you—which, of course, ended in conviction—were unanimously reversed on appeal."

"Don't start one of your garrulous speeches, counsel," the judge said testily.

"If counsel needs anything further by way of discovery in this case," Marty interrupted tactfully, "I'll discuss it with them. Perhaps we can agree on the discovery and save the necessity for formal motions."

Sabbatino and Moriarty eyed each other warily, like two brawlers parted by the crowd.

"Does that solve your problem, counsel?" Moriarty needled.

"Let me take care of this, Peter," Brill whispered to Sabbatino. "What's the sense of arguing when the prosecutor says he'll give us what we want?

"We'll accept Your Honor's kind suggestion and the prosecutor's offer," Brill added aloud. "However, a quick perusal of the prosecutor's papers indicates that there are tape recordings in this case. I'd like to ask the prosecutor for the tapes, or at least transcripts of those tapes."

"You're not entitled to any tapes at this juncture," replied the judge. "I have no authority to order the prosecutor to turn over that material."

"The tapes will eventually have to be turned over prior to trial," said Brill. "By having them now, defense counsel could save the court's time."

"I'm sure that's your reason," the judge replied acidly.

"Your Honor, I have no objection to counsel having the tapes at this time," Marty injected as diplomatically as he could.

The judge studied Marty now, with an almost imperceptible, impatient nodding of his head. He had his own idea of defendants, innocence, guilt, and trials, and any deviation therefrom was not received kindly, even when it was the act of the prosecutor.

"Well, Mr. Boxer," the judge allowed reluctantly, "I cannot stop you from turning over material to the defense. Since you have no obligation to turn such over, I certainly won't force you to do so. Have you discussed this disclosure tactic with your office?"

"I have, Your Honor."

"And Mr. Wright has agreed to this unprecedented, premature disclosure policy?"

"He has left the entire matter to my discretion, Your Honor."

Moriarty studied Marty with narrowed, steely eyes.

Sabbatino piped in. "I wish to note for the record that it is most refreshing to see such constitutionally correct procedures adopted by the special prosecutor."

"Counselor"—Judge Moriarty leaned forward on his bench, literally hissing—"this court is convened neither for your convenience nor your approval. Your remarks, which I know are meant irreverently, are totally unnecessary."

"My remarks are only intended sincerely, Your Honor."

"Are you trying to bait the court?" Moriarty leaned further forward toward the old veteran.

"Certainly not, sir. Your Honor knows me better than that."

Judge Moriarty's eyes were hard with anger, his lips pressed tightly together.

"Your Honor, if we may," said Brill, "we'll retire to the corridor to go over these documents, and perhaps discuss the tapes with the prosecution."

"You do that," said the judge, his eyes still on Sabbatino.

The defense counsel and defendants turned and walked out of the courtroom and into the corridor.

"That prosecutor seems like a decent fellow," said Judge Tauber.

"I hope he stays that way," said Brill. "Peter, I thought Moriarty was going to come over the bench at you."

"He hasn't the balls," replied Sabbatino calmly.

"Do you want to listen to the tapes today?" Brill asked.

"Where? In this corridor?"

"Let's take Boxer up on his offer before Wright changes his mind for him."

"I agree we ought to try and hear them now," said Judge Tauber.

Marty came out of the courtroom and joined them.

"I just looked through the file," said Marty. "I don't seem to have the tapes with me."

The defense group exchanged glances.

"I'll get them from the evidence vault and you can hear them at my office. If you want, supply some blank tapes and I'll make duplicate copies of the tapes for you."

"That's even better," Brill said quickly.

"Whatever other evidence there is, you can have. I want to have this case tried in the fairest possible way."

"I appreciate that very much, Mr. Boxer," said Judge Tauber. "Forgive me if it's out of line for me to speak like this, but I'm quite impressed by your fair attitude."

"It's just as it should be, judge. Nothing more."

"Unfortunately it doesn't always work that way," said Sabbatino.

"Maybe we'll start a new trend," said Marty.

"May I ask you a question?" said Sabbatino.

"Surely."

"Why are you being so cooperative? You're making me nervous."

Marty laughed. "I don't want to have to go back in front of Moriarty either," he replied. "He's not my idea of the way to spend a morning. Besides, isn't this better than the old trial by ambush that Judge Moriarty loves so much?"

"That it is," said Brill.

"In this case, there should be a search for the real truth," Marty added.

"You sound like you know something about this case that we should," said Sabbatino.

"Not really. Facts are facts, aren't they?"

"Not necessarily," Brill replied with a smirk.

SEPTEMBER 30, 1968

THE INTERCOM ON J.T.'S DESK BUZZED.

"Yes?"

"It's Marty, J.T. I have to see you."

"Just the man I wanted to see," J.T. said exuberantly. "I was about to buzz you myself. Come on in."

Within a minute, a very serious Marty took the chair next to J.T.'s desk.

"What's the matter, Otto?" J.T. asked.

"The Tauber case."

"That's just what I was going to talk to you about. I got a call from Judge Moriarty."

"What did he have to say?"

J.T. raised his eyebrows. "He said that he hadn't planned to allow the Tauber defendants all the discovery they asked for, but you up and gave it away. He is concerned we'll create an unnecessary precedent."

"That's very fair and impartial of him," said Marty.

"What does fair or impartial have to do with Judge Moriarty?" J.T. chided. "I know you're somewhat more emotionally involved than usual in this case," J.T. continued, "but we really ought not position ourselves to be embarrassed in our other cases."

"You may be in line for a great deal of embarrassment with this case," Marty said gravely.

"How's that?"

"Since you've already read the grand jury minutes in the Tauber case, I assume you remember that our phony robbery defendant, Rainone, testified that after Judge Tauber sent him to his son, Randolph concocted a phony defense for him. Rainone said Randolph wanted him to testify that the complainant was really a fag, and that he made a pass at Rainone, and because Rainone rebuffed him, the complainant went and made the original complaint."

"Yes. I remember."

"I assume you also remember that Randolph Tauber testified at our grand jury that he did *not* advise Rainone to make up a phony alibi? Young Tauber testified he told his client that he could not take the stand because he had such a bad record—the bogus one our office pumped into the computer for him. You remember that too?"

"Yes, I remember that too." J.T. listened carefully.

"And, based mainly on that conflict in the grand jury testimony, Tauber and his son were indicted."

"There's a little more to it, but basically that's correct. Come on, Marty, get to the point. I have to get to a meeting uptown. We're putting our team for the mayoral run together, and I have an appointment with the president of the Regional Teamsters Council. I want to get their endorsement. And some of their money!"

"You may need their money more than you know, when you hear what I have to tell you."

"What is that supposed to mean?"

"This tape," said Marty, taking a cassette from his pocket, "was made by Rainone when he talked to Randolph Tauber."

"What's on it?"

"Tauber very distinctly and audibly tells Rainone *that he cannot take the stand, that his record is so bad that it is impossible to let him appear before a jury.* Therefore, these was no concocted defense—just as young Tauber said."

J.T. said nothing.

"It means, doesn't it, J.T.," Marty continued, "that our undercover man deliberately lied to our grand jury? *Our own tape* makes Rainone's—our witness's—testimony perjurious. We had to know about this. It's our tape! And we let it stand! We sat back and let the indictment lodge against the Taubers and put their careers on the line. And we knew—or should have known—they were telling the truth in front of the grand jury. *They* didn't commit perjury, *our man did*."

"I knew nothing about it," J.T. said flatly.

"This was a special situation that you personally concocted. How could you not know?"

"I didn't know how Levine was going about it, Marty."

"Do you realize how embarrassing this is going to be? You can protest all you want that you didn't know what was going on, but that isn't going to relieve you of legal responsibility when the Taubers sue the State of New York and *you personally* for a jillion dollars."

"Does this tape have to get out?" J.T. asked.

"What?" Marty raged. "Are you suggesting that we suppress this tape, that we let the Taubers go to trial and be convicted, when we know they didn't commit the crimes they're indicted for? You think I'd be a party to that?"

"No, no, of course not. That's not what I meant. You don't think I'd let myself be a party to anything like that either, do you?"

"I'm wondering."

"Jesus, Marty. I said I didn't know about it," J.T. said, offended. "But you're right. I'm going to be held responsible for it. The papers will have a field day dancing on my head. Just when I don't need bad publicity." J.T. winced. "Damn." He pounded his desk with the palm of his hand. "That bastard Levine."

"Why the hell are you blaming Levine? You encouraged him to the hilt to get you this indictment."

"God damn it!" J.T. screamed, flinging everything from his desktop with one sweep of his arm. "Goddamn, goddamn, goddamn, goddamn, goddamn, goddamn."

"And that's putting it mildly," Marty said.

"Sure, you can afford to be clever. You're not the guy out front who's going to be kicked in the ass. The press will flay me. You've got to help me out of this, Marty," J.T. said desperately.

Marty wondered if J.T. was affecting this emotion for his benefit. "Excuse me, but I don't have a lot of sympathy for this situation, J.T."

"What are we going to do?"

"I'm going to turn these tapes over to the defendants."

"What? Marty, the newspapers'll kill me. How can I start a mayoral campaign if you do that? Those liberal rags will have a field day."

"What the hell do you want me to do, let the Taubers get convicted, lose their licenses to practice law, Judge Tauber be defrocked? I told you this scheme of yours was dangerous."

"Okay, okay, so you told me. Now what? I'm in a real jam, and at the wrong time. Couldn't be a worse time."

"Do you realize that all this started because Sergeant Lewis vaguely remembered a rumor that Seymour Fine might have mentioned to a client that he had given money to Judge Tauber? All this from a *rumor!*"

"What do you think we should do?" J.T. wondered absently.

"Even after Seymour Fine insisted he was only reaming a client for a bigger fee, you persisted. You wanted to indict a judge so badly that you went to this length to get a case against Tauber. Did it ever occur to you that Seymour Fine was telling the truth? That he was really just a cheap shyster trying to steal a few extra bucks?"

J.T. shuddered. "Don't mention Seymour Fine's name to me."

"Why, because he committed suicide in a fit of depression over this?"

"Let's talk about the mess we have on our hands now. What should we do, Marty?" J.T. rose and took Marty by the arm. His eyes were round with fright. "Please, Marty, please. I swear I didn't know."

"Get hold of yourself, J.T."

"Suppose, just suppose, that you were me, Marty. What special words in the English language could you use to convince your best friend that you needed help? Are there such special words?"

"All right, all right, just don't beg."

"You believe me?"

"Yes, anything, just so you stop whining. It's demeaning."

"Do you have to give them the tapes right now?" J.T. wondered.

"You're not telling me you want me to suppress these tapes and let the Taubers keep going through emotional torture until the trial?"

"The law doesn't require you to turn them over now. Not until trial, right? Delay the trial so they'll still have plenty of time to prepare. Where's the harm there? Primary's only a few months off. After that, give them their tapes over now. Our entire futures, our careers are on the line."

"*Our* futures?"

"If this office is blasted by headlines suggesting improprieties while you're the chief of staff, you're not going to get a standing ovation out in the job market either, you know. You have a stake in this too, Marty. I'm just asking for a little time."

"Why should the Taubers continue to suffer just to save our hides?"

"We didn't do anything, Marty. We didn't know. Why should we suffer for Levine's insanity?"

Marty hesitated.

J.T. saw that fatal hesitation and smiled to himself. "Besides," he said, "there are other counts to their indictment other than the one about the phony alibi, aren't there? Even if you give them the tapes now, the case wouldn't be over, would it?"

"There's nothing much to the rest of the case, J.T."

"But there is something?"

"Yes."

"Just hold on to the tapes for a little longer. I'll get my mayoral campaign moving so fast we'll fly out of here. Let's leave this hot potato for the next special prosecutor." J.T. jammed his fist down on the intercom button.

"Yes, sir?" the secretary's voice asked.

"Get Stern on the intercom for me," J.T. demanded.

For a few minutes, Marty and J.T. sat silently. J.T. stole an occasional glance at Marty, who was deep in thought. After a short wait, the intercom buzzed.

"Yes?" J.T. said into the phone.

"It's Stern. You wanted me?"

"Call Levine into your office. Fire his ass. Immediately. And make sure he's out of this building in thirty minutes."

"Right," Stern said with pleasure.

"And if he tries to see me, tell him there's nothing to discuss. Get him out of here. Now!"

J.T. looked over to Marty for approval. Marty was staring at the ceiling, unhappy with himself.

"Well, what's wrong now? Isn't that what you wanted?"

"If you fire Levine now, it'll underscore the Tauber situation, won't it?"

J.T. was pensive. "Good thinking, Marty," he said, pushing the intercom button again.

"That's what I was afraid of. I've even learned to think like you."

"Don't fire him," J.T. directed into the intercom. "Just ream him out royally for being a dumb bastard."

OCTOBER 2, 1968

"THIS BOXER FELLOW IS FULL OF BALONEY," Sabbatino said to Brill. "Not that that's a surprise, of course."

"What did he say when you called and asked about the tapes?"

"He said we'll get them. It's just that he's been tied up, and he's planning on leaving the office soon, etcetera. A lot of phony excuses."

"I thought we were actually going to get some discovery well in advance of trial this time. I guess I guessed wrong."

"I've never been a prosecutor, Joe. You have. But I just have never understood why it's skin off the DA's nose to let the defendant get a fair—I mean that—a fair trial."

"Even DAs are human, Peter. They want to win—not put people in jail necessarily, but they do want to do well. You can't do well if your opponent gets all your good stuff."

"But we're dealing with people's lives, Joe, people who are facing jail. This isn't just some business."

"As professionals, defense attorneys purposely, in order to be objective, deal with cases just as cases, not as people. Isn't that true, Peter?"

"True. I don't want to know a thing about my clients or their families. I'd get too involved emotionally, otherwise."

"DAs are in the same professional mold. They aren't dealing with people, they're dealing just with cases."

Sabbatino thought for a moment. "You think Boxer changed his mind, decided to hedge his bet, keep the material to himself until just before the trial?"

"I don't know. You say he's leaving the special prosecutor's office? Perhaps he doesn't want to tie the hands of the fellow who inherits the case."

"In any case, we'll see in a few minutes when we get to court."

"I really feel like a deadbeat," Marty said bitterly to J.T. They were in J.T.'s office, waiting for Stern to fetch the car to take them to Judge Moriarty's court.

"Look, I'm going to have a meeting with DeValen to set up the final arrangements for his retainer. I'm going to ask him for a guarantee—win, lose, or draw in the mayoral campaign—funds for at least one year. This way, at least we know that we'll have the time and the money to get our office going, even if DeValen becomes disenchanted with us."

"Does that mean you're having some doubts about being able to carry this mayoral thing off?"

"Not at all. But I can hedge against the future. Why should we take any chances?"

"I still feel like a deadbeat."

"About what?" J.T. said absently, flipping through some papers he took from a manila envelope.

"About first telling Brill and Sabbatino they could have the discovery, and then having to make up some dreary excuse for not giving it to them. Why the hell am I bothering to tell you? You're not even listening."

"Yes I am. I heard you. You're feeling guilty because you haven't turned over the tapes to the lawyers," he said casually, still studying the papers in his hand. "The papers I'm looking at are survey results on people's reaction to my campaign. We had them compiled last week. We're strong in the areas that we figured we'd be strong in—Queens, Brooklyn, Staten Island. In fact, it looks like we're picking up strength."

"When are you resigning from this office?"

"As soon as I have a piece of paper guaranteeing our retainer, with DeValen's signature on it. If I announce my resignation before we have the guarantee, DeValen will have me by the short hairs and could walk away from his promise, and we'd be out in the cold without a job or a private office."

"You don't leave too much to chance, Otto."

"Otto? You know we haven't used that in a long time. Reminds me of the days of our innocence and youth." He thought. "But I'm not that naive Otto I once was."

"We're both far from innocent anymore, J.T. The way we've been slipping and sliding through the narrow cracks doesn't leave much room for innocence."

J.T. shrugged, with a little smile. "We may not fight fair, but we don't often lose."

"I'm sorry to see that's become your philosophy."

"And not yours?"

"Not consciously. Or perhaps I should say, not by conscious choice. But, going along with your ideas without much opposition, I guess that makes me equally guilty."

"That's a rather strong word—guilty."

"Why are you coming to court yourself this morning, J.T.?" Marty asked.

"Balzano set something up with the court reporters. They're going to cover the Tauber case and catch me, accidentally-on-purpose, in action. That'll give them an opportunity to do an article about the campaign. Every bit of publicity is important."

"I should have known you had some devious reason."

"Of course," J.T. smiled. "Now where are we with the case, so I'll know what I'm talking about."

"We're exchanging discovery. At first I told the defense I'd give them the tapes. Now—thanks to you—I've told them that the turnover would have to wait because I'm resigning from the office and I didn't want to do anything that would interfere with what my successor wants to do."

"Good, good." J.T. nodded abstractly, his attention again wandering to the mayoral survey documents.

Marty stopped speaking as he saw J.T. absorbed in his statistics.

"People versus Tauber," called the clerk.

Judge Moriarty glared savagely at Sabbatino as the lawyers and defendants walked to the defense counsel table.

"What's your pleasure, Mr. Wright?" the judge asked, turning toward the prosecutor's table. J.T. was still fascinated with those statistics, which showed that he was liked, wanted, needed, by thousands of people all around the city.

Marty nudged J.T.

"That's not necessary, Marty," J.T. whispered harshly. "I heard him. I believe, Your Honor, that the people are ready for trial," J.T. said aloud.

Of course, J.T. knew that neither he nor anyone else in the office was ready to try the case. But he also knew the defense wasn't ready yet either, as the motions for a Bill of Particulars hadn't yet been decided. Thus it was safe for him to announce his readiness, putting the burden of asking for an adjournment on the defense lawyers.

"Your Honor," said Joe Brill calmly, "apparently there's some mistake on Mr. Wright's part."

J.T. looked up from his statistics. He was well aware that reporters were in the audience, listening, writing.

"The last time we were in court, Mr. Boxer advised us that we would receive all the discovery we needed in order to prepare this case. We have received nothing. While I appreciate that some might think that's what defense counsel should be allowed to prepare a case, I for one admit I am unable to do so."

"Your Honor," said J.T. "We turned over what we believed to be all the discovery material—except, of course, for the tapes. Those will be turned over. I assumed that was everything."

"Your Honor," Sabbatino countered instantly, "since Mr. Wright was not here the last time this case was on the calendar, he may not be aware that Mr. Boxer advised defense counsel that whatever was needed could be obtained without further motions or objection. I'm sure Mr. Boxer recalls that."

J.T.'s mind was absorbed in his documents, preparing for the interview that awaited him.

"That's not necessary," the judge said, smiling. "The fact that Mr. Boxer was attempting to be cooperative doesn't create a compact, bonded and copper-sheathed, which binds the prosecutor to its terms."

"J.T.," Marty whispered, "will you get your face out of those statistics!"

"What is it?"

"Tell them they're going to have everything I told them they'd have."

"You realize there are reporters here waiting to interview me?"

The eyes of the entire courtroom were centered on Marty and J.T.'s whispered conversation.

"Then you'd better announce that you're retiring from this office."

"I can't make that announcement this morning. I told you I had to get something in writing from DeValen first."

"Gentlemen?" the judge said in a kindly fashion.

"Your Honor," said Marty, turning to the judge. "Everything I said the defense would have, they shall indeed have."

The judge's eyes flicked immediately to J.T.

"The tapes, however, are not ready to be turned over at this time," Marty concluded.

"Your Honor," said Sabbatino, "I don't understand why the tapes cannot be turned over now. Particularly since they are the essence of the case."

"You know what is said about looking a gift horse in the mouth."

"I only know a little about the various ends of equine anatomy, Your Honor," said Sabbatino.

"What was that remark, Mr. Sabbatino?" The judge's eyes opened wide, his scrubbed skin turning an angry, bloodless white around the jaw muscles.

"I know little about horses' parts," Sabbatino said calmly.

"If I thought for certain that you meant something snide and insulting to the court, you can rest assured, sir, that I would have you flung into jail for contempt this very minute."

"I certainly did not mean to infer anything other than that I know almost nothing about horses," Sabbatino said innocently.

Sabbatino was at his best under adversity. It seemed to take years of age away from him as he stood straight, facing the judge directly, unafraid, bold, at ease.

"Give me a date, gentlemen," the judge said, staring with narrowed eyes at Sabbatino.

"Three weeks from today, Your Honor," suggested Brill.

"Very well, October twentieth," the judge said. "Call the next case."

"I thought he was going to leap over the bench for sure that time," Brill said softly to Sabbatino as they left the courtroom.

"J.T., J.T.," the reporter from the *Times* called as he stood in the aisle. "Can we talk with you?"

"Sure," said J.T., "let's go out in the corridor."

"I couldn't believe it when Sabbatino called the judge a horse's ass right to his face," the *Times* reporter said.

"He didn't say that, did he?" said J.T.

"He sure as hell did."

They walked to the windows in the corridor.

"What about the mayoral race?" another reporter asked directly. "Are you serious about it? Or is this just a trial balloon?"

"I'm quite serious about the need for New York to have some responsible and strong leadership," J.T. replied.

"Are you prepared to leave the Special Prosecutor's office to run?"

"I am not, at this time, making any announcement that I'm leaving my current post or that I am officially running for the mayor's office. I am considering the matter, I am seriously considering the matter. But I am not prepared right this moment to make a formal announcement."

"When do you think you might be in a position to make an announcement, one way or the other?"

J.T. and Marty exchanged glances.

"Very soon, I should think."

OCTOBER 5, 1968

"IT'S TRUE THAT I NEED GATTI for financial support," J.T. said to DeValen in the back seat of DeValen's limousine. "But I need the Teamsters' endorsement even more."

DeValen nodded agreement.

"Besides," J.T. added, "once I get their endorsement, can their money be far behind?"

"It certainly wouldn't hurt to pump some fresh money into the campaign right at the beginning. It's going to be awfully expensive."

"You won't have to foot all the bills," J.T. assured him. "I'm sure we'll get grassroots support—and contributions—as soon as the campaign is official."

"I'm not complaining about the money, J.T. But there's just so much the IRS will allow my corporations to pay your law office as legal fees."

"I don't think we have to worry about excessive fees just now. I haven't even opened my law offices yet."

"Don't you think you ought to start looking?"

"I will soon."

"When are you resigning as special prosecutor?"

"As soon as possible. The sooner I get some office space located, the sooner I can resign, and the sooner we can get the political campaign off the ground."

"There are terrific public-relations benefits in financing your own campaign out of what the public thinks are your own funds. You can represent yourself as totally independent."

"That's exactly what I have in mind," said J.T. enthusiastically. "We run the campaign with no connections to political parties; as a man of the people, a man who owes nothing to anyone except those people. People are ready for that. They're sick and tired of politicians who have nothing to offer except another freeloader on the public tit."

The limousine headed west on Canal Street, toward the river. Ponte's was a plush restaurant, set in a totally isolated location on West Street, by the Hudson River.

"How long do you think it will take them to replace you, so you can walk away from the prosecutor's job?" DeValen asked.

"It doesn't matter. I've got assistants. Someone in the office can take over temporarily until they find a new head man."

"How about Marty Boxer? He could stay on until they get someone to take over."

"Marty won't stay on. He doesn't want the headache," J.T. said with assurance.

They rode in silence for a few minutes.

"Perhaps we could set up a new corporation for you," said J.T.

"Whatever do I need a new corporation for?"

"So your tax man can justify the kind of start-up fees necessary to finance the mayoral campaign."

"That won't be necessary. At the moment I have so many corporations that as general counsel you could submit almost any kind of bill you wanted, and no one would question it. Of course, we're only talking about seed money. Once you win the nomination, big money will have to start rolling in. We couldn't possibly run an all-out mayoral campaign on the kind of money I could generate."

"I understand."

"That's why it wouldn't hurt too much if you got some Teamster money from Gatti."

"I don't think money is the important thing to push for today. His support would bring in all sorts of other benefits."

The car stopped at Ponte's canopy, and the chauffeur opened the door for them.

Ponte's was red velvet and quiet. The dining room was filled with lunching businessmen.

"May I help you?" asked the maitre d'.

"Mr. Gatti," said DeValen.

"Certainly. This way, gentlemen."

They were escorted to a table in a far corner. Charles Gatti was tall and broad, young, with a confident air and a pleasant smile. The man with him was a bit older, with graying temples. They both stood as Wright and DeValen approached.

"Mr. Wright, Mr. DeValen," Gatti said, shaking their hands, "pleased to meet you. This is Louis Spagnola," he said, indicating his companion.

Gatti was a gentleman union leader, exactly what J.T. had been told to expect. Usually, union officials were just a cut or two above the workingmen they represented. But Gatti was different—educated, bright, personable.

"Care for a drink, gentlemen?" the waiter asked when they were seated.

"We already have wine," Gatti said.

"I'll have a vodka on the rocks," said DeValen.

"I'll just have a little wine with lunch," said J.T.

The waiter turned and left the table.

"I noticed in the papers that your union is in the midst of rather serious—or should I say, sanguine—contract negotiations," DeValen said casually.

"Yes, but there won't be a strike. This will be resolved. I've noticed your office is kept on its toes these days too," Gatti said to J.T.

"Not as hectic as before. I've been putting myself as well as the criminals out of business."

The waiter came with DeValen's drink.

"Bring another bottle of Nozzole Chianti," Gatti said to the waiter.

"Very well, Mr. Gatti."

They ordered lunch from the rolling blackboard menu, and then sat talking pleasantries, avoiding talk of politics or the upcoming mayoral campaign. Their orders arrived and were set before them.

"Since the contract negotiations appear close to resolution, you must be able to concentrate on other things," DeValen said to Gatti, wanting to get the conversation headed in the right direction.

"The shoe is always pinching somewhere on this job," he replied. "I'm off to Washington right after lunch. Management is trying to get their friends in Washington to curtail the power of the unions. But of course politicians respond to votes, and there are more labor votes than there are management votes."

"This Hoffa situation doesn't help much, does it?" said DeValen.

"Bobby Kennedy began a kind of impetus—which is always there under the surface, anyway—to clean labor's house."

J.T. was fascinated by Gatti as he watched him and listened to him. It was no wonder that Gatti was a formidable labor leader. Not only was he intelligent and articulate, but a formidable person, well suited to be a spokesman for his less verbal peers.

"This calamari is terrific," said Spagnola. "Try yours before it gets too cold," he said tactfully to Gatti.

They fell silent as they ate.

After a while, DeValen looked to Gatti. "What do you think of the situation here in the city?" he asked.

"The city's got problems," he said. He sipped some wine. "Substantial problems, mainly financial. And the domino effect is that other problems follow—housing, security, sanitation, and, of course, crime."

"Perhaps the resources of the police and the court system are being dissipated," J.T. suggested.

"Perhaps," agreed Gatti. "But a stronger police department or faster court processing wouldn't eliminate the other problems that breed crime in the low-income communities: substandard housing, high rents, poor services."

"But wouldn't the average man and woman in the street be better able to cope with some of these other problems if they didn't have the fear of being struck down on their way home, if they lived in a community where people could work together in safety, resolving their other problems?"

"There's something to that," Gatti agreed.

A few more passes at the food were made in silence.

"Of course, that doesn't minimize the other problems you've mentioned, Mr. Gatti," said J.T.

"Call me Charles."

"Charles," J.T. smiled.

"Do you feel sufficiently well versed in the city's problems to be the mayor of this town?" Gatti asked J.T. right out.

"No one is born to the mayor's job," J.T. replied, launching into an answer he and DeValen had rehearsed earlier. "No one has the innate capacity to know each and every aspect of the job entirely. But I have two arms, two eyes, and a brain that works at least as well as the next man's. I'm sure I can handle or learn to handle the mayor's responsibilities. Additionally, there are people who presently head up the city's agencies and departments. I wouldn't replace them merely because another mayor appointed them. This city's government, driven by the right man, could effect changes which I think are not only necessary but reasonably within the reach of someone who has the insight and the forcefulness to push in the right direction."

"You think you can get the city's ship back on an even keel, then?"

"What I can conceive, I can achieve."

Gatti smiled. "You certainly haven't lost the silver tongue you had when you were counsel to that committee in Washington."

"Naturally," DeValen added, "we need support from people in all areas."

"Not just money," said J.T. quickly. "We're not talking money. What I'm more concerned about, if I might be frank . . ."

"Please do."

"We need a united effort, people working together to keep this great city—and I mean this sincerely, this is the greatest city in the world—to keep it strong. It's a shame that things are in such disorder now." J.T. frowned. "There has to be a new approach. I have ideas that might work if only people were inspired to believe it could be done."

Gatti sat close mouthed, listening to J.T.

After coffee, the waiter put the check in the middle of the table, like a hockey puck at a faceoff. Spagnola snared it just as DeValen reached for it.

Gatti and Spagnola rode downtown in the back seat of a dark Buick sedan. Gatti's driver was an older man, a retired teamster on pension, dressed in ordinary street clothes. Gatti had fancier cars, and could have a fancier chauffeur, but he kept his public profile toned down. A Cadillac or Lincoln and a liveried chauffeur, would not do for an American labor leader, not when his people were all working stiffs, breaking their backs to make ends meet.

"What did you think of him?" Spagnola asked.

"What did *you* think?"

"I thought the guy really meant what he was saying. I was frankly surprised. He's got a lot of guts. Maybe somebody from left field would be the right ticket. What did you think?"

"He's a treacherous opportunist without a true social conscience. He'd fluctuate into any shape or direction beneficial to himself. I don't believe his motives are as egalitarian as he makes them sound. In addition, I think he's a cocksucker."

Spagnola howled with laughter. So did the driver, still looking ahead. Spagnola, laughing hard, pounded on the back of the driver's seat.

"Hey, take it easy," the driver said sharply.

"Shut up, you old bastard," Spagnola chided the driver familiarly. "I'll have you shipped to an old-age home for broken-down fat people."

"Keep it up," the driver replied in kind. "One of these days, on my lunch hour, I'm going to take you out behind the building, and then we'll see who's an old bastard."

The three of them laughed.

"I guess that means that we don't send him any money?"

"Send him some money," said Gatti. "Not much. But send him something."

"Why are you sending him money if you dislike him?"

"Even a cocksucker could win."

NOVEMBER 1, 1968

DEVALEN AND J.T. sat at a small table near the back of Lutece. The waiter added some chilled white wine to DeValen's crystal glass. J.T. had hardly touched his.

"Of course, I understand that this is a big move on your part, J.T.," DeValen said. "It was I who suggested it, wasn't it? But I never said anything about a written guarantee of a retainer. It appears that you don't trust me."

"Trust has nothing to do with it," J.T. replied, now sipping his wine. "When people you think you can count on for support, people like Gatti, for instance, say they can't come out with an endorsement, leaving me sitting alone on that limb, I start to get a little panicky. Don't attribute my suggestion to a lack of trust in you; attribute it to fright, apprehension on my part. A written guarantee would just give me a little peace of mind, that's all."

DeValen nodded and sipped his wine again. "You certainly can string words together, J.T."

J.T. smiled slightly. "If you have confidence in me, sufficient to be as generous as you intend to be for a year, what is it to make me feel a little more secure? Besides, I'll need something to show the bank so I can make a loan to do all the things I have to do—rent furniture, that sort of thing."

"I could simply advise the bank that I guarantee the loans."

The waiter brought two orders of *saucisson en croute*. DeValen had ordered for both of them. J.T. looked at the plate unenthusiastically.

"Come on, J.T., eat. Don't be upset."

"I'm not upset. I'm just realizing that you don't give a tinker's damn about my feelings. You're going to give me the money anyway, so what's the difference if you give me a piece of paper that makes me feel more secure?"

"If a written retainer will make you feel better about going ahead with the campaign, all right, you can have it," DeValen said, rubbing J.T.'s shoulder.

J.T. smiled. He saw flashes of his campaign, his career, a fabulous office. He was on his way. "I appreciate that, George. I really do."

"Now, how about a few days rest away from all this? Rest up before the onslaught."

"I don't know . . ."

"You wanted the guarantee, you got it. I respected your feelings, didn't I? Now I feel like a few days away somewhere, and I'd like you to go with me."

"The agreement gets signed first," J.T. countered with a smile.

"Absolutely," DeValen smiled back. "Where would you like to go?"

NOVEMBER 23, 1968

J.T. STUDIED ANN BOXER, thinking far back to the first time he had met her, that weekend when he came down to New York from Millville to meet Marty, his college Little Brother. His eyes turned to Marty, who was beaming at six-year-old Muffy.

"Come on, Uncle J.T., you play too," said Muffy, coming over to J.T., taking his hand in her tiny fingers.

"Okay, Muffy," J.T. agreed, although he didn't much like playing with children.

Muffy walked J.T. to where Marty was standing. "Patty cake, patty cake," Muffy began, touching Marty's hand, then J.T.'s.

J.T. looked at Marty. There was something aloof in Marty's attitude lately. He had obtained DeValen's written agreement to finance their law office at a handsome annual retainer, he had announced his resignation from the Special Prosecutor's office, everything that Marty had wanted had been done, and yet there was some sort of unfriendliness.

". . . baker's man, bake me a cake . . ."

Marty looked away from J.T. The Tauber affair was what had started his stomach churning. Having to look the fool, in front of the court, in front of his peers, in front of everyone, was crushing. And after that, it really didn't matter what plans J.T. had, what agreements he made with DeValen.

"... as fast as you can ... pat it ..."

J.T. was watching the little girl tapping her little fist on top of her father's, his, her own, over and over. Marty said he'd stay on during the mayoral campaign as long as it lasted, he'd run the law office, but he wouldn't stay on after that. God, that was a swift kick in the ass.

"... and bake it ..."

Marty didn't know exactly where he was going to work, what he was going to do, now that he had advised J.T. that he wouldn't be practicing law with him. But J.T.'s voracious appetite for publicity and public acclaim was carrying him to reckless heights, and Marty had had enough of it.

"... mark it with an 'O' ..."

I'll have to get somebody to replace Marty in the office, J.T. thought. That was going to be tough. Plenty of people would take a high salary, but dedication was a hard commodity to come by. Phil Levine had contacted him recently, wanting to work on the campaign. J.T. looked at Marty as he thought about Phil Levine. He might not be charming, but Levine was crafty and dedicated.

"... and put it in the oven ..."

Marty truly felt badly that he wouldn't be there to sit on J.T. when his wild imagination got going. *What's going to happen to Big Brother?* Marty wondered sincerely.

Flashes of years spun through both men's minds as their eyes were directed, if not focused on, the little girl: years at Browning, congressional hearings, the law firm, Bedardo, the special prosecutor's office. They each thought different thoughts about different times, but each reminisced as he saw their curtain coming down.

"... for Daddy Otto, and Uncle Otto, and Muffy Otto three," Muffy squealed happily.

JANUARY 23, 1969

THE LAW OFFICE OF MESERVE, DEVERAUX, AND PELHAM had occupied the nineteenth floor of the Woolworth Building for forty-seven years. The chambers themselves were large by today's standards, particularly since only William Deveraux, a man seventy-five years of age—although he carried himself as if he were much older—remained in active practice, with one spinster secretary. In days gone by, the firm had thrived with three partners, five associates, and assorted secretaries, clerks, and other personnel. The other partners had long since dissolved their earthly associations and gone on to represent ethereal clients, and the firm's corporate contacts had also joined the ranks of the sublime. There was little happening in the spacious, antiquated offices on the Broadway side of the building—that is, until J.T. Wright entered the picture. J.T. wanted to take over a well-established, old-line firm, the better to jump into the middle of the lists of legal battle without delay or hesitation. Old Deveraux's firm was perfect for that purpose. Almost moribund, with a grand name and tradition, J.T. could get the firm he wanted at the price he wanted.

J.T., at several lunches, breathed some fire back into old Deveraux, convinced him that the grand old firm could rise once more;

that its respected name, typed onto legal documents, could once more be tossed across court clerks' desks, added to calendars; that the old leather couches could once again support impatient clients. Deveraux looked as antique as the office, but was always well dressed and agile, if occasionally forgetful. He was familiar with J.T.'s publicized activities over the last dozen years. He caught a glimpse of J.T.'s infectious vision of youth again, of once again being needed by clients in straits beyond their understanding. And not unwelcome was the arrangement that Deveraux would share in all fees J.T. generated, in return for J.T.'s being allowed to operate under the firm's revered banner.

Marty had quickly resigned from the Special Prosecutor's office one week after J.T. called a sprawling press conference and announced both his resignation as Special Prosecutor and his candidacy for mayor. Marty agreed to run the Woolworth Building law offices during—only during—the campaign.

Marty's first act after putting his new desk in order was to take the elevator down to the twelfth floor and make his way directly to the law offices of Peter L. F. Sabbatino.

A few minutes after the receptionist had announced Marty, Peter Sabbatino, in his shirtsleeves, a law book in his hand, appeared at the doorway of the reception room. He was looking at Marty with surprise.

"How are you, Mr. Boxer?" asked Sabbatino, extending his hand. "Come in, won't you?"

Marty followed Sabbatino through a corridor to a corner office cluttered with open law books, piles of documents, and research notes. Marty was certain the furniture was under there somewhere.

"I'm just in the middle of writing a brief," Sabbatino explained.

"Then I'll only take a minute," said Marty. "I've wound up my affairs in the special prosecutor's office, and J.T. Wright and I have joined a firm here in the building."

"Oh, really? Which one?"

"Meserve, Deveraux, and Pelham."

"Christ, is old Deveraux still practicing? That's a real old-line corporate firm."

"I don't anticipate being with them long," Marty said.

"Oh? Have something on the fire?"

"While J.T. is running his campaign, I'll be with him. After that, I'm going to find something else."

The two men were silent. Sabbatino wondered if, perhaps, Marty wanted an interview for a job.

"As I said," Marty began, realizing Sabbatino was waiting for him to start, "I've just about wound up all my affairs in the special prosecutor's office. Before I left, I wrote a letter to you in connection with the Tauber case, and I enclosed the tapes you wanted."

"I didn't get it," Sabbatino said with concern.

"Instead of mailing it, I decided to deliver it by hand." Marty opened his briefcase and produced a manila envelope.

Sabbatino could hardly conceal his surprise. He took the envelope, his eyes still fixed on Marty.

"I'm a little surprised, frankly," said Sabbatino. "Pleasantly, but still surprised."

"You shouldn't be. There are people, even prosecutors, who keep their word."

"I'm delighted. I had given up on getting these tapes much before trial. Particularly when we heard that you were no longer going to be handling the case."

"I hope they'll be helpful to you," Marty said. "J.T. and I, both of us, agreed you should have them now. He is fully aware of my being here, and approves of it. So if you get something of value out of them, it comes through the good graces of J.T. Wright."

"What are you trying to tell me, Mr. Boxer?"

"Simply that J.T. is running for mayor now, and he doesn't need any controversy coming back to haunt him about things that happened while he was the special prosecutor."

"If you're saying that you don't want me to run to the newspaper with anything that might be in these tapes, you needn't worry. I'm a lawyer, not a newspaper personality. I'll use these in court, if there's anything in them that's helpful. Is that what you were concerned about?"

"Precisely." Marty rose and reached to shake Sabbatino's hand.

"I appreciate what you've done," said Sabbatino. "Tell Mr. Wright the same. Although I doubt he was the moving force behind this."

For a few moments, Sabbatino stood still, looking at the door through which Marty had left. Then he picked up his phone and dialed Joe Brill's number.

"Come on, Marty, let's get a move on," urged J.T. as Marty entered the office. "We have to get uptown for a mini-debate and the press conference at the Roosevelt Hotel. I have a car waiting downstairs for us."

"A car? You didn't hire Stern to come over here to work, did you?"

"No, it's DeValen's car, the limousine. He's put it at our disposal for the campaign."

The two men took the elevator down to the front entrance and got into the limousine.

"When did the mini-debate come about?" Marty asked as they rode uptown. "I didn't see it on the schedule."

"I challenged the other Republican candidates to meet in a forum. Both the regular candidate and the other challenger accepted. We're going to have an open interview with all the media. The regular candidate accepted when he heard all the media would be there," J.T. laughed. "I made it short notice so the opposition wouldn't have much time to prepare."

"Did you study the position papers we drew up for you on the issues?"

"I have them with me. I didn't get a chance to read them yet, I've been so busy. Tell me about them."

"Christmas, J.T. I can't fill you in on the issues on one auto ride uptown."

"You'd better try. We're already at Canal Street and I'm going to be on the firing line in a few minutes."

"How can you run a campaign and not know what you're talking about?"

"Why should I be different from anyone else?"

"Very clever. The main issues are fiscal reform and safety in the streets. They're the issues on people's minds."

"That's easy enough. Fiscal reform—eliminate wasteful programs, overemployment by governmental agencies, cut the fat out of agencies, cut taxes. Safety in the streets—start throwing the crumbs in jails, permanently. You know," J.T. mused as the car passed through Little Italy, "I wonder if we should contact some of Bedardo's people. Maybe they could help us with the Italian vote."

"You'd let them campaign for you?"

"Not openly. But they have a lot of influence in certain areas. Italians are the biggest voting block in the city."

"I think you're crazy."

"If it weren't for being crazy, I'd have gone mad years ago," J.T. wisecracked. "Besides, I'm too clever to get my hand caught in any cookie jar."

Thinking about what J.T. had said, Marty realized that J.T. was becoming more and more reckless. His plans lately had little to do with reality. Something was driving him to higher heights, regardless of the solidity of the foothold below.

"Where is this interview supposed to take place?" Marty asked as the car pulled up to the Roosevelt Hotel.

"In one of the small conference rooms, I think. I'm not sure. We'll have to go to the Republican County Committee office, they've got their offices here."

"I'm sorry, Mr. Albanese's not here," said a woman official of the Republican County Committee. "Unfortunately, the joint press conference has been called off, Mr. Wright. We tried to call your office, but you had already left."

"Where are the reporters?"

"The media people were advised that it was called off. There's no one here."

"That's a hell of a thing," J.T. said angrily. "I called the press conference! Your candidate accepted. What happened, did he get cold feet?"

"I'm sure that's not the case. I don't know why the conference was called off. I was just advised of it by Mr. Albanese on the phone. I didn't have a thing to do with it. I'm sorry."

"Tell Mr. Albanese I'll be in touch with him," said J.T. angrily, turning to leave.

"Very well."

"Can you imagine this?" J.T. asked Marty as they made their way down to the lobby. "They probably were afraid to let their pantywaist candidate get on the same floor with me. I'd talk him through the wall."

One thing was certain, J.T. had enough gall to be mayor, Marty thought to himself.

Chauncey Delafield stood at the Reynoldses' library window, looking down at the ice floes in the river, sliding ponderously seaward on the tide. He could hear the rustling of a newspaper behind him as Archie Reynolds studied each page.

"Grand, grand," chortled Reynolds.

"What's that, Archie?"

A servant came in with a silver pot of coffee on a silver tray.

"Sure you won't have anything, Chauncey? Tea, coffee?"

"On second thought, perhaps I'll have a Bloody Mary, not too spicy."

The servant nodded and left the room.

"Not a word on this page either about that little twerp Wright," Reynolds said gleefully, turning the page.

Delafield shrugged slightly to himself, thinking that Archie was taking this nonsense of trying to block Wright's campaign a little too seriously.

"Albanese and I had cocktails day before yesterday. He told me about a joint conference Wright had put together for yesterday. I told Joe to scotch it." Reynolds laughed. "Nothing here either. Told him to let Wright go ahead and spend his money on posters, brochures, whatever. But no debates, no conferences, no opportunities for free publicity. Let the bastard go broke buying coverage." Reynolds kept turning pages. "That candidate Joe is backing is nothing to write home about. Otherwise he wouldn't have agreed to the damn press conference to begin with. Wright'd probably kick the stuffing out of him and come off looking good. He isn't going to look good anytime I can help it."

"Aren't you spending a little too much time on this? None of those Republican primary candidates are going to beat Livingston, anyway."

"Ah, but it's the *way* Wright loses, not just his defeat. I want him humiliated."

The servant entered with a large Bloody Mary.

"Thank you," said Delafield, seeking some solace.

Reynolds pored over the paper, laughing gleefully from time to time.

"The newspapers are doing a pretty good job of burying Wright's stories, too."

"You talked to the newspaper publishers, no doubt."

"Everyone I could get to," Reynolds laughed. "And buying as much advertising space as I do, I got to a lot of them. Wright bit off a bit more than he could chew when he trifled with Reynolds. I'll make sure he never has any kind of career in politics."

FEBRUARY 3, 1969

"CAN YOU EXPLAIN TO ME how a son of a bitch like Wright could live with himself?" demanded Sabbatino. A small tape recorder on Joe Brill's desk played—for the second time—the tapes Marty had turned over to them. Judge Tauber's gaze was fixed on the tape player, his head shaking slowly in disbelief. "These tapes confirm just what your son said all along, Judge. He never put together a phony defense for Rainone. He told him he couldn't take the stand."

"It's outright subornation of perjury," Brill said gravely.

"No question about that," agreed Sabbatino. "It's unbelievable that a lawyer could do something like this, jeopardize a judge's career, another lawyer's license."

"I'm just glad that Boxer is a man who still has some conscience," said Judge Tauber.

"What do you think about Boxer's part in this?" Brill asked Sabbatino.

"I go along with the judge. He wanted us to have these tapes all along. Wright was the one who held the whole thing up."

"What do you want to do now?"

"My opinion," said Sabbatino, "is that we should be very calm, do nothing precipitous. We make our motions. When this indictment is thrown out—as it must be—Wright's going to look like one hell of a fool."

"More than a fool," added Brill. "A dishonest, treacherous creature, capable of anything for his own glory. He takes the world's fame and glory as if it's real."

"You know, Joe," the judge said thoughtfully, "since the indictment, I've had plenty of time on my hands. I watched and listened as my life, my son's life, slowly disintegrated in the poisonous atmosphere of the indictment. I'd rather my leisure hadn't been forced upon me so violently. That part of it has been a nightmare. But I guess without it I wouldn't have taken the time to think, to reflect. You get so tied up in work, getting ahead, prestige, you don't realize certain things."

"Like?" Sabbatino asked. The binding pressure of the case having been eased, the three lawyers were relaxed.

"Like the fact that we're just people," the judge said. "That may not sound too profound, but it's something people in demanding, responsible positions tend to lose sight of. As judges, and trial lawyers, we get so involved in our day-in, day-out activities, they become the important force in our lives. And that constant work, those activities, a little at a time, build a shell up around us, until our work is all we're involved in. We lose touch with the reality that our so-called important tasks are so meaningless in the crucible of time. Take me, for instance, a Supreme Court judge . . ."

"And a *good* judge," Brill added.

"Good or bad, suddenly I'm indicted, I'm suspended from the bench. Who am I now? A leper. People I've known for years see me in the street and walk the other way, friends avoid me. Who am I? Who had I thought I was? Oh, the black robes surround you with a feeling of power and importance. But that's so fleeting, so ephemeral. In the face of nature, reality, eternity, it's nothing. We're all just nothing."

"That's not a very positive note" said Sabbatino.

"It really is, Peter. Because when you get past this fantasy you've been feeding yourself about how important you are, how important your work is, you suddenly see yourself clearly in reference to the rest of the world, the rest of humanity."

"And?" wondered Brill.

"And maybe that's when a person can get back his compassion." The judge lit a cigar, the flame at the end of the match leaping high as he puffed. He sat back, crossing one leg over the other. "There was a time when I was full of piss and vinegar. When I was young, first starting out. There was only black and white, no gray. And I was going to lick the world."

"We all were."

"True enough," the judge smiled. "And then we get a little older and a little jaded, too taken up with all our tasks to take much notice of things. And we get to thinking that when we were young, full of those grand ideals, we were just unrealistic, too inexperienced to realize what the real world is like."

Brill and Sabbatino were listening attentively.

"Well, with this indictment, I've had time to realize that our petty careers, our twenty years on the bench, our pensions, are nothing. Babylon, a city of a million people, disappeared, along with everything that was in it, into the desert sands. All that remains of it are a couple of stone tablets. Who knows if there were twenty Babylons before Babylon, that have disappeared into the same desert, that were literally wiped from the face of the earth? There were rich men in those cultures, and judges, and lawyers. And they all might have thought their lives, their functions were important beyond measure. But what do all their pretensions mean now?"

The judge blew out a plume of smoke, which drifted silently toward the ceiling.

"And when that worldly importance is lost, maybe the only thing that's really important is an awareness of the next person's frailty and humanity. We should look at the next person we see on the street and realize he's in the same boat, struggling just to get through the world. Stepping over people, on people, to get ahead, that's ridiculous. In the crucible of time, there's no place to go, nothing to accomplish that can't or won't disappear. So we might as well be compassionate to each other. That's where J.T. Wright comes in. He's a classic example of someone whose values are totally warped. He still thinks this game, all the trappings of worldly gain and glory, are for real. He doesn't realize how ridiculous, how transient, all his treachery is."

"*Sic transit gloria mundi*," said Sabbatino abstractly.

The three of them were silent, wistful.

"Speaking of treachery, we still have this indictment to deal with," said Brill lightly, bringing them back into focus.

"Boxer said that Wright agreed to turn over the tapes," Sabbatino said.

"I don't believe that for a moment," said Brill. "He's probably just trying to save Wright's election chances, hoping that we won't make waves at a press conference."

"That's probably true," said the judge. "But I think we ought to respect Boxer's wishes. He certainly wasn't looking to hurt us."

"Does that mean we shouldn't use these tapes to get your indictment thrown out?"

"Of course we should. We just don't have to go out of our way to get publicity. We'll just make whatever motions are appropriate, as you said, and the rest will take care of itself."

"When we make the motion, and the indictment is thrown out," said Brill, "the newspapers will pick it up all by themselves. We won't have to go out of our way."

"That's exactly what I mean," said the judge. "It will all work out by itself. Mr. Wright will get what he deserves without us having to lift a finger."

"Let's get going," Sabbatino said anxiously.

MAY 31, 1969

"THIS CITY NEEDS SOME LAW AND ORDER—now!" J.T.'s amplified voice echoed across the hot, sunlit picnic grounds. To the left of the small, flag-draped platform on which J.T. stood, frankfurters, hamburgers, and corn were being cooked on a large charcoal fire. There were tubs of cold soda and kegs of beer. Before him was a large array of eager faces, men and women, bandannaed, sunglassed, cigar-chomping, smiling, hanging on his every word. A cheer lifted to the skies.

"Tell 'em good, J.T.," urged a potbellied man from the crowd.

"Yeah," agreed another.

In the background, beyond the crowd, J.T. could see men playing softball and kids running and chasing each other.

"The present administration, and all of the other candidates, are only going to give you more of the same giveaway programs, free-loaders living off your backs . . ."

Jeers, whistles.

". . . giving away your safety to pampered criminals who go through our justice system like it's a turnstile in a subway."

The crowd roared lustily.

"Sock it to 'em, J.T."

"Giving away your taxes to people upstate. You pay the taxes, and the farmers live off them."

"He's right . . . That's it, J.T."

"Atta boy!"

"I intend to do something that other candidates wouldn't dream of doing because they haven't got the backbone to stand up to the bloodsuckers and parasites and tell them the way it's got to be. Hardworking people refuse to work half their work week just to support giveaway programs and social-service departments for lazy loafers. The parade is over. The free ride has stopped!"

Joy . . . ecstasy . . . just what the crowd wanted to hear.

J.T. watched over the crowd as someone in red shorts rounded the bases on the softball diamond.

A young boy off to the right of the platform was crying loudly. His kite had plummeted to the ground and broken. His mother bent over him, a can of beer in one hand, a cigarette in the other.

This was the Memorial Day outing for the combined Ridgewood/Jamaica Estates/Whitestone, Queens PTAs, in Alley Pond Park. Just behind the platform, DeValen and Marty listened, gauging the crowd's reactions. Marty sipped beer.

"So remember, when primary day rolls around, if you want to get the loafers off your back . . ."

"And into jail, where the creeps belong," added an overenthusiastic listener.

Cheers.

". . . to get those loafers off your back," J.T. continued, "vote for J.T. Wright. Wright can't be wrong." He raised both hands over his head in a victory salute.

The cheers grew louder. Admirers pounded J.T.'s back as he stepped off the platform. Slowly he moved through the crowd toward the car where Marty and DeValen waited.

"What did you think of the speech?" J.T. asked as they headed back to Manhattan in Marty's car. J.T. had told DeValen not to bring the limousine. It would have given the wrong impression to the people who formed J.T.'s constituency.

"You worked the crowd like a hypnotist," DeValen praised.

Marty nodded silently.

"Didn't you like it, Marty?" J.T. urged. "Didn't we say it? Didn't we say what the people wanted to hear?"

"No question. You said what the people wanted to hear."

"No question about that," said DeValen.

"What's wrong with that?" asked J.T., seeing Marty's lack of enthusiasm.

"When the media reports what you said to these people, it's going to turn off a lot of other people. I don't think you can win an election with just the support of middle-class conservatives from Staten Island, Queens, and Brooklyn."

"Do you realize what you're saying? Do you really think we can't win a citywide election with the support of three of the five boroughs of the city, two of which are the most populated boroughs in the city? You can't convince me that we can lose with that kind of support as our backbone. That backbone is the backbone of the city."

"What about the Jewish communities, the blacks, the Hispanics, who live in Queens, Brooklyn, and Staten Island? They're not going to buy your kind of programs. And remember, a lot of the people in those boroughs are Democrats. When you eliminate the hard-and-fast Democrats, and the liberals who will not buy your cutting off social services, and then eliminate the economically depressed, you're eliminating a lot of people."

"I don't see it that way, Marty. Everywhere we go, people are jumping and cheering at every word I say."

"That's true. But you're only going to select places, where you know the audiences favor your position."

"There'll be a groundswell effect, starting from word of mouth," DeValen argued.

"But is there enough time and enough word of mouth to carry us?"

"It's coming together," said J.T. "I know it is. Besides, when we get past the Republican primary, we'll tone down some of the John Birch stuff so we can pull in more of the Democrats."

"I don't think it's wise to play both sides like that."

"It's always worked before," J.T. said coolly.

JUNE 6, 1969

"MEET J.T. WRIGHT, your next mayor," an enthusiastic campaign worker called out into the early-morning sunlight as people streamed toward the subway entrance on Queens Boulevard. He pointed to the candidate, who stood by the steps wearing a big button on his lapel that proclaimed, "I'm J.T. Wright."

"Good morning, I'm J.T. Wright," J.T. said, reaching out his hand to a man in a business suit. "I need your vote in the primary." He shook the limp hand of a woman in slacks. "Good morning, I'm J.T. Wright. I need your vote, too." Two young girls giggled nervously behind their palms. "Hello, I'm J.T. Wright. I need your vote for mayor."

The crowd was a constant flow down the stairway. Some were greeted by J.T. personally, others received campaign literature from two young girls in plastic hats that were supposed to look like straw boaters with red, white, and blue hatbands.

"You sure LaGuardia started this way?" J.T. whispered to the man who stood beside him, Harold Rottenberg, the public-relations advisor DeValen had hired. He smiled and shook an elderly woman's hand.

"I certainly hope that once you're mayor, you'll do something about those awful young men who hang around on the corner at

183rd Road," the elderly woman said to J.T. "It's simply a disgrace. I think they're dope fiends. It's just awful when decent folks can't get any sleep."

"One of my first priorities is to get riffraff off the streets," J.T. assured her.

"God bless you," the old woman exclaimed, shaking J.T.'s hand again.

"I know it's tough, J.T.," said Rottenberg, "but this is the way it has to be done. You've got to get out and meet the people."

"Good morning, I'm J.T. Wright." He shook hands with a black man in shirtsleeves. He turned back to Rottenberg. "But this way I'm meeting fifty, maybe seventy people. There are millions of people in New York City. I can't shake millions of hands."

"You can try," Rottenberg laughed.

"I can't help but think this is old-fashioned, a throwback to the days when they didn't have anything but a tomtom to send out messages. Good morning, I'm J.T. Wright." He shook hands with another man, then a woman.

"Good luck, J.T.," said a man who shook his hand. "You get my vote."

"Listen, J.T., in 1954, 1953, something like that, Harriman ran for governor. There were eleven thousand districts in the state at that time, and he won the election by a plurality of only eleven thousand votes. One vote per election district. You don't know if this next person you talk to is the one that's going to put you over the top. A little personal touch is important."

"Good morning, I'm J.T. Wright. I really need your vote on primary day."

"That's not so difficult, is it?" Rottenberg whispered.

"How long are we going to stay here?" J.T. whispered back.

"About another five minutes. We have a breakfast meeting with the Fifth Avenue Association. On the way, we'll stop at the Roosevelt Avenue subway entrance. That's a big station, like this one. We'll spend ten minutes there."

"Oh brother."

"Listen, J.T., this may seem slow, but if you do this every morning for fifteen or twenty minutes, you'll have shaken hands with sixty or seventy thousand people."

After a few more minutes, when there was a lull in the flow of people, Rottenberg looked at his watch.

"Let's go, Marty," he called. Marty had been overseeing the distribution of campaign literature at the subway entrance across the street. "Let's get our people together, we're going to head back toward the city."

"Okay," said Marty, handing a pamphlet to a young man and his girlfriend. He handed another woman a campaign button. Despite his resolve, Marty hadn't totally abandoned J.T.'s efforts.

The car Marty drove toward Manhattan was covered with placards reading WRIGHT CAN'T BE WRONG. J.T. and Rottenberg were in the back seat. Another car, equally placard-covered, crammed with their workers, followed close behind. They were using rented cars now, because Rottenberg had decided that DeValen's big limousine did not project the right image. DeValen had personally hired Rottenberg because he had brought about some very impressive results in recent New York elections, and was now considered an image-maker *extraordinaire*.

"Tell me what I'm supposed to do with the Fifth Avenue Association," J.T. said as they rode.

"Naturally, they're business-oriented. They own shops and businesses in the Fifth Avenue area and they like anything that's going to make it easier to bring customers in or lighten their tax burden. They're interested in *macha leben*, making a living."

"So what are we suggesting to them? Better traffic control, more parking, a shopping mall? We'll shut Fifth Avenue to vehicular traffic . . ."

"They'd love to hear that, J.T., but you have to give them something they know is feasible."

"Is a feasibility study for such a mall reasonable? Maybe Fifth Avenue can be closed weekends. Who knows? We'll say we'll look into it."

"I think they'd like to hear that you'll impose an austerity program in the city's fiscal affairs that will result in lowered taxes."

J.T. nodded as he made a mental note. "Are these people voters, though? Are there enough of them to make a difference in the campaign?"

"It's not *them*, J.T., it's their endorsement. If we can announce a new endorsement in the media every day, one day business people, the next day labor, the public will start to move with you, get on your bandwagon. This is how we build a groundswell of support for you."

"How are we doing with endorsements?"

Rottenberg looked forward, shrugged. "We're just starting to make inroads. It takes time for people to accept an independent as a serious candidate. Especially in the primary. Usually only local party workers vote on primary day."

"How can we win then?"

"We have to create a desire on the part of the people to get the old politicians out and get some new, young blood—you—in. We have to make the election interesting, stir things up, get people who aren't the political hacks to the election booths."

"Is this the corner you want, Harold?" Marty asked.

"Stop at the far corner," Rottenberg said.

Marty found a parking space not far from the subway stairs. J.T. waited in the car while Marty and Rottenberg got out and strategically placed the workers.

"Meet J.T. Wright, your next mayor," the hawker started shouting at the crowd. "Meet J.T. Wright."

"Okay, J.T.," said Rottenberg.

J.T. adjusted his big identity button and moved out of the car. A few people cheered.

"Hello, I'm J.T. Wright. I need your vote on primary day." He shook hands with a young black girl who looked like a secretary.

"Meet J.T. Wright, your next mayor."

"Hello, I'm J.T. Wright. I need your vote on primary day, Hello, I'm J.T. Wright. I need your vote, too, on primary day. Hello. I'm J.T. Wright. I need your vote on primary day . . ."

Marty watched J.T. energetically work the crowd. He was impressed with J.T.'s capacity to exude charm and warmth at will. Marty wondered if all the world of renown and success was as much a charade as this.

JUNE 18, 1969

"I'LL TRY AND PITCH YOU SOME GOOD QUESTIONS," Sam Reiber, the *New York Post* reporter, said as an aside to J.T. "It'll give you a chance to make some points. The others are going to try to really stick it to you."

Reiber was a regular member of J.T.'s Mountaineers' Club. Since the mayoral campaign began, the club had seen a resurgence, particularly since DeValen was kind enough not only to fund J.T.'s operation, but to throw in the services of his party girls. J.T. had asked Reiber to sit in on the press conference, which he had called in response to mounting pressure from the media about the Tauber case. He wanted to neutralize the open criticism that had surfaced.

The small conference room at the Americana was crowded with media people. The TV crews were frantically setting up their cameras and lights. Marty and Rottenberg were standing by a lectern near the front of the room.

"They're ready now," Rottenberg said, walking to J.T.

"Should Marty stand with me, or should I—"

"You take it by yourself, J.T.," said Rottenberg "After all, you're the candidate."

As J.T. walked toward the lectern, a murmur arose. Camera lights flashed on and reporters moved in closer. They all seemed to have hand microphones, and all shoved them forward together.

"Let's go, gentlemen—and ladies," said J.T., a fleeting smile creasing his lips as he spied two newswomen in the audience. He pointed at a random reporter.

"Mr. Wright, what's your reaction now that the Tauber indictment has been thrown out?"

"My reaction is the same as it would be in any case. The rule of law must prevail. When a court indicates that an indictment should be dismissed, it should be dismissed. That's the judicial process."

"What do you have to say about the court's assertion that certain tapes had been withheld from the grand jury, tapes which supported the defendants' testimony?" shot another reporter over the babble of questions from everywhere.

"I was personally unaware of that. However, were I still the special prosecutor, I would investigate such a charge and prosecute the person responsible to the fullest extent of the law. I urge whomever the Governor appoints as the new special prosecutor to do so."

"Are you saying, then, that you had no idea that the Taubers were indicted on contrived evidence?" shot a voice from somewhere. A dozen handheld microphones were aimed at J.T.'s heart.

"I did not present the evidence to the grand jury, and yes, I state emphatically that I was unaware that any tapes, or any exculpatory evidence, were withheld."

"How can you absolve yourself from a situation many people in the legal profession have called a disgrace, when you were the special prosecutor in whose name the indictment was brought?"

"I don't know to whom you refer in the legal profession, and the case against Judge Tauber was brought in the name of the people of the State of New York. True, I was special prosecutor at the time, and certainly I cannot, nor would I, shirk my responsibility. However, I should note that the special prosecutor's office is entrusted only with the responsibility of securing evidence and prosecuting. Everything in this case was done according to the books, and if Judge Tauber has passed the test of law, then the indictment deserves to be thrown out."

"Do you feel in any way responsible to Judge Tauber or his son for causing such disruption in their lives for the many, many months that the case dragged on?"

"I'm sure Judge Tauber would agree with me that the processes of justice must be equally applied to all—judges, lawyers . . ."

"Even special prosecutors?" one voice shouted in the back of the crowd.

J.T. looked askance momentarily in the direction of the voice.

"That's a question for you," Peter Sabbatino said to the television set. He was watching an evening rebroadcast of J.T.'s press conference. "I wonder if Joe Brill is watching this?" He dialed the phone next to his chair as he continued to watch.

"Hello, Joe. Peter. You watching television? Good. I'll call you back as soon as it's over."

"Do you have any comments on the fact that polls show you slipping further and further behind the regular Republican candidate?" asked a reporter on the television set in Archie Reynolds' library.

Archie had his feet up on a comfortable hassock, watching the evening news, when the segment about J.T. Wright's press conference came on the air. His feet instantly hit the ground and he leaned forward to catch every word.

Chauncey Delafield was in his own apartment, watching the reflection of the television in the mirror above the library bar as he poured vodka over ice. He listened to J.T. intently as he explained:

"Polls seem to reflect the political affiliation of the pollster. We have taken our own survey recently, and it shows that rather than losing strength, we're gaining sharply."

"The *Times* poll shows you with only about seven percent of the vote."

"The attitude of the *Times* shows that I have very little popularity at the editorial offices of the *Times*, so I wouldn't doubt that their poll reflects poorly on me. As I said, it depends on whom the pollsters poll."

"Are you saying the *New York Times* poll is rigged?" asked the *Times* reporter.

"I'm saying that there are a lot of polls and many have differing results. That speaks for itself."

"The poll from the *Daily News* indicates you've declined just as much as the *Times* poll does. Are you saying they are both wrong and do not reflect the true picture?" pressed the *Times* reporter with as much indignation as he could muster for the cameras.

"Squirm, you son of a bitch," Reynolds hissed through clenched teeth at the television screen.

"I believe I've already answered that question," said J.T.

"I don't believe you have," the *Times* reporter shot back.

"Shall we take a poll to find out if I answered the question or not?" J.T. asked acidly. There was some laughter.

Delafield was seated in his chair now, sipping his drink, watching the TV impassively. He still had to admire J.T. He could fend off twenty hostile questioners and still not look like he was having his brains kicked out.

"Mr. Geofrion, please," Archie Reynolds said into the telephone as he absently watched the sports newscast giving the early season base-ball scores. "Jeff," he said happily into the phone, "I just watched that reporter of yours at Wright's throat. It was great." Pause. "Oh, abso-lutely. Keep up the good work. Yes, how about Thursday for drinks? You're on. Keep up the pressure, Jeff. He's going down for the third time," Reynolds said with delight.

"Mr. Boxer, this is Judge Tauber," said the voice on the other end of the phone. Marty was speechless. "I realize that you're probably surprised to get a call from me. I wanted to thank you personally for what you did for me."

"I did what every lawyer should have done under the circumstances."

"Mr. Boxer, you and I both know that under many circumstances not all lawyers go out of their way to help the opposition—regardless of the morality. I realize now, however, that it does happen occasionally. My case brought that point home very poignantly."

"Yes, sir," Marty said, not knowing what else to say.

"I admire how you stood up for your principles under circumstances when other people"—the judge paused meaningfully—"probably did not agree with your decision. I know our dear colleague, Judge Moriarty, did not."

"I just did what I had to do, Your Honor. I couldn't let you or your son suffer when you hadn't done anything."

"That's exactly the point, Mr. Boxer. There *are* some people, regardless of the equities of the situation, who might have permitted the case to continue to the very end, to squeeze the last moment of personal glory out of it for themselves. You did not. I admire that greatly. So does my entire family."

"Yes, sir."

"I'm sure Mr. Wright's bid for the mayoralty is going to be terminated any moment now," the judge continued.

"I don't know about that, judge," Marty said, trying to keep J.T. afloat.

"I was just looking at the television coverage, Mr. Boxer. As an old politician, seeing Mr. Wright falling further in the polls every day, I know his campaign is rapidly losing steam. The sunshine friends are already looking for safer horses."

Marty could not reply to that.

"I understand from Mr. Sabbatino that when the campaign is over you will not continue practicing law with Mr. Wright?" the judge probed.

"I'm not sure what I'll do, judge."

"I'm not trying to pry, Mr. Boxer, but I would consider it a privilege, in the event that you are looking to relocate professionally, if you would allow me to recommend you to my old firm. They can always use a man of integrity and intelligence. And if that firm doesn't interest you, perhaps I can recommend you to another in which I have some friendships and contacts."

"That's kind of you, Your Honor."

"No, Mr. Boxer. I'm just passing on the good turn."

"I'd be honored if you'd recommend me to your old firm. It's a fine firm."

"I see you did your homework on me, Mr. Boxer."

"Of course."

"Thanks to you, I'm in my chambers every day now. Please call upon me when you decide what you want to do."

A joyful feeling welled up inside Marty. He felt as though someone had just pinned a medal on him, made him Man of the Year, put his picture on the cover of *Time*.

"Look, don't let it get you down," DeValen said to J.T. in the huge living room of DeValen's elegant Fifth Avenue apartment. A television set inside a Louis XV chest was tuned to a late news program carrying J.T.'s conference. "So the mayoral thing didn't work out. You still have five months of a legal retainer that will carry you while you set up your practice in earnest now."

"I'm not concerned about that," said J.T. "Hell, the publicity in the papers, good, bad, or indifferent, didn't do me any harm. People forget what they read about you in the papers in four or five weeks. They remember you, though. I'm not worried about that."

"Is it because Marty left your office?"

"I don't know. Maybe that's it. We've been together a long time. College, law school, Washington. A long time."

"That's understandable. Perhaps another vacation would do you good. What about Capri, Italy? It's wonderful this time of year. We can wash the dust of the campaign off in the Mediterranean."

"More like mud."

"Okay, mud then. Wash off the campaign mud in the blue Mediterranean."

"That sounds fabulous," said J.T. Inwardly, however, he felt no enthusiasm. If it made DeValen happy, he'd go. Maybe he'd feel better when they got there. He had nothing holding him in New York right now, no pressing cases, no really pressing emotional ties. Now that Marty and he had split up, he had no other close friends, nothing, no one, nowhere.

"We'll have a terrific time."

When I get back, J.T. thought, *I'll have to start an entire new life.* That was going to be hard without Marty. *Come on, J.T.*, he urged himself, *there are plenty of new worlds to conquer, new mountains to climb.*

DECEMBER 23, 1969

THE MAYORAL CAMPAIGN ENDED, not ignominiously—or at least not as ignominiously as it could have, had J.T. been hacked to pieces by a hail of flying ballots intended for his opponents. Rather than face that inevitability, J.T. deftly removed himself from the race before the balloting, hinting to his media friends that his actions were prompted by an altruistic desire not to split the Republican Party and fragment any chance it might have to succeed in the general election.

Old Deveraux, shortly after J.T.'s mayoral retreat, resigned from the law firm, leaving the irascible young man with the puffy eyes and vaulting ambition to run the place himself. Deveraux was supposed to receive a check from the firm each week, but he always had to call twice before it was mailed.

J.T. kept Deveraux's old furniture. It was expensive to buy new furniture, and now that J.T. was spending his own money, he found it rather difficult to be lavish. Thus, although some chairs were wobbly and not in any sense commodious, J.T. still used them. After all, his clients didn't come to see W. & J. Sloane, they came to see J.T. Wright.

And clients did come, all kinds of clients: corporations, socialites, big name criminals, the entire fabric of humanity—well-heeled
humanity, that is.

To give the appearance of being tremendously busy, however, J.T.
never saw anyone who sought his legal assistance. Not at first, anyway. Levine would interview all new clients. Levine had joined J.T.'s
firm as soon as the hubbub about the Tauber affair died down. When
clients finally did enter J.T.'s sanctum sanctorum, they found that J.T.
had even less time and money to waste on furniture than he spent on
clothes.

Levine invariably did the research in J.T.'s office, drew the legal
papers, and put together the arguments, which he hurriedly whispered to J.T. as they ran up the stairs of the courthouse, just in time for
J.T. to repeat what he could remember to the court or jury.

J.T. missed Marty. True, Levine was useful, but theirs was nothing
more than a business relationship. It had been different with Marty.
At the end of their relationship, there was not much left of them in an
emotional sense. But they had had their days. He would never be that
close with Levine; probably not ever again with anyone. He had no
time for such things. There was too much to do, too much to take care
of, too far to go. He had no time to rest.

DeValen was still involved in acquisitions, still expanding, and J.T.
was still on retainer with DeValen, although the guaranteed retainer
had expired. J.T. saw DeValen rarely now, either socially or as his
attorney. He had new clients to pursue.

With his seemingly boundless store of energy, J.T. was able to
maintain the public image of a dynamic man on the go. But secretly
he wasn't satisfied with anything, particularly himself. There was
always something just beyond his grasp. If he could only go fast
enough and run hard enough, he'd catch up to it. He knew he'd get
there if he concentrated only on going fast, and let nothing get in
his way.

"Merry Christmas," said his secretary as she stood in the doorway
of J.T.'s office. She had her coat on, and a pile of brightly wrapped packages in her hand.

"Merry Christmas," J.T. said, a momentary smile on his face.

The girl turned happily and disappeared.

Good thing I'm going to Acapulco, J.T. said to himself. *This town is going to be absolutely deadsville for the next week and a half. No one's going to be doing anything.* He straightened out some of the papers on his desk. *Won't be able to get anything done here. At least I can meet some new clients in Acapulco.*

JUNE 15, 1970

"HELLO, MARTY," J.T. said hesitantly into the phone.

"J.T.," Marty said happily. "How the hell have you been?"

"Terrific. And you, and Courtnay, and Muffy? And the new baby?"

"They're all doing fine."

"Now that we've gotten all the small talk out of the way," joshed J.T., "where've you been keeping yourself? I haven't seen or heard from you in twelve months."

"I've been keeping up with you in the papers, J.T."

"You don't believe everything you read in the papers, do you?"

"After working with you, of course not."

"You could believe a little of it, you know," J.T. laughed tightly.

"I doubt it."

"Very funny, Otto, very funny. How's the new firm? Are you having fun?"

"It's different, J.T. Very straight, very proper, low-key."

"Sounds boring."

"In one way, it is, J.T., very pleasantly so. No mad panic ripping the office in two, no holding the ship together with string and paste. How about you?"

"You have any string or paste you can spare?" said J.T. lightly.

They both laughed.

"Listen, I'm having a party and I'd like you and Courtnay to come. I might as well have a couple of old friends at a bash where there'll be a hundred and fifty people."

"What's the occasion?"

"My birthday. Nobody has given me a birthday party in years, so I decided to give one to myself. It'll be on my yacht."

"A yacht? For a hundred and fifty people?"

"It's a hundred twenty feet long. A woman I represent got it in a divorce settlement. She couldn't use it, so she gave it to me, just to burn her husband's ass."

"I shouldn't have expected you to have anything less than a hundred-twenty-foot yacht. When is the party?"

"A week from Saturday. Can you make it?"

"Sure. Where?"

"The Seventy-ninth Street Boat Basin. The name of the boat is the *Enterprise*. We're leaving the dock about six thirty in the evening."

"We'll be there."

"Great. I" look forward to seeing you. Say hello to Muffy for me."

"I will. She'll be happy to hear from you. She asks about you all the time, asks when we're going to see you."

"Tell her I've been awfully busy. I'll be calling her real soon."

As he hung up the phone, Marty suddenly felt sad for J.T., having to throw himself a birthday party. Courtnay wouldn't be too enthusiastic about going, but how could you turn down a guy inviting his only friends to his own birthday party?

Courtnay and Marty strolled along the pier of the marina on West Seventy-ninth Street, in a crowd of other people who were heading in the same direction. Music emanated from an enormous, brightly lit yacht at the end of the pier. A crowd of people had already boarded and were standing in knots at the bow and stern, drinking, chattering, watching the arriving crowd.

"J.T. can get anything for himself with that scheming brain of his, can't he?" sighed Courtnay. They walked up the gangplank. "But he ought to spend a little time conniving some maintenance for this boat," she whispered. "It looks a little frayed around the collar."

Marty had noticed the same thing. There was none of the spit-and-polish that the true yachtsman would require his crew to lavish on a yacht like this one. The varnish on the woodwork had worn thin in places, and the bright-work wasn't polished. As they walked past the wheel-house, they saw the captain's cockpit strewn with unfolded maps, a shirt one of the crew had thrown down, empty Coke cans, and sandwich wrappings that had been rolled into paper balls.

"It isn't maintained like your father's yacht, that's for sure," Marty said.

"My father would burn his boat before he would leave it in this condition."

"Marty! Courtnay!" J.T. said, spying them making their way along the deck. They waved and walked toward him. A woman, dressed in a concoction obviously just off the designer's drawing board, with tightly bound silk leggings and a diaphanous flowing silk top that let her breasts practically fall out, intercepted J.T. and kissed him on both cheeks. He looked at Marty and Courtnay over her shoulder, and raised his eyebrows.

"Your ship is just marvelous, darling," the woman said, gushing enthusiasm. "And you look so nautical."

J.T. wagged his head boyishly. He was wearing a blue blazer, white pants, and brown penny loafers—unshined, of course.

He made his way to Marty and Courtnay. He kissed Courtnay on the cheek. She in turn leaned forward and kissed his other cheek. "How Continental you've become," he chided her.

Marty shook J.T.'s hand. They stared at each other, smiling.

"How the hell have you been?" J.T. asked, genuinely happy to see Marty.

"Great," Marty replied, equally happy. They kept shaking hands, smiling.

"This is some birthday party," said Courtnay, looking around. The crowd was splashed with people whose names and faces constantly filled the society pages, sports pages, and scandal sheets. Anybody who seemed to be somebody in New York was on board. It was another J.T.

Wright promotion, Marty thought. He had made his own birthday party into a New York "happening," and no one wanted to be left out.

A man in dungarees, sports shirt, and soiled captain's hat walked up to them. "Mr. Wright, the dockmaster wants to see you for a minute."

"What about, Captain?"

"He didn't say."

Courtnay gave the captain a fast once-over, which ended in an exchange of glances with Marty. If this was the captain of the yacht, Courtnay hoped they would stay tied to the slip all night.

"Tell him I'm too busy."

"I think it's important, Mr. Wright," the captain said urgently.

"Oh, well, tell him to come to the bridge. Come on, Marty."

Marty and Courtnay followed J.T. to the untidy, littered wheelhouse. He shut the door behind them. Clothes were strewn on the bench against the wall, and the navigation desk was covered with nuts, bolts, and an old plumber's wrench.

"This is the dockmaster, Mr. Wright," said the captain.

A bald man with a puffy face looked around, hesitating to speak in front of the others.

"What is it, Portmaster, if that's how you're called."

"I'm sorry, Mr. Wright, but I can't open the gas pump until you take care of the bill that's outstanding. It's two months overdue."

J.T., unflustered, said, "Just send the bill to my office. I'm sure they'll pay it the moment they get it. I don't own the boat," he explained to Marty and Courtnay. "It's owned by the office."

"They've already sent two bills to the office. I called personally. Your secretary said she had to wait until you told her to pay it."

"Well, I'll tell them first thing Monday."

"No good, Mr. Wright. I don't mean to upset your party, but I got orders."

Courtnay looked at Marty, amused.

"I understand, I understand," J.T. said. "I don't have a check with me, though. I don't think I can pay you now."

Marty smiled. He was sure J.T. would salvage the situation somehow.

"I can't open the pumps. That's orders."

"How much is the bill?"

"Two thousand fifty."

"I don't have that kind of cash on me."

"I'm sorry, Mr. Wright."

"Yes, yes. All right. I'll send someone over to you in a few minutes. You'll get your money."

"Very good, Mr. Wright." The dockmaster left.

"Find Mr. DeValen and ask him to come here a minute, will you?" J.T. told the captain.

"Okay."

"Some things never change," said Marty, when the three of them were alone in the wheelhouse.

J.T. shrugged. "We have a professional corporation now. I'm just an employee. I don't even draw a salary. The office pays my expenses." J.T. grinned. "This way, if anyone wants to sue me, they have to get in line with the others. I don't have any money." His grin widened. He loved that.

"Sooner or later, J.T.," Courtnay said, "like Dorian Gray, the canvas of your life is going to curdle as all your evil deeds catch up with you."

"They'll never catch me. I run too fast," J.T. said, smiling.

DeValen came into the wheelhouse, followed by the captain.

"Excuse us a minute, will you, Captain?" J.T. said.

"Huh? Oh, sure," he said, backing out the doorway.

"Hello, Marty, Courtnay," DeValen said. "What's the trouble, J.T.?"

"Trouble? Who said anything about trouble?"

DeValen smiled. "What's the trouble, J.T.?"

"They won't pump the gas because of some ridiculous bill. I don't even know if the amount is correct. It's probably too high. I told the dockmaster I'd have the office go over it on Monday."

"And what did he say?"

"No cash, no gas. And I don't have an office check with me, either."

DeValen put his hand in his pocket. He counted out several hundred-dollar bills. "I only have twelve hundred in cash with me. I do have a check. How much is the total?"

"Two thousand."

DeValen took out his wallet. Inside was a blank check. "Two thousand," DeValen said idly as he made it out.

"Give me a thousand in cash, too," said J.T.

"What for?"

"I'll show you. Captain," J.T. called out the bridge window. The captain was standing by the rail, watching the crowd. He turned and came into the cabin.

"Here," said J.T., handing him the cash and DeValen's check. "Go to the dockmaster. Tell him we scraped together a thousand in cash. That's all we have right now. See if you can get him to open the pumps. Only if that doesn't work, give him the check. Maybe he'll take just the cash. Tell him I'll send the balance by messenger on Monday."

"Okay." The captain started to leave the cabin.

"Either the cash or the check, not both," J.T. admonished.

The captain nodded.

Those in the cabin looked at each other. J.T. smiled. "Living that close to the edge must be as dangerous as it is exciting," Courtnay said.

"Not when you know how to do it," J.T. replied. "Come on, let's have a good time."

"You owe me two thousand, J.T.," said DeValen.

"Monday. Monday morning first thing."

DeValen looked at the others, but said nothing.

MARCH 15, 1971

"**JUST GIVE ME THE IMPORTANT POINTS**," J.T. said impatiently to Levine as they walked quickly up the steps of the Federal Courthouse.

"The statute doesn't apply to Birden," Levine explained quickly as he tried to keep up with J.T. "It was initially intended by Congress to apply to loan sharks and extortionists."

J.T. swung through the revolving door, leaving Levine behind.

"Go ahead, go ahead," J.T. said impatiently as Levine emerged from the next compartment.

J.T. was about to argue a criminal appeal to the U.S. Second Circuit Court of Appeals. His client, who had become wealthy in the wholesale lumber business, had a number of deadbeat customers who refused to pay for the lumber he had delivered. J.T.'s client had come up the hard way. In the present case, he'd angrily told one of the customers that he would break the customer's head if he wasn't paid. The customer complained to the FBI and was outfitted with a tape recorder so he could goad Birden even further and cause him to repeat the impassioned threats of personal violence. Such tactics made up a case for the FBI, and allowed the customer not to pay at all. A jury, on the strict interpretation of the law, convicted Birden of using extortionate means to collect his money. He was sentenced to jail for a year of weekends. The case was now on appeal.

Naturally, J.T., flooded with all sorts of other cases, interviews with prospective new clients, lunches at "21," dinner parties, and the like, did not research the law or write Birden's appeal brief. Levine did. And now Levine, in a role more and more prominent in their relationship, was briefing J.T. on the run.

"The statute was never intended for a situation like this, where a legitimate businessman—even if he did, in fact, threaten physical danger, which he never carried out—was attempting to obtain his own legitimate money back from some deadbeat."

As they rode the elevator, J.T. removed some papers that were sticking out of his pocket. "This is the Lands-burg Separation Agreement. I was going over it this morning. It's terrible. We didn't draw this up, did we?"

"J.T., shouldn't we go over the Birden case now? You're going to be arguing in a few minutes."

"I want you to draft a very strong counterproposal to this proposed separation agreement."

The elevator stopped at the seventeenth floor.

"See what number we are on the calendar," J.T. instructed Levine.

Other lawyers were milling in the lounge just outside the courtroom. They saw J.T., and many recognized him. He acted as if he didn't even notice.

"We're number two on the calendar," said Levine. "You'll go on in a few minutes."

"Court's about to be called into session," a clerk announced as he walked through the lawyers' lounge.

The lawyers began to gravitate toward the doorway leading to the large courtroom with its high bench, behind which three judges would listen to the appeal arguments.

Levine and J.T. sat on a leather couch on the side of the courtroom. The judges had not taken the bench yet.

"In the brief, I cited the statute and various cases that have been decided in the last two years. There aren't many; it's a fairly recent statute."

J.T. looked at the brief that Levine handed him, and leafed through the pages.

"Are there any precedents for the kind of prosecution against a defendant like Birden?" J.T. asked.

"Not really. That's a good point to argue. Birden's not a loan shark, he's a legitimate businessman. The statute wasn't intended to prosecute him."

"J.T.," said a man with a big smile as he approached.

"Hiya, Sidney," J.T. said enthusiastically. He stood and shook hands.

J.T. was still chatting when the three judges were announced and entered the courtroom from a door directly behind the bench.

J.T. and Sidney nodded at each other and took their seats.

The clerk announced the cases to be argued. Each lawyer answered the calendar and requested the time he desired to argue his case.

"That was Sidney Rose, chairman of the Liberal Party," J.T. whispered to Levine. "He's a good man to keep on our side."

"Appellant ten minutes," Levine said, rising at the call of their case.

As the lawyers argued the first appeal, Levine held a copy of their brief and, page by page, silently pointed to places for J.T. to read.

Bummy Carruba sat at the bar in Miami's Fontainebleau Hotel, waiting for J.T. to come down from his room. Carruba was an infamous underworld character who had only been home from jail a few months when the current alleged head of the underworld died in a hail of bullets in a New York restaurant. Thereafter, the newspapers referred to Carruba as the new "Godfather." This recognition wasn't deserved, however. Not that Carruba didn't relish the idea of being Boss of All Bosses. But there were other bosses, all of whom, like Carruba, were jockeying to become Mr. Big. If the other bosses had anything to say or do about it, Carruba was not going to succeed to the throne. He was violent, rash, hotheaded. And more than that, he was greedy, anxious to steal from other territories to expand his own. There were those who suggested, never to Carruba's face, that it was he who had engineered the death of the last Boss of Bosses in order to put himself in a position of ascendancy.

Although his usual territory was New York, Carruba was in Miami, having been subpoenaed there to answer questions before a federal grand jury. Carruba had been an associate of Pasquale Bedardo—now deceased from natural causes—and Bedardo had always spoken so glowingly of J.T.'s ability to talk, connive, influence people, that those in Bedardo's old crew who could afford to pay J.T.'s fees called him the instant there was trouble.

J.T. walked into the dimly lit cocktail lounge.

"Counselor," Carruba called.

J.T. waved and walked over to where Carruba was seated.

"Have something, counselor."

"Just a ginger ale," J.T. said. He wasn't embarrassed about drinking soda any longer. Now it was an eccentricity, respected by others.

"So what do we do tomorrow?" Carruba asked, after looking over his shoulder to see no one could overhear.

"Tomorrow I'm not going to be here," said J.T.

"What?"

"I told you I have to go to Acapulco on a merger that's going on down there. My clients are trying to take over the Acapulco Princess from the Ludwig people."

"What do I care about Acapulco?"

"You knew before I even came down here that I had to go there, that I could only spend a couple of days here."

"Yeah, you told me. But you said you would work out whatever had to be worked out."

"And I have. Everything here is fine. The prosecutor can't tell you that you can't take the Fifth Amendment. We, you and me, have the right to decide whether there's anything that might possibly incriminate you. There's no problem in the world with that."

"What happens tomorrow when I go in front of the judge?"

"My associate, Mr. Levine, is going to walk in with you."

"That funny-looking little kid?"

"I've already personally done all the research and briefed him. I've also spoken to the U.S. attorney. Everything's going to turn out fine."

Actually, Levine had done the research and had spoken to the assistant U.S. attorney. Levine had advised J.T. that Washington refused to give Carruba immunity, which meant that Carruba would be able to refuse to testify without being in contempt. Besides, J.T. wasn't going to miss Acapulco for anything. There was a huge party being thrown by an American actress who was now an Italian countess, and people from all over the world had been invited. J.T.'s true interests were always in tomorrow.

"Look," J.T. said ominously to the divorce shark on the other side of the table, "my client isn't going to accept a thing less than the house in East Hampton and the apartment in the city. Not to mention alimony for herself and child support, of course."

"That's ridiculous," said Max Hirsch, the other lawyer. He was short, with Mister Magoo's face. He was known as a tough divorce lawyer. When the husband of J.T.'s client heard that his wife had retained J.T., he had immediately run to retain the toughest divorce lawyer he could find.

"Ridiculous?" J.T. said. "Fine, we'll see in front of the judge just how ridiculous it is."

"Don't be such a tough guy, J.T. I've got your client in bed with half a dozen guys, documented up and down, back and forth. Let's talk some more and we'll make a mutually agreeable solution without going to court."

"You're not going to bluff me out of a two-million-dollar house in East Hampton or a triplex apartment in New York," said J.T.

"If you go to court, your client is going to get nothing but child support. I'll prove adultery as sure as you're sitting there. You're not doing her such a big favor, being a tough guy. My client's a *schmuck*, to tell you the truth. Even with all this evidence against her, he doesn't want to see his wife dragged through the mud, doesn't want to seem a mudslinger in the newspapers. That's why he's making what I consider an overly generous offer."

Levine, seated on the couch in J.T.'s office, was trying to catch J.T.'s attention. J.T. plunged on heedlessly.

"You'd better start getting ready for trial, then," said J.T., "because we're drawing up our papers right now for alimony *pendente lite* and child support."

"You're making a big mistake."

"If I'm making a big mistake, I'll worry about it. Don't patronize me," J.T. said annoyedly, standing up behind his desk. "I don't think we have anything else to talk about, do we?"

"We'll talk in court." Hirsch shrugged and stood. He followed a secretary to the door.

"You know, J.T., he's right," Levine said when Hirsch was gone.

"What does that mean?"

"It means our client has been sleeping all around town."

"So she's a sport. That doesn't mean she won't come out of this with the lion's share of the money."

"Not if Hirsch proves adultery. And in this case, that's like shooting fish in a barrel. Hirsch is a good trial man."

"So are you."

"Me?"

"Sure, I'm not going to try this case. It's a loser, isn't it?"

"Why not talk to Hirsch, then? He wants to settle out of court."

"You want to talk to him, you talk to him."

"Our client expects you to handle the case personally."

"So what?"

"Some of the stockholders of the Rand Paper Company are getting a little restless," DeValen said. They were dining quietly in the dim, elegant atmosphere of Orsini's.

"What's the problem?"

"They don't appreciate the fact that some of the money from their treasury is going to finance other operations and other corporations in my stable."

"Aren't the profits from all your corporations added to the general coffers in which Rand participates?"

"Yes, but they say it is illegal for us to transfer the kind of money that we're transferring."

"Let them bring suit if they want," said J.T. flatly.

"*I* don't want that, J.T., particularly not at this time. I'm working something up for the largest takeover in my career. It would be disastrous if I had that kind of lawsuit crop up now."

"Who's the lawyer for the dissidents?"

"I don't know."

"I'll find out. I'll talk to him. What do you want me to do, keep them bottled up?"

"I don't think you're going to be able to do that. They're already talking about a stockholders' derivative action. They mean business."

"When are we going to take a vacation? Portugal was all right, but it was too short."

"J.T., this is not the time to be frolicking in the sun. This is serious. Believe me."

"Don't worry about Rand. I'll take care of it."

DeValen wasn't convinced. J.T.'s assurance seemed too bold, too reckless, too hollow.

APRIL 14, 1972

ATTORNEY J.T. WRIGHT stood before the bench of Judge Gerald Wynans in one of the imposing old courtrooms of the United States District Court for the Southern District of New York. His gaze was directed disdainfully at his adversary, who was hurriedly sifting through a sheaf of papers on the counsel table. If his adversary found the paper he was searching for, J.T. was in for real difficulty. He had just sworn to the judge that it didn't exist. Despite the intense pressure he felt, J.T. was his usual calm, confident self. He still maintained his confident bearing, so familiar to all in the courtroom: the buffs, retirees who wander from courtroom to courtroom, depending on where the action is, were familiar with J.T.'s mystique; so was the clerk; the judge knew it well from the days when he'd been a member of Senator Evard Anders's Select Committee to Investigate Organized Crime. Most of all, J.T.'s adversary knew it, and trembled inwardly as he fumbled through his file, looking for the two documents that J.T. had just sworn did not exist.

Even when J.T.'s adversary actually found the two documents in his file, he felt J.T.'s intimidating stare; daring him to contradict him.

"Here are the documents, Your Honor," J.T.'s adversary announced, diffidently holding the two pages aloft. He could hardly believe his own hands, his own eyes; J.T. Wright had committed flagrant perjury.

The judge hesitated, staring at the papers in the lawyer's hand. He didn't look at J.T.

"Step into my chambers, gentlemen," he said softly. "Bring those documents with you," he added as he stood and stepped down from the bench.

The other attorney nodded uneasily, following the judge. *Why am I nervous?* he thought to himself. *Wright is the one who should be nervous.*

J.T.'s facile mind was too busy whirling, figuring his position, to be nervous. He knew he had the edge. Particularly since the judge was Gerald Wynans, old Fat Ass, as he had been referred to in committee offices years before. Hadn't J.T. collaborated with Wynans many times during those halcyon days of the committee, letting the then-congressman get some time before the TV cameras for the benefit of the constituents back home? J.T. knew Wynans remembered those days. His eyes, his hesitation on the bench just now, said so.

It would be all right, as usual, J.T. said to himself as he followed his adversary and Wynans into chambers.

Judge Wynans slowly settled in the desk chair in the privacy of the robing room. He had not removed his robe. "Mr. Wright," he said, "can you explain to me how these papers could not exist a few minutes ago?" The judge held up the two documents. "You swore on the record, under oath, that they didn't, in lieu of an affidavit to support your application to dismiss the Rand stockholder action against Mr. DeValen. And here they are.

"Mr. Briggs," the judge said to the other attorney, "you say your client obtained these papers when the defendant DeValen's corporation acquired your corporation's stock?"

"Yes, sir."

It was still all right, J.T. thought to himself, the judge had to play it for real. He was calling J.T. "Mr. Wright"; that was old Fat Ass's way of keeping it formal for appearance sake.

"Mr. Wright, these documents appear to be signed by your corporate client's chief operating officer, George DeValen, guaranteeing the board of directors at Rand Paper that no funds from Rand would be used in any way to finance outside projects without the prior specific written consent of the Rand board of directors. Without these documents, I don't believe I would see anything wrong in the actions of Mr. DeValen. With them, the scenario is completely different. And you swore they didn't exist.

"Mr. Wright," the judge continued, leaning forward, "you swore falsely before the court. A most, I repeat, a most serious offense."

He really means it, J.T. thought in disbelief.

"You and I may have known each other for a long time, Mr. Wright, but there is something far more sacred than past experiences."

This son of a bitch really believes that horse crap, J.T. thought.

"The sanctity of the law is the foundation stone of our civilization. In days gone by, simple perjury, such as you've apparently just committed, was punishable by death."

J.T. looked at his watch. He had an appointment at "21" for lunch.

"I hope I'm not detaining you, Mr. Wright," the judge said caustically. His face grew darkly serious. J.T. could see a door closing in the judge's eyes, a door closing off old days and past things.

"This is a most serious situation, Mr. Wright," the judge repeated.

"Your Honor, I can explain—"

"You're going to *have to* explain, Mr. Wright, because I am scheduling a contempt hearing for you, where you will have every opportunity to explain. And if the United States attorney participates, which I will ask him to do, you may very well also have the opportunity to explain to a jury during a trial for perjury."

"Your Honor—" J.T. was stunned at the rapidity of the judge's condemnation, the coldness of the treatment.

"Yes, Mr. Wright?"

"Your Honor, I think, most respectfully, that you have reacted a mite too harshly to an unintended oversight. You've known me a long time, judge. You know that I wouldn't purposely—"

"Mr. Wright, before you go any further, please do not bring up the fact that I've known you a long time, as if that could in some way mitigate your actions. You are indeed, and I have always thought so, a calculating individual. With you, nothing is an accident. Everything you do is thought out carefully. And yes, I do believe you could do this purposefully and willfully." The judge rose. "Now let's go out on the record again, gentlemen."

By this time the courtroom buffs had sent word to their friends in other courtrooms. They all convened in Judge Wynans's court now, buzzing in conversation as the judge and two lawyers reentered the courtroom.

The judge gaveled the courtroom to silence. J.T. sat at his counsel table, Briggs at his.

"Let the record show that I have two documents signed by George DeValen, the chief operating officer of the defendant corporation, made out to the Rand Paper Company at the time of acquisition. The actual substance of these documents is of no moment. What is significant at this time is that Mr. Wright, representing the defendant corporation, swore under oath that these documents did not exist, that there was no such agreement in existence, never was. Obviously that is not correct, unless, of course, these documents are forged. Is that your claim, Mr. Wright?" The judge looked down at J.T. "No, don't say anything at this time. Save your comments for the contempt proceeding that I am about to schedule. Where's my diary?"

The courtroom buzzed wildly as everyone looked at J.T., then at one another.

The judge was handed his diary.

"May twenty-first seems like as good a day as any, Mr. Wright. Is there any conflict in your schedule for that day?"

"I do have a meeting out of the country on that day, Your Honor," J.T. said, subdued.

"I could wait until the twenty-sixth. Is that preferable? One or the other."

"I can make the twenty-sixth," J.T. said.

"And Mr. Briggs, although you will not be a party to the proceedings, I will expect you to be in court as a witness on that day. Is that a convenient day for you?"

"Yes, sir. I'll make it," Briggs said.

"We'll stand adjourned, then," the judge said, turning back to his robing room. "Perhaps you'll want to retain counsel for yourself, Mr. Wright," the judge added acidly.

J.T. stood at his table, staring at the now unoccupied judge's bench. He shoved his papers into his briefcase, keenly aware of the noise and chatter from behind him.

"I'm awfully sorry," said Briggs, coming over to J.T. "If there's anything I can do, just ask."

"Thanks. But I don't think there's anything you can do. It'll be all right. He must have had a bug up his nose today."

When J.T. turned, he saw the crowd. They seemed a different crowd from those he was used to, with a different look. They were looking at him with that curiosity he had often seen courtroom spectators display toward his infamous clients. They were gawking at him, not admiring him. He felt quite alone. Where was Levine, he wondered. Where was Marty? Where was DeValen?

The people in the crowd didn't speak to him as he walked through the courtroom to the corridor. They hung back, wanting to see his reactions, his fear sticking out all over him like porcupine quills. *Bullshit*, he thought. He waited alone for the elevator. The goddamn thing took forever.

MAY 25, 1972

Sunlight streamed through the large window onto J.T.'s bed. The door to his cell was open. Beyond the door he could see men in red, blue, or gold coveralls gathered in conversation. Others were pacing around the recreation room.

"I had sold my interests in the corporations and had been living in Cuba for five or six years. When Castro came in, I moved to Brazil. That was where I was when the New York DA had me indicted in absentia," said Augustus Rector. J.T.'s eyes turned from the men outside his room. Flector was an old man with pale skin and puffy, alcoholic eyes. His hands shook when he raised them to make a point in conversation. Flector's coveralls were gold-colored.

"You hadn't controlled the corporations for several years and were still indicted?" J.T. asked skeptically.

"Not a single share of stock," Flector emphasized with a shaking hand. "Not the bottling companies, not the automobile companies, nothing."

"What the heck were you indicted for?" J.T.'s coveralls were red.

"You tell me. If I could get my hands on my books—fifty-two filing cabinets filled with all my papers and files were just seized out in Westbury by the FBI in 1966, and they're still under lock and key in a room in the Southern District Courthouse—if I had those books, I could prove I didn't take a red cent."

J.T. and Flector were both in "West Street" (the federal detection facility), where federal prisoners are detained while awaiting trial or further proceedings in their cases. J.T. was serving a sixty-day sentence for contempt, imposed by the Honorable Gerald Wynans in connection with the Rand Paper proceedings. The judge could have sentenced him for perjury and given him years in the can, but he'd said on the record that a sixty-day sentence should be sufficient to bring the point home to J.T.—this time.

Flector presently stood indicted for falsely submitting an affidavit claiming that he was indigent, without funds to pay a lawyer to defend him on a previous indictment for mail fraud. The government was contending that Flector had been collecting a two-hundred-dollar weekly stipend from a printing concern in Westchester when he submitted the affidavit of indigence. The printing company did pay Flector the stipend because the president of that company still admired Flector from the days when he was known as the corporate wizard of the twentieth century.

"Heck," said Flector, "I was disbarred in absentia, too, while I was in Brazil."

"How did they do that?"

"You keep asking the very same question I've been asking myself for over ten years. But they did it."

The coveralls were government issue for inmates. J.T. wore a pair of white sneakers and white socks—his own, but the mandatory footwear.

"What did you do in Brazil?" J.T. asked. There was nothing for him to do for the next fifty-five days except talk. He found Flector pleasant company. He was an intelligent man, with a wealth of stories about every industrialist, American or foreign, of whom J.T. had ever heard.

"After I escaped from Cuba—Castro had put a price on my head; I was a capitalist enemy of the state—I lived in Brazil until I came home voluntarily to face the charges, to clear my name and my family's."

If you didn't know who Flector was, you'd think he was the biggest liar in the world. But he had done it all, had made it all, and when the American government had attempted to extradite the ex-lawyer, it discovered there was no extradition treaty with Brazil. The American press carried stories that Flector had paid the Brazilian government off with part of the hoard of millions he had allegedly embezzled before fleeing the United States.

"But if you had sold the stock in all those corporations years before, what money were you charged with embezzling?"

"Beats me. Some of those companies are still in business. Heck, I didn't steal a dime. All I did was confuse them. You know, if you make too much dough just using your head, people who haven't any brains figure you're doing something illegal. Damn fools."

The only other conversations that J.T. might have would be with other inmates indicted for all sorts of crimes, hardened street people who would have liked to hobnob with him, pick his brains for their legal writs, get legal opinions they could bounce off their own lawyers. J.T. didn't want any of that; he just wanted to be left alone, get his time over, and get back in action.

"You mind if I ask why, when you came back here, you had to get court-appointed counsel?"

"There's no secret to that, J.T. I sank all my dough, a hundred and fifty million, in Cuba. And when Castro came in, I was lucky I escaped with my skin."

"How could you have put all your money in Cuba?" J.T. asked incredulously.

"You can ask that question now, J.T. But in those days, well, it would be like saying why did you put a hundred fifty million in Florida. Who the hell could ever have imagined that the United States would let Cuba, with billions of dollars in American assets sunk in there, ninety miles off the coast—who the hell would ever even have conceived that the United States would just let it go by default to the Communists?" Flector still was sadly befuddled by that. He shook his head hopelessly.

"I guess that's right."

"Hey, did you see the news on television?" Myron Weiss asked, coming into J.T.'s cell. Weiss was another inmate, whose coveralls were blue. On the outside, he was a theater producer, a financial investor who'd been extremely helpful to several mobsters with cash to launder.

"No, what's on?" asked Flector. He was a sort of Papa Bear to all the other inmates. He had been successful; he had been indicted; he had beaten three of his own cases; he was willing to help them with their legal papers. So they all trusted him.

"Your client, J.T., that guy DeValen, is being indicted for stock manipulation," said Weiss.

"What?" J.T. literally jumped off his bed to go into the recreation room, where the television was.

"It's off now," Weiss said, following J.T. Flector was third in line. "Probably it'll be on another newscast later. He's going to be arraigned on Friday."

"Jesus, I'd better give him a call," said J.T. He glanced over at the phones. They were all being used. He paced.

"Take it easy, J.T.," said Flector. "Take it easy. Don't work yourself up," Weiss said. "He isn't being arraigned until Friday."

A phone became free. J.T. dashed to it. Flector and Weiss hovered nearby.

"Is Mr. DeValen in?" J.T. asked when DeValen's office answered. "This is J.T. Wright." Pause. "He's coming here to see me?" J.T. asked. "Today? If he calls in, meanwhile, tell him I called. I'm waiting for him." J.T. hung up the phone.

"That's a twist," said Weiss. "The client is coming to jail to see the lawyer."

"That is kind of ridiculous, isn't it?" said J.T. as he and Flector went back to his cell. Weiss hadn't been admitted to J.T.'s inner circle yet.

There were several hours each day when the inmates were let out into the recreation area where they could skylark with each other.

"What are you going to do when you get out of here?" J.T. asked Flector absently.

"Get some import/export thing going with Brazil. That's a country, J.T. Just bursting with money. And they need everything. Everything! I'll make a million in the first six months I'm out, several million, just selling the Brazilians things they need down there that we have plenty of right here."

"No kidding?" said J.T., intrigued.

"Sure. Making a million is a lead-pipe cinch down there."

J.T. was impressed. He recalled that DeValen had once said something like that to him. "What do you have to do to get all this done?" J.T. asked.

"I just need someone to stake me to some walking-around money for about two months, a thousand a week, ten thousand altogether, and we'll make millions. I've got the people down there all set to buy whatever we can get them."

"You have the people down there ready to buy?"

"Sure."

J.T. nodded and thought.

"You know, J.T., just because I've lost my shingle doesn't mean I've lost my touch. I can still write a mean brief, do legal research, run an office. I might be an asset to your office while I'm setting this stuff up in Brazil. I just need a place to hang my hat."

"You fascinate me, Gus."

"Well, if you have any doubts, you know all the people I know. They'll tell you I'm the real goods. I was quite a lawyer in my day, before I stopped working for other people and made some real money for myself."

"Mr. Wright," said the prison officer in charge of their section. He wore a yellow shirt and gray pants. "You have a visitor waiting for you in the visitors' room."

J.T. stood up, straightening out his coveralls. "I'll see you in a bit," he said to Flector.

"If it's George DeValen, tell him hello for me."

"Okay, I will." J.T. followed the guard to a corridor that led to a locked metal door. The guard unlocked it and J.T. entered a narrow corridor which had seats and compartments on one side. These seats faced thick glass windows looking out to the visitors' area. Each compartment had a phone that the inmate and his visitor could use to talk to each other.

J.T. walked from one compartment to the next. He only saw other prisoners visiting with their families and friends. He didn't see DeValen. Suddenly he saw a woman, sitting alone, smiling at him. It was Dana Reynolds.

J.T. picked up the phone. "Dana? What are you doing here?" J.T. was quite surprised. They looked through the glass into each other's eyes, then looked away, then looked at each other again. They smiled again.

"I came to see you, of course," she said into the hollow sounding phone.

"I'm shocked. Delighted, believe me. But nonetheless shocked. You look great." She really did, J.T. thought. She was so distinguished-looking, so well dressed. She was still statuesque. "Gee, it's great seeing you, Dana."

"It's good seeing you too, J.T. Even if it's here." Her eyes were warm and smiling at him. Her mouth was soft and glistening.

"What a genuine, delightful surprise," J.T. repeated. "How've you been?"

"I'm excellent," she replied. "But are *you* all right?"

"Oh, sure, real fine. This'll be over in a bit. I'll be out of here and on top of the world in a few weeks. Mean-while, I have time to write my memoirs."

"Are you really writing?"

"No, just kidding. Some newspaper people asked me to do some articles, but I couldn't put anything I know into writing."

"Probably not," she smiled.

"How's the family? Uncle Chauncey? Your father?"

"Father's had a stroke."

"I'm really sorry to hear that."

"It's been a while now. He's coming along. Can't keep Dad down for very long. Right now he's walking with a brace on one leg, but the doctor thinks he'll be right as rain in a little. Uncle Chauncey is the same Uncle Chauncey."

"I'll bet."

"And that's about everything. I'm very involved in the business, as you can imagine, now that father is somewhat disabled. I'm doing all the things that he can't—meetings, conferences, travel."

"That's an enormous undertaking, a worldwide business on your shoulders. Incredible," J.T. marveled. "And you took time out to see me!"

"Why not, dear boy? You are still that to me, you know, dear. And, in a very cherished way, a boy—childlike, not childish." His eyes were captured by hers. They were so warm, so welcoming. Dana brought back memories of all sorts of things. He wished he didn't have the glass between them.

"It's great seeing you," J.T. said sincerely. "Not too many people come to see me here. The atmosphere must be too cold and damp for them."

A guard came up behind J.T. "You have another visitor downstairs, Mr. Wright," he said. The guards showed J.T. great respect and deference, particularly in front of his VIP visitors.

"Excuse me a minute, Dana," J.T. said, turning.

"I have to get going anyway," she said, looking at her watch. "I've got a tight schedule."

"Stay another minute or two," he asked into the phone.

"Of course."

J.T. asked the guard, "Who is the visitor, do you know?"

"Let me ask on the phone, Mr. Wright."

The guard locked the steel door and went to the phone on the desk. J.T. watched him talk. He couldn't hear what the guard said.

The guard opened the steel door again.

"It's Mr. George DeValen."

"Can you have him wait until Miss Reynolds goes down? A couple of minutes?"

"That's the way it has to be anyway, Mr. Wright," said the guard. "They won't let nobody up until this lady goes down."

"Thanks."

The guard nodded and went back to his desk.

"Do you know a man named Augustus Flector?" J.T. asked Dana on the phone.

"Oh, 'Mr. Reflector' I used to call him," Dana smiled. "Of course. I knew him when I was a little girl. He was a good friend of Daddy's. Don't tell me he's in trouble again."

"Yes, he's here," said J.T. "He sent his regards."

"That poor man. He's been involved with litigation for the longest time—ten or twelve years now."

"He's here again, indicted for falsely swearing he didn't have any money to pay a lawyer. They say he was getting two hundred dollars a week stipend."

"Oh, dear God! What a sweet man, too. I knew him when he owned the world," Dana recalled with a smile. "I went to one of his daughter's birthday parties when I was just a girl. At his place in Old Westbury. That was my first plane ride. He had his own plane and pilot, and flew a bunch of children out from the city. His lands were immense. The horses—oh, my God, the horses—they were magnificent. He must have hired Ringling Brothers for his daughter's tenth birthday—elephants, clowns, the works. He was truly on top of the world then. How is he?"

"Old, shaking."

"That's too bad. He always did drink. I remember Daddy telling me stories about when he would see him sitting at the bar in Orsini's with a beautiful girl who had a little dog in her purse. You know how chi-chi Orsini's is. Well, Mister Reflector was so important at the time that they let him bring in his girlfriend's dog. How's that for important?"

J.T. smiled. "It's good to see someone from the old days, when we were all young."

Dana's smile became wistful. "You've got another visitor, and I really do have to run." She looked at her watch again. "I'll come in again, if you'd like."

"If you have nothing better to do," J.T. tried to say casually.

"Is there anything I can do for Mr. Flector?"

"Maybe mail in a money order for commissary so he can buy candy or razor blades. Nothing big. Ten or twenty dollars."

"Surely more than that."

"No, it wouldn't do him any good. He can't use it or spend it. I'll tell him you were asking for him."

"Yes, please. Tell him if there's anything I can do. You call me if there is. Even if there isn't," she said as a second thought. "Let me give you my private number. Eldorado five, six three four two.

J.T. memorized the number.

"Is there anything I can do for *you?*" she asked. Her face was so compassionate, J.T. thought. He was being drawn toward the warmth of it.

"No. Heck, I'm great," he said. "I'll be out of here in no time, on top of the world, making millions. That's a lead-pipe cinch." He stunned himself with that remark.

"Dear boy," Dana said, leaning close to the window as if that would make their conversation on the phone more private. She whispered softly, "I already have millions. And I still have a broken heart."

J.T. drew back and looked at her. Her forehead wrinkled, her eyes quivered as if she were about to cry. Then Dana took a deep breath, pulled herself tall and regal. She smiled. "Goodbye, J.T. Good luck." She put down the phone and stood.

The guard let Dana out through the steel door. J.T. watched her go out through another steel door to the elevator that would take her downstairs. He remained at the window panel, staring at blank whitewashed cinderblock walls on the other side. He felt like a kid with his nose pressed against a store window.

"Hell," he repeated to himself. "I'll be out of here in no time, on top of the world, making millions. A lead-pipe cinch . . ."

He heard Dana's voice reverberate contrapuntally. *I already have millions. And I still have a broken heart.* He realized at that instant that there wasn't anything on the other side of the glass.